Tall, Tatted and Tempting

By Tammy Falkner

Night Shift Publishing

For my own personal heroes:

My current hero: My husband, Thomas
My first hero: My dad, Glenn Switzer
My heroes in training: JT and Stephen

Copyright © 2013 by Tammy Falkner

Tall, Tatted and Tempting
First Edition
Night Shift Publishing
Cover design by Tammy Falkner
Cover photo by Yuri Arcurs - Fotolia.com
ISBN-13: 978-0-9887429-4-9

This book is a work of fiction. Names, characters, places, and incidents either are products of the author's imagination or are used fictitiously. Any resemblance to actual persons, living or dead, events, or locales is entirely coincidental.

Dear Readers,

I found myself in a little bit of a quandary as I wrote this book. If you've read any of my books before, you know that my writing tends to run toward the hot end of thermometer. I write heat because it's also what I like to read. However, when I was writing this book, my eighteen-year-old son was intrigued by the premise, and he asked if he could read some pages early on. As I wrote more and more, he asked for more pages, and finally I got to the point where he could no longer feel comfortable reading it. He asked me for a version "just for him." He's not a prude by any means, but he was more comfortable with a "sexy-lite" version of the book. My mother is also someone who skips the sex scenes, and she was intrigued when I told her about this special version.

Since it was already written, I have included both versions in this compilation. The first version is a hot read, not meant for anyone under the age of eighteen and not meant for those who don't enjoy explicit sex scenes. You can go straight to it by turning to page 4.

The second version is my son's version. By no means is it meant for anyone under the age of eighteen, since it has adult content, adult language, and adult situations. But it's sexy-lite. You can go straight to it by turning to page 190.

I hope you like and appreciate that the choice of which one to read is entirely yours!

Best regards,

Tammy

Tall, Tatted and Tempting

By Tammy Falkner

(Sexy Version)

Logan

I don't know her name, but she looks familiar to me. She's a tight package in a short skirt that makes me imagine the curves under her plump little ass. That skirt is made to draw attention, and she has all of mine. I'm so hard I can't get up from behind the table where I'm drawing a tat for a client on paper. I reach down and adjust my junk, the metallic scrape of the zipper against my dick not nearly enough to calm my raging hard on. I shouldn't have gone commando today. I hope Paul did some laundry this morning.

Her nipples are hard beneath the ribbed shirt she's wearing, and she pulls her sleeve back to show me something. But I can't take my eyes from her tits long enough to look at them. She shoves her wrist toward my face, and I have to jerk my eyes away. Shit. She caught me. I would tell her I'm a guy, I can't help it. Or at least I would if I could talk.

I see her mouth move out of the corner of my eye. She's talking to me. Or at least she's mouthing something at me. No one really talks to me since I can't hear. I haven't heard a word since I was thirteen years old. She's talking again. When I don't answer, she looks at my oldest brother Paul, who rolls his eyes and smacks the center of his head with his fist.

"Stop looking at her tits, dumbass." He says the words as he signs them and her face flushes. But there's a grin tugging at the corners of her mouth at the same time.

I roll my eyes and sign back. *Shut up. She's fucking beautiful.*

He translates for her. I would groan aloud, but I don't. No sound has left my throat since I lost my hearing. Well, I talked for a while after that. But not for long. Not after a boy on the playground said I sounded like a frog. Now I don't talk at all. It's better that way. "He says you're beautiful," he tells her. "That's why he was ogling your tits like a 12 year old."

I flip him off and he laughs, holding out his hands like he's surrendering to the cops. "What?" he asks, still signing. But she can hear him. "If you're going to be rude and sign around her, I'm going to tell her what you say."

Like I have another choice besides signing. *You never heard of a secret code between brothers?* I sign.

"You start whispering secrets in my ear, dickhead, and I'll knock your head off your shoulders."

You can try, asswipe.

He laughs. "He's talking all romantic to me," he tells her. "Something about kissing his ass." She's grinning now. The smile hits me hard enough I'd be on my knees, if I wasn't stuck behind that table. She brushes a strand of jet black hair back from her face, tucking it along with a lock of light blue behind her ear.

I watch her open her mouth to start to speak. But she looks over at my brother instead. "He can read lips?" she asks.

"Depends on how much he likes you," my brother says with a shrug. "Or how ornery he's feeling that day." He raises his brows at me, and then his gaze travels toward the tabletop. Shit. He saw me adjust my junk. "I'd say he likes you a lot."

This time, she closes her eyes tightly, wincing as she smiles. She doesn't say anything. But then she looks directly at me, and says, "I want a tattoo." She points toward the front of the store. She's still talking, but I can't see her lips move if she's not looking at me. I want to follow her face, to jump up so I can watch those cherry red lips move as she speaks to me. To me. God knows she's speaking to me. But I don't. I force myself to keep my seat. She looks back at me as she finishes talking and her lips form an O. "Sorry," she says. "You didn't catch any of that, did you?" She heaves a sigh and says, "The girl up front said to see you for a tattoo."

I look over at my brother who just finished a tat and isn't working on anything at the moment. Friday – really, that's her name -- laughs and signs, "You're welcome."

I scratch my head and grin. Friday set me up. She does it all the time. And sometimes it works out well. She sends all the hot girls to me. And the not so hot girls. And the girls who want to sleep with the deaf guy because they heard he's amazing in the sack. I'm the guy they don't have to talk to. I'm the guy they don't have to pretend with, because I wouldn't know what they're saying regardless.

If this girl is just there to sleep with me, we can skip all the tattoo nonsense.

"Don't even think about it," my brother says. "She wants a tat. That's all."

How do you know what she wants?

I just know, he signs. This time he doesn't speak the words. *Don't try to lay this one.*

I hold my hands up in question asking him why. "She's not from around here," he says, but he signs *not our kind.*

Oh, I get it. She's from the other side of the tracks. I don't mind. She might be rich, but she would still love what I can do for her. I reach for her hand and squeeze it gently so she'll look at me. I flip her hand over and point to her wrist. My fingers play across the iridescent blue veins beneath her tender skin, and I draw a circle with the tip of my finger asking her *Here?*

Her mouth falls open. Goose bumps rise along her arm. Hell, yeah, I'm good at this.

I stand up and touch the side of her neck and she brushes my hand away, shaking her head. Her lips are pressed tightly together.

I look directly at her boobs and lick my lips. Then I reach out and drag one finger down the slope of her breast. *Here?* I mouth.

I don't even see it coming. Her tiny fist slams into my nose. I've had girls slap me before, but I've never had one punch me in the face. Fuck, that hurt. The wet, coppery taste of blood slides over my lips, and I reach up to wipe it away. My nose is gushing. Paul thrusts a towel in my hands and tilts my head back.

Fuck, that still hurts. He presses the bridge of my nose, and I can't see his mouth or his hands over the bunched up towel, so I have no idea if he's talking to me. Or if he's just laughing his ass off. He lifts the towel but blood trickles down over my lips again. I see her standing there for a brief second, her fists clenched at her sides as she watches me suffer.

Shit, that hurts.

Then she turns on the heels of her black boots and walks away. I want to call out to her to get her to stay. I would say I'm sorry, but I can't. I can't call her back to me. I start to rise, but Paul shoves me back into the chair. *Sit down*, he signs. *I think it might be broken.*

I see a piece of paper on the floor and it's crumped. I take the towel from Paul and press it to my nose, pointing to the piece of paper. He picks it up and looks at it. "Did she drop this?" he asks.

I nod. It's damp from her sweaty palms. I unfold it and look down. It's an intricate design, and you have to look hard to find the hidden pictures. I see a guitar, the strings broken and sticking out at odd angles. And at the end of the strings are small blossoms. I turn the picture, looking over the towel I'm still holding to my nose with one hand. Paul replaces it with a clean one. My nose is still bleeding. Son of a bitch. I look closer at the blossoms. They're not blossoms at all. They're teeny tiny shackles. Like handcuffs, but more medieval. Most people would see the beauty of that drawing. But I see pain. I see things she probably wouldn't want anyone to see.

Shit. I fucked up. Now I want more than anything to know what this tat means. It's obviously more than just a pretty drawing. Just like she might be more than just a pretty face. Or she might not be. She might be a bitch with a mean right hook that will eat my balls for lunch if I look at her the wrong way.

I spin the drawing in my hands and look around the shop. It's late and no one is waiting. I punch Paul in the shoulder and point to the drawing. Then I point to the inside of my own wrist. It's the only place on my whole arm that's not tatted up already. I have full sleeves because my brothers have been practicing on me since long before it was legal to do so.

"No," Paul signs with first two fingers and his thumb, slapping them together. "You've lost your mind if you think I'm going to put that on you."

He walks toward the front of the store and sits down beside Friday. He's been trying to get in her pants since she started there. It's too bad she has a girlfriend.

I get out my supplies. I've done more intricate tats on myself. I can do this one.

He stalks back to the back of the shop, where I'm setting up. "I'll run it," he says. "You're going to do it anyway."

I hold up one finger. *One change?*

What do you want to change? He looks down at the design and his brow arches as he takes in the shapes and the colors and the handcuffs and the guitar and the prickly thorns. And I wonder if he also sees her misery. *That's some heavy shit,* he signs. He never speaks when it's just me and him. I'm kind of glad. It's like we speak the same language when we're alone.

I nod, and I start prepping my arm with alcohol as he gloves up.

Emily

It has been two days since I punched that asshole in the tattoo shop and my hand still hurts. I've been busking in the subway tunnel by Central Park, and it's somewhat more difficult to play my guitar when my hand feels like it does. But this tunnel is one of my favorite spots, because the kids stop to listen to me. They like the music, and it makes them smile. Smiling is something left over from my old life. I don't get to do it much, and I enjoy it even less. But I like it when the kids look up at me with all that innocence and they grin. There's so much promise in their faces. It reminds me of how I used to be, way back when.

I'm considering singing today. I don't do it every time I play. But I am seriously low on funds. The more attention I get, the more change I'll get to take home with me. Home is a relative term. Home is wherever I find to sleep that night.

I'm sitting on the cold cement floor of the tunnel; back a ways from the rush of feet, with my guitar case open in front of me. In it, there are some quarters, and a little old lady stopped a few minutes ago and tossed in a fiver while I played *Bridge Over Troubled Water*. Old ladies usually like that one. They haven't seen troubled waters.

I'm wearing my school girl outfit, because I get more attention from men when I wear it. It's a short plaid skirt, and a black ribbed short sleeve top that fits me like a second skin. Ladies don't seem to mind it. And men love it. I sure got a lot of attention from that asshole two days ago. He was hot, I had to admit. He had shoulders broad enough to fill a doorway, and a head full of sandy blond curls. He towered over me when he stood up from behind that table, at least a head and shoulders taller than me. Tattoos filled up all the empty space that used to be his forearms, and it was kind of hot. He had lips painted on his left arm, and I wanted to ask him what those were. Were they to remember someone? A first kiss, maybe? Or did they mean something the way the tattoo I wanted did?

I dropped my tattoo design as I ran out of the shop, which pisses me off. I thought I had it clutched in my hand and when I'd stopped to take a breath, it was gone. I almost expected the asshole to follow me. But he was still bleeding when I left him.

I shake out the pain in my hand again. A towheaded boy stops in front of me, his hand full of pennies. He is a regular, and his mother stopped to pray over me once, so I switch my song to *Jesus Loves Me*. Jesus doesn't. If He did, He wouldn't have made me like I am. He would have made me normal. The boy's mother sings along with my tunes and the boy dips his face into her thigh, hugging it tightly as she sings. When the song is over, he drops his handful of pennies into my guitar case, the thud of each one hitting the felt quiet as a whisper.

I never say thank you or talk to the kids. I don't talk to the adults unless they ask me something specific. I just play my music. Sometimes I sing, but I really don't like to draw that much attention to myself. Except today, I need to draw attention to myself. I had saved up three hundred dollars, which would pay for a place to sleep and that tattoo I thought I needed, but someone stole it while I was asleep at the shelter last night. I'd made the mistake of falling asleep with it in my pocket, instead of tucking it in my bra. When I woke up, it was gone. I don't know why they didn't take my guitar. Probably because I was sleeping with it in my arms, clutched to me like a mother with her child.

I wish I'd gotten the tattoo yesterday. It was a useless expense, but it was my nineteenth birthday, and it's been a long time since anyone has done anything for me. So, I was giving it to myself. And trying to free myself in the process. Who was I kidding? I'll never be free.

This city is hard. It's mean. It's nothing like where I came from. But now it's home. I like the noise of the city and the bustle of the people. I like the different ethnicities. I'd never seen so many skin colors, eye shapes, and body types as I did when I got here.

A girl reaches her chubby hand to touch my strings, and I smile and intercept her hand by taking it in mine, instead. Her hands are soft, and a little damp from where her first finger was shoved in her mouth just a minute ago. I toy with her fingers while I make an O with my mouth.

Her mother smacks her hand away with a sharp, cracking blow to her forearm, and her eyes immediately fill with tears. You didn't have to do that, I think. She didn't mean any harm. But the mother drags the crying child with her toward the subway and picks her up when she doesn't move quickly enough.

I draw a small crowd between subway arrivals, and one man yells out, "Do you take requests?"

I nod, and keep on smiling, playing with all I'm worth. He calls out, "I think you should suck my dick, then." One of his buddies punches him in the shoulder and he laughs.

College kid. His mama never taught him any manners. I let my eyes roam over the crowd and no one corrects him. So, I start to play *All the Wishing in the World* by Matt Monroe. The irony is lost on the jock, and they walk away as the train pulls in behind them.

The platform fills with new people getting off the train, so I switch to some more familiar tunes. Money drops into my case, and I see a dollar float down. I nod and smile as the person walks by, but she's not looking at me.

A big pair of scuffed work boots steps up beside my case. I look at them for a minute, and then up over the worn jeans and the blue T shirt that's stretched across broad shoulders. And then I'm looking into the same sky blue eyes as the other day. My pic stumbles across the strings. I wince. His eyes narrow at me, but he can't hear my mistake, can he? His head tilts to the side, and I turn my body to face the other direction.

My butt is freezing and my legs are aching from sitting on the cold floor for so long. But I don't have anywhere else to go. My three weeks at the shelter were up yesterday. So, I have to find somewhere new to sleep tonight. I look down into my case. There's enough there for dinner. But not for anything else. So, I keep playing.

Those boots move over so that he's standing in front of me. I scoot to the side, and look everywhere but at him. But then he drops down beside me, his legs crossed criss-cross-applesauce style in front of me. He has tape across the bridge of his nose and that makes me feel competent for some reason. There are very few things in my life that I can control, and someone touching my body is one of them. I say when. I say where. I say with who. Just like in *Pretty Woman*. Only Stucky would never get to backhand me. I'd take him out first.

He leans on one butt cheek so he can pull out his wallet, and he throws in a twenty. He doesn't say anything, but he points to my guitar and raises his brows. I don't know what he wants, and he can't tell me, so I just look at him. I don't want to acknowledge his presence. But he's sitting with his knee an inch from mine.

When I don't respond, he puts a hand on my guitar. He points to me and strums at the air like he's playing a guitar. I realize I've stopped playing. But he did put a twenty in my case, so I suppose I owe him. I start to play *I'm Just a Gigolo*. I love that tune. And love playing it. After a minute, his brows draw together and he points to his lips.

I shake my head because I don't know what he's asking. Either he wants me to kiss him, or I have something on my face. I swipe the back of my hand across my lips. Not that. And the other isn't going to happen.

He shakes his head quickly and retrieves a small dry-erase board from his backpack.

Sing, he writes.

I have to concentrate really hard to read it, and there are too many distractions here in the tunnel, so I don't want him to write anymore. I just shake my head. I don't want to encourage him to keep writing. I read the word *sing*, but I can't read everything. Or anything, sometimes.

He holds his hand up to his mouth and spreads his fingers like someone throwing up. I draw my head back. But I keep on playing.

Why does he want me to sing? He can't hear it. But I start to sing softly, anyway. He smiles and nods. And then he laughs when he sees the words of the song on my lips. He shakes his head and motions for me to continue.

I forgot he can read lips. I can talk to him, but he can't talk back. I play all the way to the end of the song, and some people have now stopped to listen. Maybe I should sing every time.

He writes something on the board. But I flip it over and lay it on the concrete. I don't want to talk to him. I wish he would go away.

His brows furrow and he throws up his hands, but not in an "I'm going to knock you out" sort of way. In a "what am I going to do with you" way. He motions for me to keep playing. His fingers rest on my guitar, like he's feeling the vibrations of it. But what he's concentrating on most is my mouth. It's almost unnerving.

A cop stops beside us and clears his throat. I scramble to gather my money and drop it in my pocket. I've made about thirty two dollars. That's more than the nickel I had when I started. I pack up my guitar, and Blue Eyes scowls. He looks kind of like someone just took his favorite toy.

He starts to scribble on the board and holds it up but I'm already walking away.

He follows after me, tugging on my arm. I have all my worldly possessions in a canvas bag over my right shoulder and my guitar case in my left hand, so when he tugs me, it almost topples me over. But he steadies me, slides the bag off my shoulder in one quick move and puts it on his own. I hold fiercely to it, and he pries my fingers off the strap with a grimace. What the heck?

"Give me my bag," I say, and I plant my feet. I'm ready to hit him again if that's what it takes. But he smiles, shakes his head and starts to walk away. I follow him, but getting him to stop is like stopping a boulder from rolling downhill once it gets started.

He keeps walking with me hanging on to his arm like I'm a Velcro monkey. But then he stops, and he walks into a diner in the middle of the city. I follow him, and he slides into a booth, putting my bag on the bench on the inside, beside him. He motions to the other side of the bench. He wants me to sit? I punched him in the nose two days ago and now he wants to have a meal with me? Maybe he just wants his $20 back. I reach in my pocket and pull it out, feeling its loss as I slap it down on the table. He presses his lips together and hands it back to me, pointing again to the seat opposite him.

The smell of the grill hits me and I realize I haven't eaten today. Not once. My stomach growls out loud. Thank God he can't hear it. He motions toward the bench again and takes my guitar from my hand, sliding it under the table.

I sit down and he looks at the menu. He passes one to me and I shake my head. He raises a brow at me. The waitress stops and says, "What can I get you?"

He points to the menu, and she nods. "You got it, Logan," she says, with a wink. He grins back at her. His name is Logan?

"Who's your friend?" she asks of him.

He shrugs.

She eyes the bandages across his nose. "What happened?" she asks.

He points to me, and punches a fist toward his face, but he's grinning when he does it. She laughs. I don't think she believes it.

"What can I get for you?" she asks me.

"What's good?" I reply.

"Everything." She cracks her gum when she's talking to me. She didn't do that when she talked to Logan.

"What did you get?" I ask Logan. He looks up at the waitress and bats those thick lashes that veil his blue eyes.

"Burger and fries," she tells me.

Thank God. "I'll have the same." I point to him. "And he's buying." I smile at her. She doesn't look amused. "And a root beer," I add at the last minute.

He holds up two fingers when I say root beer. She nods and scribbles it down.

"Separate checks?" she asks Logan.

He points a finger at his chest, and she nods as she walks away.

"They know you here?" I ask.

He nods. Silence would be an easy thing to get used to with this guy, I think.

The waitress returns with two root beers, two straws and a bowl of chips and salsa. "On the house," she says as she plops them down.

I dive for them like I've never seen food before. Now that I think about it, I can't remember if I ate yesterday, either. Sometimes it's like that. I get so busy surviving that I forget to eat. Or I can't afford it.

"How's your brother doing?" the waitress asks quietly.

He scribbles something on the board and shows it to her.

"Chemo can be tough," she says. "Tell him we're praying for him, will you?" she asks. He nods and she squeezes his shoulder before she walks away.

"Your brother has cancer?" I ask, none too gently. I don't realize it until the words hang there in the air. His face scrunches up and he nods.

"Is he going to be all right?" I ask. I stop eating and watch his face.

He shrugs.

"Oh," I say. "I'm sorry."

He nods.

"Is it the brother I met? A the tattoo parlor?"

He shakes his head.

"How many brothers do you have?"

He holds up four fingers.

"Older? Or younger?"

He raises his hand above his head and shows me two fingers. Then lowers it like someone is shorter than he is and makes two fingers.

"Two older and two younger?" I ask.

He nods.

I wish I could ask him more questions.

He writes something on the board and I sigh heavily and throw my head back in defeat. This part of it is torturous. I would rather have someone pull my teeth with a pair of pliers than I would read. But his brother has freaking cancer. The least I can do is try.

I look down at it and the words blur for me. I try to unscramble them, but it's too hard. I shove the board back toward him.

He narrows his eyes at me and scrubs the board clean. He writes one word and turns it around.

You, it says. He points to me.

I point to myself. "Me?"

He nods and swipes the board clean. He writes another word and shows it to me.

"Can't," I say.

He nods and writes another word. He's spacing the letters far enough apart that they're not jumbled together in my head. But it's still hard.

My lips falter over the last word, but I say, "Read." Then I realize that I just told him I can't read. "I can read!" I protest.

He writes another word. "Well."

He knows I can read. Air escapes me in a big, gratified rush. "I can read," I repeat. "I can't read well, but..." I let my words trail off.

He nods quickly, like he's telling me he understands. He points to me and then at the board, moving two fingers over it like a pair of eyes, and then he gives me a thumbs up.

My heart is beating so fast it's hard to breathe. I read the damn words, didn't I? "At least I can talk!" I say. I want to take the words back as soon as they leave my lips. But it's too late. I slap a hand over my lips when his face falls. He shakes his head, bites his lip and gets up. "I'm sorry," I say. I am. I really am. He walks away, but he doesn't take his backpack with him.

While he's gone, a man approaches the table. He's a handsome black man with tall, natural hair. Everyone calls him Bone, but I don't know what his real name is. "Who's the chump, Kit?" he asks.

"None of your business," I say, taking a sip of my root beer. I fill my mouth up with a chip, and hope he goes away before Logan comes back. And I hope deep inside that Logan will come back so I can apologize.

Logan slides back into the booth. He looks up at Bone and doesn't acknowledge him. He just looks at him.

"You got a place to sleep tonight, Kit?" Bone asks.

"Yeah," I reply. "I'm fine."

"I could use a girl like you," Bone says.

"I'll keep that in mind." It doesn't pay to piss Bone off. He walks away.

"You all right?" I ask Logan.

He nods, brushing his curls from his forehead.

"I'm sorry," I tell him. And I mean it. I really do.

He nods again.

"It's not your fault you can't talk. And..." My voice falls off. I've never talked to anyone about this. "It's not my fault I can't read well."

He nods.

"I'm not stupid," I rush to say.

He nods again, and waves his hands to shut me up. He places a finger to his lips like he wants me to shush.

"Ok," I grumble.

He writes on the board and I groan, visibly folding. I hate to do it, but I can't take it. "I should go," I say. I reach for my bag.

He takes the board and puts it in his backpack. He gets it, I think. I'd rather play twenty questions than I would try to read words.

He opens his mouth and I hear a noise. He stops, grits his teeth, and then a sound like a murmur in a cavern comes out of his mouth.

"You can talk?" I ask. He put me through reading when he can talk?

He shakes his head and bites his lips together. I shush and wait. "Maybe," he says. It comes out quiet, and soft, and his consonants are as soft as his vowels. "Just don't tell anyone."

I draw a cross over my heart, which is swelling with something I don't understand.

"What's your name?" he asks. He signs while he says it. It's halting and he has to stop between words, like when I'm reading.

"People call me Kit," I tell him.

He shakes his head. "But what's your name?" he asks again.

I shake my head. "No."

He nods again. The waitress brings the burgers and he nods and smiles at her. She squeezes his shoulder again.

When she's gone, I ask him, "Why are you talking to me?"

"I want to." He heaves a sigh, and starts to eat his burger.

"You don't talk to anyone else?"

He shakes his head.

"Ever?"

He shakes his head again.

"Why me?"

He shrugs.

We eat in silence. I was hungrier than I thought, and I clear my plate. He doesn't say anything else. But he eats his food and pushes his plate to the edge of the table. He puts mine on the top of it, and looks for the waitress over his shoulder. I'm almost sorry the meal is over. We shared a companionable silence for more than a half hour. I kind of like it.

He gets the waitress's attention and holds up two fingers. He's asking for two checks. I should have known. I pull my money from my pocket. He closes his hand on mine and shakes his head. The waitress appears with two huge pieces of apple pie. I haven't had apple pie since I left home. Tears prick at the backs of my lashes and I don't know how to stop them. "Damn it," I say to myself.

He reaches over and wipes beneath my eyes with the pads of his thumbs. "It's just pie," he says.

I nod, because I can't talk past the lump in my throat.

Logan

Black shit runs down from her eyes and I wipe it away with my thumbs, and then drag my thumbs across my jeans. She's crying. But I don't know why. I want to ask her, but I've already said too much.

I haven't talked since I was thirteen. That was eight years ago. I tried for a while, but even with my hearing aids, it was hard to hear myself. After the kid on the playground teased me about my speech, I shut my mouth and never spoke again. I learned to read lips really fast. Of course, I miss some things. But I can keep up. Most of the time.

I'm not keeping up right now. "Why the tears?" I ask, as she takes a bite of her pie. She sniffs her tears back, and she smiles at me and shrugs. This time, it's her who won't talk.

Hell, if pie will make her cry, I wonder what something truly romantic would do to her. This is a girl that deserves flowers and candy. And all the good shit I can't afford. But she likes to talk to me. I can tell that much, so she's not with me simply because I wouldn't give her bag back.

She asks me a question but her mouth is full of pie, so I wait a minute for her to swallow. She gulps, smiles shyly at me and says, "Were you born deaf?" She points to my ear.

I point to my ear and then my cheek, showing her the sign for deaf. I shake my head.

"How old were you when it happened?" Her brows scrunch together, and she's so damn cute I want to kiss her.

I make a three and flick it at her.

"Three?" she asks.

I shake my head and do it again. She still doesn't get it. So, I put one finger in front of the three and she says, "Thirteen?"

I nod.

"What happened when you were thirteen?"

"High fever one night," I say, wiping my brow like I'm sweating, hoping she'll understand.

She opens her mouth to ask me another question, but I hold up a finger. I motion back and forth between the two of us, telling her it's my turn.

I can't figure out how to mime this one so that she'll understand, so I say very carefully, "Where are you from?"

She shakes her head and says, "No."

I put my hands together as though in prayer.

She laughs and says, "No," again. I don't doubt she's serious. She's not telling me. I have a feeling I could drop to my knees and beg her and she still wouldn't tell me.

"So, Kit from nowhere," I say. "Thanks for having dinner with me."

"How do I say thank you?" she asks. "Show me."

She looks at me, her eyes bright with excitement. I show her the sign and she repeats it. "Thank you," she says. And my heart expands. Then she looks at her bag beside me and says, "I should go."

I nod and stand up, and then I put my backpack on, and throw her bag over my shoulder.

"I'll take that," she says as she picks up her guitar case.

But I throw some bills on the table and wave at Annie, the waitress. She throws me a kiss. Kit is following me, but Annie doesn't throw her a kiss. I laugh at the thought of it. Annie loves me. And she's known my family since before our mom died and our dad left.

I stop when we get out to the street and light a cigarette. Kit scrunches up her nose, but I do it anyway. I take one drag from it, show it to her, pinch the fire off the end, letting the embers fall to the ground, and throw it in a nearby trash can. What a waste. But I can tell she doesn't like it. My brothers don't like it either. At least now they're in good company.

She holds her hand out for her bag, and I position her under a street light so I can see her mouth.

"Where do you live?" I ask. "I'll walk you home."

She looks confused for a minute. She glances up and down the street. Cars are rushing by and she's looking at me like she's suddenly lost.

"I live around the block," she says. "Give me my bag." This time, she stomps that black boot of hers and gives me a rotten look. She shakes her hand at me like that'll matter.

I lean close to her, because I'm kind of scared someone I know will see me talking to her. My brothers would be hurt if they thought I could talk and just chose not to. I let them think it's a skill I unlearned, instead. "You can't walk home alone. It's not safe."

She glares at me. "I'm not taking you home with me, you perv," she says, and she tries to take the bag from me. But I don't let her. She's tiny. And I'm not. I win. She balls up her fist, and I know I'm in trouble.

I lean close to her. "I don't want to sleep with you," I say. "I just want to make sure you get home safe." I hold up my hands like I'm surrendering. I draw a cross in the center of my chest like she did before and say, "Promise."

It's pretty late. It was already dark when we left the subway tunnel. Now it's really late. Later than she should be on the streets by herself. Particularly in this neighborhood. This is my neighborhood. I'm perfectly safe here. But she's not from here. This I can tell without ever hearing her voice. She's not my kind of people.

I put my fingers down, and pretend they're someone walking. "Let's go," I say.

She stands there, and crosses her arms in front of her. "No."

There's one thing I'm already sure of and it's that this chick means no when she says no.

Suddenly, the guy from the diner, the one she called Bone, walks up beside us. "Need some help, Kit?" he asks.

His lips are dark in the night, and I can barely see them. But I can see hers. She smiles what I know to be a phony smile at him, because her real smile will drop a man to his fucking knees, and she says, "Fine."

"This your guy for the night?" he asks.

She looks at me and steps forward, running the tips of her fingers down my chest. I go hard immediately, and I catch her hand in mine. She startles for a second, but then I cover her hand with mine, pressing it against my heart, tight and secure. She looks up at me and bats those brown eyes. I hadn't realized how dark they are. But they're almost black in the darkness of the night. "This is my guy," she says. But I can tell she's talking to him, and not to me.

The hair on her arms is standing up, and so is mine. But it's probably for very different reasons.

Bone walks away, looking over his shoulder at her ass. I want more than anything to punch him in the face. But I have a feeling that wouldn't be a good idea. "I'm your guy?" I say to her.

She deflates, and lifts her hand from my chest. "He's gone," she says. She slips her bag off my shoulder and puts it on her own. She stands up on tiptoe and kisses my cheek, her lips lingering ever so briefly. I want to turn my head and catch her lips with mine, but she'd run if I did that. I'm sure of it. *Thank you*, she signs. My heart leaps when I realize she's speaking my language. I just taught it to her, but still.

"Where are you going?" I ask.

"Home," she says with a shrug. Then she turns on her heel and leaves me standing there. I shake out a new cigarette and light it, and I watch her walk away. She doesn't look back. Her black bag is bouncing against her leg, and her guitar case is in her other hand. She hunches down against the wind. Does she own a coat? I wish I'd given her mine.

I follow her. I can't help it. I need to see where she's going, or I won't be able to find her again. Not to mention that her being alone in the night in the city scares the shit out of me. She's not hard enough for this place or for these people. If I let her get away from me, I might not ever find out what that tattoo means to her. And I sort of need to know now that it's on my arm. I might be able to find her in the subway tunnel. I realized when I saw her today that must be why she looked so familiar. I've seen her in the tunnel, busking for change.

She crosses the street and goes toward the old bank building, the one that was turned into a shelter for the homeless a few years ago. There are people in a line outside, and she gets in line with them. She doesn't have anywhere to stay. She's going to a fucking homeless shelter? But before she can go inside, they close and lock the doors. The people in line stand and protest. But they're full.

The throws her head back, her long dark hair falling even longer, reaching her ass. She's frustrated, I can tell. But she doesn't complain. She picks up her case, and starts down the street. There's another shelter a few blocks over, but my guess is that it's full, too. The shelters sprung up around here like fast food restaurants when the city began to change. But there are too many homeless and not enough places for them to stay.

I follow her, finishing my cigarette while I do. But instead of going to the next shelter, she stops and sits down on a bench, dropping her face into her hands. She's tired. And I feel weighed down by her burden, too. I approach her and sit down beside her. She looks up, her brown eyes blinking in confusion.

"You followed me," she says, looking up and down the street like she's not sure where I came from.

I nod.

Her chest bellows with air, and I'm guessing that was a heavy sigh. "You don't have to sit with me," she says.

I look at her, and I make sure to use my voice. "Come home with me," I say.

She looks into my eyes, hesitates for a moment, and then says, "Yes."

Emily

He's going to expect me to sleep with him. They usually think they can get in my pants if they give me a bed and a meal. He's given me food, and now the bed is the next part of it. He wouldn't be hard to sleep with. He has those dreamy blue eyes and curly locks of blond curls spring about in wild disarray all over his head.

I retrieve the money he gave me earlier from my pocket and try to give it to him. "For the place to sleep," I say. So he'll know I don't plan to sleep with him.

He shakes his head, looking at me like I have lost my mind. He slides my canvas bag off my shoulder again and puts it on his. His building is surprisingly close. All this time, I've been staying at shelters right around the corner from this guy. And I didn't even know he was there.

He opens the door and motions for me to step inside. "Do you live alone?" I ask.

He shakes his head no.

I stop him and press on his shoulder. "Who do you live with?"

He does that thing again where he shows me two people taller than him and two shorter than him. He lives with his brothers. Shoot. I'm not going to an apartment filled with men I don't know. "I can't," I say, but he rolls his eyes at me. Then he bends at the waist and drives his shoulder very gently into my midsection. He hefts me over his back like I'm a sack of potatoes. I'm still holding on to my guitar, and I knock him against the backs of his legs with it, because I know I could be screaming at him right now and he would have no idea. I can't talk to him. I can't tell him to put me down.

He carries me like that up four flights of stairs, and he's huffing a little when we get to the fourth floor. I expect him to keep climbing, but he doesn't. He stops and opens a door, and we're suddenly in a hallway.

My struggling has ceased, because it's no good. He can't hear me. He can't respond. So, I brush my hair out of my face with one hand and hold on tightly to my guitar with the other. He opens a door and steps inside, closing it behind him.

Four men turn to look at me, flopped there like a sack of potatoes over his shoulder. I'm turned to face them as he closes the door, so I wave. What else can I do? The one I met at the tattoo parlor gets to his feet. "Who's that?" he asks.

The tattoo guy bends over to look in my face. "Shit, Logan, that's the girl who clocked you."

The other men get up and walk over, too.

One of them says, "Dude, she's got Betty Boop on her panties." I can't even reach back to cover my ass.

Logan lowers me to my feet. I stumble as he sets me upright, when all the blood rushes back to my head. He reaches out to steady me, and he smiles. I realize that they could all see my panties when he had me upside down, not just the one of them. The rest were just nice enough that they pretended not to look.

Logan points to each of his brothers in turn, and motions for them to talk. "Paul," the biggest one says, as he extends his hand.

"I remember you," I say.

"I'll never forget you," he says, with a laugh as he smacks Logan on the shoulder. "And neither will his nose." He feints as Logan makes like he's going to punch him. But he doesn't. He stops right before he gets to his face.

The second to largest one, and they're all big boys, sticks out his hand and says, "Matthew." Matthew looks tired and a little green. I look at Logan and he nods subtly. This is the one who has cancer and is going through chemo. Paul slaps Matthew's hand away and says, "You're not supposed to be sharing any germs right now."

"Fuck you," Matthew says, and then he walks toward the hallway and goes in his bedroom and closes the door. He doesn't look back at me, but I don't mind.

The last two brothers have to be twins. They're younger than Logan, and they look identical. "Sam and Pete," Paul says.

They huddle around me, and I end up sandwiched between them, which they think is hilarious. They jiggle me around for a minute, until Paul barks at them. "Let her go," he says. He pops them both on the backs of their heads and says, "They don't know how to act when company comes over."

Company? That's what I am? "Nice to meet you," I say. I'm a bit overwhelmed. This is a lot of testosterone in one room. There's shooting and fighting blasting from the television and I look over at it. I know Logan can't hear it, but there are subtitles playing at the bottom of the screen. I don't know why, but that makes me smile.

Logan motions for me to follow him and I do, presumably toward his bedroom.

One of the twins (I can't tell them apart) calls out for us to wait. But Logan can't hear him. I follow him down the hallway, and the other of the twins is standing at the end of the corridor laughing like hell. Something is up, but I don't know what. Logan opens his bedroom door, and steps inside. I follow him. And that's when I see a form move in the bed.

"Who the fuck is that?" a female voice shrieks. Logan turns around and slaps at the light switch, and the room goes bright. A book flies across the room and hits his shoulder just as the light comes on. I step back out of the room, because whoever that is in his room is throwing shit like crazy. She's blonde. And she's naked. Completely and starkly naked. Shoot.

She jumps out of bed and starts grabbing for her clothes. Logan swipes a hand down his face and sticks his head out of the room. He motions toward Paul, who is leaning casually against the wall, a grin on his face. Paul walks down the hallway, his stride full of swagger, and he removes me from the doorway and goes in himself. The door closes with a thud.

"I thought you knew she was coming!" Paul says with a laugh. I imagine him doubled over, because that's how the twins are, they're laughing so hard. They're high fiving each other and listening to what's going on behind the door.

Logan must have signed something to him. Because he says, "She said she was going to surprise you."

Well, she did that, apparently.

Paul heaves a sigh and says, "He wants you to go."

More thuds in the room make me think she's throwing stuff again. Good God.

"He doesn't want you to surprise him again," Paul says quietly, but I can hear it. I want to press my ear against the crack in the door, because things have gotten quiet. I can hear her sniffle.

"You don't have to worry about that," she says with a loud inhale. "I'll never sleep with you again." The door flies open and she steps out it, and then she attempts to crowd me back against the wall. The twins freeze, their mouths falling open. She's almost six feet tall. I'm not.

"Oh, shit," one of them says.

I tolerate her until a piece of spittle flies out of her mouth and hits me in the cheek. "You better back the fuck up, bitch," I say. And I draw my fist back. I don't hit like a girl. I never have. I never will.

Like one of those hooks on the gong show my grandma used to watch, Logan wraps his arm around her waist, picks her up and spins her away from me. He shakes a finger at me. He better be glad he caught her, or she'd have my fist up her ass.

"Don't shake your finger at me," I warn. I'm pushing against him to get to her. "I'll rip every extension from your head." She actually has nice extensions. I'd love to ruin them. "I'll wrap them around your skinny neck and strangle you with them." I'm still reaching for her, and Logan can't sign, because he has her on one side and me on the other. I swipe at my cheek. The bitch spit on me. He hands her to the twins, who try to calm her down.

He holds up one finger at me. I think he wants me to wait. Wait for what? That skinny little no account whore just spit in my face. He shakes that finger at me again. I grab it and bend it back, until he winces and makes me let go. He's stronger than me and I know it. But it felt good. I could get tired of that finger really quickly.

He bites his lips together and sets me back from him. Then he walks to her, takes her by the elbow and escorts her to the door. She slides her shoes on as she goes, and her pants are still unbuttoned. She's going to be doing the walk of shame and she didn't even get laid. I take a good bit of joy in that. I'm more content than a cat in a windowsill. Logan signs something to Paul.

Paul turns to the twins and says, "One of you walk her home. It's late."

They both volunteer by raising their hands and jumping up and down. He calls on the one on the left. "Pete, you take her." He glares at him. "Don't stay long."

"Asswipe," the other one grumbles as he stalks back to the couch. "Pete gets to do everything." He clunks his feet down on the table. Then he changes his mind, stomps down the hallway and slams the door to his bedroom.

"Pete's not a man whore," Paul calls in the wake of his departure, deadpan.

"Since when?" Sam complains, sticking his head back out his door. "I'll have you know-" But he shuts his mouth when Paul glares at him. The door slams closed behind him again.

Logan swipes a hand down his face and then grabs my arm, leading me into his room. He closes the door behind us. "I didn't know she'd be here," he says. His voice is halting and slow.

I pout, crossing my arms beneath my breasts. He looks down at them. He is such a guy. "When was the last time you slept with her?" I don't know why I want to know this.

He holds up three fingers and points behind him. He's not quite meeting my eyes.

"Three days ago?" I clarify.

He nods. "But I didn't invite her tonight."

"Is she your girlfriend?" I ask.

He shakes his head. He holds up that finger again and I roll my eyes.

He leaves the room and comes back with a stack of clean sheets. He jerks the slut sheets off the bed and throws them in the hallway. He motions for me to walk around to the other side of the bed, and then he snaps the sheet open and makes a movement like he wants me to help him. I might as well.

I work quietly with him to make the bed. Then he crosses to me and tilts my chin up. I think he's going to try to kiss me and I'm balling up my fist to deck him again. But he just looks into my eyes. "I'm sorry," he says. His voice is clear. Halting, but clear.

"I'm not sleeping with you," I say.

He jerks his head back, clearly surprised. He steps back and shakes his head, and I think he's biting back a smile. "I brought you here to keep you safe. Not to have sex with you." He smiles again, and then he walks out of the room.

I follow him, because I don't think we're done yet. He goes to the fridge and pulls out a beer, pops the top of it and offers it to me. At the last second, he takes it back. "How old are you?" he asks, his brows drawing together.

"Nineteen," I admit. He puts the beer back and hands me a cold bottle of water. I take it. It's cool. And I'm thirsty. "What now?" I ask. He takes a sip of his beer.

He shrugs, and goes to sit on the couch. I look around. The place is a mess. There are pizza boxes everywhere, and dirty laundry piled up in the hallway. There are dishes in the sink, and the counter is full of clutter. There hasn't been a woman in this place for a really long time.

"Can I use your shower?" I ask. It has been a few days since I had a shower. It's hard to protect my stuff when I'm wet and naked, but I'm not too worried about it now.

Paul looks over his shoulder and then signs something to Logan. Logan looks at me and nods, pointing down the hallway. He makes a two with his finger and points, and I assume he means the second door. So, I grab my bag and head that way.

I open the door without knocking and I find Matthew hunched over the toilet. I move to step back and he looks me in the eye, his watery and red. "Don't tell my brothers," he warns. He starts to wretch again, and I step in the room and close the door. I open the cabinets and find a wash cloth, wetting it with cold water. I pass it to him and he wipes his face. He closes the toilet, flushes it and sits down on it. "Fucking chemo," he says. "It's a bitch."

"Do they know you're sick?" I ask.

He shakes his head and flushes the toilet again when it stops running. "Please don't tell them. They have enough to worry about."

"I won't."

"Did you need to use the bathroom?" he asks. He doesn't look like he has enough strength to stand.

"I was going to take a shower," I say. "But I can wait."

He gets up, groaning. "I think I'm good for now." He smiles a watery smile. "But I might have to barge in on you." He removes a towel from the cabinet and lays it by the sink for me.

"You'll be here to puke and not to look at me naked," I say.

"I don't mess with Logan's women," he says. Then he goes on to say, "Ever. It's a brother thing." He burps and I worry that he's about to toss up his cookies again, but he doesn't. He smiles at me and walks out, closing the door behind him.

"I'm not Logan's," I say more to myself than to him.

He opens the door back up, startling me. "Yes, you are."

Logan

Kit's in my bathroom and she's naked. Or she will be in just a minute. I look down the hallway at the closed bathroom door. If it was any other girl, I'd be in there with her. But with the tattoo this girl wanted, I already know there's a vulnerability there that no one gets to see. I don't want to make her run away. I want to get to know this one. I've never had this kind of curiosity about a girl before. I usually sleep with them. Then I send them home. That's one of the reasons why it surprised me so much to find Terri in my bed tonight. She knew what we did wasn't the start of a relationship. I never bought her flowers or candy or took her on a date. I never bought her dinner. I just said *let's go* with my eyes and led her back to my room. Why she thought I might want a repeat performance is beyond my comprehension.

I go get another beer and Paul glares at me like the time I let the toilet lid fall on his dick when he was seven and I was four.

"How did you end up with her?" he asks.

I shrug. *I found her in the subway tunnel busking for change.*

"And she followed you home like a lost puppy?"

No. I had to carry her. You saw me. Why is he asking so many questions? It's not like I've never brought a girl home before. *I followed her to see where she was going after I bought her dinner. And she stood in line at the homeless shelter until they closed the doors. They were full. She didn't have anywhere to go, so I brought her here.*

He's still glaring at me.

What? I ask.

"I told you not to mess with that one." He sits back, huffing out a big breath. "She's not like the others."

I know that. I'm going to sleep on the couch, dickwad. I'm not going to sleep with her.

His brows shoot up.

Shut up, I sign.

"You're going to sleep on the couch." He might need a two ton jack to pick his jaw up off the floor.

I nod. *How's Matt?*

"Sick." He takes a swig of his beer. "I don't think he wants anyone to know."

I nod.

His brows are still up. "You're really going to sleep on the couch?"

I nod again, raising my hands in the air to say what the fuck.

He shakes his head. "I just don't believe it."

I have a heart.

"Yeah, but it usually gets overruled by your dick." He takes a sip of his beer. "Does she know you put her tattoo on your wrist yet?"

I shake my head. *Not yet.*

"Are you going to tell her?"

Why should I?

"Maybe because it's personal to her. I still don't understand why you wanted it."

He's going to get a permanent crease between his eyebrows if he keeps scowling like that.

I don't understand it either. I look toward the bathroom door again. *Does she look familiar to you? Like you've seen her before?*

He shakes his head. "I don't think so."

I nod and shrug. I would say she just has one of those familiar looking faces, but she's so fucking beautiful that can't be the case. She's gorgeous. She would stand out in a crowd. And that's not just because she's in my bathroom naked.

"How's your nose?" Paul asks.

I shrug. It's fine. Nothing I can do about it either way. And I kind of deserved it.

The bathroom door opens up and she comes out. She's wrapped in a towel and her hair is wet and hanging down over her shoulders. She looks like she just brushed a comb through it. She doesn't have any makeup on. There's no black stuff around her eyes and I see she has a line of freckles across the bridge of her nose. She ducks quickly into my bedroom, and I sit back, forcing myself not to go and see her. She probably wanted to get dressed somewhere that's not all steamy.

I get up and go to the bathroom, closing the door behind me. The mirror is fogged up from the steam of her shower. The countertop is clean for the first time in months, and she even cleaned the toilet and the shower before she got in it, apparently. Everything is all clean and shiny. I assume it's because she's a girl that she felt the need to clean it before she used it. It looks nice and I remind myself to tell her thank you.

She left her shampoo bottle in the shower, and her soap. It smells nice in the bathroom for a change and I realize it's her stuff that left that clean scent in the air. Makes me want to go and sniff her. I want to bury my face in her hair to see if it smells as good as the bathroom does.

She's had enough time to get dressed now, hasn't she? I knock on my bedroom door and I crack it open, peeping in. She's sitting on the edge of my bed wearing the towel. It's open over her thigh, showing a long expanse of naked leg.

I motion to her, asking her silently if I can come in. She grips the towel where it's tucked between her breasts and hitches it higher. But she nods.

She looks toward my closet, which is standing open, and then back at me. I raise my brows at her in question. Does she need something?

"Can I borrow a shirt?" she asks. She looks down at her bag. "All my clothes are dirty, and I hate to put on dirty clothes when I just got out of the shower."

I must have looked at her funny. Because she rushes on to say, "I'll return it to you tomorrow, before I leave. I just want to sleep in it. Do you have a washing machine?"

I nod.

"Which question are you answering? The shirt? Or the washer?"

"Both," I say. She smiles at me. I'd talk to this girl all day long if it means she'll smile at me like that. I take a shirt from a hanger and toss it to her. She catches it and pulls it over her head. After she tugs it down toward her knees, she tugs the towel and jerks it from beneath the shirt. She sits down on the side of my bed and removes a pair of pink panties from her bag.

"Can you turn around?" she asks.

I do, and the fact that I did makes me grin like a kid in a candy store. I hope she can't see me.

I feel her hand on my shoulder and I turn back around. She's wearing my AC/DC shirt, and it hangs down around her knees. Damn she's pretty.

"Can I throw some things in your washing machine?" she asks.

"I can do it for you," I offer.

She shakes her head. "You are not fondling my panties, perv," she says, grinning. "Next thing I know, you'll be sniffing them." She laughs. I wish I could hear it, because it's probably the most beautiful sound in the world. It's not often I wish I could hear, because I can do almost anything I want. But right now, I wish I could hear the sound of her laughter.

I motion to her and she walks out with me to the hallway, where I open the door to the laundry closet. I take what's in the dryer out, and put it on top. Look like Sam and Pete's stuff and they can handle their own clothes. I flip what's in the washer to the dryer, and ask her for her things by holding out my hands. She shakes her head. I step to the side and she starts to take a few things from her bag. She doesn't have much – just a few shirts, some shorts, a pair of jeans, and what she was wearing today.

And the throws in a few pairs of panties. There's more Betty Boop and I grin at her and shake my head.

I dump in some laundry soap and she starts it, and then she walks back toward my bedroom. "Do you have a blanket I can put on the floor?" she asks.

What the hell? "Why?" I ask.

She looks at me like I've grown two heads. "To sleep on?"

"You are not sleeping on the floor," I tell her. "You take the bed. I'll sleep on the couch."

"The couch is about five feet long. You're too tall. I can sleep on the couch." She nods like she's made up her mind.

I grab her arm gently as she goes to walk by me. "No," I say. "You take the bed."

The bed is full size, so it's not the biggest bed in the world. She draws her lower lip between her teeth and nibbles it. That has to be one of the most erotic things I've ever seen. I reach out and touch her lower lip with my thumb, gently pulling it from between her teeth. She licks her lips and looks everywhere but at me.

"Are you sure this is all right with you?" she asks.

I lean close to her and pull her into my chest. I don't know why I feel the need to do that, but I do. She hesitates briefly and then wraps her arms around my waist. I kiss her gently on the forehead. She looks up at me and she looks almost lost. The color is high in her cheeks and she steps back. "Thank you," she says. She stands up on tiptoe and kisses my cheek almost like it's an afterthought.

That kiss touches me like the deepest tongue kiss never has. It's like my breath is trapped in my throat and I can't draw it in or out.

"Are you all right?" she asks.

"Fine," I say. But I'm anything but fine. She raises her arms to lift her wet hair from her neck and her boobs shift beneath her shirt. I'm instantly hard. "Let me know if you need anything?" I say. But I'm not looking at her anymore. I'm walking toward the door as fast as I can, before she notices that I'm getting hard just thinking about the fact that she doesn't have a bra on.

She touches my arm and says, "Logan, please don't tell anyone that I can't read, ok?" She looks worried and I hate it for her. I hate that she even has to worry about things like this.

"That was between me and you," I tell her. I like that it's our secret. Kind of like my talking is.

She closes the door behind me and I hear the thumb lock on the door click. She just locked me out of my own room. I can't say I blame her really. She's in a strange place. And she's surrounded by strange men. But there's a piece of me that's glad she locked the door.

I walk back to the living room, taking a blanket with me from the linen closet.

"I still can't believe you're going to sleep on the couch," Paul says.

I can't believe it either. But I am.

Emily

I've been lying in Logan's bed for what feels like hours, but I can't sleep. I heard Pete when he came home, and I heard Paul tell him to go to bed. Then the apartment got quiet. No one has made a sound for hours, until now. I think it's Matthew, because it sounds like quick, muffled footsteps and then an awful gagging noise.

I open the door and look out, the bathroom door is open about an inch, and I'm pretty sure that's Matthew in there getting sick. He's miserable, and I want to help him, but I also don't want to intrude. I tiptoe into the kitchen because I'm thirsty, and I look over at the sofa, where Logan is sleeping. His feet are hanging off the edge by about a foot, and he's flat on his back, his head bolstered by the arm of the couch. He doesn't even have a pillow.

I open the fridge and bend over see what they have to drink, and when I stand up, Matthew is looking at me over the top of the door. "What are you doing?" he asks. His eyes are rimmed in red and bloodshot, and his face is pale.

"Getting something to drink," I whisper. "Can I get you anything?"

He shakes his head. His gaze darts down to my bare legs, and I tug on the hem of Logan shirt. "Nice shirt," he says. He jerks a thumb toward Logan. "Did you two have a fight?"

I look over at Logan too. He's sleeping soundly, his mouth hanging open. "No," I whisper. "Why would you think that?"

"Wait." He stops like he's thinking about something. "Why are you still here? Are you spending the night?"

I nod, lifting a bottle of water to my lips.

"Logan's girls never spend the night." He looks amused. But I don't understand why.

"He insisted," I whisper.

"Why are you whispering?" he whispers loudly and dramatically.

"Logan's asleep," I reply.

"He's deaf." He grins.

Oh, yeah. I forgot. It's so easy to forget that he can't hear. I laugh and shrug.

Suddenly, he turns on his heel and runs back to the bathroom. He's sick again, but it sounds like his stomach is empty. I open drawers beside the sink until I find a drawer with towels in it. I wet one with some cool water, and I meet him when he's coming out of the bathroom with it. He takes it from me with a heavy sigh and dabs his face with it. "Do you need anything?" I ask.

"Ginger ale," he says. "There's some in the fridge."

I nod and go back in that direction. While I'm there, I grab an empty margarita mix bucket off the counter. I start down the hallway, and assume his door is the one with the open doorway. He's sitting on the edge of the bed, his head in his hands. I put the bucket in front of him. "For later," I say.

"Thanks," he says as he takes a sip of the ginger ale. I take the towel from his hands and go back to the bathroom, getting it cold again. When I go back in the room, he's laying down, so I gently put the towel on his forehead and turn to walk out. "Don't break his heart," he says.

He's puking his guts out and all he's worried about is me breaking Logan's heart.

"I'm just here for the night," I say.

He snorts. It comes out more like a snuffle. But I get it. He doesn't believe me. "I'll see you tomorrow," he says.

I turn out his light as I leave the room, and close the door behind me.

The washer has stopped quite some time before, and I take what's in the dryer out and see that the pile on top of the washer is growing. I can't see letting their things get all wrinkled, so I stand there and fold them, and I fold what's coming out of the dryer, too. I flip my laundry into the dryer, and then I remember the huge pile of laundry in the hallway, so I start a load of their things. Might as well. I'm not doing anything else.

I walk back to the kitchen, and Logan is snoring. His hair hangs all tousled over his forehead, and I wonder if his mother ever used to watch him sleep like this.

The kitchen is a mess, so I grab a trash bag from the pantry and start packing pizza boxes away. Then I put up all the food that's on the counter, and give it a good scrub. The kitchen is all nice and sparkly before I go back to bed.

I yawn and close the bedroom door behind me. But this time, I don't feel the need to lock it.

***

The bed dips in the middle of the night, and I startle awake. My heart starts pounding like a jackhammer and I scoot to the edge of the bed. "What are you doing?" I ask.

It's Logan, and the room is dark, so he can't see my face or hear my voice. He rolls to his side, away from me, snuggling deeply into the pillow. He makes this adorable smacking noise with his mouth as he settles. He reaches back and jerks the blankets off of me, tugging them onto him.

He doesn't really think he's going to sleep in here, does he? I could go and get on the couch, but he's already snoring. He's sound asleep. I lean up and look into his face. He doesn't stir. He's not going to try to put the moves on me. He's just going to sleep.

I roll over, curling into myself, because it's chilly without a blanket. I could go and get the one from the couch, I guess. I know he had one out there. But I'm afraid I'll wake him if I get up. I grab the edge of the blanket he just stole from me and pull it back over to my side, just enough to cover half of me. He doesn't move. So, it must be all right.

Logan

I wake up slowly, immediately aware there's a warm body pressed against mine. I raise my head and look down at the leg thrown across my thighs. There's a delicate arm wrapped across my chest, and a black head of hair with a blue streak tucked under my chin, right beside my heart.

Her thigh is naked and it feels so fucking good that I don't want to move. Her shampoo tickles my nose and I wonder how I ended up in bed with her. I know all we did was sleep. My guess is that I got up to pee in the middle of the night and came back to my bed by accident. How she got wrapped around me is another story.

I lay my head back against the pillow and look up at my cracked ceiling. I didn't mean for this to happen. And I don't want her to think that I just want her in my bed. That I only want to sleep with her. But I do want to sleep with her. Right now, I want to roll her over and slide the pink panties she made me turn around for last night slowly down her legs. I want to kiss her from the soles of her feet to the insides of her thighs. I look down at her thigh again. I can't resist it. I reach out and lay my hand on it. She wiggles and presses harder against me, her breasts cushioned by my chest.

I'm so freaking hard that all the blood in my body is pulsing in my dick. Shit.

The sun is coming up, so my brothers will be moving around soon. They'll never let me hear the end of it if they find me in here. I started off on the couch, and swore I would stay there.

Shit.

I just wanted to keep her safe and now she's in bed with me. Or I'm in bed with her.

Involuntarily, I clench her thigh in my grasp. I turn onto my side to face her, and hitch her thigh up higher over my hip. I need to slide out from under her arm. But then her brown eyes blink open. We're face to face. She doesn't seem startled. "You stole the covers," she says.

She has morning breath, and I've never wanted to kiss someone so bad in my life. "Why are you in my arms?" I ask.

She looks around like she's not quite sure, and she bites her lower lip between her teeth again. I pull it out very gently with my thumb and she licks her lips, just like she did last night. "I was cold. And you were warm."

"I started out on the couch," I say.

She nods, leaning close to me, burying her face in my chest. She inhales deeply, her breath moving through the thin material of my t-shirt when she exhales. Did she just sniff me?

"You smell good," she mouths, looking up at me so I can see her lips.

She did just sniff me. I can't help it. I palm her ass and draw her closer to me. "Do you always wake up so sweet?" I ask. She's like cotton candy in my arms. She smells soft and clean and she's not shoving me away.

"I'm not awake yet," she mouths. She spins over in my arms, facing away from me. My forearm is under her head and her bottom is tucked against my groin. Her head is beneath my chin, and I can't see her face anymore. But I doubt she's talking. She's soft in my arms, and her breath rushes out of her open mouth with every exhale, searing my forearm with her every breath.

The bottoms of her feet are cold against the tops of mine, so I unfurl the blanket over us both, tucking it around her, throwing it over our feet.

I don't want to let her go. But I know I need to get up. I need to go back to the couch. I close my eyes and brush her hair down between us.

She lets me wrap around her, and by her own admissions she's still asleep. Will it hurt to stay there? I keep holding her. I've never had a girl sleep the whole night in my bed before. Ever. I've never woken up with someone. I've never wanted to. Until now.

I settle my arm around her waist. I'll just stay a few more minutes.

***

My bedroom door slams open, and I feel its *thwump* as it hits the wall. Paul is a bear in the morning, and he doesn't wake anyone up easily. He goes around, throwing open doors and turning on lights until the twins are up and ready for school. They're both seniors in high school and have to be there early. I look up at him as he stops in my doorway.

I knew you wouldn't stay on the couch the whole night, he signs to me. He doesn't say it out loud. Probably so he won't wake her up. Kit's asleep on her stomach, her hand tucked beneath the pillow and one leg pushed out to the side. I sit up and look down at her. My AC/DC shirt has risen up around her waist, and one side of her pink panties has migrated to tuck in the crack of her ass. Her left ass cheek is on display, the firm, round globe taught but relaxed. I toss the blanket over her bottom as I get up.

Shut up, I sign to Paul.

I reach over and grab my jeans, shoving my legs into them quickly. I put on my boxers before I went to sleep last night.

Paul is wearing a pair of lounge pants and no shirt. When I get to the kitchen, the twins are eating bowls of cereal, both in their boxers.

Put some clothes on, I sign to them. *Kit's still here.*

"That's her name? Kit?" Sam asks.

I shake my head. *I don't think so.* I'm pretty sure that's not her name. *It's what some guy on the street called her.*

"Where's she from?" Pete asks.

I don't know. She won't tell me.

Paul motions to the couch. "How'd you sleep?" He grins.

My neck still hurts from being on the couch. *Fine*, I say.

"She slept in your bed. With you." Paul's grin has turned into a glare.

I nod. *Not the whole night. Just part of it.* I fumble for a cup of coffee, but the coffee pot's not where we left it. What the fuck happened to the kitchen?

Paul has his hip hitched against the counter top and he's staring at me. "We woke up to it looking like this." He motions toward the expanse that is our clean countertop. I can't remember the last time I saw the Formica.

Where is all the stuff?

He opens the pantry door and points inside. She put it all away? The sink is empty of dishes, until Sam puts his bowl in it. *Put it in the dish washer*, I tell him. If she worked this hard to clean the kitchen, we can try to keep it looking like this, can't we?

"Aww, man," Sam complains. But he opens the dish washer and puts his bowl in there.

"You two get to school," Paul says. He shoos them toward their room so they can get dressed. "Next time, put some clothes on before you come out of your rooms," he warns. He looks at me. "How long will Kit be here?"

Paul looks over my shoulder and smiles at something. I turn around and see that it's Kit. She's all rumpled and she has a dent in her cheek from the crease of the pillow case. "I'll leave today," she says. She walks toward the coffee pot, which is now on a different counter. Granted, it's more convenient where she put it, but it's still not where it goes. She takes out a coffee cup and pours herself a full mug, and then she turns and says, "Thank you for letting me stay last night. I appreciate it."

I want to ask her about cleaning the kitchen and tell her thank you, but I can't use my voice in front of my brothers.

"She cleaned the bathroom, too," Sam says as he comes around the corner. His hair is wet and he leans toward me. "Do I smell too much like a girl?" he asks. He looks slightly abashedly at Kit. "I used your shampoo. And your soap."

Paul shoves him in the shoulder. "He would have used your tampons if you'd left any in there."

Her face colors prettily.

"Stay out of her stuff, dickwad," Paul warns.

Paul adjusts his jeans. "She folded my jeans. It doesn't feel quite right wearing something that wasn't rolled up in a ball in the basket in the corner of the room."

I glare at her. She did all this while we were sleeping? I want to tell her she doesn't have to work to stay here.

"What?" she asks. "I couldn't sleep."

She was sleeping pretty well in my arms. I don't want to think about that, because I can't get over the fact that I liked it as much as I did.

Sam leans over and kisses her on the cheek, just as Pete kisses her other cheek. She scrunches up her face, but she doesn't slap either of them. "I vote that we let her stay another day," Pete says. He looks down at her naked legs. Honestly, I've seen women at night clubs show a lot more skin than she's showing. "She's cute," he says. Then he grabs a banana off the counter and runs for the door. Sam is right behind him. He closes the door behind him and Sam sticks his head back in. "I second that vote," Sam says. Then the door slams and they're gone.

Kit smiles and looks over my shoulder. Matt is up, and he looks like death warmed over. "I third," he says as he sits down in a chair and puts his face in his hands.

Paul shrugs. "It's fine with me," Paul says. "But it's Logan's call. It's his bed."

Paul leaves to get ready for work. I have to do the same, but I don't have to go in until eleven. Paul goes early every day because he has to do paperwork.

Kit gets a ginger ale from the fridge and pours it into a glass. She hands it to Matt and he smiles faintly, and says, "Thank you." She doesn't say anything back, but she squeezes his shoulder. What's going on with the two of them? He won't let us do a damn thing for him, but he's letting Kit get him something to drink?

She smiles and walks back to the bedroom, taking her coffee with her.

"She's going to break your fucking heart, man," Matt warns after she closes the door.

I know. She's going to break my fucking heart. Because I've never wanted anything with anyone the way I want something I can't even define with her.

Emily

Waking up in his arms was one of the best moments of my life. I didn't want to wake up. I wanted to stay like that forever. So when he asked me questions about how we came to be tucked into one another, I pretended like I was asleep and rolled over, hoping he would wrap his arm around me. He did. He wrapped his whole body around me. I purposefully chose to turn away so I wouldn't have to explain. Because I didn't want to tell him about how I felt him when he got in bed with me. Or how I reached out to touch him in the night, and he let me put my head on his chest.

I didn't intend to wrap my body around him, but he didn't seem displeased by it. If the tent in his boxers was any indication, he was very pleased by it.

But even after, he was nothing but respectful about my body.

I come out of his bedroom dressed in my school girl outfit. It's clean now, so I didn't mind putting it back on. Aside from the fact that putting it on means I'm leaving his apartment. My bag is over my shoulder and my guitar case is in my hand. No one is there aside from the two of us. Paul went to work an hour ago. And Matt is staying home today, I'm sure. He's too sick to hold his head up, much less go work with the public. He must be in his room, because Logan is sitting at the table reading the newspaper. He looks up when I walk out of the bedroom, and his face falls.

He makes a gesture with his hands like he's asking me what.

"I have to go," I explain. I hold up my guitar. "I have to go to work. And you have to go to work. And I'm sure you don't want me hanging out while you're not here. What if I steal something?" I try to laugh it off, but he's not amused.

"You don't have to go," he says. "Stay." He gets up and comes to stand in front of me.

I hold up the guitar again. "I can't. I have to work." I only have thirty two dollars to my name. I can't find a decent place to stay on that. Not even for a night.

Like he can read my mind, he pulls out his wallet and flips it open. He takes money out of it and tries to press it in my hand. I can't take his money. "Stay," he says. He wants me to stay instead of going to busk for change.

I shake my head. It's hard to explain it to him. I want so badly to stay. But I can't. I can't get comfortable anywhere. Because tomorrow, I might have to leave again. "Thank you for letting me sleep here," I whisper. I know he can't hear the quality of my voice, but he can still read my lips. He tips my chin up with his forefinger under my jaw so that I look at him. "Thank you," I repeat.

"Come back tonight?" he asks. He's holding my hand, his thumb swiping back and forth across the surface of it. "I'll sleep on the couch. I promise."

I look up at him, swallowing hard. "I liked it when you were in the bed with me," I admit.

His eyes narrow and he looks closer at me than I think anyone ever has. But he doesn't say anything else.

"I think I'm in like," I admit softly. That's probably the wrong thing to say. But I need to tell him. I didn't just use him for a place to sleep. I genuinely could care about him if my situation was different. But it's not. And I can't.

He doesn't understand the terminology, I think, because he looks confused. "What?" he asks.

"I think I'm in like," I repeat. But he still looks just as confused.

He looks like he's going to get Matthew to translate. I stop him by jerking on his arm. "I like you," I say clearly. "That's why I'm leaving. I wouldn't be any good for you or for your brothers. I like you too much to stay."

"That's ridiculous," he says.

Yeah, it's ridiculous. But he doesn't know where I come from. He doesn't know how many people are looking for me and why. And when he does find out – I have no doubts that he will – he'll hate me for not telling him everything up front.

"Have dinner with me?" he says, his brows shooting up. He looks hopeful, and that's not what I want for him. He bends his knees so he can look into my face. "Dinner?" he repeats, like I might not have understood him. "A date," he says. "Go on a date with me."

I shake my head. I shouldn't like him so much after such a short time, but I see possibilities there where before I had none. He makes me believe I could have a real connection with someone. Well, maybe if I was someone else. But I'm not. So I can't.

"Thank you for letting me sleep here," I say. "And do my laundry and take a shower. I really appreciate it. Will you tell your brothers thank you for me?"

His hand falls away from me, and I feel like someone just untethered my anchor and I'm going to float away. He nods. He walks back over to the table and sits down, and begins turning the pages of the newspaper. He's not looking at me anymore and I feel the loss like someone chopped off my arm.

I let myself out and lean heavy against the wall outside his door. I can't bring him into my life. It's not good for him. Not for any of them. This is the way it has to be.

***

My ass is cold again, even though I'm wearing black leggings under my plaid mini skirt. It's freezing in the subway, and I'm sitting on my bag to keep my butt off the cold concrete. But it's still seeping into me. I have made forty-two dollars today, though, and it's a good day. I must have looked utterly miserable, because people have been putting money in my case like I'm homeless. Well, I am, but it's not like I'm holding a sign that says "I'm hungry."

It's a little after seven o'clock, and I've been here since I left Logan's apartment. My hands are tired, and I can't help but think to myself that I had better get moving. The after-work crowd has passed, and the drunks tend to come out after dark. So, I never feel safe in the subway when it starts to get late. I gather up my things and put my guitar away. I pocket the money I made today. It's getting colder outside as fall settles on the city, and I don't have a coat. So, I can either use the money I have to get a motel room, or I can go to the thrift store and try to find a used coat that I can use to keep warm as the weather changes. If I do that, I'll be sleeping in the shelter again, provided that they have room.

So, it's coat, shelter, and back to the subway for me tomorrow.

Someone calls my name as I walk up the steps of the tunnel and I turn to find Bone standing by the lamppost. "How's it going, Kit?" he asks. His eyes rake down my body, and my insides revolt.

"Fine," I say quickly. "Did you need something?"

He shakes his head, biting his lips together. "You have somewhere to stay tonight?" he asks.

He asks me this every time he sees me, like he's going to catch me at a vulnerable moment and I'll take him up on whatever he's offering. I don't even know what he's offering, but I know it won't do me any good. "I do, but thanks for asking."

"Any time, Kit," he says. He turns and walks away, his arm around some girl's shoulders. She looks strung out. And I'd be willing to bet that's how he likes them.

I walk through the city, wandering toward the shelter. I know it's right around the corner from where Logan works. I can't help but walk by there. The lights are on inside and there are still people walking around. I slow down, hoping I can get a look at him. I just want to see him. I know he probably hates me. But I want to see that he's walking around, breathing and maybe even laughing.

The neon sign over the building says Reed's. Makes me wonder if that's their last name. Paul walks to the door and lifts a hand at me without opening it. He tilts his head and looks at me. A bit too closely. He pushes the door open and speaks through the crack. "Are you coming in?"

I shake my head. "I shouldn't."

He nods. "You shouldn't. But you are." He motions me forward. "He's in the back."

It's like my feet have a mind of their own. I walk toward the back of the store, and the girl at the front desk shoots me a heated glance. I ignore her. There's a curtain in the back of the shop, and I'm guessing that's where he is. I push it slowly to the side. He can't hear me and he's facing away. But there's a woman on the table who's naked from the waist up. He's standing in front of her with his arm wrapped around her; his hand is busy around her right breast.

"Shit," I say. I feel like someone has just punched me in the gut. The lady on the table startles and Logan looks up. I have no choice but to leave. I've done nothing but think about this man all day long, and he's with one of his skanks. I knew he had them. But seeing his hands on one of them is worse. I have no right to claim him. I didn't even plan to come and find him. Paul insisted. Did Paul know what I would walk into?

Paul steps into my path as I run toward the door. "Kit," he says, blocking me from leaving with his body in front of me.

I put up my hands to ward him off. I can't take a deep breath, much less stop to talk to him. Before I can get to the front door, Logan runs from the back of the shop to the front, chasing after me. I can hear his feet on the laminate floor.

Logan reaches for me, taking my elbow in a tight but gentle grip.

Tears are stinging the backs of my lashes. I don't know why they are. But they are. And I don't want him to see. He holds up a finger telling me to wait. I can't wait. If I wait, he'll see me break down.

He takes my hand in a firm grip and starts to tow me toward the back of the store. He pushes the curtain to the side, and I see that the woman is still sitting exactly like he left her. Only now she's holding a thin piece of paper over her breasts. "Hi," she says. He points toward a chair and indicates that he wants me to sit.

I shake my head. "No."

He points toward the chair again. I drop into it because I feel like my legs won't hold me up anymore and that's the only reason.

He turns back to the woman and urges the paper down. He's tattooing her nipple. I look away. "It's all right," the woman says. "He did beautiful work. I don't mind if you see it."

He's doing a tattoo. Of course he is. All the breath rushes from my body in a huge exhale. He's doing a tattoo. I look over his shoulder as he's finishing up. He's not just tattooing her nipple. The tattoo is her nipple. What the hell?

"Double mastectomy," she explains. "Logan does free tattoos for mastectomy patients." She arches her back, pressing her breasts out. "What do you think?"

They look like real nipples. The shading around the edges is perfect, and he's drawn a simple nipple with a large areola. But there's nothing simple about it. It's a work of art. The color is the same shade as her lips, and I can't believe how real they look. "Wow," I say. What do you say? Nice nipples? Beautiful boobs? "That's amazing."

Logan holds up a mirror for her, and she looks from one to the other. "They're perfect!" she squeals. She throws her arms around his neck, and he hugs her tightly, smiling over her shoulder at me. He steps back from her, and bends down, softly placing a kiss on the top of her breast. Her eyes fill up with tears, and so do mine. "I'm going to show everybody," she says. She holds the paper over her breasts as she walks out into the shop. The girl that runs the front of the shop comes over to admire them, and Paul pretends to look everywhere but at her boobs. There's no one in the shop, but I get the feeling she wouldn't care if there was.

"She wanted to feel sexy again," he says quietly, yanking the curtain so that we're behind it.

"You did beautiful work." I bat my guitar case against my shins, not sure what else to say. It really was remarkable how lifelike they looked. The shading and the colors and the way they fit the size of her new breasts – it was all perfect.

"She needed them." He shrugs. He's so humble.

She bounces back behind the curtain, looking so pleased. She tugs her shirt over her head and takes money out of her purse. "I don't have much," she starts.

He presses it back into her purse, shaking his head.

"He won't take it," I say.

She narrows her eyes at me. "Who are you?"

"No one."

She nods. She kisses Logan on the cheek, waves at me and leaves.

He starts to clean up his supplies. He looks over at me out of the corner of his eye and says, "Why are you here?"

I open my mouth, but can't think of the right thing to say. I close it again. He stops and leans his hip against the table, crossing his arms over his chest.

"Can I buy you dinner?" I blurt out. I have no idea where that came from. But there it is.

He smiles. "Yes."

Logan

"What do you want to eat?" I ask as we leave the shop. Kit asked Paul to join us, but I think he saw the pleading in my eyes when I looked in his direction. I need some time alone with her. I need to take her on a date. Technically, she asked me out, but I'd never let her buy dinner for me. Ever.

"I don't care," she says with a shrug.

I realize I have no idea what she likes. "Italian?" I point to an Italian restaurant on the corner by my apartment.

She nods, smiling at me.

"I didn't think you were going to come back." I hold the door open for her, and she walks into the dark restaurant ahead of me. The waitress leads us to a corner booth and she slides in across from me.

"I shouldn't have." She puts her guitar under the table, banging me in the shin with it in the process. "I'm sorry," she says, wincing. She's suddenly uncomfortable with me.

Is she sorry for knocking me in the shin or for leaving me this morning? "What did you do today?" I ask.

She makes a face and points toward her outfit. "Playing in the subway."

"How did it go?"

She shrugs. "It was cold. My butt is still freezing," she admits. I get an immediate and strong image of me helping to warm up her ass. I saw that perfect globe that is her ass cheek this very morning. "What?" she asks.

My thoughts must have played out on my face. "Nothing," I say. But a grin tugs at the corners of my lips.

"What's so funny?" she asks, her head tilting to the side.

I shake my head. "My mind was in the gutter if you must know," I admit. "I'm sorry. It won't happen again. Please go ahead." I motion for her to keep talking using my hands.

"You were thinking about my butt," she says. And now she's grinning too.

Heat creeps up my cheeks. She's so damn pretty.

The waitress comes to the table with menus, and lays one in front of each of us. "Welcome," she says. "Do you want to know our specials?" She blinks at me, trying to catch my eyes. I make it a point not to look at her.

Kit nods in answer to her question. She rattles off some menu items and their prices, and I see Kit reach into her pocket and count her money beneath the table. There's no fucking way I'm letting her buy dinner.

"What can I get for you to drink?"

Kit arches a brow at me and I motion from her to me and back so she'll get me what she's having. "Root beer?" she asks.

I nod. The waitress leaves us with the two menus. I open mine and she doesn't. "Do you know what you want?" I ask.

"What are you having?" She smiles at me.

I open the other menu in front of her and point to the word at the top. "What do you see when you look at that?"

She scrunches up her nose. "I see someone who thinks he can teach me to read." She closes the menu. "Believe me, better people than you have tried."

"Who tried?" I ask.

She takes a sip of her root beer through a straw, her lips pursing around it. "A better question would be who didn't try. I have been poked and prodded and put through special ed and been to therapists who thought they could unlock my brain. No one could."

She doesn't look upset by this. She just looks resigned to it. I open the menu back up, just because I'm curious. I point to the word at the top of the page again. "What does that say?" I ask.

She looks down at it and closes it. "I know words," she says. She looks like she really wants to explain it to me, and I really want to hear it. "I can spell words. And I know what they mean. It's just the way they lay on the page that's hard for me." She shrugs. "I don't expect you to understand." She's looking everywhere but at me now, and I wish I hadn't pushed it.

"So, you know the words, and how to spell them in your head?" That baffles me.

"Crazy, isn't it?" She laughs, but there's no smile on her face. "Dyslexia's a bitch."

The waitress reappears with a basket full of bread and places it in the center of the table. Kit reaches for a piece and I wonder if she ate today.

"Did you decide what you want?" the waitress asks. I point to the chicken parmigiana. She nods and looks at me funny. She's catching on that something isn't right. But apparently, she still finds me intriguing.

"What's good?" Kit asks her. She did this same thing at the diner. It must be how she copes.

"The chicken parmigiana is amazing," she says, smiling down at me. Kit's not impressed. "But the alfredo is my favorite."

I raise my brows at her in encouragement. She laughs. "Ok, but if I don't like it, I'm taking your chicken," she warns. I nod. "I'll take the alfredo," she says to the waitress.

Kit lifts a piece of bread to her lips and takes a bite. A crumb sticks to her lip and I want to reach over and catch it, and bring it to my lips. But I don't dare. I have her at dinner with me. If I push her too hard, she's going to run away.

"Did you eat today?" I blurt out.

Her face flushes and she nods. She's lying. I'm sure of it.

I push the bread basket toward her and say, "Eat." She takes another piece.

She chews silently for a minute and then she looks at me. Her face is soft when she says, "What you did for that woman in the shop, with the tattoos…" I nod when she stops. She's referring to the nipple tats. "That was amazing and beautiful. Where did you learn to do that?"

I shrug. I don't remember learning it. I just knew I could draw it. And if I can draw it, I can run a tat of it. "I think she was pleased."

"Are you kidding?" She slaps the table. "She was ecstatic. And they really were beautiful. Like art. Can I see your tattoos?" she asks hesitantly.

I'm wearing my coat, so I have to shrug out of it to show her. I want to show her my art. I drew most of them, and my brothers put them on me. But I take my coat off and lay my hands face down on the table. She leans over, looking closely. I have full sleeves, which means I have tats from my neck all the way to my wrists.

She touches the lips on my forearm with a light finger. The hair on my arms stands up, but I pretend I don't notice. "Why did you get this one?" she asks.

I smile. "That one goes with this one." I point to my other arm. "It's something my mother used to say."

Her forehead crinkles as she looks at the cross on my other arm.

"From your lips to God's ears," I explain. "In my case, I have a lot of distance between my lips and God's ears. That's why they're on different arms."

"Do you see your mother often?" she asks. She's still eating bread, and that's good. I want to keep talking to her so she'll keep eating. I know she hasn't eaten today.

I shake my head. "She died a few years ago."

"Oh." Her mouth stops moving, and she swallows hard. "I'm so sorry."

I shrug. It was a freak accident.

"And your dad?" she asks.

"He left after Mom died," I explain. This part is always difficult. "There were just too many of us, I think." I laugh. But it's not funny.

"So, it's just you and your brothers?" she asks.

I nod. "Paul took responsibility for everyone when our dad left. He had to so we wouldn't all be split up."

"Wow." That's all she says. Just wow. She looks baffled.

"We make do," I explain. I don't want her to feel sorry for me. "How about you? Where's your family?" I wait, like a kid in a candy store.

But she shakes her head. "No," she says.

"That's not fair," I say.

She holds up a finger, just like I do to her all the time. "I know it's not fair," she says. "But it's better if you don't know."

"Better for who?" I ask. I'm a bit irked that she's keeping secrets. She has a right to them. But I don't have to like it.

"My situation is difficult," she begins. "And I can't explain it to you."

She looks back down at my tats. Her eyes play across them. There are too many to count. But I need to show her the one that's hers. "I want to show you something," I say. "But I'm afraid you're going to be angry at me."

She's suddenly on guard. "Why? What is it?"

I turn my wrist over and point to her tattoo on my inner wrist. It's a bare spot I'd been saving for something special. She leans toward it and all of her breath rushes from her body. I can feel it across my hand when she exhales. "That's my tat," she says.

She takes my hand in hers and lifts it toward her face. "Are you angry?" I ask.

She looks up at me briefly and then back down at the tattoo. She's taking in every facet of it. Her hand trembles as she holds tightly to mine. "You changed it."

"I felt like you needed a way out."

I put it on my wrist because I was intrigued by the secrets inside. It's art. And I appreciate art in all its forms.

She swallows. Hard. Then her eyes start to fill with tears. She blinks them back for as long as she can. And then she gets up and runs toward the bathroom.

Shit. Now I fucked up. I made her cry. She runs by the waitress, who startles. The waitress starts in my direction, a sway in her hips. I get up and follow Kit. I stop outside the door to the ladies' room and press my hand against it. I don't know what I'm waiting for. She's in there crying and I can't hear her through the door to be sure she's all right. Fuck it. I'm not leaving her in there upset. I push through the door and I don't see any feet in the stalls when I bend over.

Where the fuck did she go? I push doors open, but the last one is locked. I stand up on my tiptoes and look over the top. She's standing there with her forearms pressed against the wall, her head down between her arms, and her back is shaking. She's crying.

I knock on the stall door and say, "Let me in, Kit." She doesn't say anything. I wouldn't be able to hear her if she did. I step back onto my tiptoes and look over. She's still crying. "Let me in," I repeat. She doesn't move, so I walk into the stall next to hers and stand up on the toilet. I rock the partition between the stalls gently. It might hold my weight. There's only one way to find out. I hoist myself up and over the wall, bringing my legs over the top slowly and carefully, and then I hop down.

Before I can reach for her, she's in my arms, her arms sliding around my neck. She's still sobbing, and her body shakes against mine. I tilt her face up to mine because I can't see her lips to tell if she's saying anything to me or not. I need to apologize. I didn't expect her to get so upset. I'll have it covered up with something else if it bothers her this much.

My heart twists inside my chest. I really fucked up. "I'm sorry," I tell her, looking down into her face. Her face is soaked with tears and she freezes, looking up at me. I can feel her like a heartbeat in my chest. She steps on the toes of my boots, and then rocks onto her tiptoes. She pulls my head down with a hand at the back of my neck.

Her brown eyes are smoldering, and black shit is running down her cheeks, but I don't care. She's never looked more beautiful to me. I hold her face in my hands and wipe beneath her eyes with my thumbs. Her breath tickles my lips and she leans over even closer. She's standing on my fucking boots, and I don't care. She can do whatever it takes to get her closer to me.

"Why did you do it?" she asks, moving back enough that I can see her lips.

I already told her. I thought she needed a way out. All I added to the tattoo was a keyhole right in the center of the guitar. It's a simple design really. "I don't know," I say. I want to explain it to her, but I can't. Not right now. Her breath is blowing across my lips and she smells like yeast from the bread and root beer. And I've never wanted to kiss a girl so much in my life. But she was fucking crying. I can't take advantage of her.

She pulls my head toward hers and she kisses the corner of my mouth. Then she kisses the other corner. I can't take much more. I chase her lips with every move she makes. She's smiling when she finally presses her lips to mine. I can feel it against my mouth. I keep my eyes open, because I need to see her face. I'm holding her in my hands, and I slide my fingers into the hair at her temples.

I want so fucking bad to kiss her softly. I want to treat her like the treasure she is. But I can't. She smells so good and she feels so good and she's in my arms and I don't know if I can stop. Then she draws my lower lip between hers and sucks it gently. Her eyes are closed, and she's making love to my mouth. I'm afraid if I close my eyes, that I'll realize this was all a dream when I open them back up.

I tilt my head and press my lips harder against hers. She's soft and warm in my arms, and she's pressed against me from head to toe. Kit starts to tug my shirt from my jeans and I raise my elbows to help her. Her hands touch my waist, and I freeze. I hoist her in my arms, wrapping her legs around my waist, holding her up with my hands palming her ass. I press her against the wall and she laughs against my lips. I can feel the sound of it through her throat, like a gentle hum.

Her hands skim up my chest between us, but I'm still making love to her mouth. Her tongue slides against mine and I press inside the cavern of her mouth. This is the first time my body will enter hers, and I want to take it slow. I want to enjoy every second of it, but she's not having that. She's hot in my arms, and wiggling to get closer to me. Her hands stop as she skims up my chest, and she withdraws her lips from mine. I take a moment to try to catch my breath, because I feel like I just ran a five mile sprint. I even have the stitch in my side to prove it. She lifts my shirt up, and touches my piercings with her fingertips.

My breath leaves me. She's curious and I love that she's taking the time to look at me. She's intent upon her task and she explores my nipples, looking down, her bottom lip drawn between her teeth. I pull it free with my thumb, just like I have so many times before. Only this time, I lean forward and draw it into my mouth, nipping it gently. She rolls my piercings between her fingertips, and she's going make me disgrace myself if she doesn't stop. I pull back and bury my head in her shoulder, breathing harder than I ever have. This woman has completely undone me.

A hard wrap on the bathroom stall startles me, because I can feel the heavy shake of the metal partition. Kit looks up and says, "Just a moment."

I'm breathing so fucking hard that I can't catch my breath. But I put her down when she unwraps her legs from around me. She opens the stall door and steps out, wiping her still-wet face. The guy who banged on the door startles when he sees how wrecked she is. She was crying really hard there for a minute. I close the door and let her talk to him, because I need a minute to compose myself. I reach into my pants and adjust my junk. I have to cover it up with my shirt, because my dick is reaching up past the button on my jeans. Shit.

She felt so fucking good in my arms. I lean back against the wall and try to take some calming breaths. But there's not much that can calm me at this point. The only thing that would make this better is if she came back in here and we finished what we started.

I open the door and look out. The man is gone, and she's standing at the sink washing her face. She looks up at me, a soft smile on her lips as she sees me in the mirror. I walk up behind her and put my arms around her, resting my chin on her shoulder. "I'm sorry I made you cry," I say.

She shakes her head and talks to me in the mirror. "No one has ever done anything like that for me before," she says. Her eyes fill up with tears again, and I'm sorry that I came out of the stall. I'll go back in there if she'll stop crying. But I'm not leaving her. I can see that now. I'm not leaving her, no matter what.

"The lock?" I ask. She's leaning back against me, and she wraps her arms over mine.

She nods. She wipes her eyes with a paper towel, swiping the black makeup from under her eyes. Her face is splotchy, but she's never looked more beautiful. For that one split second, she isn't hiding anything from me.

"The minute I saw the tattoo, I knew it needed to be changed. I'm sorry if I defiled your art." She could take exception to my change. But I have a feeling she doesn't.

"It's perfect," she says. She lifts my arm from around her waist, and looks down at it. "It's perfect," she repeats, sniffling. "I don't know how to tell you what I'm feeling."

I'm the one with the hearing impairment and she can't tell me something? I laugh and lift her hair from her neck, and press my lips there. "You don't have to say anything," I tell her.

She turns around and cups my face in her palm, her hand stroking across my five o'clock shadow.

I take her hands in mine and lift them to my lips, kissing them one by one. Then I look into her eyes and open my mouth to ask her the one question I need to know the answer to. "What's your name?" I ask.

She freezes. It's like there's suddenly a wall between us and I haven't even let her go. "No," she says.

I feel like she's kicked me in the gut. I let her go and take a step back. "Why not?" I ask.

"I just can't," she says.

I nod and let myself out of the bathroom. My legs are shaking. The waitress shoots me a glance as I walk back to the table. I sit down. Kit's still in the bathroom and I can't help but wonder if she's ever going to come out. Her guitar is still under the table. So, she has to come back, right?

Emily

I lean heavily on my palms, putting all my weight on the bathroom countertop. My pulse is pounding so loudly that I can hear it in my ears, and drawing in a deep breath is burning my lungs like someone has set a fire inside them. Perhaps that's what he did. Or maybe he'd just shaken the pieces of me loose and now my body had to work to put me back together.

Either way, I feel like someone has torn me into two pieces. There's the one piece of me that wants to give Logan everything he wants. It's the piece that so very desperately wants to bare my soul to him, to tell him all of my problems. He would take them inside himself and then breathe them back out, and all my problems would vanish like in *The Green Mile*. I know he would. But my problems are too big for him. They'd eat him alive. And I can't let that happen. Because there's the other piece of me that knows I need to run like hell. I need to leave him before I hurt him.

I touch the tips of my fingers to my lips. They're red and swollen from his kisses. I've never been kissed like that before. I've never had a man make love to my mouth. I've never had a man try to work his way inside my body, kissing deep inside me, while touching nothing but my mouth. But that's what Logan did.

I need to go out there and collect my guitar, and then go. That would be the fair thing to do. But he put the tattoo on his wrist. He marked himself with my brand, and he changed it. Tears flood my eyes again, and I blink them back, using a wet paper towel to wipe the eyeliner smudge from beneath them. I look like a raccoon.

I heave a sigh. It's no wonder the manager looked at me like I deserved all the sympathy in the world. I told him someone important had died. That's why I looked like this. But in reality, I'm the one who died. When I left home, I died. I like the peaceful existence I've been creating here. I know what to expect. And I expect to face life alone. Now Logan is ruining my almost perfect existence.

I haven't felt hope in a really long time. But I am hopeful. And that isn't a good thing.

I push off the countertop and fluff my hair. His hands have been all over it, and it looks like I'd been tumbled in a drier. Laughter falls from my lips, completely unbidden.

I go back to the table, and he's there. He's eating a piece of bread, and looking up at me, quiet like he normally is. I slide into the booth across from him and settle against the seat back.

"Are you all right?" he asks.

I nod. "I'm fine." I close my eyes tightly, trying to find the right words to explain it.

He takes my chin in his grip and I open my eyes to look at him.

"You don't have to tell me anything," he says.

I shake my head. The words are right there on the tip of my tongue, but I can't force them past my teeth. "I want to talk to you," I start. But then I wince and bite the inside of my cheek.

The waitress comes with two warm dishes, and puts them in front of us. She refills our root beers and leaves.

Logan looks down at his food and smiles. He takes a bite of his chicken, and he's happy. He points to mine with his fork. I don't want to eat right now. I want to hash all this out.

"I'm just glad you're here," he says as I fill my mouth up with alfredo. "I was afraid you'd run."

I was afraid of that, too. And I probably still will. I circle my fork in a pile of noodles and hold it out to him. "Do you want to try mine?" I ask.

His blue eyes get all smoldery there for a minute. Then he grins and leans forward. He leans his head back after his mouth is full and chews thoughtfully. "Yours is better than mine," he says.

I take my fork and dip it into his plate, and he grins and shakes his head. It doesn't stop me. I chew thoughtfully on a piece of his chicken. "Mine's better than yours," I agree.

He shrugs and smiles. "Eat," he says.

We eat quietly, and I steal food off his plate so often that he puts up a fork to block me. But I feed him just as much of mine as he will accept. I like this time with him. But I also liked the time in the bathroom.

When the waitress takes the plates away, I have to force myself not to ask for a to-go box. There might not be anything for me to eat tomorrow, and I hate to see food go to waste. But there won't be anywhere for me to keep it at the shelter. That is, provided that I can find a shelter that's not crowded already.

The table is clear between us, and the waitress comes and leaves a leather-bound folder. I reach for it, but he intercepts it. "No," he says, shaking his head.

"But I wanted to pay," I complain.

He shakes his head again. "No." He slides his credit card into the slot and lays it on the edge of the table.

I reach over and take his hand, and he startles for a minute, but then his grip is strong on mine. I turn his hand over gently, looking at the inside of his wrist.

You can tell it's a fresh tattoo, and it's looking a bit like Fruity Pebbles, all rough and crinkly. But the design is still there. "I love this," I say. "Will you put one on me one day?" I ask. I want one just like this one. And I want the keyhole. "How much does this cost?"

"Nothing, for you," he says.

"I wouldn't let you do it for free."

He smiles. "I wouldn't let you pay for it."

"Do you do tattoos like the one today often?"

His brows draw together like he's not sure what I'm referring to.

I point to my boobs. And then heat creeps up my face when he looks down at them. He grins.

"Oh, jeeze," I say, burying my face in my hands.

He pulls my hands away. "What?" he asks. He must have thought I said something when my face was buried.

"Nothing." I shake my head.

"I don't do those often. Just once in a while. They give my name out at the cancer center."

"You never charge them."

He shakes his head. "I can't. They need it."

"So, how many boobs do you touch a day?" I ask playfully.

He grimaces. "Some," he says.

"Really?"

He nods. "It's a popular place for tats. Even when people aren't getting new nipples." His face colors. I think he's embarrassed.

Our discussion about boobs makes me think of what we'd just done in the bathroom. When I ran my hands up his chest, I'd discovered his piercings. He'd even let me look at them. "How many piercings do you have?" I ask.

He starts to count on his fingers. He stops at seven. "Seven?"

"Where?"

He points to each nipple, then his ears, then the shell of his ear. And then his gaze goes down to his crotch. He's not smiling, and his eyes narrow, like he's waiting to see my reaction.

I gasp, and nearly choke on my inhale. "Down there?" I whisper, a grin tugging at my lips.

He nods, taking a sip of his root beer.

"Did they hurt?" I suddenly have the most obnoxious desire to see every last one.

He shrugs.

"Can you do one for me?" I ask. Then I rush on to say, "Not today. Or any time soon. I don't have enough money."

"Where would you want it?" he asks.

I've only had my ears pierced, and never thought of doing any other part of my body. My nipples go hard just thinking about it. "Did your nipples hurt?" I whisper. Then I realize he can't tell I'm whispering, since he's just reading my lips.

"It hurts a little when you do it. But it goes away. Just like any other piercing."

I can't stop thinking about the one down there. Heat creeps up my cheeks again.

"I could pierce you. Anywhere you want," he says. And his face floods with color.

"Anywhere?"

He closes his eyes and takes a deep breath. When he opens them, he only opens one and he looks at me like he's wincing when he says carefully. "Anywhere." He looks at my boobs again and licks his lips. "Take your pick of places."

Suddenly, I'm curious. "You do a lot of those?" I don't know why that bothers me. "The… ones… down there?"

He shrugs.

I don't like the idea of him touching anyone's private places. Not at all. Although the idea of him touching mine… I squirm in my seat, and he arches a brow at me. "Something wrong?" he asks. He's smirking.

I shake my head, biting my lips together. "Can anyone get a piercing like that?" I point toward my lap. I don't know why I'm being so bold about this. But I'm curious.

"Most people can." He plays with the salt shaker. "We'd have to take a look to see what type of piercing would be best for you."

My face flames at the thought of him taking a look down there. He pushes my root beer toward me and says, "Drink. Before you pass out." He's grinning, though, and I've never seen such a look of confidence on a man. The awkwardness of a moment before has passed. And he's enjoying making me squirm.

"Are there, like, different kinds?" My words don't want to come out of my mouth gracefully.

He nods. He takes my hand in his and drags his thumb across the back. "There are as many kinds as there are types of women."

I take a deep breath.

"Is there, like, a purpose for it?"

He grins. "There can be." He takes a sip of his root beer. "Some people just like the idea of it. Then others like to play with it."

"Play with it?" I choke out. His thumb is still stroking across the back of my hand, and he might as well be touching me right where a piercing might go. Because it's thumping like crazy.

He leans closer to me, speaking softly. "Lips. Tongue. Fingers." He licks his lips again. "Teeth." He arches a brow at me. "I can go on, if you like."

I hold up a hand. If he goes on, I might just spontaneously combust. "No thank you."

"Another time," he says.

He threads his fingers through mine.

"You scare me," I blurt out.

He startles, jerking his hand back from mine. "Me? Why? What?" he asks, leaning forward.

He's worried. I can tell, so I feel the need to fix the error I just made. "I have all these feelings for you," I say.

He sits back, laying a hand on his chest, heaving a sigh in relief. "Oh, you scared me," he breathes. "I thought I offended you with the sexy talk."

"You didn't offend me. But you make me want things I can't have." There. I admitted it. I want him. I want all the things that come with him. But I can't have them.

"I feel like I need to tell you something," he says. He's thinking about his next words, and he's talking very slowly, like the weight of them is hard for him to carry.

"Ok," I say hesitantly.

"I want you more than I want air," he says. My heart starts to beat a tattoo rhythm in my chest. I open my mouth to speak, but he holds up that damn finger. "But I can't act on my feelings. Not while I don't even know your name."

He takes a deep breath and waits for me. I can't say anything. I wouldn't know what to say even if I could.

"I want to take you to bed, and make love to you all night long." He cocks a grin at me. "Lips. Tongue. Fingers. Teeth." He makes a circle motion with his hands. "Should I go on? Or do you understand?"

I nod. I get it. He reaches over and lifts my jaw to closes my mouth. His touch is tender.

"I want to do things to you that you probably couldn't imagine." His blue eyes are dark and the centers big and wide.

"I don't know," I start. I am imagining all sorts of things right now. And my clit is thumping so hard I have to push my legs together to ease some of it. It doesn't help.

"But even more than I want to lick you all over and make you cry out my name and swear you see God, I want you to trust me. And you don't. Not yet. But you might one day."

I'm breathing so hard I feel like I just ran a mile. "I trust you," I say.

He shakes his head. "No you don't." He smiles at me, and my heart flips over. "But you might one day."

The waitress brings the receipt to the table, and gives him a pen. I see that she's written her name and phone number on the bottom of the receipt. He tears that part off and gives it back to her. He shakes his head, and tilts his at her, and she looks disappointed. Her heavy bottom lip pokes out.

I look up at her and blink. "I absolutely hate it when skanks try to give my boyfriend their contact information," I say.

Logan chokes, coughing into his fist.

The waitress steps toward me, but Logan gets between us. That's good, because I will take that bitch out. "Have you ever slept with her?"

He looks up at her and takes in her features. "I don't think so," he says quietly, by my ear.

He's slept with that many women that he can't tell one from another?

She huffs away. He tugs me to my feet. "You shouldn't have called her a skank," he says with a laugh.

"What do you call a woman who gives her number to a man who's been holding hands with someone else?" I ask crisply.

"And you shouldn't have called me your boyfriend." He looks down at me as he opens the door of the restaurant for me.

"I'm sorry," I start. "I shouldn't have said that. I just wanted her to go away." And I wanted to stake my claim, even though I had no right to one.

He looks down at me beneath the street light. "You shouldn't have said it because you gave me hope," he says.

I can't speak. I can't utter out a sound.

"Come home with me," he says.

I shake my head.

He sighs heavily. "You know how this is going to end."

"I shouldn't." I really, really shouldn't.

"Fine," he says, and then he bends at the waist and tosses me over his shoulder, just like the night before. Only this time, his hand is on my ass, under my skirt, instead of holding the backs of my legs. It's hot, pressed against my panties.

I can't say a word to him, because he wouldn't hear me. So, I just hang there, all the way to his building, and up four flights of stairs.

He opens the door and walks inside. His brothers are there, and they look up. Sam and Pete snicker, and Paul shoots them a look. Matthew is on the sofa, and he shakes his head.

Logan puts me down. Apparently, I'm not a side show attraction tonight. "Hi," I say tentatively to them all.

"Hi," they call back. They don't get up and rush over to me, not even when he sets me on my feet and steadies me. "You're back," Matthew says as he walks to the fridge.

He looks better tonight. Not quite as green.

Sam walks to the kitchen and Paul snarks at him when he reaches for a beer. He takes a soda, instead, grumbling to himself.

Logan signs something to them. Pete tells him the name of the movie, and it's one I haven't heard of. Logan points to the TV and then to me asking me if I've seen it.

I shake my head. He sets my bag and my guitar on floor, and laces his fingers with mine. He tugs me gently toward the couch. Logan bumps Sam and Pete's knees until they scoot down. There's barely enough space for him, much less for me. "I'm going to go take a shower," I complain.

But he sits down and pulls me into his side, his arm around my shoulders.

Matt gives me a look I don't understand. He doesn't seem completely pleased by my being there. Did I do something to offend him?

But Logan looks down at me and smiles, and then places his lips against my forehead. Matt gets up and goes to his room, but not before shooting me a glance that I couldn't help but take as a warning.

Logan

She fell asleep curled into my side. The credits roll on the TV and I don't want to move. I don't want to set her away from me. My arm is sweating where she's pressed up against me, and her hairline is damp. I reach over and brush her hair back, and she blinks her brown eyes at me. "Is it over?" she asks.

She stretches, her arms raising high above her head.

I nod. The movie's over. But my feelings for her are not. They're just beginning. I like having her on my couch. And I like it even more that she's so soft in my arms.

"Good movie," Paul says.

She looks over at him like she's surprised he's there. Sam and Pete went to bed as soon as the credits rolled, and Matt is in bed, too. "Sorry I fell asleep," she says. She wipes the side of her mouth, and I draw her in to give her a hug. She pulls back all too soon, looking askance at Paul. "I'm going to take a shower," she says.

I nod and help her to her feet. She picks up her bag and goes into the bathroom, closing the door behind her. I flop back onto the couch and cover my face with my hands. This girl will shred me. I already know she will. And I'm jumping in with everything I am despite the fact that I know it.

"Want to talk about it?" Paul asks. Matt comes into the living room and drops down on the sofa beside me.

You too? I sign and then throw my hands up in surrender.

Matt grins and shrugs his shoulders.

You guys like her, right? I ask. Their opinions do matter to me.

Paul nods, while Matt shakes his head. What the fuck? It's like they're at opposite ends of the spectrum.

Matt lays a hand on my knee so I'll look at him. "I like her," he says. He's talking while he signs, which makes it easier to listen. "But how much do you know about her?" His eyebrows draw together.

I don't know anything about her. *Nothing,* I admit. *I don't know a damn thing about her.* I lean forward so I can prop my elbows on my knees. I feel like I can't breathe. *She won't tell me anything. Not even her name.*

"What's she hiding?" Matt asks.

I wish I knew. I flop back against the couch again.

"She looks so familiar to me," Paul says, looking toward the closed bathroom door. He shakes his head. "I wish I could place her."

She busks in the subway tunnels every day, I sign with a shrug.

"It's more than that," Paul says. He shakes his head, like he's shaking his crazy thoughts away. There's no way he could know her from anywhere else.

"She staying over again?" Matt asks.

I nod.

"Don't fall in love with her," Matt warns.

Paul nods his head in agreement. "Fuck her and be done with her," he says.

She's not like that.

Paul exhales heavily. "You haven't slept with her yet, have you?"

I slept with her. I hang my head. *But all we did was sleep.*

"You've never *slept* with anyone, dumbass," Paul says.

I haven't. Not since my mom died. I used to crawl in bed with her when I was young. Her bed was always warm and smelled like her. After she died, I used to crawl in her empty bed just so I could smell her, until Paul changed the sheets and took that room as his own.

I know. I've had plenty of women in my bed. But none of them stayed.

"Stay smart," Paul says, tapping his temple.

"He'd have to be smart to stay smart," Matt says, bumping my knee with his. "He's already half in love with her." He looks down at his fee and then glares at me. "If you don't want her, can I ask her out?"

She's mine! I sign.

He holds his hands up to fend me off. "I know! I know! I said *if*, asshole. I just wanted to see where your head is." He heaves a sigh. "Apparently, you really like this one." He shakes his head. "I don't think she has bad intentions. But I'm worried about you. Be careful."

Matt's in love with April. But she dumped him when she found out he was sick. Self-serving bitch.

"She brought me a bucket when I was sick last night," Matt admits. "It was nice of her."

Paul's eyebrows draw together. "That was you, puking your guts out?" Paul asks.

This is Matt's second round of chemo. The first didn't work. This is his last chance. He nods.

Why didn't you tell us? I ask.

He scrubs a hand down his face. "I'm scared," he admits. He looks me in the eye and then his gaze moves to meet Paul's. "I'm going to fucking die," he says. He grins but there's nothing funny about it. "So you don't have to worry about me asking her out."

"Don't joke about that shit," Paul bites out.

"I'm not joking," Matt says. He's serious.

Paul leans forward and squeezes Matt's knee in his hand. "You have to believe it's going to work. If you don't, you don't stand a chance."

Matt pushes forward to perch on the edge of the sofa. "You guys believe for me, ok?" he says. "Because I'm too fucking tired to do it." He gets up and goes to his room, closing the door behind him.

"When did he start admitting he's afraid?" Paul asks.

I shrug. *It's the first time I've heard him say it.* I look up at Paul. Fear clutches my heart in a death grip. *He's going to be all right, isn't he?*

"I don't know," he admits. He swipes a hand down his face.

I pat my shirt pocket, reaching for my cigarettes.

"Matt has fucking cancer, dumbass," he snarls at me, his hands flying wildly. "And you want to smoke?"

I jerk the pack from my pocket and toss it across the room, into the waste basket.

Paul nods. "Thank you," he signs dramatically. He sags back into the lazy chair.

He's going to make it, right? I ask.

He nods. "Of course he is."

I believe him. Because I can't imagine a life without Matt in it. I won't allow myself to think he's going to die. I just won't. If Matt can't believe he's going to live right now, I'll believe enough for the two of us.

Paul stands up and ruffles my hair, and it quickly changes into a noogie. I brush his hand away. "Don't worry," he says.

The starts down the hallway, and I clap my hands to get his attention. He turns back to me, scratching his stomach. "What?" he asks.

"I want to talk to her," I admit.

His eyebrows draw together. "Yeah?" He shrugs. "So talk."

I want to tell him about her dyslexia, so he won't feel like I've been holding out all these years, but that's not my story to tell. It's hers. I shake my head. It's just too hard to explain. She's making me feel things I've never felt before. She makes me want things.

"I wish you'd just fuck her and get it out of your system. Then you can be done with her. And stop wishing for things you can't have."

She gasps behind him. Her mouth falls open and her eyes fly open wide. I can imagine her gasp, even if I can't hear it. But Paul must hear it. His eyes clench shut. "She's right behind me, isn't she?" he asks. He opens one eye and looks at me.

Kit's wrapped in a towel with another turbaned around her head. Paul turns to her, but I can't hear what he's saying. It had better be a profuse apology.

She glares at him for no more than a moment, and then she ducks into my bedroom and closes the door behind her.

"Shit," Paul signs. "I fucked that up."

He knocks on the bedroom door. He knocks again. His hand wraps around the doorknob, and he starts to turn it, but she's wrapped in a towel. I can't let him in there. I leap over the back of the couch, and put myself between him and the door. I push his chest back and point toward his bedroom door.

"I need to apologize," he says. He's grimacing, and his face is flushed. He didn't mean it. Well, he did mean it. But he didn't. "I didn't know she was there."

I sign the word *tomorrow*. I place my hands on his chest and push him back gently. I couldn't manhandle Paul even if I wanted to. He's a great big son of a bitch. Even bigger than me. And twice as mean. *Tomorrow* I say again. *I got this. I'll talk to her. I'll tell her you didn't mean to hurt her feelings.*

He nods and runs a frustrated hand across the stubble he calls hair. "Sorry," he says.

I nod, and let myself into my bedroom. I lean back against the door. I expect to see her angry and throwing things. Or crying. I really don't know what to expect. I don't know her well enough to have a clue. She's doing neither. She's standing there looking at me. She unrolls the towel from her hair and her locks spill down over her shoulders. Her hair is all wet and tangled and she fluffs it with the towel, blotting it dry. She looks at me, but she hasn't said anything yet.

"He didn't mean that," I start.

"I think he's right," she says. Then she raises her arms, pulls the towel free of where it's tucked between her tits, and drops it to the floor. She kicks it across the room with her delicate little naked toe. She's starkly, completely, beautifully, perfectly, delectably naked. "I think you should fuck me and get it out of your system. Then you can be done with me."

Emily

I'm shaking like a leaf, and I desperately want to cross my arms over my chest. But I force myself to stand there. He looks at my pointed toe as I kick the towel to the side. My heart leaps in my chest, kicking like an angry mule. I expect his eyes to drag up my leg, and then to the rest of me, and my body heats in anticipation of his gaze. But he doesn't. Instead, he rushes to the closet, yanks a t-shirt from a hanger and hands it to me.

I finally do cross my arms, but it's so that I can more effectively glare at him. He looks everywhere but at me, and then bunches the shirt up in his hands, rucking it up until he can slide it over my head. He tugs it down until my hips are covered. Then he steps back, falls against the door and takes a breath.

"Damn," he breathes. Then he grins.

I shove my arms through the armholes of the shirt, and glare at him. He's laughing. Seriously? I arch my brows at him. "Beg your pardon?"

He chuckles into his closed fist, and then shakes his head. "He didn't mean to hurt your feelings." He bends over at the waist, trying to catch his breath, he's laughing that hard. I pick up a pillow and throw it at him, then sit down on the end of the bed and cross my legs. I still don't have any panties on. And I'm too angry to care.

I just stood naked in front of this man and he's laughing. Tears prick the backs of my lashes. "This isn't funny," I say.

He sits down beside me on the bed and turns my chin so that I have to face him. "I didn't see what you said," he tells me. His thumb touches the corner of my eye, and his brows come together in confusion. "Did Paul hurt your feelings?"

I shake my head, pinching my lips together.

He reaches over and lifts my wet hair from the collar of his shirt. "Your hair's still wet," he says, as he picks up a towel. I brush his hand away as he tries to dry my hair.

"It's fine," I say. "Stop," I warn.

"He didn't mean to hurt your feelings," he says.

He thinks Paul hurt my feelings. What crap. Paul didn't hurt my feelings. Logan did, when he completely ignored my offer. And he laughed.

I reach into my bag and pick up my panties, then shimmy into them. Logan looks away, and I roll my eyes. I was naked in front of him. Does he really think I care if he sees me put my panties on? I tug the blanket from the bed and glare at him for a moment, and then I open the door and head for the couch. I'll sleep out there. It's better than sleeping in here with a man who doesn't want me.

Matt's at the kitchen table with his head in his hands when I come out of the hallway. I falter and tug on the length of Logan's shirt. He looks down at my legs and smiles. "I've seen more skin at the club," he says. "You might as well be a nun."

I sigh heavily and throw the blanket onto the edge of the couch. Then I walk into the kitchen for a cup of water. "Can I get you anything?" I ask.

He looks better today. But he still doesn't look good. "No thanks."

"Did you eat anything today?" I ask. Now I sound like Logan, but I can't help it.

"I did," he says with a nod.

"Did you keep it down?" I tilt my head and look at him.

"Some of it," he admits.

Logan walks out of the bedroom and skids to a halt in the kitchen. He looks from Matt to me and back again. He signs something to Matt.

"Dude, you can't talk around her unless you want me to interpret," Matt warns.

Logan clenches his hands together and bites his lips just as hard. He looks like he wants to say something. But he can't. Not with Matt there. "Go to bed, Logan," I say.

Logan shakes his head. He starts to sign, and Matt starts to talk. "He doesn't want you to sleep on the couch," Matt says. Matt sighs heavily. He gets to his feet. "How do you two communicate normally?" he asks, exasperated.

I can't tell him that Logan talks to me. So, I just shrug. Everyone else in this family shrugs all the time. I might as well take up the habit. Become a master at evasion. "He can go fuck himself," I say. "I'm sleeping on the couch."

"Shit, man, what did you do?" Matt asks.

Logan signs something quickly.

"Damn. You should make Paul sleep on the couch." He chuckles. "Seems like he deserves it."

Logan stalks back into his room. Matt looks at me, grinning. "You're turning him inside out," he says.

Apparently not. He didn't even look at me when I was naked.

"What are your intentions with Logan?" he asks. His voice is quiet. He's not threatening me. I think he's genuinely curious.

"I don't have any intentions. He tossed me over his shoulder both times I've been here. It's not like I had much choice in the matter."

"You could have said no," Matt clarifies. He holds up a hand to stop me when I open my mouth to talk. "Paul was just trying to protect him. He's never brought a girl home before. Not one he really likes."

"I'm the first one he won't sleep with, I guess," I murmur, more to myself than to him.

Matt nods. "Yes, you are. That means you're special." He tweaks my nose as he walks by and I make a face at him. He has cancer. I can't be mad at him. Particularly not when he's being so sweet. He turns back to face me. "He's never wanted something real with a girl. Give him time to explore it before you start expecting more from him."

"That's just it," I argue. "I don't expect anything."

"Yes, you do." He looks sorry for me, and it pisses me off.

"Apparently, I'm the only girl in the city of New York that he won't sleep with." I harrumph like a two year old who just dropped her ice cream.

"I can't believe I'm discussing my brother's lack of sexual appetite with his girlfriend," Matt mutters.

"I'm not his girlfriend."

"Oh, honey," he says, shaking his head. "You're his first girlfriend."

I turn to look toward Logan's room. I don't know what to do.

"Don't fuck with him," Matt warns. He's suddenly very direct. And the intensity in his face is almost scary. "And don't break his heart."

"He'd have to love me for that to be an issue."

Matt snorts. "You're clueless, aren't you?" he asks.

"Apparently," I say.

Matt wraps my head in his arm and squeezes me against him, rubbing my head playfully with his knuckles. He stops and sniffs me. "You smell good," he says. He laughs. "We don't have much around here that smells good."

"Thank you," I grumble.

He pops me on the tail and points me toward Logan's room. "Go talk to him," he says.

I yelp and look back at him over my shoulder. I can't believe he just did that.

"That was a 'get your ass in the game' smack. Not an 'I want to see you naked' smack," he warns. I didn't doubt what he meant.

"I don't mess with Logan's women," he says. He told me that the first night.

"It's a brother thing," we both say at the same time.

Matt grins. "Exactly," he says.

When I walk in Logan's room, he's laying back on the bed with his arm laid over his eyes. He doesn't look up when I walk in, so I touch his knee. He uncovers his eyes and lifts his head, looking up at me. His blue eyes blink for a moment, and then he sits up. He tangles his fingers with mine and pulls me closer to him. "Don't sleep on the couch," he says.

"Matt says we should wake Paul up and let him sleep on the couch."

Logan's eyes get wider and he smiles. "I like that idea. But I would rather sleep with you any day."

"You could have fooled me," I spit out.

"What?" he asks. Could he not see my lips? Or did he not understand what I said?

"I was standing stark naked in front of you, Logan. And you didn't have any interest in me." I hold up a hand to stop him when he opens his mouth. "I get it. You don't have feelings like that for me. It's all right."

Suddenly, Logan jerks my hand, rolling me gently onto the bed. His body covers mine, and his face is a breath away from me. "You think I don't like you that way?" he asks. He's looking into my face like he'll find something he's missing there.

"You laughed at me."

"I laughed because the one girl I do want to fuck is naked in my room and I can't have her!" he growls. "It's like divine intervention."

He wiggles a knee between my knees and kicks my legs open wider. He settles there between my thighs and rocks forward so that he presses against my panties. He's hard. So hard.

"I was naked and you wouldn't even look at me," I start. I close my eyes.

"I didn't want to disrespect you," he says.

He rocks his hips against me again, and this time the length of him notches against my cleft. My breath catches.

"I want you so bad it hurts." His voice is quiet, and harder to understand than it normally is.

"You didn't even look at me," I protest.

He sits up on his knees and lifts my leg up by his shoulder. He's not looking at my body. "You have pink toenail polish. And you have a bit of stubble on your legs." He grins. "You can use my razor if you want." His hand slides up my calf, toward my knee, leaving a wake of goose bumps behind. "Your thighs are firm, and you have a generous flare to your hips. His hand slips to the front of my panties, where he drags his thumb back and forth for a moment. "You have this tiny dusting of hair, here." His thumb presses against my cleft and I arch my back to press harder against him. He chuckles. His hands drift up my sides, lifting the shirt. He tugs it up, until it rests just beneath my breasts. He presses a kiss to my belly. My nipples are hard and standing tall. He licks his lips. "Your nipples are pink and puffy and perfect. And your breasts will fit in my hands." He throws the shirt back down, groaning as he lies back down on top of me, rocking his length against me again. "I saw everything," he says. "I was just trying to be a gentleman." He laughs. "You thought I didn't look." He kisses the tip of my nose. "Silly woman," he scolds.

"You looked." That's all I can say. And it comes out as a croak. Thank God he can't hear the quiver in my voice.

"I looked," he admits. "You were naked. And so fucking beautiful that I could barely breathe. Of course, I looked."

"You look at a lot of naked women?" I don't want the answer to that question after it's out of my mouth.

"Not anymore," he breathes against my lips. His lips touch mine, tentatively, and then he retreats. He's making me crazy. His hips press insistently, pushing him closer and closer to my heat. "I haven't seen a single naked woman since the day I met you."

"Do you want to see any naked women?" I ask. My voice is still doing that quavery thing. His hand lies on my throat, almost like he's listening with his fingertips for the sound of my voice.

He shakes his head, looking directly into my eyes. "Just one."

I reach down to tug his shirt over my head, but he stops me with a grunt.

"What?" I ask.

He looks into my eyes. "What's your name?" he asks.

This time, it's me who throws her arm over her eyes. I want to scream. I can't tell him anything. "I can't tell you," I say.

He tugs the shirt back down around my hips. "Then your clothes stay on." He kisses me, his lips nibbling at mine until I'm breathless. "And so do mine."

"Your brother said you should fuck me and get it over with."

He heaves a sigh. "That's because he thinks I'll fuck you and not want to see you anymore. But I can assure you, that's not the case." He presses against me again, rocking against my cleft, the ridge of his manhood pressing against my clit. "Once I get to be inside you, I'll never want to give you up." He kisses the side of my neck, suckling gently as he moves across the front of my throat. His five o'clock shadow abrades my tender skin. But I don't want him to stop.

I reach down to cup him through his jeans, and he stills.

"Don't play with me," he warns. His voice is strong but quiet. "If you want to be my friend, you can be my friend. We can sleep in the same bed, we can have meals together, and we can spend time doing things we both like."

I lift his head so that he's looking at me. "I want to be your friend," I say.

"I want you to be my girlfriend."

"What does that mean?" I cry, slapping the bed with my open palms in frustration.

He looks confused. "I'm not sure. But I think it's the same as being my friend, but I get to make you come." He rocks against me once again. Then he lifts away. I want to scream.

"Where are you going?"

"To get the blanket off the couch. Unless you want me to sleep out there?" He looks unsure.

I want him inside me. But that's not going to happen. "Go get the blanket," I grumble. He chuckles and leaves the room.

My panties are wet. Soaked. I reach into my bag and put on a fresh pair. I'm adjusting them over my hips when he walks back in the room.

"Fresh panties," I explain. "All your fault," I taunt.

He groans, and flops back on the bed. "Why did you have to tell me that?" he asks. He lays there for a minute with his hands clenched. Then he motions me forward and pulls my head down to lie on his chest. He takes a deep breath and hugs me to him tightly, then releases me and relaxes. He picks up a book from beside his night stand and holds it in one hand. He reads quietly to himself.

"What are you reading?" I ask.

He looks down at it and tells me the title. "Will you read it to me?" I ask.

He lifts his head long enough to look at my face and finds that I'm serious. I can learn. And I love books. I just can't read them. I have an amazing memory.

"Start at the beginning?" I ask.

He turns to page one and begins to read. I settle against him, wrapping my arms around his chest, snuggling as tightly against him as I can. And he reads. His voice is strong and sure, and he reads long into the night, long after he's yawning, because I don't want him to stop. When he finally lays the book to the side, I roll toward him and he turns to face me. He tucks me beneath his chin and I can hear his heart beating in his chest. "When you're ready for what I want," he says, "let me know."

I'm ready. I'm ready now. But I'm not ready for the same thing he is. I nod against his chest, and he heaves a sigh. His lips touch the top of my head, soft as a whisper.

***

I wake up the next day and lift my head. Sunlight pours into the room, and I know I've slept much later than I normally would. But then again, we were up really late last night reading. My heart clenches inside my chest when I realize that he hasn't used his voice in eight years, but he spent hours last night reading to me. It makes me feel warm all over, and I look around, wondering where he is. The bed is empty, and there's not even an impression of his head on the pillow. That's probably because we shared the same space last night. I draped myself across his chest, and then we adjusted, and I had my head on his belly. All the time he read, his fingers had trailed across one body part of mine or the other. It was a tiny tickle, but it touched the center of me.

I know he wasn't unaffected by it. He was rock hard, and he had to ball the covers up in his lap more than once. But he ignored it. I ignored it. I wanted to reach over and touch him, but he doesn't want that from me. He wants all of me. And I'm not free to give it away. I'll never be free.

I roll over and brush my hair from my eyes. I still can't get used to the black hair. It's so different from my natural color. Every time I look at myself in a mirror, I have to do a double-take and try to figure out who I'm looking at. Maybe I'll never know.

My eyes land on a sketch pad that's propped against the lamp on Logan's end table. I crawl closer to it on my hands and knees, and close my eyes tightly, wincing when I see that he's drawn a naked woman. She's drawn in pencil, and he has shaded all the parts of her naked body. But what immediately grabs my attention is that there's one streak of color on the whole thing. It's down the left side of her hair. It's blue.

Oh, crap. It's me.

I sit up on the edge of the bed and pick it up. It's me. Definitely me. My arms are down by my sides, and my fists are clenched tightly. There's a look of defiance on my face. I've never seen an artist capture a look like that. But he's done it. There's a towel on the floor beside my toe and my foot is pointed like I just kicked it to the side.

He's drawn shadowing around my boobs, and my nipples are standing tall, sticking out like they've been kissed tight. My stomach clenches and I have to force myself to take a breath. There's a small triangle of hair at the vee between my thighs. I close my eyes. It's almost lifelike.

It's me. He drew me. From memory. At the bottom are some scribbled words. They're written in all caps and the letters are spaced far apart.

I LOOKED

Yes, apparently he did. There's no doubt about it. He saw me naked. And he remembered every dip, every curve and every strand of hair. Or lack of hair. Yikes. I close the sketch pad so no one else will see it. I'm feeling a bit over-exposed, like he somehow peeled back a layer of me and forced me to look at it as closely as he did.

I can't believe I accused him of not wanting to look at me. He obviously did. He looked closer than anyone ever has. I take a deep breath and sit there for a minute with my eyes closed.

I slide on a pair of jeans beneath Logan's t-shirt and put on a bra. I like his brothers, but I'm not one hundred percent sure who's in the house. And I don't want to walk out there to get a cup of coffee to find everyone dressed appropriately and for me to be the one who's not. Padding around in the middle of the night is one thing. This is different.

I let myself out of the room and look around. The apartment is empty. I'm kind of glad that Logan's not there, since my face is flaming just thinking about how closely he perused my body. If he was there in the flesh, I'd be a puddle on the floor.

I don't think I've ever seen the apartment when it wasn't full of testosterone and male bodies. It's a mess, like usual. I pour myself f a cup of coffee and load the dishwasher, and then clean the countertops. I can't help it. They might not even want me to do it. But I do it anyway. My life is such a mess, and what I want most in the world is to tidy it up. Since I can't tidy my own life, I'll tidy their apartment instead. I remove a rubber band from a stack of mail and twist my hair up out of my face. If I'm going to clean, I'm going to do it right.

I start a load of laundry, and fold what's in the dryer. I don't know which shirt goes to which man, since they're all big boys. So, I just make a neat pile of them and stack them on the kitchen table. The pile grows as the day goes on, and by the end of the afternoon, the house is still empty and quiet, and it's clean from top to bottom. I didn't clean any of their bedrooms, because that would be an invasion of their privacy, and my cleaning at all might be, now that I think of it. I bite my fingernails and look around. They won't be mad, will they?

I go into the bathroom and look beneath the sink. There were cleaning supplies there the other day, and it could use refreshing. I lift a bucket of baby toys out of the way and then I stop. I shuffle through them. There are tiny boats, bath crayons, and a rubber ducky. I give it a squeeze and it goes flat, a hiss of air escaping it. Why do they have baby toys?

The curiosity is killing me. Do they have a little sister? They couldn't possibly. Logan said he lived with four brothers the day I met him. He didn't say anything about a sister. I put the bucket back under the sink, and keep cleaning.

The timer on the dryer goes off, and I fold the last load of laundry, blowing a lock of hair out of my eyes. I look toward the window, and see that the day is nearly gone. So much for busking in the subway. And Fridays are usually my best days, since people just got paid and they're feeling generous. I have wasted the whole day cleaning Logan's apartment, but I feel good about it. I put my hands on my hips and look around the room. I did a good job. I've mopped, and vacuumed, dusted, and put things away. Of course, I had to guess where a lot of stuff goes. The stuff I'm not sure about, I've been putting on the kitchen table with the stacked laundry.

I open a kitchen drawer and stumble back when I see that it's full of condoms. Nothing but condoms. They're in every shape, every size and every color. And every flavor, if the banana on the front of one is any indication. My face fills with heat. Why on earth do they have a drawer filled with condoms? I slam it shut, and walk away. It's none of my business.

I carry the mop bucked toward the sink so that I can dump it. I pick it up, and just as I'm walking across the kitchen floor, the door of the apartment opens, and Logan walks through. Only he's not alone. On his shoulders, there's a blonde with two squiggly pony tails. He ducks to get through the door, and she giggles when he wiggles her feet and pretends to dump her off his shoulders.

He stops in front of the closed door and freezes when he sees me standing there. He must not have expected me to still be there. And I certainly didn't expect for him to have a child. He starts toward me, one hand holding on to her feet tightly at the base of his neck. And the other reaches for me. But I'm so startled by the girl that the bucket of sudsy water slips from my hands.

"Stop!" I warn, because I don't want him to slip with his daughter on his shoulders.

Logan

I'm so damn happy to see Kit that I want to run to her and pick her and spin her around. I wonder if she'd giggle like Hayley does when I jostle her. Probably not. I wasn't sure Kit would still be here, and I was really worried she'd vanished when she didn't come to see me at the tattoo parlor.

Water crashes over the toes of my boots, and Kit rushes to right the bucket. She slumps, looking down at the mess. But her dejection only lasts for a second. She gets herself together and rushes to the table, where there are piles of folded laundry and she grabs towels, throwing them down over the spill.

She's saying something but I can't read her lips. I walk toward her and she warns me to stop, holding up her hands. Her eyes dart to Hayley, and then back to my face, and she doesn't look too happy with me. I set Hayley on the counter and put a cookie in her hands, and she settles there to watch us, her mouth full of chocolate chips. Hayley's three, and she's a cool kid.

I move the towels around with my boots, and Kit drops to her knees to mop up all the water. She pushes the towels around frantically, until it's all cleaned up. Then she throws the wet towels in the mop bucket and starts a load of wash with them in it. She comes back to the kitchen and looks at Hayley, who's still perched on the counter, happily munching on her cookie. Paul's going to have my ass when he finds out I gave her chocolate, but I needed to entertain her for a second.

Kit blows her hair out her eyes with a frustrated breath and glares at me. "You're home," she says. Her hands are on her hips, and she's not wearing any make up and her hair's a mess and she has a line of dirt streaked across her forehead. But she's never looked prettier.

I nod. The knees of Kit's jeans are wet, and her shirt's damp now, too. "What have you been doing?" I ask. I look around. The apartment is clean. And I don't just mean "straighten it up because Grandma's coming over" clean. I mean spotlessly clean. Like showroom floor clean. But better. It smells nice. And it looks nice. And she's here. God, I'm so happy she's here.

She shrugs. "How was your day?" she asks. Her gaze zips between me and Hayley. Hayley's making a mess, but I don't care.

"Better, now," I admit. I feel like someone took a weight off my chest when I walked into the room and saw her here. I reach for Kit, and squeeze her to me, kissing her on the forehead. She scrunches up her face, and pushes back from me, her gaze jumping to Hayley again.

"Who's that?" she asks warily.

I wet a kitchen towel and wipe Hayley's mouth and hands clean. She hasn't gotten it on her dress yet, but I know it'll happen any second. Her mother will shit a brick if we send her back with dirty clothes. I tickle Hayley's tummy and she giggles, her belly clenching as she arches into my hands. "This is Hayley."

Hayley looks a little confused, and I pick her up, putting her on my hip. She wraps around me, and one hand covers my mouth. I kiss her palm and make noises at her. She wiggles in my grasp. She's probably confused about the noises coming out of my mouth. I've never talked in front of her before.

"How old is she?"

"How old are you Hayley?" I ask her, jostling her on my hip.

She holds up three fingers.

"Three?" Kit says, like she's amazed. "Such a big girl." Kit looks at me. "Does she talk?"

"I don't know," I admit. Her lips are really hard to read, so I don't know if she talks or if she's just making noises. She knows how to sign simple words like food, milk, bath, water, and other things she needs. She and I do pretty well together. Most of it is just me trying to figure out what she needs, but Hayley doesn't seem to mind. "She might."

Kit bends down to her level and asks, "Do you talk?" Kit smiles and she's so damn pretty making faces at Hayley that I want to kiss her. I grab Kit quickly around the waist and jerk her into my side with a hand on her hip, and she laughs, looking up at me. I kiss her on the forehead and Hayley bats the side of my face with her open palm. "I don't think she likes that," Kit says, backing away from me.

"She'll have to get used to it." Kit's eyes meet mine, and then they skitter away.

"She's adorable," she says, but she's not looking in my eyes. We'll have to talk about that later.

"What happened to the apartment?" I ask, a grin tugging at my lips. She looks unsure of herself as she brushes her hair back from her face. That streak of dirt is still across her forehead and I reach out to wipe it away with my thumb.

She wrings her hands together and doesn't look me in the eye. "I did a little cleaning."

I take her chin in my hand and tip her face up to mine. "I'm glad you're still here."

"You're not mad, are you?" she asks. She bites her bottom lip.

"That you're here?" I ask softly. "I'm fucking ecstatic."

She scowls and looks at Hayley. "Language," she says. "And I meant about the cleaning. I started it this morning and... well... I couldn't stop."

"You shouldn't have."

"I know," she says with a shrug. "I wanted to. And I sort of feel like I owe you guys for letting me stay here."

"You don't owe us anything," I try to explain. I tug her to me again. I like the feel of this girl in my arms so much more than I should. "I like having you here."

She smiles up at me, and then Hayley starts to jump in my arms. She's excited, and reaches over my shoulder. I look back and Paul's coming in the door. She gets so excited to see Paul.

Kit starts smiling beside me, and then she grins, and air escapes her in one big relaxed breath. I'm not sure what that's about.

"You met Hayley, I see," Paul says to Kit. She nods as Paul takes her from me. "See, Hayley," he says to his daughter, "now you won't be the only girl in the house." He dances around in a circle with her. I'm reading his lips, because it's really hard to sign when your hands are full of baby. I can't see what he says when he dances around in a circle, but whatever it is makes Kit smile.

Kit points a finger at Paul and smiles. "She's yours?" she asks.

Paul looks from me to her. "You're not trying to use my daughter to score with chicks again, are you?" Paul asks, punching me in the shoulder. "I can't let him take her to the grocery store. He gets too much attention from the ladies."

Paul looks around the apartment and grins. "What the fuck happened here?" he asks.

Kit scowls at him, too. "Language," she says, looking toward Hayley. She's smiling now, though, and she looks like she's taking deep breaths, which she wasn't doing when I first walked into the house.

"Who cleaned?" Paul asked. He wipes a spot on Hayley's cheek with his thumb and says, "And who gave you chocolate?" He scowls at me. I shrug my shoulders and grin.

Kit cleaned up. I pull her into my side, and she wraps an arm around my waist, lays one hand on my chest, and looks up at me. *Isn't she amazing?*

Paul looks from me to her and back again, sticks his finger down his throat like he's going to hurl and walks away with Hayley toward his bedroom. He looks back at me long enough to say, "You're going to be late for work if you don't hurry." He looks down at Hayley. "Tell Uncle Logan he's going to be late." He shows her the sign for late and she does it. She's adorable when she signs. They disappear into his bedroom and I look down at Kit. I bend my head and touch my lips to hers. I don't want to pull back, but I do have to hurry. "I have to go out," I say.

Her brows raise, and she looks wary. "Out?" she says.

I nod. "I have to work tonight. Do you want to go with me?"

She looks down at her wet shirt, and brushes a lock of hair from her forehead. "I haven't even had a shower today."

"How quickly can you get ready?" I ask, looking at my watch. I have thirty minutes before I have to be there.

Emily

Warm water sluices over my body, and I force myself to hurry up. Logan is probably dancing from foot to foot in the living room waiting for me so he won't be late for work. Apparently, he's a bouncer at some club around the corner on Friday nights. And he wants me to go with him.

I hear the door to the bathroom open and I freeze. "Matt?" I call. He's the only one who might come into the bathroom with me, and that's only if he's sick.

I open the bath curtain an inch and look out. Logan is standing there, looking at me. He changed clothes, and now he's wearing a pair of jeans, his boots, and a blue t shirt that says "Bounce(r)" on the front of it. It strains across his broad shoulders. His eyes are a startling shade of blue against the azure shirt, and he looks at my face as I poke my nose through the curtain. My hair is full of suds, and soap is burning one of my eyes. "Is something wrong?" I ask.

He shakes his head and smiles at me. He doesn't say anything else, but he stands there with one shoulder against the wall with his arms crossed. "I have a question," he finally says.

I lean back and wash the soap from my face and hair, and then poke my head back through, blowing water from my lips. "Ask it," I say.

"It bothered you when you thought Hayley was mine," he says. His face doesn't change. He's still appraising me closely. But he's not leering, or trying to look at my naked body. He's totally respectful, just like always.

It did bother me when I thought Hayley might be his. They have the same deep blue eyes, and their hair color is similar. And he was so familiar with her. But then she's called Paul Daddy, and everything was suddenly all right. I know he can't read my lips unless I stick my head out of the shower. "What makes you say that?" I ask.

He snorts. "I read people every day, all day, and I have to tell how they feel by the way they hold themselves, rather than the inflections in their voices. And something tells me that you didn't like thinking that Hayley was mine."

He looks closely at me, and I know he's still appraising my reactions.

"Either you don't like kids, or you didn't like the idea of me having a kid." He shuffles his feet. "I just wanted to tell you that I might not be able to hear, but I'm fully capable of taking care of a child. If I wasn't, Paul wouldn't leave her with me."

He heaves a sigh, and then he turns to walk out of the door. I call his name, but he doesn't hear me. So, I jump out of the shower and grab for the towel, letting it fall open in front of me, but I don't have time to wrap it around me. I clutch it to my chest, and grab his arm. He turns back toward me, one eyebrow rising as he looks at me.

"It wasn't that I don't think you're capable of taking care of her," I say. "It wasn't that at all."

"Then what was it?" he asks.

It's so hard to explain, but if I don't tell him the reason it bothered me, he'll go on thinking it's because I think he can't do the kid justice with his disability, and that couldn't be farther from the truth.

"I thought she was yours," I say with my eyes closed. He tips my chin up with an insistent finger.

"What?" he asks.

"I thought she was yours," I repeat. This time, I make sure he can see my lips; although that's the last thing I want him to see me say. "I thought she was your daughter."

He grimaces. "Again, I'm fully capable of taking care of a child. I can watch the lights on a monitor just like anyone else. And changing diapers doesn't require my ears." He's irritated. And I can tell it. "She cries, and I can figure out what she needs."

"It's not that." God, I'm so stupid. I bury my wet face in my hands and he urges them down, watching my lips. "I was jealous," I admit. There. I said it.

"Jealous?" he asks. "Of Hayley? She's three, for Christ's sake."

"I know." I don't know how to tell him. "It made me wonder what kind of a stupid woman would ever let you go." And made me realize someone else has had him. Probably a lot of someone's. A lot of someone's I can't compete with.

He chuckles, the air in the room lightening. "That's all it was?" he asks, his voice incredulous. That's not really all it was. I also wondered how in the world I would do sharing him with someone else. But he's not mine to share, is he? Not really. Not at all.

I nod. "That's all. It's not because you're deaf. I was just jealous." I shrug. "I'm sorry. Really, really sorry. I didn't mean to offend you." I want to tell him that I want him all to myself. But I'm not free to do that.

"I don't have any kids," he says. "In case you were wondering."

The thought hadn't even crossed my mind until I saw Hayley. "All right."

"I want kids someday," he says. His voice is soft and he's looking into my eyes. "Do you?"

"I don't know." The idea of trying to help a kid of my own with homework, and spelling, and school is sometimes overwhelming to me. "I don't think I'd make a great mother."

His lips press against my forehead and he lays his hands on my naked hips. I draw in a breath. My hips are bare and his hands cover them completely as he pulls me toward him. The towel that was draped in front of me gets sandwiched between our bodies.

"I'm glad you came to talk to me," I croak out.

He dips his head, and kisses the side of my jaw. I don't even think about it; I tilt my head to give him better access. "I am, too," he says against my skin.

I could say more, but he's not looking at my face. He's not looking at anything. His eyes are closed. His hands slide around to my bottom and he lifts me against him. "I have never wanted to have sex with someone I care about," he says.

He's hard against my belly, and I can barely think or take in a breath.

I lift up his shirt, and lay my hands on his stomach. The muscles ripple under my fingertips. I want to touch him. I want to touch him so badly. "Pretend I'm someone you don't care about," I say impulsively.

He must have seen my lips, because he stills. "You think I can do that?" he asks, his voice incredulous. He lifts a hand and runs it through his hair. "I don't think you realize how very much I like you."

He likes me a lot if the rather impressive size of him pressed against my stomach is any indication.

He must read my mind, because he sighs heavily, and says, "I don't mean like that." A muscle ticks in his jaw for a moment, and then he steps back from me, lifts the towel and wraps it around my naked body. "I've had sex. Lots of sex. But I've never had it with anyone who matters to me."

He's only known me a few days. "Why do I matter so much? What makes me different?" Now I'm dying to know.

He shakes his head.

"Tell me," I prompt.

"I've been locked in my own world for a really long time," he says. "I have an excuse to keep people away, because of my disability. And then I saw your tattoo." I turn his wrist over and trace my finger across it. He shudders at my touch, closing his eyes tightly. "And I felt like maybe, just maybe, we were each locked in our own little worlds and we could let each other out."

He's pouring his heart out here, and I have nothing of encouragement to say. "But there's nothing wrong with you," I start. I look up at him, and he looking at me with a warning in his eyes.

"That's not true." He shakes his head.

"There's nothing wrong with you. So, we're not on equal footing, and we never will be."

He shakes his head again, like there's something on the tip of his tongue that he wants to say but won't.

"I can't read. I can't get a job. I can't go to school. I can't do any of the things my family wanted for me." Actually, they'd wanted me to get married and have babies, because all I was good for was being a trophy wife. But I refused. That's why I left. They'd compartmentalized me, deciding I couldn't play my music because it was "beneath our class" and I couldn't further my education, because it was too hard for them to watch me struggle. It was all about them. Always about them.

"Don't underestimate your own value, dummy," he says.

I stiffen. I hate that word. Absolutely hate it. He stiffens when I do.

"What?" he asks. "What's wrong?"

"Don't ever call me a dummy, Logan," I say, my teeth grinding together so hard they hurt.

"Oh, God, I'm so sorry," he rushes to say. He takes my face in his hands, holding it tightly as he looks into my eyes. "I didn't mean it." He chuckles, but there's no mirth in the sound. "It's a term of endearment in our family. I didn't mean to hurt your feelings. Really I didn't. I don't think you're stupid. You have a fucking learning disability. But you're not stupid. I know that."

I wish I knew it. He sounds so sure about it. "It's all right," I say, but I'm already pushing back from him. Tears are pricking at the backs of my lashes.

"Don't pull away from me," he warns.

That makes me laugh. "I'm not the one who's always pulling away, Logan," I remind him. I push him back again, but he's not having any of it. Suddenly, his hands clutch my bottom and he hoists me up onto the bathroom countertop.

"Forgive me," he says.

I nod, and he kisses the corners of my eyes where tears have formed. That word hurts me. It always has. And it was the final straw that made me leave my parents' house. That word and others like it. I've heard them for too long.

He bends his head and his lips touch mine. He licks into me, his tongue soft but insistent. I lay my palm flat on the side of his face and he keeps kissing me. He's taking my mind off that word. I already know what he's doing. I applaud him for it. Because he's stealing the pain along with my wits.

He jerks the towel from between us, and looks down at my naked body. I'm perched there on the countertop, and he stands between my legs. He licks his lips, and my heart beats double time. God, he's sexy. I pull his mouth back to mine, and he allows it, but not for more than a moment. Then his head dips, and he takes my nipple into his mouth. He's not gentle. He's rough. His five o'clock shadow rubs against the underside of my breast as he suckles my nipple, drawing it deep into his mouth, touching something inside me that I didn't even know existed.

"Do you want me to stop?" he asks, lifting his head to look into my face.

I shake my head. "Don't stop," I say. I thread my fingers into his hair, and hold him tight to me, tugging his hair gently, and he moans around my nipple. My head falls back, and I lean against the mirror, watching his face as he sucks on the turgid flesh. His other hand slides down my belly, toward my curls, where it slips between my legs. I open my legs wider for him. Logan raises his head, and buries his face in the curve of my neck as he dips a finger inside me and brings it forward, using my own wetness to slicken his way. His finger strums across my clit, and I nearly leap off the counter. He presses his body closer to mine, his free hand plucking at my nipple, elongating it with his urgent tugs, as his middle finger strokes me.

If he doesn't stop, I'm going to come. "Logan," I say. He can't see my lips, so I tug his head up until he looks at me. I can barely get the words to form on my lips. "I'm going to come before you do, if you don't stop." I start to work at the button on his jeans and he brushes my hands away.

He looks deep into my eyes and asks, "What's your name?"

I can't answer. I don't answer. I close my eyes tightly and arch against his fingertips, which are still taking me higher. When I don't respond,

Logan growls, drops onto his knees in front of me, and shoves my legs apart. Then he licks me from bottom to top.

I sink my hands into his hair, tugging him up when he goes down, and he takes the hint. He latches onto my clit with his lips and tongue, suckling softly as he stares up at me, his eyes as blue as the sea. I look into his face as he pushes me, and pushes me, and pushes me and then finally I'm crying out. He doesn't stop when I start to come. Instead, he slides a finger inside me and strokes me from the inside, while his mouth feasts on me. "Oh, God!" I cry.

My body quakes and I shake uncontrollably, pressing his face closer to me as I come. He slows his licks and nudges as my body stills. Now when he licks me from bottom to top, I like it, and I tremor as he passes my clit. He does it over and over until my body stills. I lie back limply against the mirror, and pull him up to face me. "Your turn," I say, and I reach for the button of his jeans.

He shakes his head. "No."

"What?" I don't understand.

He lifts me to stand in front of him.

"You don't want me?" I ask.

"Fuck, girl, I want you more than I have ever wanted anyone or anything." He presses his forehead against mine and he's breathing hard. His lips touch mine softly, but there's an urgency there, too. He bends over and picks up the towel, wrapping it around me, tucking it tightly between my breasts. Then he opens the door, shoves me out into the hallway, and locks the bathroom door behind me.

Logan

Fuck!

I scrub my hand down my face, and then run my fingers through my hair, squeezing my head in my hands like a big pimple that's ready to burst. That's not the only thing that's ready to burst.

I've never been as fucking turned on as I am right now. Kit was wet, and warm, and she was willing. She would have let me fuck her right here on the countertop if I'd said yes. I know she would have. And she wouldn't have had any regrets. But I would. Although right now, I'm rethinking my decision to put her outside the door. I reach for the handle and get ready to turn it so I can beckon her back into the room, but I jerk my hand back.

I desperately needed to take that look off her face, and the only thing I could think of was to put her mind on something else. But now I can't get my mind off the look on her face when she came. Or how tightly she gripped my finger when she trembled. Good God, that girl can undo me.

My junk is so hard I could pound nails with it.

The door vibrates as someone pounds on it. Probably Paul telling me to hurry up so I won't be late for work. But my dick's so hard that I can barely stand up straight, much less walk.

I run my hands through my hair again. Deep breaths.

Shit. I'll never get out of here this way.

I take a towel from under the sink and lay it in front of me, and unzip my jeans. This won't take but a second. Because I know I'll think about her while I do it. I spit into my palm and take the head of my dick in my hand, pulling away from me with a tight grip.

God, I'll never get the sight of her coming out of my mind. She'd cried out once. I'm sure of it. I could feel her throat move through the side of my cheek. It was a soft vibration, and it happened when she started to squeeze around my finger.

It only takes a few pulls, and I rise up on my tiptoes, spilling onto the towel on the sink. I think about how it would feel to be inside her right now, and my balls lift up tight against my body as I come. Oh, God. God, I want to be inside her so bad.

I sink back down onto my heels, spent. I lean heavily against the door, trying to catch my breath. The door shakes with the pounding of a heavy fist. I wash my hands, and throw the towel in the hamper. Shit. I'm glad I did that. But I wish it had happened differently.

I tuck myself back into my jeans, and I'm still semi-hard, but not so hard that I can't walk. I open the door, and Paul greets me with an arched brow. "Better?" he asks, grinning.

Fuck you, dumbass, I sign.

"Fuck you," he repeats, laughing. "Oh, wait. You already got fucked." He tilts his head at me. "How was it?"

I jerk him into the bathroom with me. *I didn't fuck her.*

He rolls his eyes. "Yeah, tell it to someone who couldn't hear her crying out in here." He pushes against my chest playfully. "Next time, warn a guy so he can leave. That shit was loud."

What was loud? I'm confused.

Very dramatically, he signs, "Oh, God! Oh, God! Oh, God! Logan! Logan! Logan!" He punches me again. This time it hurts. I rub at the spot. "That shit would have been hot if it hadn't been my brother on the other side of the door. As it was, it was just awkward."

I couldn't hear her. Sorry. I am. Well, sort of.

"No shit," he says. He's looking very closely at me. "You all right?"

I nod. Then I shake my head. *Fuck, I don't know.*

"What's wrong?"

She's making me crazy, man. Stark-fucking crazy.

"You just got laid, and you're complaining?" He waves his hands in dismissal. "I don't even want to hear it. Do you know how long it's been for me? Shit, asshole. You don't get to be all torn up inside when you just got some."

I didn't get any.

"Shut up. And stop rubbing it in."

I run a frustrated hand through my hair and close my eyes.

He taps my chest with his open palm, forcing me to open my eyes. "Wait. You're serious."

I nod. *I said something stupid to her. She was crushed. And it was all my fault.*

"So..." he prompts

So, I wanted to make her feel better. I'm not giving you details.

"It's like you're being re-virginized. That shit's fucked up." He has this mock look of abjection on his face.

I can't hold back my grin. *Tell me about it.*

"You're going to be late for work," Paul warns.

Shit. I am going to be late for work. I run out of the bathroom just as Hayley runs in. Paul picks her up and dances around with her in his arms. He has her every other Friday until the next Friday. And he loves every second of it.

Pete's standing beside Kit in the living room. "You ready?" he asks.

Kit's shuffling from foot to foot, avoiding my eyes. I walk over to her, tip her face up to mine and kiss her. It's a kiss full of promises of what could be. And what's not possible yet. She's breathless and clutching my shoulders when I pull back. "Thank you," she says. She signs it at the same time and my heart swells.

Ready, I sign to Pete.

He follows us into the hallway and I catch him looking at Kit's ass. *Knock it off*, I sign to him.

He grins and shrugs. *I can't help it.*

I can, I warn. I mock punching my fist into my open palm.

He looks away somewhat sheepishly. I motion for him to look at me. *Help me take care of Kit tonight? In case I get busy with something.*

Pete nods. He understands exactly what I mean.

Emily

The name of the club is Bounce. Logan leads me by my fingertips through the back door, but on the way from the street, I see a huge line out front, and a few men about Logan's size watching the door. This place is nothing like I expected. It's a lot bigger.

A big, burly guy in an apron stops us as we walk inside the rear entrance and puts a hand in the middle of Logan's chest. He looks at me and lifts his brow.

Logan starts to sign something and Pete translates. "She's with me." Pete sheepishly looks over at me and points a thumb toward Logan. "Well, with him," Pete admits. "She's 19," Pete interprets. The guy motions over a man with a stamp pad and he stamps the word "no" on the back of my hand. I roll my eyes. Seriously?

"It's a bar sweetheart. I'll get in all sorts of trouble if someone serves you when they shouldn't." He has him stamp Pete's hand too.

I nod. I understand.

"Is she deaf, too?" he asks.

Logan shakes his head.

I think he says something like "flavor of the night" as he walks away, rolling his eyes. Pete goes with him.

Logan leads me to the end of the bar and shoves a really big guy off his stool. The man teeters, complains, and turns to find Logan standing behind him. The man holds up both hands like he's surrendering to the cops, turns and walks away. "Why did you that?" I ask.

He shrugs. "You needed a seat."

He says it like I needed a soda. "But you just shoved him off the chair."

Logan follows him with his yes. "He didn't care."

"He didn't care because he thought you would kick his butt if he said anything."

He nods. Like he would kick his butt. Seriously?

"What?" he asks. He pats the stool. I slide onto it slowly and look at him.

"You want me to stay here?" I point to the stool. The bar. The general area.

He nods. He tips my face up so that I look at him. "Don't drink anything unless the bartender gets it for you. Do you understand?"

Not really, but I nod.

"I'm serious," he says.

"Where are you going?"

"To work." He presses his lips to my forehead, holding there for a moment. Then he bends his head and says close to my ear. "Just so you know -- I can still taste you on my lips." He looks down toward my lap. Heat floods my face. I'm probably as red as a tomato, but I force myself to look into his eyes.

"Wish I could say the same."

He groans, pushes back from me, winks, and walks away.

I look down at the bar counter, and see the perky blonde who's making drinks. She shoots me the stink eye and says, "What can I get for you?"

"Root beer?" I ask. She raises a brow, nods, and pours one from the tap on the bar.

"How do you know Logan?" she asks as she slides my drink over to me.

The words "he's my boyfriend" come unbidden to my lips. But I bite them back. "I'm staying with the boys for a bit."

Her brows shoot up toward her hairline. "Really?"

I nod, taking a sip of my root beer. "Thanks," I say absently, pointing toward the drink.

She drops two cherries with stems into it and smiles. "I'm Abby." She holds out her hand and I take it. She has a firm grip. I like that.

"Kit," I say. "So, are you one of the thousands of women Logan has slept with?" I ask. I try to make a flippant sound, but if the look on her face is indication, I fail. I don't really want the answer. But then again, I do.

She laughs. "Honey, I have more respect for myself than that." She looks at me for a moment as she pours someone else a beer with a perfect head. "You?"

I feel much better about her knowing she hasn't slept with him. "No. But girl, do I want to." I force a chuckle that I don't really feel past my lips.

"He has that effect on all the girls." She laughs. "Hang in there."

I don't want to be like all the girls.

Someone taps the bar in front of her rudely, and she looks up scowling. "Don't ever bang on my fucking bar again, asshole," she says, but there's a smile under her words, I can tell.

"Oh, come on, Abby," he says. "You know you love it when I bang you."

Snickers erupt around the bar. He leans over the bar and she stands up on her tiptoes, putting all her weight on her arms, so she can touch her lips to his. She points to me. "Ford, this is Kit."

Ford looks over at me and smiles.

"Kit came in with Logan," Abby explains. She shoots him an odd look and he narrows his eyes at her, and then looks over at me.

"Say it ain't so," he says with a laugh.

I press my lips together, not sure what he's insinuating.

"It's about time somebody caught that bastard." He laughs, rubbing his hands together with excitement. "Payback's a bitch," he says. Then he saunters off into the crowd.

"Ford works with Logan in the front," she explains in between pouring drinks. She takes a twenty from a guy and presses it down her top. I can see the tip of it sticking up from her cleavage. And so can her customer. He licks his lips. "Oh, did you want change?" she asks sweetly. He shakes his head, laughs and walks away.

"Have you worked here long?" I shout. The band is just getting started on the stage, tuning their instruments and playing some snippets of music. I turn around to look toward them. The lead singer is already shirtless. But the crowd seems to love it.

"About a year," she says. She's working quickly to fill drinks, and the club is getting busier and busier. I almost wish I could go and help her. I feel pretty useless sitting on the sidelines like this with nothing to do.

"Who's the band?" I ask, jerking a thumb over my shoulder.

She shrugs. "They're new."

I hear the beginnings of *Free Bird* start to play and my fingers itch. I swipe the tip of my finger across the calluses on my thumb and wish it was me on that stage. But it can't be. They're just doing cover songs, anyway. But they're songs that make my fingers twitch and make my heart start to beat faster.

I turn around to watch them.

They're really very good. But there's one problem. Their lead guitarist is stinking drunk. They barely got through their warm up, and he's already stumbling over the cords. Their bassist turns to glare at him, and he grins and keeps on playing. But he can barely stay on his feet. He motions to a waitress and she brings him a shot. He tips it back and keeps on playing.

The bass guitarist is pissed. I can tell. I would be too. You don't mess with the music. Ever. I'm itchy on the stool, and I want to go and take the guitar from him and take over. I force myself to sit still.

Logan stalks close to me from across the room and stops half way. "You ok?" he mouths. I nod at him and shoo him away with my hands. He grins at me, and stays where he can look my way. I hope he's not planning to hover all night.

I twitch for a completely different reason when I see a girl walk up to Logan. She's wearing a short skirt and a skimpy top, and her boobs are sitting up like they're stacked on a shelf for people to look at. Logan's eyes skim across her chest, and she lays her hand on his arm, leaning close to him. I scoot to the edge of the chair, watching to see how he reacts. He watches her lips for a moment, and then puts his hands on her shoulders and pushes her back. She scowls. He takes a step back from her, and my heart thrills.

"Damn," Abby says. "Never thought I'd see that happen."

I look over at her. "What do you mean?"

"I've never seen him push one away."

Logan looks over at me and winks.

The girl glares at me, and turns to say something sharp to him. He looks at her kindly, but there's no heat in his gaze. At least not the kind she was looking for. She huffs off.

Suddenly, the band's amp screeches loudly and their lead guitarist stumbles, falling to his knees. His buddies stop playing and try to stand him up, but he just lays there laughing.

The crowd starts to shout, pushing toward the stage. They are not happy. And I can't say I blame them.

I motion to Logan, and he rolls his eyes as he walks toward the stage. The crew staggers the lead guitarist to his feet and lifts the guitar strap over his head, but he's too wobbly to stand. Logan bends, shoves his shoulder into the man's middle, and hoists him over his back. Logan winks at me as he walks toward the back of the bar and disappears behind a curtain. The band members are huddled in a circle, trying to figure out if they can continue or not without their lead guitarist.

My fingers twitch and I wiggle my feet, trying to keep away. But it's impossible. I slide from the stool, my legs wobbly as I walk over, and very nonchalantly step onto the stage. My heart is pounding in my ears and I couldn't utter a sound if I wanted to, my throat is so tight. But I pick up the abandoned guitar, slide the strap over my head, and look at the band members. I pull my pic out of my pocket and hover over the steel strings. One of them reaches to take the guitar from me. But I start to play before he can.

Sweet Child of Mine rolls off my fingertips, the sound of it filling the space, and the men step back, aghast at the little girl who's playing the big boys' guitar. Truth be told, it's too big for me, but I don't let that stop me. "We going to play or what, boys?" I yell. But I don't stop playing, no matter what. The crowd is hooting, and I do a quick show for them.

The boys of the band all rearrange themselves, and the lead singer comes to me and asks, "What can you play?"

"I can play anything you can sing," I say with a laugh. My blood is surging in my veins, and the rhythm of the music is taking me away with it.

"Can you be more specific?" he asks. But he's smiling and watching my fingers as they fly around on the guitar. He shakes his head. "Never mind."

He goes back to the mic and says, "We have a surprise for you, folks!" He motions toward me. "She's a whole lot prettier than our usual lead guitarist, don't you think?"

The crowd yells and claps. I keep playing, until I wind down *Sweet Child of Mine*. I stop and look up the lead, grinning. "What's next?" I ask.

He raises a brow. "*Hotel California?*" he asks.

I nod. I was playing that when I was eight. But I wait for the drummer to pick up the beat, and then I fall in with it. Their bass guitar duels with me for a minute and then we find a rhythm.

I haven't had this much fun in a long time. Not since I left my band back home. I forgot how much I missed this.

We finish up the song and the lead singer mouths at me, "*Welcome to the Jungle?*"

I nod, laughing. I look out over the crowd and see Logan leaning against a post in the middle of the room. His arms are crossed over his chest, and his mouth is open slightly. I blow him a kiss and he shakes his head, smiling. Goodness, that boy is pretty. He gives me a thumbs up and walks away.

I wish I could share this with him, because this is the best feeling ever. The fans, the sound, the way I feel complete when I do this... there's nothing that compares. I'm not scared. Not in the least bit. I love this. I love music. I love the guitar. And I'm afraid I'm a little bit in love with Logan.

Logan

I turn around to watch Kit as she plays. Her cheeks are all rosy, and she's smiling. Every now and then, they give her a quick solo, and she strums the guitar, dancing around, her knees bending as she works it. By the way the crowd's going crazy, I'd guess she's really good at this.

I can feel the thump of the music in the floor and on the walls, and I stop and rest my hand on one of the speakers.

Kit's hair is all wet, and her face is shining. She's never looked more beautiful to me. This is obviously what she was born to do. And I can't help but wonder why she's busking in a subway for pennies rather than doing this full time. This is where her future lies. This is her passion.

I'm happy just watching her. And I have to keep reminding myself to keep an eye on the crowd, rather than both my eyes on her.

Someone chucks my shoulder and I look over to find Pete standing beside me grinning. "Damn, she's good," he says. He plays some air guitar, and I can't help but laugh at him. He waves at me and says, "Hell, I'll leave it to the pro." He points a finger toward Kit. "Did you know she could do that?"

I shrug. *I knew she could play. But they apparently think she's really good.* I motion to the crowd.

I watch as the lead singer walks toward Kit and says something in her ear. He's shirtless and sweaty, and she brushes him away like he's a pesky fly. He goes, but he's laughing when he does it, and I don't like it. I don't like it at all. I stand up taller.

"He's not worth it," Pete says.

I know. But I still don't like it.

"You got it bad for this one, don't you?" he asks. He's smiling, but his question is serious.

I nod. I don't need to say more than that. I do have it bad for this girl.

The band breaks, and Kit wipes her hairline with her forearm. The lead singer walks toward her, but I go that direction and hop onto the stage before he can get to her. He nearly bumps into my back. But he stops and goes the other way.

"Oh my God!" she says, excitement in her eyes as she jumps in place in front of me. "Did you see that?" she asks.

Then she grabs my shoulders, jumps, and wraps her legs around my waist. She kisses me. She tastes like root beer and excitement as she licks into me. I hold her ass, and jerk her tighter against me. The owner of the club waves and I catch him out of the corner of my eye. He jerks his thumb toward the back of the club. I nod and carry Kit in that direction. But she's all hyped up on nerves and attitude. And she hasn't taken her lips from mine. I carry her with her legs still wrapped around my waist into the storage room, and back her up against the wall. She's tangling her tongue with mine, and I don't ever want her to stop.

She finally pulls back and looks at me, her hands clutching my face. "Did you see that?" she asks.

"See what?" I have lost all my wits in her kiss.

"Me playing. Did you see it?"

I nod, nuzzling my nose into her neck. "You were amazing."

"I know! Wasn't I? Oh my God, I want to go back out there." She unclenches her legs from around my waist and drops her feet to the floor. She starts to pace back and forth across the room, chewing on her fingernail. I can't see her lips moving at all, but I lean against the wall and smile at her. "What's so funny?" she asks, stopping to look at me.

"Nothing," I say. I walk to her and brush her sweaty hair from her neck. "You're just so fucking beautiful." She shivers as I blow across her neck.

Her hand comes up to cover mine where it lays on her shoulder, and I get more comfort from that little touch than I ever have from a girl I've been inside. "Thank you for bringing me here," she says.

"Thank you for coming with me."

"I haven't had this much fun in a really long time," she admits. She's glowing.

I lean down and kiss her, because she's that damn pretty. She hears something from the doorway, and turns to look that way. "I'll be right there," she says, holding up a finger. She looks up at me. "They're ready to get started again."

"I have to get back to work, anyway. The owner just sent us back here because he was afraid I was going to fuck you on the stage."

She covers her mouth with her hand. "So, they think we're having sex back here. Are you serious?" Her eyes are wide.

I can't keep from grinning. "Probably."

"Do you do that back here often?" she asks.

I freeze. I don't want to answer her. Because I have done it. She doesn't push for an answer. But she heaves a sigh and shoves herself away from me. I feel the loss of her immediately. "Don't do that," I say, taking her face in my hands. "I can't change my past."

She looks deep into my eyes and says, "I know. I didn't ask you to. I just have to go back on stage." She kisses me softly. "Can we come back to this later?" she asks, grinning. She's nearly vibrating with excitement.

She's not mad at me. Thank God. "We can come back to this as often as you want." Any time. Any place.

She darts away from me, and I tug on her fingers to hold her back. She pulls back from me slowly and I ache with wanting to jerk her back into my arms. But she turns and runs away.

She hops back up on the stage and I follow her. The lead singer turns to her, scowling. "You and Logan, huh?" he asks. I can read his lips from where I'm standing.

She grins and nods her head.

He says something that looks like, "Figures," before he scowls and turns toward me. I point to her and point to my chest and mouth the word "mine" at him. He gets it. He totally gets it. He might not want it to be true. But he knows she's not in his future. She's my future.

I go see Abby and get Kit a root beer. She's been sweating up there for an hour, and they have another set to do. I point to the root beer lever on the fountain and raise my brows. "For you?" Abby asks, with a pointed finger as she fills a glass. I point to Kit. She nods and drops two cherries into it. I turn to take it to Kit and Abby tugs on my sleeve. "Where did she learn to play like that?" Abby asks.

I shrug. I have no idea where she learned to play. All I know is that she's good. I can tell by the way the crowd is reacting to her. My heart is filled with pride for her. And it's filled with a lot more. A lot more that she's probably not ready to address yet.

I take her root beer to her and stand by the side of the stage to wait until she's done with the song. But she marches down the steps, her fingers flying over the strings, and she leans over, taking the straw into her mouth. She sucks it greedily, and there's not a man in the room who's not envious of me right that moment. She never stops playing, but she drains the glass. Then she smiles at me, kisses me quickly and struts back up the steps and onto the stage.   Great. Now I have a hard on and so does every man within a twenty foot radius. Suddenly, she runs back down the steps. She nods toward a cherry in the glass and I lift it to her lips. She takes it against the tip of her tongue and closes her lips around it. She pops it off the string with a gentle tug. She nods to the other, and looks at my lips. She taunts me with her grin, and I lift it to my lips and open my mouth for it. I tongue it from the stem, taking my time with it, playing with her, until she leans over, opens her mouth over mine, and takes it back from me.

I pretend to look offended, but I'm so fucking turned on that all I can do is look like an idiot.

Emily

I crash onto the stool at the end of the bar I'd vacated when I took over the band's guitar, and lean my elbows on the table. A grin I can't suppress tugs at my lips. Abby clinks a root beer down in front of me. "That was amazing!" she says as she tosses in two cherries.

I nod. It was pretty damn amazing. I'm still trying to catch my breath. I lift my wet hair off my neck and roll it into a lump, then let it go.

"You been playing for a long time?" Abby asks. She wipes the bar down with a rag.

"I think I was playing before I could walk," I admit. I can't remember a time when I didn't have a guitar. "My grandfather gave me my first guitar." My dad was all for it, until it became the only thing I was good at.

"Well, you can tell." She raises a hand to give me a high five. "That was fantastic." She clenches my hand for a second and meets my eyes, smiling. I don't quite know what to do with that. Yet.

I look around the bar. The place is finally quiet and Logan is stacking chairs on tables for the cleaning crew. He raises the tail of his t-shirt and mops his brow with it. His abs ripple as he bends and a whistle escapes my lips. "Goodness gracious," I breathe.

"That boy is one fine piece of man candy," she says, stopping to lick her lips.

"Makes me want to lick him from top to bottom," I reply softly, more to myself than to her. My face floods with heat when I see that she heard me.

She laughs and keeps cleaning. "What's stopping you?"

I point to Logan. "He is."

Her brows shoot up toward her hairline. "Logan won't scratch your itch?" She points a finger toward him. I'm afraid I'm going to have to give her mouth to mouth, she looks that shocked.

I shake my head. "He scratched my itch. But he won't let me scratch his," I whisper fiercely. I have no idea why I'm talking to this girl. Probably because she's a bartender. They have a natural way of making people open up and spill their guts. Consider me eviscerated.

Abby steps back, her chin dropping toward her chest. She regards me like I just grew two heads. Then she smiles. "It's about damn time," she says, throwing her head back with a laugh.

"It's not funny," I pout. "And don't say anything to Ford, ok?" I add.

She holds up a hand like she's raising it to God and says, "I promise not to say a word." She laughs again. "Even though it's the news of the century, I'll keep it to myself."

I look up as Pete walks out of the back, but he's deep in conversation with Bone and another man. I watch them closely. Pete reaches over and shakes hands with Bone. What in the world is that about? You never, ever shake hands with Bone. Ever. That would imply that you made a deal with him. And Bone's deals never turn out well for anyone but Bone.

Logan smacks his hands together to get Pete's attention. He signs something really quickly, but Pete brushes him off with a wave. Logan sets down the mop he was wielding, and steps toward the pair of them. Bone squeezes Pete's shoulder and then Bone walks away from him and straight toward me.

Bone leans back against the counter beside me, and Abby tries to make herself look really busy. I watch Logan as he yells at Pete in sign language. I have no idea what he's saying, but it's not pleasant, whatever it is.

Bone looks at me over his shoulder and says, "You got a place to stay tonight, Kit?"

I nod. "Yep. But thanks for checking."

Bone looks closely at me for a minute. So closely that my skin crawls. "Let me know if you ever need anything."

"Sure will." I don't say more than that. I just play with my straw and wait for him to walk away. It's best not to antagonize him.

Bone stands up tall, nods at me, and walks toward the back entrance. He leaves. Logan is still yelling at Pete. And Pete's finally deflating a bit. Logan's bigger than he is. But that's not all. Pete looked like he wanted to argue with Logan when they first started talking. But then Logan wraps his fist up in Pete's shirt and jerks him into his chest. He's not signing a word. He's just glaring at Pete until Pete holds up his hands in surrender. If looks could kill, Pete would be a dead lump on the floor.

Logan releases him and Pete falls back off his tiptoes onto his heels. He signs something that calms Logan down, but he's still pissed, and he starts shoving chairs from place to place. He was stacking them. Now he's stacking them forcefully. Pete walks toward me and grumbles.

"What were you doing with Bone, Pete?" I ask.

"Nothing," he mutters.

"That man's no good. Don't let him get you into trouble," I warn quietly.

"Why does everyone think I'm going to get into trouble?" Pete asks, affronted. He pats his chest. "I can take care of myself."

"Not with the likes of him," I say.

He looks up at me, and asks, "What do you know about Bone?"

"More than I want to know," I admit. I've seen what he's capable of. I've seen what he's done to girls at the shelters. I've seen how he uses them.

"Mmm hmm," Pete hums.

Just then, the band members walk out from the back of the building. The lead singer walks toward me and slaps a small pile of bills in front of me. He sits down on a stool next to me, his shoulder a little too close to mine for comfort. I shift away. He doesn't take the hint.

I look down at the stack of money. "What's that for?" I ask.

"That's your cut of the door."

"What's that mean?" I ask.

He nods toward the front door. "We get a percentage of the cover charge. That's your cut. We split it five ways."

A grin steals across my lips. "Seriously?"

He smiles and nods. "Seriously." He lays a hand over mine. "You did a good job tonight."

I slide my hand from under his and wipe it on my jeans. He doesn't notice. He looks at me like he's hungry and I'm cake.

I pick up the stack of bills and fan them out in my hand. There's more than three hundred dollars here. My mouth falls open. "Thanks," I say. I can live for weeks on this much money.

He shrugs. "You earned it."

Abby jumps in. She's watching Logan across the room. And warning me by shooting her eyes in Logan's direction. "Logan's girlfriend is an amazing guitar player, huh?" she asks.

"Girlfriend, huh?" he asks me quietly.

I smile and nod. "Girlfriend." I look over and see Logan walking toward us. He's not smiling. He's doing the opposite. I get up and step between him and the lead singer. I didn't even get his name. Nor do I really want it. I tuck the money in my pocket and put my hands on Logan's chest. He looks down at me and tries to brush me to the side, but I won't let him. "When can we go home?" I ask, purposefully tugging him toward me by the loops in his jeans. He finally looks down at me. His brow is furrowed as he glares at me. "What's the sign for home?" I ask.

He shows me, looking into my eyes as he signs it. I point to me and then repeat the sign. Logan nods.

The lead singer walks by us, and says softly so that I can hear, but Logan can't see his lips. "When he's done with you, give me a call, sweetheart," he says.

Abby gasps. He looks over at her and winks and she flips him the bird. He laughs louder, and then he leaves, taking his band mates with him.

Logan wants to talk to me, I can tell. But he won't do it with everyone looking. "When can we go home?" I ask.

He looks around. The chairs are all put up and Ford took over with the mop. Logan claps his hands at Pete and Pete turns around. He makes the sign he just showed me for home and Pete nods. He's still pissy but he comes with us.

I wave at Abby and she waves back. She's lifting her purse from beneath the bar, so I think she's about to leave, too. "Don't be a stranger!" she yells at me. I smile back and nod. She's nice. I like her.

We walk through the bar to the back exit, and let ourselves out. It's after four in the morning, and I'm tired, but the cold air wraps around me, and I feel more invigorated than I have in a really long time. I just got to play with a band for hours. And I have over three hundred dollars in my pocket.

Logan takes my hand in his and looks around. The streets are dark and more than a little scary at this hour. I'm suddenly really glad I'm with these two men. They're both built like mountains, and the tats make them look much fiercer than they are. I want to talk to Logan, but I know he can't walk beside me and see my lips. So I stay quiet all the way to his apartment. He motions for Pete to go up the stairs, and we stand in the stairwell for a moment. He brushes back a strand of hair that's stuck to my lip. "You really enjoyed tonight, didn't you?" he asks as soon as Pete's gone.

I nod, and bury my face in his chest for a moment, squealing inside with excitement. I want to bite his chest, but I lift my head and say, "Thanks so much for taking me with you."

"What did Bone want with you?"

I shrug. "Same thing he always wants."

"Have you ever worked for him?" He appraises me closely, his blue eyes searching my face.

"Never." It's true. I have never fallen that far. Although I came close more than once.

He takes my hand in his and starts up the stairs. I kind of like holding hands with him. It's nice. He pushes me up the steps before him and I turn around to say, "Do you know this is the first time I've ever walked up these steps of my own free will?"

He turns me around, slaps me on the ass, and I hear him chuckle. It's more of a murmuring sound, but it's all Logan and it warms my heart.

Logan

I'm so pissed at Pete that I can barely keep from running up the stairs and strangling the living shit out of him. He has something going on with Bone, but he won't tell me what they were talking about. Bone's no good and Pete knows it. So I have no idea what his purpose is for talking to the loser. He should have stayed far away from him.

But Kit's hand is in mine, and it jerks me from my thoughts about strangling Pete. I stop at the top of the stairs and draw her to me. She laughs and falls into me, her hands landing to lie flat on my chest. Her thumb scrubs across one of my piercings and my breath catches. "Kit," I warn.

"What?" she asks playfully, a grin tugging at her lips. "After what you did to me on the bathroom counter, you still won't let me touch you? Seriously?" She's playing. And I know it. But I don't want to explain it. I cup her neck with my hand, and I feel a soft purr in her throat. God, I want her so bad.

"I enjoyed what I did to you on the bathroom counter," I say as I touch my lips to hers. I lick across the seam of her lips, and she opens for me. Her tongue is a velvet rasp against mine, and I can imagine her taking my dick in her mouth and licking across it the same way. I groan into her mouth, and she steps up on tiptoe to get closer to me. Her hands slide around my neck, her tits pressed against my chest.

She lifts her head so I can see her lips. "When do I get to return the favor?" she asks. Her cheeks color prettily, and I can tell asking the question embarrasses her. God, she's so damn cute.

I shake my head. "Not going to happen."

She pulls back farther, her brows drawing together into a crease. "How long are you going to stick to that rule?" she asks.

"As long as it takes for you to trust me."

"I trust you now," she protests.

She doesn't. If she did, she would tell me her secrets. "No, you don't."

"There are just some things I can't tell anyone." She takes my face in her hands. "Even you." Her breath rushes against my lips and it's all I can do not to press her against the wall and sink inside her right here and now. I could have her jeans off in seconds. Her legs around my waist. She breaks me from my haze of lust when she says, "I want to tell you everything."

"You don't have to tell me everything. But you can't hold back from me."

She lets me go and steps back, her breath rushing from her. I can feel the blast of it against my chin. "You mean like you're holding back from me."

I jerk her back to me, and she pushes away. She's irked. I try to explain. "If I ever get to fucking be inside you, I want to know what to call you. I want to at least know your name. Because when that happens, you're going to fucking own me." I tip her face up so she's looking at me. "Do you understand?"

She looks unsure.

"You're going to own me." I jerk her hips to mine, letting her feel how much I want her. "And there's nothing I want more."

I step back, brush her hair from her face, and open the door, tugging her by her fingertips until she follows me. She's dragging. She tugs on my hand until I look at her.

"I want everything you want," she says. She's not looking me in the eye. So, I wait for her eyes to open. They finally do. She meets my gaze. "I do want everything you want. I just can't have it."

I lay her hand on my chest, and spread her fingers over my heart. "You already have me." I laugh. "You had me from that first moment in the shop." I hold up my arm, so she can look closely at her tat. "I'm wearing your fucking brand, damn it." I tip her face up to mine. "What are you afraid of? You're hiding from something. I know it. But I don't know what."

She bites her lower lip between her teeth and worries it. I tug it free with my thumb and lean down, sucking it between my lips. She steps onto her tiptoes and growls against my lips. I set her back and away from me, and I can feel the rumble in her chest as she moves.

"I'll tell you. I can't tell you everything. But I can tell you some of it," she says.

My heart swells. I take her hand and lead her into the apartment. The whole place is quiet. Everyone is already in bed. "Want to take a shower?" I ask her. She sweated the night away.

"I thought you wanted to talk," she says, looking everywhere but at me.

"I do." And I don't. Now I'm really afraid. "Take a shower and then we can talk until the sun comes up, if you want."

She nods and bites her lower lip, which sends a kick straight to my gut. Then she turns from me. Suddenly she spins back. She grins and jerks her thumb toward the bathroom. "You want to join me in the shower so we can talk in there?"

Something tells me that if we end up in the shower, we won't be doing much talking. "We'll talk when you get out."

Her bottom lip pokes out. But then she shrugs and says, "Can't blame a girl for trying."

Emily

I shower quickly, trying to put my thoughts in order. I have to be really careful about what I tell Logan, mainly because there are so many people looking for me. I still see the lost posters at times. And there are news blasts sometimes with pictures of the old me. They're of the me who had dark blond hair, pretty headbands, and shoes that cost more than the Reeds' monthly budget. I ignore them, telling myself that person no longer exists. It's easier that way.

I miss home with the longing of a toothache. But I've been gone so long now that I can't go back. I left out of anger. And I can't go home out of shame or necessity. I will only go home when I'm strong enough to stand up for myself. And I haven't felt like that for quite some time.

I wrap a towel around my head and one around my body, and I step into the bedroom. Logan's reclining on the bed wearing nothing but his boxers. He tosses me a clean shirt, and I pull it over my head. He closes his eyes as I slide his shirt on and step into my panties. I can hear the hiss of his heavy breaths across the room, and it's a heady feeling to know how I affect him.

"You still want to talk?" I ask. "Or are you too tired?" I shake out my hair and run a comb through it.

"There's no way you're taking back your offer," he warns. "You can't tease me like that."

I laugh. "I'm not taking it back. I just thought you might want to wait until tomorrow."

He sits up and crosses his legs in front of him. I crawl onto the bed and mirror his position.

His gaze darts down to my panties, where he can probably see the strip of fabric between my legs. But I still sit criss-cross-applesauce. He groans. "You're killing me here."

I tug his shirt down over my knees. "You're making me spill my guts. You can take some torture, too." I glare at him until his gaze becomes indecipherable. "What is it?" I ask.

He heaves a sigh.

I hold up a hand to stop his melancholy mood. "If you could do anything, what would it be?" I ask.

His brows shoot up. "We're supposed to be talking about you."

"We will," I warn. "I promise. Just tell me, if you could do anything, what would you do?"

He doesn't even blink. But his eyes darken, and he says, "I'd lay you down, move your panties to the side and slide inside you."

I freeze. My gut clenches and my belly quivers and my face heats up. I want what he wants. I want it so badly.

He laughs. "Oh, you meant the thing I want second-best?"

"That'll do," I croak.

"I'd go back to college," he says over his laughter.

"Back to college? When were you in college?"

He scrubs a hand down his face. "Before Matt got sick. I had a scholarship."

"But you had to come back home because of Matt and his cancer?" I lay a hand on my chest. My heart is breaking for this family. For Logan.

He shrugs. "We had to get some loans against the shop to pay for his treatment. And then he couldn't keep doing tats because of the germs. So, we couldn't pay the loans. Pete and Sam weren't old enough to work there. Not doing tats."

"What school did you go to?" I ask.

"NYU." His brows furrow. "Why does any of his matter?"

"You gave up your scholarship for Matt. For your family."

He shakes his head. "I got a deferment. I didn't give up. I can go back once things are good here."

"Did it cost a lot of money for Matt's treatment?"

He nods. But he doesn't elaborate. I can guess what a lot of money is to them.

"I wanted to do that, too," I say quietly. No one knows this. No one else knows I had dreams once. "Well, not to NYU. I wanted to go to Julliard. But my dad said it was a worthless endeavor and he refused to pay for it." I hold up a finger when he opens his mouth to protest. "But he was willing to pay for a wedding that cost four times what Julliard ever would." I shake my head.

Logan looks a bit shell shocked. "A wedding?" he asks.

I nod, looking up at him from beneath lowered lashes.

His breath hitches. "Please tell me you're not married."

I shake my head. "No. That's why I'm here." I scoot forward so my knees are touching his. I don't touch him anywhere else. But I need a connection with him. "My father arranged a marriage for me. That's all I was good for, being on the arm of a senator or a high powered attorney. I had no worth of my own, aside from being someone's arm piece. Since I can't read, that was supposed to be my future."

"But you said no."

I nod. "I said no. And he didn't like it. So, he went on without me. The wedding was planned. The dress was purchased. The church was decorated."

His brows shoot toward the ceiling. "But you ran away."

I nod, biting my lower lip. He pulls it free with the pad of his thumb and strokes across it. I kiss his thumb, and he leans back. "I ran away," I confirm. "On the morning of the wedding, I ran away. I took a bus from home to here."

"With nothing."

I show him my empty hands. "I took some clothes, my guitar, and bus fare."

"Where are you from?" he asks.

I shake my head. "I can't tell you." Yet. I know I'll tell him eventually. But I can't risk him calling my family. I can't risk them finding out where I am. My father is one of the richest men in the country. He would spare no expense in bringing me home."

He nods. He's not happy about it, but he understands. "Julliard, huh?" he asks, smiling. His thumb trails across the back of my hand.

"Julliard," I say with a smile. "I struggle with reading," I admit. "But Julliard didn't care. I even auditioned for them without him knowing. They wanted me. And offered special services for my dyslexia. But my dad found it to be a worthless endeavor. He's of the opinion that I can't learn. Anything."

"Your dad is an idiot." Logan says it deadpan.

I laugh. It's a watery sound. He believes in me. Logan believes I could do it.

"What's stopping you from going now?"

"My social security number," I explain. "My father is looking for me. And I'm afraid he'll force me back there if he knows where I am. He can track my movements if I go to the doctor or get a bank account or register for school."

Logan shakes his head. "You're an adult. You're not under your father's thumb."

"I know." I'm starting to realize that. "I don't think I'll ever go back."

"Do you miss them? Your family?"

I miss them like crazy. "Almost every day."

"Your dad?"

I nod.

"Your mom?"

I nod, and tears prick at my lashes when I think of her. But she didn't help me when I begged and pleaded for her to do so. She sided with my father.

"Siblings?" he asks.

I shake my head. "My parents didn't have more children. I'm their only one. Poor things got robbed, huh?"

"Don't say that," he warns sharply.

"It's the truth. I've never been what they wanted."

"What did they want?"

Someone else. "Someone who can read. Follow in their footsteps. Someone who doesn't struggle to read street signs or financial statements. I can't do any of those things."

"Have they ever seen you play?" he asks.

I shake my head. "Not like I played tonight."

"Then they're even bigger idiots than I thought. You were amazing tonight. You had the crowd eating out of the palm of your hand."

"Thank you for saying that."

His eyes narrow. "It's the truth."

"I appreciate you so much," I say. I know I've only known him for a few days, but it feels like forever. "Did I tell you enough?" I ask.

"Not by a long shot," he says with a laugh. "I want to know everything."

Maybe someday. "Can we take this slow?"

I can't give him enough info that he could contact my parents. Because I'm afraid he would, thinking he was helping me.

"You're worried that I'll betray your confidence?" he asks. He sits back, affronted.

"Some people have good intentions. I know you do. But you don't understand how much I have to keep my anonymity. I can't trust anyone." If I do, my parents will suddenly have the info they need to sweep down and snatch me back into their world.

He nods. He's somber. I should have known how this would affect him.

"Now that you know where I came from, I understand if you want me to leave." I turn to reach for my bag, so that I can gather my things.

"What the fuck?" he says, his arm snaking around my stomach as he picks me up and lifts me into his lap. I turn to face him, my legs over his thigh. "Where do you think you're going?"

I heave a sigh. "I have no idea."

He tips my face up and looks into my eyes. "I want you here. Will you stay?"

"Will you be satisfied with what I told you?"

He nods. "For now, yes."

His eyes narrow and I know what his next question is. "Will you tell me your name?"

I shake my head. I can't. "I'm sorry," I say.

He nods, settling me against his shoulder. He holds me like that for a minute, and then he jostles me out of his arms. He pulls the covers back and picks me up, tucking me. He climbs in behind me and turns me to face him. "I had hoped for more. But I'll take what I can get. Thank you for telling me what you did."

"Thank you for listening."

I lean forward and touch my lips to his. He's hesitant. "What's wrong?" I ask, leaning back.

He pulls me into him, and I feel the length of him against my hip.

"Oh," I say. My belly clenches. My need matches his.

He brushes my hair back from my face with gentle fingers. "Yeah," he says with a laugh. "It's like this crazy torment, having you this close to me."

"You know we could-" I start. But he puts a finger against my lips to stop me.

"I can wait," he says. He reaches over and turns off the light. He rolls me into him, and the light dusting of hair that's on his chest tickles my cheek.

"I think I might love you, Logan," I say to the darkness.

His head lifts. I can see it in the sliver of light that's falling from the open curtain. "Did you say something?" he asks.

I shake my head, letting my nose brush his chest so he can feel my answer.

"You sure?" he asks.

I nod, my nose brushing him up and down. He kisses the top of my head, and hitches my leg up over his hip. I wrap an arm around him and snuggle in deeply. "Go to sleep," he says softly.

So I do.

***

I wake the next morning to a gentle tap, tap, tap on the side of my nose. I blink my eyes open and startle when I see a face looking into mine. Hayley grins at me. "You sweepy?" she says quietly.

I was, until she tapped against my face like a hungry bird. I scrub the sleep from my eyes and look over at Logan. He's lying beside me with one arm flung over his head, his mouth hanging open. I snuggle deeper into my pillow. "Where's your daddy?" I ask.

"Sweeping," she says. She's dragging a bunny by the ears. "I'm hungwy," she says.

I cover a yawn with my open palm. I probably have awful morning breath. "Can you go and wake your daddy?"

She shakes her head. "He said to go back to sweep."

I look toward the window. The sun is just barely over the horizon. "I want a pancake."

A pancake? "How about some cereal?" I ask, as I throw the covers off myself and get up. I take a pair of Logan's boxers from his drawer and put them on.

"Dos are Logan's," she says, scowling at me.

"Do you think he'll mind if I borrow them?" I whisper at her.

She shakes her head and smiles, taking my hand in her free one so she can lead me from the room. "You don't got to whisper. Logan can't hear," she says.

I laugh. She's right. And what's funny is that it took a three year old to remind me. I hold a finger to my lips, though, as we step out into the hallway. "But your daddy can. Shh."

She giggles and repeats my shush.

She runs down the hallway, her naked feet slapping softly against the hardwoods until she's in the kitchen. I search through the cupboards to find a box of cereal.

"Not dat one," she says, shaking her head. "I don't wike dat one." She points to a different box. One with a cartoon character and the word fruit on it. But I know there's no fruit in this cereal. Or anything else healthy.

"Does your daddy let you eat this?" I ask.

She grins and nods. I shrug my shoulders and pour her a bowl of cereal with milk. She gets her own spoon from the drawer. She knows where everything is. She digs into her cereal, her feet swinging back and forth beneath the chair.

I go and lay down on the couch. I am tired. I think Logan and I got to sleep around five in the morning, and it can't be much later than that now. I lay back with a groan and close my eyes. I am just getting comfortable when two sharp elbows land in my midsection. Hayley crawls on top of me on the couch. I think she must be part monkey. She holds a kid-sized board book in her hand. "Wead," she says, shoving it in my face.

I sit up, tucking her into my lap. I take the book from her and open it, but the words jumble. I turn it upside down. "Once upon a time," I begin.

"Dat's not how it goes," she complains.

She's a smart girl. "I know," I explain. "But books are magical and if you turn them upside down, there's a whole new story in the pages."

"Weally?" she asks, her eyes big with wonder.

No, not really. But it's the best I can do, kid. "Really," I affirm.

She wiggles, settling more comfortably in my arms.

I start to make up a story, based on the upside down pictures. She listens intently. "Once upon a time, there was a little frog. And his name was Randolf."

"Randolf," she repeats with a giggle.

"And Randolf had one big problem."

"Uh oh," she breathes. "What kind a problem?"

"Randolf wanted to be a prince. But his mommy told him that he couldn't be a prince, since he was just a frog."

I keep reading until I say, "The end." She lays the book to the side and snuggles into me. I kiss the top of her head, because it feels like the right thing to do. And she smells good. "Your story was better than the book's story," she says.

My heart swells with pride. "Thank you." If only it was this easy to please the adults of the world.

"Want to watch TV?" she asks.

I yawn. "Sure. Why not?"

She goes over and picks up the DVD. "You go start it," she instructs.

The DVD player is under the TV, and it doesn't look that complicated. I put the movie in and turn the TV on. The movie starts, but it's not a typical kids' movie. It's a movie that teaches sign language to children. I drop onto the floor to sit beside her. There's a lady teaching each of the signs, and there are pictures. There are words at the bottom of the screen for people who can read. But it's an instructional DVD made for kids.

Hayley sits beside me and she starts to repeat the signs. "You do it?" she asks. "We wearn signing for Logan."

I am enraptured. "We learn sign language for Logan," I repeat with a nod.

When the first DVD ends, we move on to the second. I have an amazing memory, because I have to have one. So, I think I can remember some of this. I'm giddy with excitement. I practice some of the more basic signs with Hayley.

We're almost done with the second DVD when Paul walks into the room. "Hayley, what are you doing?" He scratches his stomach. His hair is a mess, sticking out all over the place.

She pats my cheek. "I wearning signing with Logan's girl," she says.

I like that. I like it a lot.

"Did she wake you up?" Paul asks, smothering a yawn.

I wave him off with a breezy hand. "It's no big deal. She was showing me the DVD's."

He nods, his brows arching. "Well, I'm sorry she woke you. You should go back to bed."

"Do you think it would be all right if I watch the rest of them later?" I ask, suddenly feeling shy about it.

He chuckles. "Of course. That's how we all learned."

I nod. He picks Hayley up, jiggling her until she giggles. He laughs at her. "Next time I tell you to stay in bed, I mean stay in bed, little girl," he says. She laughs all the way down the hallway, until he takes her in his room and closes the door.

I yawn. The bed is calling to me. I go back in Logan's room, and he's lying exactly like I left him. I draw the shades closed, so the room isn't quite so bright. Then I take off his boxers and slide back into bed with him. He reaches for me immediately, pulling me into him as he rolls and covers me with his leg, his thigh across the backs of mine. "You all right?" he asks.

I nod. I'm all right. I can't help but think that I'm where I'm supposed to be.

He brushes my hair from my face and nuzzles me with his lips. I settle deeper into him and go back to sleep with him wrapped around me.

It seems like only moments later when the bed begins to vibrate.

Logan

The bed vibrates and I reach over and smack the alarm clock. I hate early Saturday mornings. But I promised Sam that I would go and run some plays with him in the park before the shop opens. Sam's a football player, and he's being scouted by a few colleges. He thinks he might get a full ride, and I couldn't be happier for him. He doesn't have the grades to get a scholarship like I did. But he's capable of getting an education through sports, and that works too.

The purr of Kit's throat tells me that she's saying something. I look down at her lips, but she's laying with her face smushed into the pillow. "Did you say something?" I ask, rolling her to her back. I throw my leg across her.

She doesn't speak, but she signs the word no at me. My heart leaps. She smiles, then her brown eyes open and she blinks at me. "Did I do that right?" She signs the word for right, but nothing more.

"Yes, it's right. Where did you learn that?"

"I watched some DVD's with Hayley this morning when she woke me up." She yawns and turns toward me. "Will you sign with me? I want to learn your language so we can talk around your brothers."

My heart swells.

"I can learn to sign," she begins, like she has to justify her ability to learn. I put my finger over her lips.

"Shh…" I say. "I'll sign with you any time you want."

She's lying on her back with my t shirt sliding up to expose a strip of skin over her panties. I reach out, and run my hand along the seam of her panties, dipping the tips of my fingers below the elastic. She squirms and her eyes open. They're soft and warm and pleading with me.

I should move away from her. But I can't. I haven't been able to get away from her since I met her, and I can't start now.

I bend my head and press my lips to that little strip of skin, lingering there as I kiss my way from one hip to the other. She arches her back, pressing her heat closer to me. If she were anyone else, I would be pulling her panties down her legs by now. But she's not anyone else. She's mine. And she's special. I groan out loud, flip her shirt down and move up to kiss her quickly. I'm sure I have morning breath, so I don't linger. But as I move to roll off of her, she grabs my shoulders and pulls me back to her. "I'm not a virgin, you know?" she says.

I still. I didn't know. And I don't care. "Ok." I don't know what else to say.

She closes her eyes so she doesn't have to look at me as she says, "I just wanted to be sure you know in case that's why you're hesitating so much."

"Ok." I pry her hands from my chest and roll away from her. She taps my shoulder and I look at her.

"It's not like I've been with a lot of guys or anything." She hesitates.

"I didn't ask." I smile at her in encouragement. But I'm sort of reeling from her declaration. I look into her eyes. "Did you ever do it with someone you were in love with?" I drag my crooked finger down the line of her jaw.

"Not yet," she says.

I can't bite back my smile. "Good." Neither have I.

My dick is so hard that I have to shove it down into my jeans. I turn away from her long enough to do it and zip.

"Where are you going?" she asks.

"To toss the football with Sam."

She throws the covers off and her face lights up. "Can I go?"

I stop. "You want to go toss a football in the park?"

She nods enthusiastically, her eyes shining. "There are a lot of things I can't do. But football isn't one of them."

"You play football?"

"Played," she clarifies. She takes on a strong man pose. "Four years with the pee wee league."

I laugh. "Get dressed. You can come with me."

She jerks on a pair of jeans and lifts her hair into a messy pony tail. Damn, she's pretty. She picks up her bra, turns her back to me and hides her arms in the shirt, adjusting the bra beneath the fabric. Within seconds, she's ready to go. She slides on her boots and nods. "Ready?" she asks. "You look like you've never seen a woman get dressed quickly."

"I've never woken up with a woman," I say. She stops moving and stares at me. "So, no, I've never watched one get dressed to start the day." It's usually a quick shrug into clothing after I kick someone out of my bed. Correction – after I make her come and then kick her out of my bed. But one day soon, I hope to watch her get dressed without holding the shirt over the best parts. "It seems really intimate, and I've never paid attention to anyone getting dressed after getting out of my bed." I shrug. "I like it."

"I'm your first," she teases, her face going soft.

I nod, unable to speak past the lump in my throat. "You're my first," I say, walking toward her. She thinks I'm going to squeeze her into a hug, and she leans into me. But I jerk her into the crook of my arm and give her a noogie instead. "That's for messing with me," I growl.

She jerks back, running her hand over her hair. She bends and takes her toothbrush from her bag.

"We don't have time for tooth brushing, woman," I say. "It's time for football."

"I am not leaving here without brushing my teeth," she says pertly. Then she signs the word no.

I point her toward the bathroom and smack her ass. She jumps and turns back to me, walking backward. She shakes her finger at me and I chase her into the bathroom. She brushes her teeth standing two feet away from me while I brush mine. I imagine her humming, and I find that I'm right when I place my hand on her throat. "Don't stop," I say.

She mouths something at me, but her mouth is full of toothpaste and I have no idea what she's saying.

"Don't stop humming," I say.

"Why do you care?" she asks after she spits. "You can't hear it."

"You look happy when you do it. So, don't stop."

She freezes, nods at me and rinses her mouth. I do the same. I grab her by the belt loops and tug her to me. "Is it safe to kiss you now?" I ask.

"Unless you want to be late," she warns, but she's smiling and she's already threading her fingers into the hair at the nape of my neck.

I slam the bathroom door shut. "Let's be late," I say.

Emily

Sam is irked because we're running later than he'd planned. I can't say I blame him. But when Logan kisses me, I can't think about anything but him. He always calls for the stop before I do. I can't figure out what to do about that, aside from giving him time to trust me. We just met a few days ago, but I feel like I've known him my whole life. He's kind, considerate, and he doesn't treat me like I'm somehow lacking because of my dyslexia. He doesn't seem to care.

Ahead of us, Hayley walks alongside Paul, her fist clutching his index finger. She's dressed warmly in a pink coat that has fur around the hood. She's adorable. Paul looks at her like she hung the moon and stars in the sky. Sam and Pete walk side by side in front of them, and they stop to shove one another across the sidewalk every few seconds. Logan tosses a ball in the air as we walk together. I bite back a shiver.

He makes the sign for cold, asking me with his brows raised if I am. I show him my fingers about an inch apart. He hands me the ball, unzips his hoodie and puts it around my shoulders. I pass the ball back to him, tug the hoodie more tightly around myself, and slide my arms into it, and zip it up to my chin. I lift it and sniff. It smells like him.

Why he asks in sign, then he mimes my sniff. Why did I smell it? I know the sign for why, and my heart thrills that I do.

I don't know how to sign the words, so I say, "Smells like you. I like it." I shrug my shoulders. I turn around backward and walk facing him because I'm sure it's hard for him to read my lips from the side. He holds a hand in warning. He shakes his head.

No need, he signs. He mouths the words while he does it, so I get it.

"Don't let me run into anything," I warn. I like looking at him. Apparently, a lot of other women do, too. His arms are naked, his t shirt straining across his shoulders. You can see his tattoos, which go all the way to his hairline on the back of his neck. He attracts a lot of attention. "Women really love you, don't they?" I ask. He's drawn more than one pair of eyes, from the teenagers to the cougars. They all stop to stare as he walks past. And having his brothers with him doesn't help any. They're a good looking group of boys.

He shrugs, looking sort of put out by my question.

When we get to the park, Matt goes and sits on a bench and I drop down beside him. Logan goes with Sam and Pete to toss the ball around. Paul chases Hayley over to the swings. "How are you feeling?" I ask of Matt.

"Fine," he says quickly. He doesn't elaborate.

"You don't look fine," I blurt out. I can't help it. He doesn't.

"Thanks," he says, his voice droll. "I love to hear how bad I look from beautiful girls." He nods. "Appreciate it."

"Why didn't you stay home to rest?"

"Honestly?" he asks, looking at me out of the corner of his eye. He's leaning forward so that his elbows rest on his knees. He plucks a blade of grass.

"No, lie to me," I respond. Then I roll my eyes.

He chuckles. "I don't know how many more moments I'll have to do this. I want to suck every bit of life from the moments I have."

Tears prick at the backs of my lashes. "Are you afraid?" I ask quietly.

"Only every fucking day," he says on a heavy sigh.

"Oh." I don't know what else I can say. "What's your prognosis?" I ask. I don't know why I'm being so nosy. I just want to know what Logan will be up against. And Matt. But mainly for Logan. I might be able to do something to cushion his blow.

"Don't know. I go back in two weeks and they'll tell me if the chemo worked."

I nod. What can you say to that? *Hope it's good news. Hope you're going to live. Oh, you're going to be just fine.* None of those seem appropriate.

He turns so that his knee is facing me, his arm lying along the back of the bench. "I've been trying to plan. For when I'm gone."

Shoot. What should I say to that? "That's smart." I'm an idiot.

"I have letters for all my brothers. I already wrote them."

"Is that what you've been doing all day?"

He nods, playing with the piece of grass, rolling it between his fingers.

"They'll appreciate them if anything ever happens to you."

"*When* something happens to me," he says, correcting me. "It's just a matter of how long I have at this point, I think. I can feel it."

I cover my hand with his on the back of the bench, and give it a squeeze. "Is there anything at all I can do for you? Anything to help you plan?"

He looks at me, hard. His green eyes bore into mine. "If you're still around when it's time, can I give you the letters? To share with them when I'm gone?"

"I'll still be around," I say. I'm not going anywhere. Not any time soon. "And yes, I can take your letters. Just tell me how and when you want them delivered."

He nods. "I have one for this girl, too. April is her name. Logan will be able to find her. But he won't give her a letter from me. He sort of hates her."

"She probably deserves it," I mumble.

He chuckles. "You don't get to pick who you fall in love with." He sits silent for a minute. Then he says, "Don't let them put me on the mantel or anything," he says. "I fucking hate the idea of being stuffed in an urn."

"What would you want them to do with your ashes, if they could?" I kick at a rock that's near my toe.

"I don't give a fuck, as long as I'm not stuck on the mantelpiece." He chuckles.

"Don't give up yet, all right?" I ask.

He nods. "I'm fighting 'til the day I die. But there are things I need to plan for."

I nod. I understand.

Logan walks over and stands in front of me. He signs something. The only sign I recognize is the word *girl*.

"No, I'm not putting the moves on your girl," Matt complains. Then he laughs. "She's putting the moves on me."

Logan turns to me, his mouth hanging open wide. But his eyes dance with laughter. He pulls on my hands until I stand up. Then he bends and tosses me over his shoulder and spins in a circle. I scream, covering my eyes. I know he won't drop me, but still.

He runs around, and Sam and Pete chase us. Pete -- or Sam – I still can't tell them apart – slaps my butt. I flail around, trying to reach out and grab him, but Logan is running with me over his shoulder. He spins, holding tightly to my legs. I cover my eyes and squeal, but I know he can't hear me.

I hit Logan on the butt, but he pays me no mind. Suddenly, he stops and starts to lower me down his body. I slide down him slowly, my body contours rubbing against his until my feet hit the ground. "Hi," he says quietly. He signs it, too, but his free arm is around me holding me against him.

"Hi," I say, and I sign it just like he did. Then I smack his chest. "I can't believe you did that." I turn and motion toward Sam. "Throw me the ball," I say. Sam looks at me like I'm nuts, so I say, "What? Are you afraid to play with a girl?"

He smiles and hurls the ball at me. I take off running with it cradled in my arm. Logan runs after me, but I'm faster than any of them expected. Just before I reach the bench Matt's sitting on, Logan snakes an arm around my waist, swinging me around. While he holds me tightly, Sam wrestles the ball from me. "That's cheating!" I scream.

"Cheating is allowed!" Sam yells back.

"In whose rule book?" I ask, stamping my foot.

"What rule book?" Matt says with a chuckle. He hefts himself to his feet. "Me and you against them?" he says. He grins at me.

"We can take them any day," I say, throwing my arms around him. He squeezes me gently and sets me away from him. He rubs my head, messing my hair all up.

Logan runs down the field, and I chase him. He turns to catch the ball Sam throws, and as soon as he has it, I tackle him. I hit him as hard as I can. He stumbles with me holding on to his shirt, until I can wrap around his legs. He goes down like a big oak tree falling. He lies on his stomach, but he's smiling at me. I climb on his back and sit on him, plucking the ball from his grip. I hold it in the air and cheer, flailing my feet wildly. He lets me sit there on top of him for a minute as his breath heaves in and out under me. But then he upends me. He rolls me under him. "You cheated." He says. His hands hold my wrists in a strong grip.

"There's no rule book, remember?" I giggle when he tickles beneath my ribs. "Stop!" I cry.

He looks into my eyes. "I think I might be falling in love with you," he says softly.

My breath catches. "Yeah, me too," I say.

He smiles and gets to his feet, tugging me up beside him. His face is flushed, and he's grinning.

"If you two are done playing lovey dovey," Matt yells, "we have a game to win." He waggles his brows at me. Suck every moment from life. We should all do more of that.

Logan

It has been almost two weeks since her declaration in the park. She hasn't said it again, and neither have I. But I know she loves me. There's no doubt in my mind. She sleeps in my bed every night, and we spend every waking moment together when we're not working. I'm so used to having her at my side, I'm not sure I'll survive it at this point if she leaves me. I'm hopeful that she'll be ready for what I want soon. Because I want all of her. I want her past, her present and her future. I want to ask her to marry me, but I can't. Not yet.

Sometimes, there's a look in her eye that I don't fully understand. She's longing for something she doesn't have. I'm not sure if it's home or something else.

She's learned to sign in the past two weeks, and she can carry on conversations. She's actually really good at it, and she's found that spelling isn't as hard for her when she's fingerspelling as it is on paper. Something about the spacing of the letters, she says.

She's sitting on the couch now with Hayley in her arms. She's holding a book upside down, and telling a story she has made up. The corners of my lips tip up and I can't bite back my grin. She fits so well into my family.

She still busks in the subway every day while I work at the tattoo shop. And last Friday night, the band encouraged her up on the stage when the crowd started chanting for her. They passed a hat through the audience and she got to keep the money they put in it. It was just over one hundred dollars and she only played one or two songs.

She saves every dime of the money she has made. We won't let her pay rent. My brothers and I had a frank discussion about it and we all agreed. She does too much for us to charge her rent. She cooks often. And she can't seem to keep from cleaning, even though we tell her not to.

Pete's on the couch across from Kit with a girl he met a couple of weeks ago. They've been necking for about ten minutes. I'm standing in the kitchen with Paul. I jerk my thumb toward them and Paul scowls. He says something to Pete, who looks up sheepishly. He adjusts his junk and lifts the girl up, taking her down the hallway toward his room. Paul yells at him, and he comes back and takes a few condoms from the drawer, grins and goes to his room.

"Great," Sam grouses. "I'll have to sleep on the couch."

Paul smiles. "There are two beds in there."

"Yuck," Sam says. "I don't want to have to hear them."

At least the boy is getting some, I sign.

Kit scolds me with a glance from across the room. I rue the day I taught her to speak sign language. I can't keep anything a secret anymore. I shrug at her and she grins.

You would be getting some too if you'd quit being such a prude, she signs to me.

Did you really just call me a prude? I ask as I stalk toward her. She sets Hayley to the side and jumps over the back of the couch. By now, she knows I'm coming for her.

She darts around the sofa and dodges back and forth, trying to avoid my hands. But I catch the tail of her shirt and jerk her to me. Linking my arm around her waist, I pick her up and take her to our room, slamming the door behind us. I toss her onto the bed and she bounces, laughing at me. "Did you really just call me a prude?" I ask, using my voice.

"No, definitely not." She laughs as I tickle her and she squirms in my arms.

"I think you did." I keep tickling her, because I know it drives her crazy.

"Prove it," she says. She's signing the whole time she's talking. So, I don't miss anything with her anymore. She grabs my hands to keep me from tickling her.

I growl as I press my lips to her throat. "Don't tempt me," I warn.

She taps my shoulder until I look up at her. "I want to tempt you. I want to tempt you really bad." She throws her head back on the last word and I can feel her throat vibrating as she growls. "You're making me crazy."

I chuckle. "I think that's my line."

"How much longer will you make me wait?"

I wake up with her wrapped around me every fucking morning. I go to sleep with her in my arms every night. I take long, cold showers every day, just so I can take some of the pressure off. She's making me nuts. But she's not ready for me yet. She's not. She knows it. I know it.

I change into a pair of jeans while she watches. I don't even try to hide my erection from her anymore. She knows it's there. She knows how much I want her. I think she knows how much I love her. I feel certain she loves me just as much. I just don't know why she's still hiding. "I have to work tonight at Bounce. Are you coming with me?"

She shakes her head. "I don't think so. I have a date with Hayley to read a book." She doesn't look at me.

No she doesn't. "Paul has a date tonight and he's taking Hayley with him," I remind her.

"Oh." She avoids my gaze.

"You're worried about Matt, aren't you?" I ask her. I frame her face with my hands and look into her eyes.

She nods. "He's been sleeping too much. I don't think it's good."

We all dance around the fact that Matt will be going back to the doctor two days from now to find out his prognosis. Everyone but Kit. She thinks about it a lot, I think. I try not to think about it at all. "You want to stay home so you can keep an eye on him?" I run a hand down the length of her hair and press a kiss to her forehead.

"Would you mind?" she asks. She looks hopeful.

"You know Pete's here," I remind her.

"Pete's knocking boots in the bedroom. How's he going to know if Matt's ok or not?"

She's right. "Thanks for staying," I say. I kiss her forehead again. "I'm taking Sam with me. Send for me if you need me for anything, ok?"

She nods. She flops back on the bed and I want to climb on top of her. But I have to go. Sam beats on the wall. I can feel the vibration of it. "What do you want, Sam?" I ask.

"Her," he says, grinning. He waggles his brows at Kit.

I punch his shoulder. "She's taken."

Kit grins, shaking her head. She has gotten used to all of us. I walk over to her and tip her head up to look into her eyes. "I'll see you later."

"Count on it," she says.

Emily

I step closer to Matt's door, listening intently for signs of life. He's been really tired for the past few days, and I'm worried for him. I'm *really* worried for him. And for Logan and the rest of them. None of them have come to terms with the fact that Matt is dying. They all overlook it, like pretending it's not going to happen is going to help him.

His voice, weak and tired, funnels through the crack in the door. "Don't just stand there breathing hard. Come on in."

I open the door and smile at him. "You could not hear me breathing."

He chuckles, but it's a hollow sound. "I heard your footsteps. You should learn to be more stealthy. Like Paul. He came in last night and stood over me, watching me breathe for about an hour." He adjusts, fluffing a pillow and jamming it behind his head. "He thinks I was asleep."

"Why didn't you tell him you were awake?" I ask. "You two could have talked."

He harrumphs. "He doesn't want to talk. He wants to fix everything. But I'm afraid I can't be fixed."

"You don't know that."

He heaves a sigh. "I know it."

I can't say anything past the lump in my throat.

"How's it going?" he asks.

I still can't find my tongue, so I nod.

"That good, huh?" he rolls toward me, his arm beneath his pillow.

"Matt," I start. But I stop, bite my lower lip and shake my head. "I don't know what to say to you."

"You still running Logan in circles?" he asks.

I bite back a smile. "I don't know what you're talking about."

He laughs. "It's good for him. Keep up the good work." He narrows his eyes. "He's never had to work for anyone before. Women came easily for him."

My face floods with heat when I realize what he said.

He laughs. "Yeah, that, too." He points across the room. "You remember those letters I told you about?" he asks.

I nod. I don't want to talk about letters. Because when I deliver the letters, he'll be gone.

"They're in my top drawer. My dresser." He nods his head in that direction. "When the time is right, be sure they get them?"

I nod. "I will. I promise."

"There's one for you too."

I don't want mine. "Ok."

He takes my hand in his and squeezes it tightly. I can tell the action takes a lot out of him. "What do you want to do tonight?" he asks.

I shrug. "Sit here with you."

He smiles at me. And I see so much of Logan in him that it hurts. He rolls to the edge of the bed and lifts himself up to sit. "Let's go watch a movie."

I nod, taking his hand in mine to help him to his feet. He lets me, but he groans as he gets up. "You sure you can do this?" I ask.

"Remember when I told you I was going to suck every minute out of life that I could?" He stares at me. I am a little worried that he's trying to gather enough energy to walk into the living room.

"Let's go suck at life," I say. "Do you want some popcorn?" I ask over my shoulder. He's following me.

"Why not?" he asks flippantly. "Popcorn and I'm going to snuggle with Logan's girl." His voice is farther behind me. But he's coming, so I start the popcorn. The steady pop, pop, pop has started when I realize he hasn't followed me into the kitchen.

There's a thud in the hallway, and I jump. "Matt?" I ask, walking back in that direction. But Matt's lying on the floor. He's drooling, and his body is convulsing. "Oh, shit," I say. "Matt!" I yell. I roll him onto his side, because I heard that's what you do when someone convulses. Or maybe it's that you're supposed to roll him onto his back. Shit, shit, shit. I don't know. "Pete!" I yell.

Pete opens his door, he's in a pair of boxers and he drags his shirt over his head. "What?" he asks. Then he sees Matt lying on the floor. "What the fuck?" he says, and he drops down beside Matt.

"Go call 911," I say calmly. When he sits there and doesn't move, I shove him and yell in his face. "Go call 911!"

He shakes out of his fear induced stupidity and runs to the phone.

He gives them the address and stays on the phone with them until the ambulance arrives. He gets dressed while he talks to them, stepping into his jeans in front of me, but I don't care. His girlfriend leaves. She's not worth the air she's breathing, apparently.

Matt calms and I lift his head into my lap. I wipe the spittle from his face with my sleeve and brush his hair back from his forehead. He's still. Too still. I hadn't realized how much hair he'd lost with the chemo. It's thinner than I thought it was. I brush across his face. "Not yet. It's too soon," I whisper to him.

I follow the paramedics as they carry him downstairs. "One of you can ride along," the paramedic says.

Pete looks at me and says, "I need to get my brothers." He runs a heavy hand through his buzz cut.

He knows where they are and I don't know how to get there. None of them carry cell phones because it's not in their budget.

"Go get some shoes," I say. He looks down at his naked feet and nods.

He shoves me into the ambulance and they close the door behind us. The rest of the world falls away, and I can no longer hear the sounds of the street or the blaring horns. All I can hear is the unsteady beat of Matt's heart on the monitor. Every time it stutters, mine flips in my chest, my breath leaving me. I lean over and take Matt's hand.

"It would be better if you don't touch him," they say.

I nod and sit back, buckling the seat belt in the jump seat they pointed me toward.

My hands are shaking and I don't know what to do with myself. They start IV's and look into his eyes and do a lot of things I don't understand.

He doesn't wake up. I worry that he never will.

Paul gets to the hospital first, and he's carrying Hayley on his hip. She's frantic, and she wants to know why they can't finish their date. I hold out my hands and she comes to me, settling against my chest. "What happened?" Paul asked.

"He just fell down in the hallway and started to shake," I try to explain. But I'm trying to be strong since I'm holding Hayley.

"Can we see him?" he asks.

I shake my head. "Not yet. They took him back and they're working on him."

Paul goes to the payphone and drops in some change. He turns his back to me and talks for a minute. Then he comes and takes Hayley back from my arms. "Now we wait," he says.

Hayley pats his cheek, and I see tears well up in his eyes. "Where's Matt?" Hayley asks.

"Matt's with the doctors," he explains, blinking hard.

"Dey gonna make him all betta?" she asks. She's following his gaze with hers, not letting him off the hook. She frowns when he doesn't answer.

"They're going to work hard to make him better," I tell her.

"Thank you," Paul chokes out. I nod. I can't say more than that. Hayley holds out her arms to me again, and I take her to sit down. We read upside down books until a woman comes rushing through the doors. She runs to Paul. Her hair is up in a ponytail and she's almost as tall as he is.

But she's stunning. Hayley has Paul's hair color and eyes, but everything else about her is her mother.

She leans into Paul to her and he hugs her tightly. I hear them murmuring to one another but I can't hear what they're saying. She comes to me and takes Hayley in her arms. "Thank you," she says.

I look into her eyes. She's kind. I can tell. And I can also see that she's head over heels in love with Paul. She walks over to him, whispers something in his ear, and he nods. She kisses him on the lips, and he kisses her back. "I'll call you when I find out what's going on," he says.

She leaves with Hayley. Paul takes a deep breath and sits down beside me, his elbows on his knees. "He wasn't in a lot of pain, was he?" he asks.

"Not that I could tell." He was convulsing. But not in pain. I doubt he was feeling much.

"That's my biggest fear. That he'll be in a lot of pain when it happens. It scares me to death."

"So you've thought about it," I blurt out. I want to take it back immediately. But it's too late.

"Thought about it." He snorts. "It's all I ever fucking think about. Ever." His voice cracks on the last word. "I'm his big brother. I'm supposed to be able to save him from anything that could hurt him. But I can't save him from this."

I just listen, because there's nothing I can say to comfort him.

A tear drop rolls down his cheek and he brushes it away with a hurried swipe. "He knows how much you care," I say. It's probably the wrong thing to tell him.

"The fucker better know how I feel about him. I'd die for every last one of them. I wish it was me instead of him. I'd trade places with him in a heartbeat."

"He wouldn't let you." It's the truth.

Paul chuckles. But it's a sound without any merriment.

The doors of the hospital slide open and Logan, Pete and Sam run in. I hop out of my chair fall into Logan's arms, because I know he'll catch me. He squeezes me to him and rubs my hair for a second. Paul walks over and starts to speak to him. They're all signing, but I can follow it. He explains.

Can we see him? Logan asks.

Paul shakes his head. "Not yet. They'll let us know when we can."

If we can. But no one says that out loud.

Logan drops his arm around me and pulls me into him. His face is in my hair and I can feel the warm caress of his breath against my neck. I lift my head and look up at him. "It's bad," I say.

He closes his eyes and lays the tips of his fingers against his temple. He knows.

Now we wait.

They're all draped over the furniture in the waiting room, taking up a ton of space. But no one else is there, so it hasn't mattered. Any one of these boys would give their seat up for someone else. Pete took Sam's socks about an hour ago, and Sam put his shoes back on with none. Pete was barefoot. I somehow knew he wouldn't go back inside. He went for his brothers instead.

It seems like days later when a doctor comes to talk to the family. It could have been minutes. It could have been hours. It feels like days.

The doctor sighs heavily and starts to talk. I hear snippets of it over the pulse that's pounding in my head.

The chemo didn't work.

He's worse than he was.

They can call hospice.

"There's nothing else you can do?" Paul asks.

The doctor sits down with them. "We've exhausted every opportunity. There are some trials that he could get into, but the chances are small. And the one that would most benefit him is very expensive."

He waits. A pregnant silence falls over the room. "How expensive?" Paul asks.

"Hundreds of thousands," the doctor says. "He doesn't even have medical insurance."

So that's it. They don't have hundreds of thousands of dollars so their brother dies.

I wipe a tear from my cheek. "This treatment, it could save him?" I ask. "Or would it just prolong the inevitable?"

He looks at me like I'm the most ridiculous person he's ever met. "They're having good success with it. There are no guarantees, however."

"But it would give him a chance?"

"The best he could have."

I nod. Logan squeezes me to him. *I'll be right back*, I sign to him. I know what I have to do. My heart is breaking in two. But I know what my choices are.

Where are you going? he asks.

Restroom. I'll be right back.

You ok?

I nod. He watches me walk away, his gaze boring into my back. I can feel it all the way down the hall. I don't stop at the bathroom, though. I keep walking until I find a payphone.

I pick up the handle and a weird sort of peace settles over me. I press the button for the operator. "Collect call to California, please," I say. I rattle off the number. It's Saturday afternoon. My dad will be in the office.

Ring.

Ring.

Ring.

"Mr. Madison's office," a chipper voice says.

"You have a collect call from – caller, state your name?" the operator says.

"I'd like to talk with Mr. Madison, please," I reply.

"We'll accept the charges." There's a stillness on the other end of the line. "Emily, is that you?" the voice says. There's hope in her voice. She's been my dad's secretary for as long as I can remember.

"Can I talk with him, please?" I ask.

The line goes dead for a moment, and then my dad picks up. "Emily?" he asks. I can almost hear the beat of his heart through the phone in the stillness.

"Dad," I say.

"Em," he says on a long sigh, like he's deflating. There's a clank and I imagine him taking his glasses off his nose and laying them on the table. "Where are you?"

"I need some help, Dad," I say. I lay my forehead against the cool tiles on the wall and try not to cry. I want to cry for all that I'm giving up. I want to cry for all that I'm giving them. But mostly, I want to cry for me.

"Anything, Emily," he says. His breath catches. "You're not hurt, are you?"

"No, I'm fine. But I'm coming home."

"Tell me where you are. I'll send the jet." His voice is urgent.

"Dad, first, I need for you to do something for me." Please, please, please do this for me.

He doesn't say anything for a minute. "What do you need, Emily?"

"I need for you to take care of something for me, Dad." I tell him some of the story. "I need for you to get him in the trial. And I want to take care of his treatment. We'll use my money, Dad." I have enough to spare. And then some. A lot more than I need.

He chuckles. "We don't need to touch your trust fund, Em," he says. "Why does this young man matter to you?" he asks.

"He just does, Dad."

I hear his pen click. "What's his name?"

"Matthew Reed." My voice clogs in my throat. He's going to do it. *He's going to do it.* I tell him the name of the hospital. "I don't know more information than that. I don't even know who his doctor is."

He chuckles. "I can get the information I need."

"You're going to do it, right, Dad?" I ask.

"Emily," he sighs. "If I do this, you're coming home."

My voice is a whisper. "Yes, Dad. I understand."

"I'm sending the jet for you now."

"I need a day, Dad. I need for you to handle this now. And I need another day. If you'll give me that much time, I'll come home and I'll do whatever you want." I'm pleading with him now.

He waits. And I hear his pen click over and over. "Ok," he breathes. "I'm sending the jet now. It'll be waiting when you're ready at the airport."

"Take care of this for me, Dad." I roll my forehead back and forth across the tiles. "Please. Promise me."

"I'd do anything for you, Em," he reminds me.

"I'll see you in a couple of days," I whisper.

"Two days, Em," he says. "No longer." And before the line goes dead, I hear him yelling details to his secretary. I hear Matt's name. And I hear him tell her to handle it. It'll get done. I'm sure of it.

I walk back to the waiting room. The doctor is gone and all the boys are standing there with their arms around one another. "What happened?" I ask.

They move away from one another. "They're moving him to a room. He's awake. We can go see him in just a minute," Paul explains.

I drop into a chair. My legs will no longer support me.

A few minutes later, a nurse summons the boys to follow her. Logan takes my hand and tugs me along with them. "I'm not family," I say.

"Shut up," he murmurs. He brushes a strand of hair back that's stuck to my lip.

I let him tow me along.

"You can only stay for a few minutes," the nurse warns.

The boys are giddy with excitement. She pushes back a curtain and Matt's there in the bed. There are tubes and wires and he's hooked up to monitors. "What's up, guys?" he asks. He winces and adjusts himself in the bed.

"The next time you want to die, don't do it on Kit's watch, you sorry fucker," Logan says out loud. The room goes quiet. A tear rolls down Logan's cheek and Matt reaches out a hand for him. Logan grabs it, palm to palm, their thumbs wrapped together like men do, and falls into his chest. Sam and Pete put their arms around one another and Paul is just standing there, so I lean into his side. He throws an arm around my shoulders and pulls me into him.

Matt finally lets Logan go and says, "Shit, when did you learn to talk?"

Logan shrugs.

"This girl is teaching him all sorts of new shit," Paul says, squeezing me tightly.

"What happened?" Logan asks. He's signing while he talks out loud.

"I had a date to snuggle with your girl on the couch and we were going to watch a movie," Matt says. "Next thing I know, she has my head in her lap, instead." He looks over at me, an impish twinkle in his eye. "If you wanted to hold me, Kit, you could have just asked." He chuckles.

"You remember?" I ask.

He grins this unrepentant grin. "I'll never, ever forget the day you threw Logan over to hold me in your arms."

Logan chuckles. Out loud. Everyone looks at him and he shrugs.

"You going to keep talking, bro?" Paul asks cautiously.

Logan shrugs again.

Paul squeezes me.

Suddenly, a team of doctors rushes into the room. "What's wrong?" Paul barks.

The doctor comes in a moment later. "We're going to be moving Matt to a different facility," he explains. "So he can begin that treatment we discussed."

"What?" Matt's dumbfounded. As are the rest of them.

The doctor holds up his hands to silence them. "Don't get too hopeful," he says. "But now there's a chance where there wasn't one before."

"There's a chance he might live?" Paul asks.

The doctor smiles and claps Paul on the shoulder. "A small one, yes."

"How?"

"I'm still working all that out." The doctor looks at me, but I break eye contact.

The room is barraged with activity, and the nurses get ready to move Matt. "There's a helicopter waiting," the nurse explains.

"How?" Paul asks again.

Matt reaches for each of them in turn. He hugs his brothers. Then he hugs me to him last. "Take care of them," he says. "No matter what."

I nod. I'm doing that the only way I know how.

Logan

My brothers are solemn on the way back home. It's early afternoon on Saturday, and I look down at my watch. "Shit," I say.

"What?" Paul asks.

"I have an appointment for a tat this afternoon." Kit's walking beside me but she has been lost in her own world since we left the hospital. "I guess I can cancel."

"Are you too tired to do it?" Paul asks.

Honestly, I'm so full of adrenaline right now I could climb mountains. And pick them up and throw them. I shake my head.

"So, why not do it?" he asks.

"Matt," I say. Just that one word.

Paul claps me on the shoulder. "They won't let us see him for forty eight hours, dummy," he reminds me.

That's right. They are going to do a bunch of tests and scans and shit and told us that he can't see anyone until at least Monday. Until he's settled in. I'm hopeful. I'm so hopeful and I haven't been hopeful for weeks. I've watched Matt decline more and more, and I was at the point where I was coming to terms with it. But hope has bloomed within me. It's not fair. It's not fair at all. What if he still doesn't get better? I have to believe he'll make it.

"He said he'd call when he gets settled," Paul reminds me. "Until then, we wait."

Kit looks up at me, her eyes focusing for the first time since we left the hospital. "I think you should open the shop. Do your tat. You're going to need the money." She doesn't look me in the eye when she says the last part of it. "Can I go, too?" she asks. "I want to watch."

I wrap my arm around her and she smiles up at me. "You ok?" I ask.

She nods and leans in. I can feel the warm wind of her inhale against my skin. "Stop sniffing me, you little pervita," I say.

Her eyebrows lift and she repeats the word. "Pervita?" She laughs. I hug her to me, never wanting to let her go. She's a part of us now. All of us. And she's mine.

Sam and Pete are walking behind us with their heads pushed together, talking softly. When they do that, there's usually trouble brewing. "What are you two up to?" Paul barks. Their heads snap apart, and they try not to look guilty. They're terrible at it, though.

"Nothing," they say in unison.

Paul narrows his eyes at them. "I don't believe you."

They look at him sheepishly.

"I don't believe you either," I say.

"I think I liked you better when you didn't speak," Pete says. Then he grins.

I flip him the bird and he flies at me, jumping on my back. He bounces up and down, and leans over my shoulder so I can see his lips. "My feet are cold," he says, batting his golden lashes at me. "You should carry me the rest of the way."

He's latched onto me like a koala. And he's fucking heavy. It's like carrying a load of bricks. But I hitch him up higher and start walking.

Sam turns his back to Kit and bends down. "You look tired, Kit," he says. "Want a ride?" He waggles his brows at her. She laughs, and jumps onto his back.

"I'm not sure I got the good end of this deal," I croak, as we all walk along together.

I can't help but wish Matt were here. I miss the gentle giant already.

***

I've been working on this tat for weeks. It's a huge bald eagle that goes from shoulder blade to shoulder blade. Not to mention that it's on a really big guy. I drew the outline, and then I started shading it last week. I need to finish it today. It's a five hundred dollar tat, and we could use the money. Particularly now.

I settle down to work on it, and Kit watches over my shoulder for a few minutes. But then she goes to the front of the store to sit down with Friday and Paul. Paul is updating Friday on Matt's condition. Friday adores Matt; if there's one of us she hangs with the most, it's him. She wipes a tear from her eye.

I can read her lips from there. "What are the odds that he gets accepted in that trial? It's so strange," she says. I can't see what Paul says in response.

Kit ambles up to the front of the store and says something to Paul. He looks shocked for a minute and then he pulls her forearm down to look at it. She's not hurt, is she? I move to set my gun to the side, but she looks over her shoulder and smiles at me. She's fine. Paul motions for her to follow him and he takes her behind a curtain. I see his lips when he says, "Keep him out of there," to Friday. Keep who out of where? Then he pulls a curtain around the two of them to separate them from us and I have to put the gun down. I start in that direction. Friday gets between me and them. "She's just getting a tat," she says, turning me around.

"What kind of tat?"

"A tiny little butterfly or something equally as cute. Maybe a Disney princess. She hadn't decided yet." She rolls her eyes. Friday has skulls and crossbones, and turtles, and all sorts of weird shit all over her body.

"I want to help her pick something," I say, trying to push past Friday.

"Stop," she says. "She wants to surprise you."

I run a frustrated hand through my hair.

"Tats mean different things to different people," Friday says. "This means a lot to her and she should be the one to decide what she gets."

I already know this, but I want to be involved. Damn it.

"You don't trust Paul to take care of her?" Friday asks, her brows crashing together.

Of course I trust him. "But this is my girl," I say. I know I sound like a baby. But there it is.

She pats me on the arm. "Suck it up, buttercup," she says. Then she narrows her eyes at me. "Wait a minute! When did you start talking?"

My face flushes with heat. "Don't get used to it," I grumble. "I may never talk to you again."

"I could only be so lucky," Friday says, rolling her eyes. But she jumps up onto her tiptoes and hugs me tightly. "I'm so happy for you," she says.

I can't figure out what she's talking about. Kit? Me? Our relationship? My talking? I brush her off when the guy I was working on starts waving his arms from the back of the shop. I have a lot of work to do. So, I had better get busy.

An hour later, Kit comes out from behind the curtain with Paul. She's smiling, and her forearm is covered with a large bandage. She walks over to me. I finished my tat ten minutes ago and have just been waiting for her. "You're going to wear a hole in the carpet," Kit teases.

Paul walks out behind her. He's smiling, but he won't meet my eyes.

"What did you put on her?" I ask.

He scowls at me and says, "Shut up." He points to a sign on the wall that says, "Tattoos are as individual as the people who get them." Then he points to another that says, "One man's ink is another man's purpose in life." Then he points to a third. "We do not tattoo drunk clients." Then he points to a roll of duct tape below a sign that says, "Keep whining and I'll use it."

"You are not amusing," I say.

Kit falls into my side and wraps her arms around me.

"What did you get?" I ask.

She looks into my eyes. "Something that will keep me from ever forgetting you and what you mean to me."

"It's about me?" My heart lurches and my breath catches and I suddenly can't think.

She smiles and she nods. "It's about you."

"Can I see it?" I'm dying here.

She shakes her head. "Not today."

"When?" Still fucking dying here.

She shrugs and she suddenly looks sad.

"What's wrong?" I ask, tipping her face up to mine.

She reaches into her pocket and pulls out a folded piece of paper. She hands it to me. Her face flushes with heat.

"Is this the tattoo?" I ask.

She shakes her head. "No."

I open it slowly.

MY NAME IS EMILY.

Emily

My heart is pounding so loudly that I can hear it. Logan opens the piece of paper and he freezes. He looks down at it for a long time, longer than I expected. I try to take it back from him. He jerks it away. Then he takes my hand and pulls me from the shop. I don't get a chance to say goodbye to Paul or Friday. I don't even get my feet under me before he's tugging me down the street.

"Wait," I call. But he can't hear me. His gaze is fixed on his route to wherever he's taking me. I tap his shoulder. He doesn't stop. He just pulls me through the crowd. I dig my heels in and stop. He turns to me and reaches for my hand again. I'm afraid he's going to toss me over his shoulder one last time. But I want this to be my choice. I want this to be our choice, together. "Wait," I say, framing his face with my hands. He looks down at me. "Why the rush?"

"Because I want you so fucking bad that I hurt, you silly woman." He makes me smile. He'll probably never call me a dummy again, but I do realize that it's a term of endearment with him, and not a set-down.

"I want you too," I admit.

He looks down at the piece of paper that's in his hand. "You trust me," he says.

I nod.

"Can we go to the apartment and talk?" he asks. "I promise not to molest you the minute we walk in the door. We have some things that need to be said."

Yes, we do. I nod.

He takes my hand in his and raises it to his lips to kiss my knuckles. He walks a little slower this time. He points to my arm. "What did you get?"

I smile. I'm not telling him. It's for me. It's for me to take with me when I go. It's a piece of him. Of all of them really. It's mine. And I'm not sharing it. Not right now.

"Come on," he cajoles.

I shake my head. "Not happening."

He looks crestfallen for a moment. But then we reach his apartment complex and we run up the stairs side by side. He's barely winded.

We step into the empty apartment. No one is there.

"Can you believe that they admitted Matt into the trial program?" he asks as he walks toward the bedroom.

"Amazing, isn't it?"

"So fucking amazing," he says. He's giddy about it and I love the way he wears his heart on his sleeve.

I don't want to talk about Matt because I'm afraid I'll break down crying and tell him what I did. Tell him what I committed to in order to give Matt a chance, in order to be sure Logan's world stays complete and full with all his brothers. "I'm so glad he's going to get a chance," I say. My voice clogs in my throat and I'm glad Logan can't hear it.

He picks up on my feelings, though, because he walks across the room and brackets my face with his fingers. "I'm sorry you were the one here when he got sick."

I'm not. Not at all. I'm so glad I was here. I'm glad I could help. In more ways than one. "I am glad I was here. Wouldn't trade the time I spent with his head on my lap for anything." I can't bite back my grin.

"I love you so fucking much," he says. Then he bends his head and kisses me. His lips are soft, but urgent.

Tears well in my eyes, because I know this is our last day together. "I need to take a shower," I say, stalling. I need a moment to compose myself. Not to mention that we spent the night at the hospital. I need to get cleaned up.

He nods and points at my arm. Shoot. I have a new tattoo and a bandage. "You can get it wet if you take the bandage off," he says.

I don't want to take the bandage off. "Can we just wrap it up?"

"Why don't you want me to see it?" He's looking deep into my eyes. I can't explain it to him.

He heaves a sigh and comes back with some plastic wrap and some waterproof tape. He wraps my arm and says, "There. That'll keep it completely dry."

I'm not worried about getting it wet. I'm worried about the bandage falling off. "Thank you," I say. I kiss him quickly. "I'll be out in a few minutes."

I take off my clothes and step into the shower. Warm water sluices over me and I realize that the fear in my heart has been replaced by longing. I was afraid to love Logan. Now I long to love Logan. And I do. And always will. But I have to give him up to protect something precious to him. I know that. I don't have a choice. The warm water steams over my back, and I lean both forearms against the wall, trying to compose myself. Tears track down my face, melding with the water. There's a draft and I feel the curtain move behind me.

I jump when Logan steps into the bath with me. His body envelopes mine, completely naked. "Logan!" I screech.

A warm chuckle makes his chest move against my back. "I don't want to be away from you," he says, pushing my wet hair to the side so he can press his lips to my naked shoulder.

He's hard against my bottom, the rigid length of him teasing me. He takes my washcloth from my hands and gets it soapy. Then he drags it down my spine, slowly, ever so slowly. My breath catches in my throat when he abandons the washcloth and runs his soapy hands over my bottom, squeezing my butt cheeks in his gentle grip. He doesn't leave a spot unwashed, his hands finding every crevice and dip, all the way down the backs of my legs, across the backs of my knees, which I had no idea were so ticklish, and over the heels of my feet. I stand there with my eyes closed, unable to look at him. He stands back up and lathers the soap in his palms again. This time, he doesn't take the washcloth at all. He uses his fingers to skim my body. His fingers tickle all the way down my left arm, all the way to my fingertips. Strong fingers lace with mine and he gives me a squeeze before he turns me to face him.

I keep my eyes closed. I am overwhelmed by what he's doing to me. If I look into his eyes, I don't know what will happen right now. I might combust. I might shatter. I might break. I might just come from the sheer pleasure of his touch. I can feel his smile against my shoulder as he presses his lips there. His hands circle my breasts, and gentle thumbs stroke across my nipples, which are straining for his touch. I arch my back, pressing my breasts into his hands and I hear him chuckle. My eyes fly open.

His hair is wet and he's dripping with water. I lean forward and lick his chest. He groans, freezing. His fingers pluck at my nipples, elongating them with his gentle tugs. "Logan," I cry. He looks up at me and stills.

"Did you say something?" he asks.

"I don't know," I say. Laughter breaks from my throat. "I can't even think. You want me to repeat myself?"

"I felt you say something," he says. He grins. "I just wanted to be sure you're all right."

I lay my head back against the wall. I'll never be all right again. He rubs his soapy hands over my belly, and then his fingers dip into the cleft between my legs. I reach for his shoulders.

He picks up the wash cloth again, and gets it sudsy. "Open your legs for me," he orders, tapping my inner thigh.

This is more intimate than anything I ever dared dream of. He uses the wash cloth to gently clean between my legs. He spreads me open with his fingertips, growls low in his throat, and washes me clean. The cloth drags across my clit, and my knees almost buckle. He throws the cloth to the side and uses his soapy hands to slide across my folds, front and back, front and back, front and back. "Logan!" I cry. This time, I tap on his shoulder. He looks up and grins. "Something wrong?" he asks. He strokes across my clit again, and then opens me to the spray of the shower. His fingers rub back and forth until I'm no longer slippery. Or at least not slippery from the soap.

"I think I'm clean," I say. I can't take much more.

Logan stands up and kisses me. "I want to be inside you so bad," he says. He pushes me under the spray to get my hair wet, and then washes my hair, rinsing it gently. "Your hair is growing out," he says. "Is it blond?"

I nod. "Not platinum. But a dark blond color."

"I'd like to see you like that," he says. "Maybe someday." He smiles and kisses me. He moves me to the side and starts to wash his own body, his movements quick and efficient.

"Let me help you," I say, reaching to take the soap from him.

"If you touch me right now, I'll come," he warns. "And I really want to do that while I'm inside you."

My belly flips. "Oh."

He chuckles. "Just stand there and watch," he says.

He washes and rinses his hair, and I let my gaze drag down his body. He told me he had a piercing down there. But he didn't tell me he had a bar through the skin at the base of his penis. "That's the piercing you were telling me about?" I ask.

He nods, blowing water from his lips. He's hard. So hard. And long. And thick. And I have no idea how he's going to get that inside me. But one thing is certain. He's going to be inside me tonight. I opened that door when I told him my name.

"Emily Madison," I say. "My name. It's Emily Madison."

He stills. "Where are you from?" he asks. He turns the water off, but never looks away from me.

"California."

"The opposite coast," he breathes. He takes my face in his hands. "Emily," he says again. "It suits you."

I grin. "I'm glad."

Logan steps out of the tub, and comes back with two towels. He dries me off and wraps me in one towel. The other he uses on himself, and then wraps it around his hips.

"Do you want to go to bed?" he asks. He fakes a yawn. "I'm really tired."

I laugh. God, this man makes me laugh. "If you think you're getting any sleep tonight, you are sadly mistaken." I shake my finger at him.

"Promises, promises," he growls as he lifts me from the tub with strong hands around my waist.

Logan

She's so fucking beautiful that I can barely breathe. "Emily," I say. I want to say it over and over and over. She told me her last name, too, but for the life of me all I can remember is what was written on the piece of paper.

"That's my name. Don't wear it out," she teases.

I pick her up, and she wraps her legs around my waist. My dick reaches for her, and I slide against her heat. But I'm not ready yet. I want to savor every second. I carry her into the bedroom. She kisses me as I walk, and I can barely take a step, I'm so wrapped up in her.

"Is anyone here?" She sits back from me long enough to ask.

God, I hope not. "Don't think so," I say.

"What if they are?" she asks.

"Then you're going to have to be quiet." I laugh. Because the odds of her being quiet during all the things I plan to do to her is ludicrous.

She buries her head into my shoulder and I can feel her breath against my neck. She kisses me softly, suckling my skin. "Give me a hicky," I urge. I'm kidding, but then I feel the scrape of her teeth against the tender skin and I really, really want her to keep doing what she's doing. She bites down gently, and then sucks the pain away. "Jesus," I moan. My dick pulses and I bite back a groan. I slam the bedroom door behind us and fall onto the bed with her, holding myself above her. My fucking arms are shaking and for the first time in my life, I don't know what to do next.

So I can collect myself, I take a moment to stop and I unwrap the plastic and tape from her arm. I start to peel the bandage back, but she catches me and slaps my hands away. I freeze, burying my face in her neck. I can barely breathe.

"What's wrong?" she asks, taking my face in her hands.

"I feel like a fourteen year old fumbling with his first girl," I admit. "I don't know what to do next."

I lift up and open her towel, and unhook mine, shoving it from between us. "You've done this so many times," she reminds me, rolling her eyes.

I still. "I have never done this before."

Her eyes narrow.

"I've never done this with someone who matters. With someone I'm in love with. Jesus, girl, you make me crazy."

"Can we turn the light off?" she asks. Then it dawns on her that I can't see her lips if we don't keep the light on. "Never mind," she says.

"Will the light bother you?" I ask. I kiss her, cupping her breast in my palm. I gently heft the weight of it, and watch her face as I plump it and bring her nipple to my lips. I tongue it quickly, rasping her tender flesh with care, but force. She arches her back, her eyes closing as she moves to get closer to me.

Her naked thighs wrap around my hips, and I feel the slickness of her against my dick. "Shit," I say.

"What?" She freezes.

"I forgot to get a condom."

She counts on her fingers and shakes her head. "It's all right. We don't need one." She stops and bites her lip. "Unless, um, you need one."

I got tested just a few weeks ago when we all had bone marrow testing for Matt. I'm clean. "I've never done this without one." I'm afraid. More afraid than I've ever been.

I press into her cleft, sliding back and forth through her wetness, but not slipping inside. I notch my dick against the top of her cleft, and press gently, rocking against her clit. She's so wet she's slippery and so, so sweet.

I don't know what to do next, I want her so bad. My breath falters, and my arms quiver under my weight.

"Emily, can you take me inside?" I ask. I can do this with finesse later. We have a lifetime to perfect this.

She reaches between us and takes my dick in her hand. She shuttles her hand up and down the slippery length of me, and then points me toward her heat. She raises her hips so I slip inside.

I take it slow. I want to remember this moment forever and ever. I can't hold in a groan as I bury my face in her neck. "Fuck, Emily. You're so fucking tight. I don't think I can stand it."

She rocks her hips, and takes more of me. I'm buried to the hilt inside the woman I love. I look up at her face and there are tears in her eyes. "Have I hurt you?" I ask. I bracket her face with my hands and swipe her tears away with the pads of my thumbs.

She shakes her head and pulls me into her with her feet on my ass. I start to move.

Emily kisses me, her tongue sliding into my mouth as I slip in and out of her heat. I can feel the little stutters of her breath as I push forward and retreat. She rocks to meet my movements. "Emily, Emily, Emily," I chant.

I'm closer to coming than she is, but not by much. I reach between our bodies and stroke across her clit. She lifts for me, her hips pushing her harder against me. She cries out. I can feel the vibration in her chest. I look into her face. She's saying my name over and over and over.

Her feet lock around me as she tightens on my dick. "Em," I rasp. My voice hurts from overuse. "I need you to come, Emily," I say quietly. "Come on my dick. Please, Em." I'm not above pleading with her. I'm finally inside the woman I love, but I can't hold out forever. She feels too fucking good.

She throws her head back when she comes, and her pussy pulls at my dick. I shove myself inside her pushing in as far as I can go. She sucks at me from the inside, pulling me into her with the quivers of her channel as it closes tightly, so tightly, around me. She falls apart in my arms and I covet every clench. I look into her face, because I can't hear her cries. I can feel her, though, as she milks me, coming harder than I ever imagined. But then again, so do I. I feel like my balls are being pulled out through my throat. It's almost painful how she takes all of me. I pump slowly in and out of her, not wanting to stop, but my dick is so sensitive that I have to stop moving.

Her arms wrap around me when I collapse on top of her and she squeezes me, but then her arms fall away. She says something. I can feel it. I lift myself up. "What?" I ask. "I didn't hurt you, did I?" Fear clutches at my gut with eager talons.

"If that's hurting me, I want you to do it over and over and over, all night long." She chuckles, her body shaking with laughter.

I roll to my side, but I don't want to be far from her, so I roll her to face me. I brush her hair back from her face with both hands. "I love you," I say.

She smiles at me, hiding her face abashedly in the pillow. "I love you too," she says. "No matter what happens, please know that what I feel for you is real. That I don't know how I could live without you."

I lean back, appraising her closely. Why would she say such a thing? But she reaches for me and pushes me onto my back. I was still semi hard, and I go fully hard immediately. She rocks on my dick and then takes me inside her. "Jesus Christ, woman," I say. She's hot, and wet from where I just came inside her.

She squares her hands on my chest, and begins to ride me. Her movements are unsure, so I take her naked hips in my hands and guide her movements. She slows until she finds a rhythm, drawing her lower lip between her teeth. I tug it free, and pull her down to kiss me. I fuck her while she's on top of me, her tits pressed tight against my chest. She meets me, and her throat vibrates with sound every time I push in and pull out.

She cries out my name. I can read it on her lips. She says it over and over and over, but I can't imagine ever tiring of hearing it.

She squeezes my dick within her depths, and I need to come. She sits up, rising and falling on me again, and then she shatters. She comes on top of me, her arms shaky as she quakes with pleasure.

She protests when I pull from her depths. I roll her onto her stomach and shove a pillow under her hips. She smiles at me over her shoulder, a simple encouragement. I need none, but I take great pride in the fact that she offered me her blessing. I slide into her from behind, and she's so tight this way that it wouldn't take me but a moment to come. I reach around her hip for her clit. She grabs my hand and won't let me touch it. I fight with her for a moment. I want to please her. I want to please her so bad. "Please?" I say in her ear. Her hand pushes mine toward her heat and I rub her to completion, and only when I feel her orgasm wreck me do I follow. I collapse on top of her. She lets me lay there for a minute, but she wants to turn over and say something to me, I think.

I fall to the side and pull her to lie on my chest. I place my lips against her forehead and hold them there.

She sits up with her elbows on my chest and looks down at me. "I love you so much, Logan," she says. Then she dips her head, settles against my chest, and falls asleep.

Emily

I wake before the sun comes up. The light is still on and Logan's on his back. I'm lying on top of him, and there's sweat between us. I need to get cleaned up and get out of there before he wakes up. My gut clenches at the thought of leaving him and tears fill my eyes. I look at him through my crying until he's a big blur. A big, beautiful blur. I love him so much. I love him so much that I can't stay. I love him too much to make him do without Matt for a lifetime. I just can't do it. I have to give him up to save Matt. I know it can't be avoided. Someone might as well cleave me into two pieces – it wouldn't hurt any less.

I let my tears fall, not bothering to wipe them away as I go and shower. I move as quietly as I can, and get dressed in the bathroom. I brush through my wet hair, but I don't do much more than that. There's no need to put on any makeup. It'll be washed away by my misery.

I sneak back into the bedroom and look down at him lying there. He's so beautiful. He's everything I want and everything I could ever need. But I'm not sure what he needs. Yes, I am. He needs Matt. He needs for me to see that Matt gets everything he has to have to get better. To live. And I'm giving him this the only way I can.

His hair is tousled over his forehead. I remember looking at him as he slept that first night and wondering if his mother ever watched him like I do. She had to. He's just so pretty. Both inside and out. He took care of me for so long. And I trust him so much. But I need to do this.

I brush the tears from my cheeks and steel my spine. I can do this. I have to do this. I pick up my guitar and my black canvas bag. There's still not much in it. There's not much of me that I won't be leaving here, so I don't guess it matters.

I look down at my guitar. I want to leave him a part of myself. Something that will let him know how very much I love him. I lean the guitar against the wall. He'll take care of it for me. My father will never let me use it again anyway. There will be no Julliard for me. There will be a wedding. There will be me as arm-candy. There will be a future, but not the one I want.

I leave with nothing but my black canvas bag and a few articles of clothing. I don't take anything else, except for his AC/DC t-shirt, the one I wore the first night I met him. I know it's silly, but I want it. I call for a cab before I walk downstairs. In the city, you never can be too careful.

I bounce from foot to foot. I still don't have a coat and it's cold. It's still dark out. There are no stars in the sky because of all the street lights. The cab slows to a stop in front of me and I walk out onto the sidewalk. I look up at his building, and I say a little prayer for Matt. Logan will be all right. He'll survive this. I'm not sure I will, but Logan will have Matt and the rest of his brothers.

I take a deep breath and get in the cab. I tell the cabbie to take me to the airport, and I need to go through a private entrance. He looks at me closely in the mirror. Then he shrugs and takes me where I tell him. I bypass security inside the airport, but we still have to go through security checks. They call the plane, and the pilot assures the security guards that I will be traveling privately, and that they have my identification. I hadn't even thought of that. But my father would have thought of everything.

My father's own security guard is waiting at the bottom of the steps of the plane. "Miss Madison," he says.

"'Sup, Watkins?" I ask flippantly.

He smiles. "I like the hair."

"Look at it while you can, because Daddy will make me change it as soon as I get home." I heave a sigh. I'm so tired. I buckle up, because it's what I'm supposed to do until we take off and stabilize. The pilot comes to greet me. I know him, too, but can't remember his name.

"Miss Madison," he says with a nod. "I'm glad you're flying with me today."

"I'm not," I mutter.

He doesn't respond. He just goes and gets things started. It's early and still dark, so I can't even watch the city pass me by as we take off. I see the lights, but they're not what the city is to me. This city is so much more.

After the pilot says it's ok, I unbuckle and go lay down in the bedroom. "Can I get you anything, Emily?" Watkins asks. I bury my face in my pillow so he won't see my tears. I shake my head. "Let me know if you need anything, Em," he says softly. Then more firmly, "Anything."

I nod, my face still buried in my pillow.

I sob until I am too exhausted to do more. Then I sleep the rest of the flight. They wake me up to buckle when it's time to land. I go to the bathroom and wash my face, brushing my hair and cleaning up. My dad is going to have a shit fit no matter what. But I can at least look presentable.

The limo pulls up beside the plane just as soon as it lands. Watkins opens the door and I slide inside. But then I stop. My mother is inside. She's perfectly put together, as always. Her brown eyes are not the ones I want to be looking into. I want Logan's blue gaze. His are the eyes I want to see. She looks at me, and at Watkins, who closes the door behind me and goes to sit with the driver. He never does that. But my mother can accomplish just about anything with nothing more than a look. "Emily," she says crisply.

"Mom," I reply.

"You look like hell," she says. And her face finally cracks into a smile.

"Where's Dad?" I twirl a lock of my black hair around my finger.

"Your father is in the doghouse I'm afraid. He bungled this terribly. And so he's no longer in charge of this little matter."

My mother never does this. I didn't think she had a spine at all. "What?"

"Your father is the reason why you ran away from home. Your father is the reason why you have been gone for more than six months. Your father and his conniving are the reason why I lost my daughter." Her voice cracks on the last word. My mother never falls apart. Ever. But she does now. Tears roll down her cheeks and she reaches for me. I fall into her. My mother is offering me everything I need right now.

"I'm going to mess up your clothes," I warn, sniffling.

"Mess me up. I don't care." She squeezes me to her. "Tell me everything."

I sit back. "You don't want to hear everything."

She sighs. "I can't help you if I don't know what's wrong."

"Mom," I complain.

"I'll start it for you," she says, smiling. She mocks my bored tone and says, "Well, there's this boy…" She motions for me to finish.

I tell my mother the story about why I left, where I've been, what I've been doing.

At the end of my story, she says, "Your father still expects you to marry that boy."

I nod. "I know."

"But that will never, ever happen."

My gaze shoots to her.

"We're going to the salon. And then we're going to take care of this."

"Mom," I breathe. "I promised Dad."

She pats my hand. "You'll see. Trust me." And for some reason, I do.

For the next four hours, we change my hair color back to its natural shade, paint my nails a glossy pink instead of black, "because we don't want to buck the system but just so much," and she sends someone to get me a new outfit. She has a flock of people doing her bidding.

When we're done, I feel like my old self. But I'm not. I never will be.

We pull up to our home and the gates are open. I'm so confused. There are news vans everywhere. "What's this, Mom?" I ask.

"This is me handling this situation for you." She absently runs a hand down the length of my hair. "You're a smart girl, Emily. You can make your own choices."

Tears prick at the backs of my eyelids. I'm a smart girl. Someone other than Logan said it.

Logan

I'm terrified. Emily is gone, but her guitar is still here. She was gone before I got up this morning. Her black bag is gone. And all of her belongings, except her guitar. She wouldn't have left, would she? Not for good. Paul sits beside me on the couch and he knocks my hand from my mouth when I chew my fingernails. "She'll be back," he says. "Stop worrying."

She won't be back. I'm sure of it. I realized that by telling me her name last night and letting me inside her, she wasn't telling me she loves me. She was telling me goodbye. It hurts like nothing ever has when I realize that, but it's true. I'm sure of it.

The phone rings. I jump when the lights flash, signaling the ringer. Paul runs to answer it. "Matt says to turn the news on," Paul says, as he turns the TV on and flips the channels.

The new anchor starts to talk. I read the captions as they play across the bottom of the screen.

IN CELEBRITY NEWS TODAY, THE PRODIGAL DAUGHTER OF ONE OF THE UNITED STATES' MOST INFLUENTIAL BUSINESSMEN HAS BEEN FOUND ALIVE TODAY.

"What does this have to do with us?" I ask Paul.

YOU MAY REMEMBER THE MEDIA CIRCUS MORE THAN SIX MONTHS AGO WHEN EMILY MADISON DISAPPEARED.

The TV switches to a picture of a blonde.

Paul slaps my chest hard to get my attention. It hurts like a mother fucker but my gaze is stuck on the TV.

EMILY MADISON DISAPPEARED MORE THAN SIX MONTHS AGO, BUT SHE RETURNED HOME TODAY.

"That's my Emily," I breathe. Her hair is blond. And she has on a million dollar smile, along with some million dollar earrings.

Paul smacks me harder so I have to look at him. "That's Kit?" he asks.

I wave at him to shut him up. He turns the TV up. I watch the words at the bottom of the screen. I scoot forward so my ass is balanced on the edge of the couch.

EMILY HAS AGREED TO ANSWER A FEW QUESTIONS, the captions say.

I watch as the woman I love steps up to the podium. She blinks and holds her hand up to block the sun. I can see the freckles across the bridge of her nose, and my heart lurches. She's in California. "Good afternoon," she says.

The crowd starts firing off questions. They only print the ones in the captions that get to her. "Where have I been?" she repeats. "I have been in New York for six months. There's a bit of a story to go with that, but I won't bore you with it. Sometimes a girl just needs a break." The captions indicate that she's laughing. But there's no laughter in her eyes.

ARE YOU WELL, EMILY?

She's not well, but she's alive.

"I'm perfectly well," she says, smiling. "Never been better."

ARE YOU MENTALLY ILL, EMILY? DID YOU HAVE A BREAKDOWN? HAVE YOU BEEN IN REHAB?

She looks at the person with surprise. "The last time I checked, I wasn't." She looks down at her body and pats her hips and stomach. "I think I'm all in one piece."

WAS THERE FOUL PLAY, EMILY?

She shakes her head. "No. No foul play. I was perfectly safe the whole time."

Someone steps up to the podium to pull Emily away, and I ache as I watch her take a step back. One more question scrolls across the screen.

WHAT ARE YOUR PLANS FOR THE FUTURE, EMILY?

She smiles. Then she looks directly into the camera. Directly at me. She might as well have kicked me in the gut. "In the spring, I'm going to Julliard to study music."

My stomach drops down toward my toes.

WHY NEW YORK, EMILY?

Thank God someone asks before she can walk away.

She tilts her head to the side and looks right at me. She raises her hand into the sign for I love you and I see the tattoo that takes up her forearm. It's a key, and written down the center of the key shaft are the letters of my name. I look at Paul. "Did you do that?"

He grins and shrugs. "It's nothing."

It's everything. It's every fucking thing.

The reporter repeats the question.

WHY NEW YORK EMILY?

"That's simple," she says. "It's because I love New York. I love New York with all my heart and I can't wait to get back to it. I needed to come see my Dad so he could take care of something for me. But I'm going back to New York." She leans close to the microphone. "I love you New York. Never doubt it. I'll see you soon."

Then she waves and she's gone.

I fall back against the couch, trying to put it all together in my head.

"Shit," Paul says. "She paid for Matt's treatment."

"What?" I'm still dumbfounded.

"She went back home for you," he explains. He still has Matt on the phone and he's talking to both of us at the same time.

She did it all for me. "She did it for me," I say out loud.

"You lucky fucker," Paul says, punching me in the arm.

"She'll be back for the spring session at Julliard." Warm happiness settles around me like a blanket fresh out of the dryer.

Paul nods. "Matt will be home by then."

We all hope Matt would be home by then. Matt has a chance to come home and it's all because of Emily. I jump up and Paul pulls me into a hug.

"She'll be back?" I ask. I can't wrap my head around it all. "She's not gone for good."

"She just told the whole fucking world how much she loves you, you jackass." Paul punches me in the shoulder again.

She's coming back. To Julliard. To me.

THE END

Tall, Tatted and Tempting

By Tammy Falkner

(Sexy-lite version)

Logan

I don't know her name, but she looks familiar to me. She's a tight package in a short skirt that makes me imagine the curves under her plump little ass. That skirt is made to draw attention, and she has all of mine. I'm so hard I can't get up from behind the table where I'm drawing a tat for a client on paper. I reach down and adjust my junk, the metallic scrape of the zipper against my dick not nearly enough to calm my raging hard on. I shouldn't have gone commando today. I hope Paul did some laundry this morning.

Her nipples are hard beneath the ribbed shirt she's wearing, and she pulls her sleeve back to show me something. But I can't take my eyes from her tits long enough to look at them. She shoves her wrist toward my face, and I have to jerk my eyes away. Shit. She caught me. I would tell her I'm a guy, I can't help it. Or at least I would if I could talk.

I see her mouth move out of the corner of my eye. She's talking to me. Or at least she's mouthing something at me. No one really talks to me since I can't hear. I haven't heard a word since I was thirteen years old. She's talking again. When I don't answer, she looks at my oldest brother Paul, who rolls his eyes and smacks the center of his head with his fist.

"Stop looking at her tits, dumbass." He says the words as he signs them and her face flushes. But there's a grin tugging at the corners of her mouth at the same time.

I roll my eyes and sign back. *Shut up. She's fucking beautiful.*

He translates for her. I would groan aloud, but I don't. No sound has left my throat since I lost my hearing. Well, I talked for a while after that. But not for long. Not after a boy on the playground said I sounded like a frog. Now I don't talk at all. It's better that way. "He says you're beautiful," he tells her. "That's why he was ogling your tits like a 12 year old."

I flip him off and he laughs, holding out his hands like he's surrendering to the cops. "What?" he asks, still signing. But she can hear him. "If you're going to be rude and sign around her, I'm going to tell her what you say."

Like I have another choice besides signing. *You never heard of a secret code between brothers?* I sign.

"You start whispering secrets in my ear, dickhead, and I'll knock your head off your shoulders."

You can try, asswipe.

He laughs. "He's talking all romantic to me," he tells her. "Something about kissing his ass." She's grinning now. The smile hits me hard enough I'd be on my knees, if I wasn't stuck behind that table. She brushes a strand of jet black hair back from her face, tucking it along with a lock of light blue behind her ear.

I watch her open her mouth to start to speak. But she looks over at my brother instead. "He can read lips?" she asks.

"Depends on how much he likes you," my brother says with a shrug. "Or how ornery he's feeling that day." He raises his brows at me, and then his gaze travels toward the tabletop. Shit. He saw me adjust my junk. "I'd say he likes you a lot."

This time, she closes her eyes tightly, wincing as she smiles. She doesn't say anything. But then she looks directly at me, and says, "I want a tattoo." She points toward the front of the store. She's still talking, but I can't see her lips move if she's not looking at me. I want to follow her face, to jump up so I can watch those cherry red lips move as she speaks to me. To me. God knows she's speaking to me. But I don't. I force myself to keep my seat. She looks back at me as she finishes talking and her lips form an O. "Sorry," she says. "You didn't catch any of that, did you?" She heaves a sigh and says, "The girl up front said to see you for a tattoo."

I look over at my brother who just finished a tat and isn't working on anything at the moment. Friday – really, that's her name -- laughs and signs, "You're welcome."

I scratch my head and grin. Friday set me up. She does it all the time. And sometimes it works out well. She sends all the hot girls to me. And the not so hot girls. And the girls who want to sleep with the deaf guy because they heard he's amazing in the sack. I'm the guy they don't have to talk to. I'm the guy they don't have to pretend with, because I wouldn't know what they're saying regardless.

If this girl is just there to sleep with me, we can skip all the tattoo nonsense.

"Don't even think about it," my brother says. "She wants a tat. That's all."

How do you know what she wants?

I just know, he signs. This time he doesn't speak the words. *Don't try to lay this one.*

I hold my hands up in question asking him why. "She's not from around here," he says, but he signs *not our kind.*

Oh, I get it. She's from the other side of the tracks. I don't mind. She might be rich, but she would still love what I can do for her. I reach for her hand and squeeze it gently so she'll look at me. I flip her hand over and point to her wrist. My fingers play across the iridescent blue veins beneath her tender skin, and I draw a circle with the tip of my finger asking her *Here?*

Her mouth falls open. Goose bumps rise along her arm. Hell, yeah, I'm good at this.

I stand up and touch the side of her neck and she brushes my hand away, shaking her head. Her lips are pressed tightly together.

I look directly at her boobs and lick my lips. Then I reach out and drag one finger down the slope of her breast. *Here?* I mouth.

I don't even see it coming. Her tiny fist slams into my nose. I've had girls slap me before, but I've never had one punch me in the face. Fuck, that hurt. The wet, coppery taste of blood slides over my lips, and I reach up to wipe it away. My nose is gushing. Paul thrusts a towel in my hands and tilts my head back.

Fuck, that still hurts. He presses the bridge of my nose, and I can't see his mouth or his hands over the bunched up towel, so I have no idea if he's talking to me. Or if he's just laughing his ass off. He lifts the towel but blood trickles down over my lips again. I see her standing there for a brief second, her fists clenched at her sides as she watches me suffer.

Shit, that hurts.

Then she turns on the heels of her black boots and walks away. I want to call out to her to get her to stay. I would say I'm sorry, but I can't. I can't call her back to me. I start to rise, but Paul shoves me back into the chair. *Sit down*, he signs. *I think it might be broken.*

I see a piece of paper on the floor and it's crumped. I take the towel from Paul and press it to my nose, pointing to the piece of paper. He picks it up and looks at it. "Did she drop this?" he asks.

I nod. It's damp from her sweaty palms. I unfold it and look down. It's an intricate design, and you have to look hard to find the hidden pictures. I see a guitar, the strings broken and sticking out at odd angles. And at the end of the strings are small blossoms. I turn the picture, looking over the towel I'm still holding to my nose with one hand. Paul replaces it with a clean one. My nose is still bleeding. Son of a bitch. I look closer at the blossoms. They're not blossoms at all. They're teeny tiny shackles. Like handcuffs, but more medieval. Most people would see the beauty of that drawing. But I see pain. I see things she probably wouldn't want anyone to see.

Shit. I fucked up. Now I want more than anything to know what this tat means. It's obviously more than just a pretty drawing. Just like she might be more than just a pretty face. Or she might not be. She might be a bitch with a mean right hook that will eat my balls for lunch if I look at her the wrong way.

I spin the drawing in my hands and look around the shop. It's late and no one is waiting. I punch Paul in the shoulder and point to the drawing. Then I point to the inside of my own wrist. It's the only place on my whole arm that's not tatted up already. I have full sleeves because my brothers have been practicing on me since long before it was legal to do so.

"No," Paul signs with first two fingers and his thumb, slapping them together. "You've lost your mind if you think I'm going to put that on you."

He walks toward the front of the store and sits down beside Friday. He's been trying to get in her pants since she started there. It's too bad she has a girlfriend.

I get out my supplies. I've done more intricate tats on myself. I can do this one.

He stalks back to the back of the shop, where I'm setting up. "I'll run it," he says. "You're going to do it anyway."

I hold up one finger. *One change?*

What do you want to change? He looks down at the design and his brow arches as he takes in the shapes and the colors and the handcuffs and the guitar and the prickly thorns. And I wonder if he also sees her misery. *That's some heavy shit,* he signs. He never speaks when it's just me and him. I'm kind of glad. It's like we speak the same language when we're alone.

I nod, and I start prepping my arm with alcohol as he gloves up.

Emily

It has been two days since I punched that asshole in the tattoo shop and my hand still hurts. I've been busking in the subway tunnel by Central Park, and it's somewhat more difficult to play my guitar when my hand feels like it does. But this tunnel is one of my favorite spots, because the kids stop to listen to me. They like the music, and it makes them smile. Smiling is something left over from my old life. I don't get to do it much, and I enjoy it even less. But I like it when the kids look up at me with all that innocence and they grin. There's so much promise in their faces. It reminds me of how I used to be, way back when.

I'm considering singing today. I don't do it every time I play. But I am seriously low on funds. The more attention I get, the more change I'll get to take home with me. Home is a relative term. Home is wherever I find to sleep that night.

I'm sitting on the cold cement floor of the tunnel; back a ways from the rush of feet, with my guitar case open in front of me. In it, there are some quarters, and a little old lady stopped a few minutes ago and tossed in a fiver while I played *Bridge Over Troubled Water*. Old ladies usually like that one. They haven't seen troubled waters.

I'm wearing my school girl outfit, because I get more attention from men when I wear it. It's a short plaid skirt, and a black ribbed short sleeve top that fits me like a second skin. Ladies don't seem to mind it. And men love it. I sure got a lot of attention from that asshole two days ago. He was hot, I had to admit. He had shoulders broad enough to fill a doorway, and a head full of sandy blond curls. He towered over me when he stood up from behind that table, at least a head and shoulders taller than me. Tattoos filled up all the empty space that used to be his forearms, and it was kind of hot. He had lips painted on his left arm, and I wanted to ask him what those were. Were they to remember someone? A first kiss, maybe? Or did they mean something the way the tattoo I wanted did?

I dropped my tattoo design as I ran out of the shop, which pisses me off. I thought I had it clutched in my hand and when I'd stopped to take a breath, it was gone. I almost expected the asshole to follow me. But he was still bleeding when I left him.

I shake out the pain in my hand again. A towheaded boy stops in front of me, his hand full of pennies. He is a regular, and his mother stopped to pray over me once, so I switch my song to *Jesus Loves Me*. Jesus doesn't. If He did, He wouldn't have made me like I am. He would have made me normal. The boy's mother sings along with my tunes and the boy dips his face into her thigh, hugging it tightly as she sings. When the song is over, he drops his handful of pennies into my guitar case, the thud of each one hitting the felt quiet as a whisper.

I never say thank you or talk to the kids. I don't talk to the adults unless they ask me something specific. I just play my music. Sometimes I sing, but I really don't like to draw that much attention to myself. Except today, I need to draw attention to myself. I had saved up three hundred dollars, which would pay for a place to sleep and that tattoo I thought I needed, but someone stole it while I was asleep at the shelter last night. I'd made the mistake of falling asleep with it in my pocket, instead of tucking it in my bra. When I woke up, it was gone. I don't know why they didn't take my guitar. Probably because I was sleeping with it in my arms, clutched to me like a mother with her child.

I wish I'd gotten the tattoo yesterday. It was a useless expense, but it was my nineteenth birthday, and it's been a long time since anyone has done anything for me. So, I was giving it to myself. And trying to free myself in the process. Who was I kidding? I'll never be free.

This city is hard. It's mean. It's nothing like where I came from. But now it's home. I like the noise of the city and the bustle of the people. I like the different ethnicities. I'd never seen so many skin colors, eye shapes, and body types as I did when I got here.

A girl reaches her chubby hand to touch my strings, and I smile and intercept her hand by taking it in mine, instead. Her hands are soft, and a little damp from where her first finger was shoved in her mouth just a minute ago. I toy with her fingers while I make an O with my mouth.

Her mother smacks her hand away with a sharp, cracking blow to her forearm, and her eyes immediately fill with tears. You didn't have to do that, I think. She didn't mean any harm. But the mother drags the crying child with her toward the subway and picks her up when she doesn't move quickly enough.

I draw a small crowd between subway arrivals, and one man yells out, "Do you take requests?"

I nod, and keep on smiling, playing with all I'm worth. He calls out, "I think you should suck my dick, then." One of his buddies punches him in the shoulder and he laughs.

College kid. His mama never taught him any manners. I let my eyes roam over the crowd and no one corrects him. So, I start to play *All the Wishing in the World* by Matt Monroe. The irony is lost on the jock, and they walk away as the train pulls in behind them.

The platform fills with new people getting off the train, so I switch to some more familiar tunes. Money drops into my case, and I see a dollar float down. I nod and smile as the person walks by, but she's not looking at me.

A big pair of scuffed work boots steps up beside my case. I look at them for a minute, and then up over the worn jeans and the blue T shirt that's stretched across broad shoulders. And then I'm looking into the same sky blue eyes as the other day. My pic stumbles across the strings. I wince. His eyes narrow at me, but he can't hear my mistake, can he? His head tilts to the side, and I turn my body to face the other direction.

My butt is freezing and my legs are aching from sitting on the cold floor for so long. But I don't have anywhere else to go. My three weeks at the shelter were up yesterday. So, I have to find somewhere new to sleep tonight. I look down into my case. There's enough there for dinner. But not for anything else. So, I keep playing.

Those boots move over so that he's standing in front of me. I scoot to the side, and look everywhere but at him. But then he drops down beside me, his legs crossed criss-cross-applesauce style in front of me. He has tape across the bridge of his nose and that makes me feel competent for some reason. There are very few things in my life that I can control, and someone touching my body is one of them. I say when. I say where. I say with who. Just like in *Pretty Woman*. Only Stucky would never get to backhand me. I'd take him out first.

He leans on one butt cheek so he can pull out his wallet, and he throws in a twenty. He doesn't say anything, but he points to my guitar and raises his brows. I don't know what he wants, and he can't tell me, so I just look at him. I don't want to acknowledge his presence. But he's sitting with his knee an inch from mine.

When I don't respond, he puts a hand on my guitar. He points to me and strums at the air like he's playing a guitar. I realize I've stopped playing. But he did put a twenty in my case, so I suppose I owe him. I start to play *I'm Just a Gigolo*. I love that tune. And love playing it. After a minute, his brows draw together and he points to his lips.

I shake my head because I don't know what he's asking. Either he wants me to kiss him, or I have something on my face. I swipe the back of my hand across my lips. Not that. And the other isn't going to happen.

He shakes his head quickly and retrieves a small dry-erase board from his backpack.

Sing, he writes.

I have to concentrate really hard to read it, and there are too many distractions here in the tunnel, so I don't want him to write anymore. I just shake my head. I don't want to encourage him to keep writing. I read the word *sing*, but I can't read everything. Or anything, sometimes.

He holds his hand up to his mouth and spreads his fingers like someone throwing up. I draw my head back. But I keep on playing.

Why does he want me to sing? He can't hear it. But I start to sing softly, anyway. He smiles and nods. And then he laughs when he sees the words of the song on my lips. He shakes his head and motions for me to continue.

I forgot he can read lips. I can talk to him, but he can't talk back. I play all the way to the end of the song, and some people have now stopped to listen. Maybe I should sing every time.

He writes something on the board. But I flip it over and lay it on the concrete. I don't want to talk to him. I wish he would go away.

His brows furrow and he throws up his hands, but not in an "I'm going to knock you out" sort of way. In a "what am I going to do with you" way. He motions for me to keep playing. His fingers rest on my guitar, like he's feeling the vibrations of it. But what he's concentrating on most is my mouth. It's almost unnerving.

A cop stops beside us and clears his throat. I scramble to gather my money and drop it in my pocket. I've made about thirty two dollars. That's more than the nickel I had when I started. I pack up my guitar, and Blue Eyes scowls. He looks kind of like someone just took his favorite toy.

He starts to scribble on the board and holds it up but I'm already walking away.

He follows after me, tugging on my arm. I have all my worldly possessions in a canvas bag over my right shoulder and my guitar case in my left hand, so when he tugs me, it almost topples me over. But he steadies me, slides the bag off my shoulder in one quick move and puts it on his own. I hold fiercely to it, and he pries my fingers off the strap with a grimace. What the heck?

"Give me my bag," I say, and I plant my feet. I'm ready to hit him again if that's what it takes. But he smiles, shakes his head and starts to walk away. I follow him, but getting him to stop is like stopping a boulder from rolling downhill once it gets started.

He keeps walking with me hanging on to his arm like I'm a Velcro monkey. But then he stops, and he walks into a diner in the middle of the city. I follow him, and he slides into a booth, putting my bag on the bench on the inside, beside him. He motions to the other side of the bench. He wants me to sit? I punched him in the nose two days ago and now he wants to have a meal with me? Maybe he just wants his $20 back. I reach in my pocket and pull it out, feeling its loss as I slap it down on the table. He presses his lips together and hands it back to me, pointing again to the seat opposite him.

The smell of the grill hits me and I realize I haven't eaten today. Not once. My stomach growls out loud. Thank God he can't hear it. He motions toward the bench again and takes my guitar from my hand, sliding it under the table.

I sit down and he looks at the menu. He passes one to me and I shake my head. He raises a brow at me. The waitress stops and says, "What can I get you?"

He points to the menu, and she nods. "You got it, Logan," she says, with a wink. He grins back at her. His name is Logan?

"Who's your friend?" she asks of him.

He shrugs.

She eyes the bandages across his nose. "What happened?" she asks.

He points to me, and punches a fist toward his face, but he's grinning when he does it. She laughs. I don't think she believes it.

"What can I get for you?" she asks me.

"What's good?" I reply.

"Everything." She cracks her gum when she's talking to me. She didn't do that when she talked to Logan.

"What did you get?" I ask Logan. He looks up at the waitress and bats those thick lashes that veil his blue eyes.

"Burger and fries," she tells me.

Thank God. "I'll have the same." I point to him. "And he's buying." I smile at her. She doesn't look amused. "And a root beer," I add at the last minute.

He holds up two fingers when I say root beer. She nods and scribbles it down.

"Separate checks?" she asks Logan.

He points a finger at his chest, and she nods as she walks away.

"They know you here?" I ask.

He nods. Silence would be an easy thing to get used to with this guy, I think.

The waitress returns with two root beers, two straws and a bowl of chips and salsa. "On the house," she says as she plops them down.

I dive for them like I've never seen food before. Now that I think about it, I can't remember if I ate yesterday, either. Sometimes it's like that. I get so busy surviving that I forget to eat. Or I can't afford it.

"How's your brother doing?" the waitress asks quietly.

He scribbles something on the board and shows it to her.

"Chemo can be tough," she says. "Tell him we're praying for him, will you?" she asks. He nods and she squeezes his shoulder before she walks away.

"Your brother has cancer?" I ask, none too gently. I don't realize it until the words hang there in the air. His face scrunches up and he nods.

"Is he going to be all right?" I ask. I stop eating and watch his face.

He shrugs.

"Oh," I say. "I'm sorry."

He nods.

"Is it the brother I met? A the tattoo parlor?"

He shakes his head.

"How many brothers do you have?"

He holds up four fingers.

"Older? Or younger?"

He raises his hand above his head and shows me two fingers. Then lowers it like someone is shorter than he is and makes two fingers.

"Two older and two younger?" I ask.

He nods.

I wish I could ask him more questions.

He writes something on the board and I sigh heavily and throw my head back in defeat. This part of it is torturous. I would rather have someone pull my teeth with a pair of pliers than I would read. But his brother has freaking cancer. The least I can do is try.

I look down at it and the words blur for me. I try to unscramble them, but it's too hard. I shove the board back toward him.

He narrows his eyes at me and scrubs the board clean. He writes one word and turns it around.

You, it says. He points to me.

I point to myself. "Me?"

He nods and swipes the board clean. He writes another word and shows it to me.

"Can't," I say.

He nods and writes another word. He's spacing the letters far enough apart that they're not jumbled together in my head. But it's still hard.

My lips falter over the last word, but I say, "Read." Then I realize that I just told him I can't read. "I can read!" I protest.

He writes another word. "Well."

He knows I can read. Air escapes me in a big, gratified rush. "I can read," I repeat. "I can't read well, but…" I let my words trail off.

He nods quickly, like he's telling me he understands. He points to me and then at the board, moving two fingers over it like a pair of eyes, and then he gives me a thumbs up.

My heart is beating so fast it's hard to breathe. I read the damn words, didn't I? "At least I can talk!" I say. I want to take the words back as soon as they leave my lips. But it's too late. I slap a hand over my lips when his face falls. He shakes his head, bites his lip and gets up. "I'm sorry," I say. I am. I really am. He walks away, but he doesn't take his backpack with him.

While he's gone, a man approaches the table. He's a handsome black man with tall, natural hair. Everyone calls him Bone, but I don't know what his real name is. "Who's the chump, Kit?" he asks.

"None of your business," I say, taking a sip of my root beer. I fill my mouth up with a chip, and hope he goes away before Logan comes back. And I hope deep inside that Logan will come back so I can apologize.

Logan slides back into the booth. He looks up at Bone and doesn't acknowledge him. He just looks at him.

"You got a place to sleep tonight, Kit?" Bone asks.

"Yeah," I reply. "I'm fine."

"I could use a girl like you," Bone says.

"I'll keep that in mind." It doesn't pay to piss Bone off. He walks away.

"You all right?" I ask Logan.

He nods, brushing his curls from his forehead.

"I'm sorry," I tell him. And I mean it. I really do.

He nods again.

"It's not your fault you can't talk. And..." My voice falls off. I've never talked to anyone about this. "It's not my fault I can't read well."

He nods.

"I'm not stupid," I rush to say.

He nods again, and waves his hands to shut me up. He places a finger to his lips like he wants me to shush.

"Ok," I grumble.

He writes on the board and I groan, visibly folding. I hate to do it, but I can't take it. "I should go," I say. I reach for my bag.

He takes the board and puts it in his backpack. He gets it, I think. I'd rather play twenty questions than I would try to read words.

He opens his mouth and I hear a noise. He stops, grits his teeth, and then a sound like a murmur in a cavern comes out of his mouth.

"You can talk?" I ask. He put me through reading when he can talk?

He shakes his head and bites his lips together. I shush and wait. "Maybe," he says. It comes out quiet, and soft, and his consonants are as soft as his vowels. "Just don't tell anyone."

I draw a cross over my heart, which is swelling with something I don't understand.

"What's your name?" he asks. He signs while he says it. It's halting and he has to stop between words, like when I'm reading.

"People call me Kit," I tell him.

He shakes his head. "But what's your name?" he asks again.

I shake my head. "No."

He nods again. The waitress brings the burgers and he nods and smiles at her. She squeezes his shoulder again.

When she's gone, I ask him, "Why are you talking to me?"

"I want to." He heaves a sigh, and starts to eat his burger.

"You don't talk to anyone else?"

He shakes his head.

"Ever?"

He shakes his head again.

"Why me?"

He shrugs.

We eat in silence. I was hungrier than I thought, and I clear my plate. He doesn't say anything else. But he eats his food and pushes his plate to the edge of the table. He puts mine on the top of it, and looks for the waitress over his shoulder. I'm almost sorry the meal is over. We shared a companionable silence for more than a half hour. I kind of like it.

He gets the waitress's attention and holds up two fingers. He's asking for two checks. I should have known. I pull my money from my pocket. He closes his hand on mine and shakes his head. The waitress appears with two huge pieces of apple pie. I haven't had apple pie since I left home. Tears prick at the backs of my lashes and I don't know how to stop them. "Damn it," I say to myself.

He reaches over and wipes beneath my eyes with the pads of his thumbs. "It's just pie," he says.

I nod, because I can't talk past the lump in my throat.

Logan

Black shit runs down from her eyes and I wipe it away with my thumbs, and then drag my thumbs across my jeans. She's crying. But I don't know why. I want to ask her, but I've already said too much.

I haven't talked since I was thirteen. That was eight years ago. I tried for a while, but even with my hearing aids, it was hard to hear myself. After the kid on the playground teased me about my speech, I shut my mouth and never spoke again. I learned to read lips really fast. Of course, I miss some things. But I can keep up. Most of the time.

I'm not keeping up right now. "Why the tears?" I ask, as she takes a bite of her pie. She sniffs her tears back, and she smiles at me and shrugs. This time, it's her who won't talk.

Hell, if pie will make her cry, I wonder what something truly romantic would do to her. This is a girl that deserves flowers and candy. And all the good shit I can't afford. But she likes to talk to me. I can tell that much, so she's not with me simply because I wouldn't give her bag back.

She asks me a question but her mouth is full of pie, so I wait a minute for her to swallow. She gulps, smiles shyly at me and says, "Were you born deaf?" She points to my ear.

I point to my ear and then my cheek, showing her the sign for deaf. I shake my head.

"How old were you when it happened?" Her brows scrunch together, and she's so damn cute I want to kiss her.

I make a three and flick it at her.

"Three?" she asks.

I shake my head and do it again. She still doesn't get it. So, I put one finger in front of the three and she says, "Thirteen?"

I nod.

"What happened when you were thirteen?"

"High fever one night," I say, wiping my brow like I'm sweating, hoping she'll understand.

She opens her mouth to ask me another question, but I hold up a finger. I motion back and forth between the two of us, telling her it's my turn.

I can't figure out how to mime this one so that she'll understand, so I say very carefully, "Where are you from?"

She shakes her head and says, "No."

I put my hands together as though in prayer.

She laughs and says, "No," again. I don't doubt she's serious. She's not telling me. I have a feeling I could drop to my knees and beg her and she still wouldn't tell me.

"So, Kit from nowhere," I say. "Thanks for having dinner with me."

"How do I say thank you?" she asks. "Show me."

She looks at me, her eyes bright with excitement. I show her the sign and she repeats it. "Thank you," she says. And my heart expands. Then she looks at her bag beside me and says, "I should go."

I nod and stand up, and then I put my backpack on, and throw her bag over my shoulder.

"I'll take that," she says as she picks up her guitar case.

But I throw some bills on the table and wave at Annie, the waitress. She throws me a kiss. Kit is following me, but Annie doesn't throw her a kiss. I laugh at the thought of it. Annie loves me. And she's known my family since before our mom died and our dad left.

I stop when we get out to the street and light a cigarette. Kit scrunches up her nose, but I do it anyway. I take one drag from it, show it to her, pinch the fire off the end, letting the embers fall to the ground, and throw it in a nearby trash can. What a waste. But I can tell she doesn't like it. My brothers don't like it either. At least now they're in good company.

She holds her hand out for her bag, and I position her under a street light so I can see her mouth.

"Where do you live?" I ask. "I'll walk you home."

She looks confused for a minute. She glances up and down the street. Cars are rushing by and she's looking at me like she's suddenly lost.

"I live around the block," she says. "Give me my bag." This time, she stomps that black boot of hers and gives me a rotten look. She shakes her hand at me like that'll matter.

I lean close to her, because I'm kind of scared someone I know will see me talking to her. My brothers would be hurt if they thought I could talk and just chose not to. I let them think it's a skill I unlearned, instead. "You can't walk home alone. It's not safe."

She glares at me. "I'm not taking you home with me, you perv," she says, and she tries to take the bag from me. But I don't let her. She's tiny. And I'm not. I win. She balls up her fist, and I know I'm in trouble.

I lean close to her. "I don't want to sleep with you," I say. "I just want to make sure you get home safe." I hold up my hands like I'm surrendering. I draw a cross in the center of my chest like she did before and say, "Promise."

It's pretty late. It was already dark when we left the subway tunnel. Now it's really late. Later than she should be on the streets by herself. Particularly in this neighborhood. This is my neighborhood. I'm perfectly safe here. But she's not from here. This I can tell without ever hearing her voice. She's not my kind of people.

I put my fingers down, and pretend they're someone walking. "Let's go," I say.

She stands there, and crosses her arms in front of her. "No."

There's one thing I'm already sure of and it's that this chick means no when she says no.

Suddenly, the guy from the diner, the one she called Bone, walks up beside us. "Need some help, Kit?" he asks.

His lips are dark in the night, and I can barely see them. But I can see hers. She smiles what I know to be a phony smile at him, because her real smile will drop a man to his fucking knees, and she says, "Fine."

"This your guy for the night?" he asks.

She looks at me and steps forward, running the tips of her fingers down my chest. I go hard immediately, and I catch her hand in mine. She startles for a second, but then I cover her hand with mine, pressing it against my heart, tight and secure. She looks up at me and bats those brown eyes. I hadn't realized how dark they are. But they're almost black in the darkness of the night. "This is my guy," she says. But I can tell she's talking to him, and not to me.

The hair on her arms is standing up, and so is mine. But it's probably for very different reasons.

Bone walks away, looking over his shoulder at her ass. I want more than anything to punch him in the face. But I have a feeling that wouldn't be a good idea. "I'm your guy?" I say to her.

She deflates, and lifts her hand from my chest. "He's gone," she says. She slips her bag off my shoulder and puts it on her own. She stands up on tiptoe and kisses my cheek, her lips lingering ever so briefly. I want to turn my head and catch her lips with mine, but she'd run if I did that. I'm sure of it. *Thank you*, she signs. My heart leaps when I realize she's speaking my language. I just taught it to her, but still.

"Where are you going?" I ask.

"Home," she says with a shrug. Then she turns on her heel and leaves me standing there. I shake out a new cigarette and light it, and I watch her walk away. She doesn't look back. Her black bag is bouncing against her leg, and her guitar case is in her other hand. She hunches down against the wind. Does she own a coat? I wish I'd given her mine.

I follow her. I can't help it. I need to see where she's going, or I won't be able to find her again. Not to mention that her being alone in the night in the city scares the shit out of me. She's not hard enough for this place or for these people. If I let her get away from me, I might not ever find out what that tattoo means to her. And I sort of need to know now that it's on my arm. I might be able to find her in the subway tunnel. I realized when I saw her today that must be why she looked so familiar. I've seen her in the tunnel, busking for change.

She crosses the street and goes toward the old bank building, the one that was turned into a shelter for the homeless a few years ago. There are people in a line outside, and she gets in line with them. She doesn't have anywhere to stay. She's going to a fucking homeless shelter? But before she can go inside, they close and lock the doors. The people in line stand and protest. But they're full.

The throws her head back, her long dark hair falling even longer, reaching her ass. She's frustrated, I can tell. But she doesn't complain. She picks up her case, and starts down the street. There's another shelter a few blocks over, but my guess is that it's full, too. The shelters sprung up around here like fast food restaurants when the city began to change. But there are too many homeless and not enough places for them to stay.

I follow her, finishing my cigarette while I do. But instead of going to the next shelter, she stops and sits down on a bench, dropping her face into her hands. She's tired. And I feel weighed down by her burden, too. I approach her and sit down beside her. She looks up, her brown eyes blinking in confusion.

"You followed me," she says, looking up and down the street like she's not sure where I came from.

I nod.

Her chest bellows with air, and I'm guessing that was a heavy sigh. "You don't have to sit with me," she says.

I look at her, and I make sure to use my voice. "Come home with me," I say.

She looks into my eyes, hesitates for a moment, and then says, "Yes."

Emily

He's going to expect me to sleep with him. They usually think they can get in my pants if they give me a bed and a meal. He's given me food, and now the bed is the next part of it. He wouldn't be hard to sleep with. He has those dreamy blue eyes and curly locks of blond curls spring about in wild disarray all over his head.

I retrieve the money he gave me earlier from my pocket and try to give it to him. "For the place to sleep," I say. So he'll know I don't plan to sleep with him.

He shakes his head, looking at me like I have lost my mind. He slides my canvas bag off my shoulder again and puts it on his. His building is surprisingly close. All this time, I've been staying at shelters right around the corner from this guy. And I didn't even know he was there.

He opens the door and motions for me to step inside. "Do you live alone?" I ask.

He shakes his head no.

I stop him and press on his shoulder. "Who do you live with?"

He does that thing again where he shows me two people taller than him and two shorter than him. He lives with his brothers. Shoot. I'm not going to an apartment filled with men I don't know. "I can't," I say, but he rolls his eyes at me. Then he bends at the waist and drives his shoulder very gently into my midsection. He hefts me over his back like I'm a sack of potatoes. I'm still holding on to my guitar, and I knock him against the backs of his legs with it, because I know I could be screaming at him right now and he would have no idea. I can't talk to him. I can't tell him to put me down.

He carries me like that up four flights of stairs, and he's huffing a little when we get to the fourth floor. I expect him to keep climbing, but he doesn't. He stops and opens a door, and we're suddenly in a hallway.

My struggling has ceased, because it's no good. He can't hear me. He can't respond. So, I brush my hair out of my face with one hand and hold on tightly to my guitar with the other. He opens a door and steps inside, closing it behind him.

Four men turn to look at me, flopped there like a sack of potatoes over his shoulder. I'm turned to face them as he closes the door, so I wave. What else can I do? The one I met at the tattoo parlor gets to his feet. "Who's that?" he asks.

The tattoo guy bends over to look in my face. "Shit, Logan, that's the girl who clocked you."

The other men get up and walk over, too.

One of them says, "Dude, she's got Betty Boop on her panties." I can't even reach back to cover my ass.

Logan lowers me to my feet. I stumble as he sets me upright, when all the blood rushes back to my head. He reaches out to steady me, and he smiles. I realize that they could all see my panties when he had me upside down, not just the one of them. The rest were just nice enough that they pretended not to look.

Logan points to each of his brothers in turn, and motions for them to talk. "Paul," the biggest one says, as he extends his hand.

"I remember you," I say.

"I'll never forget you," he says, with a laugh as he smacks Logan on the shoulder. "And neither will his nose." He feints as Logan makes like he's going to punch him. But he doesn't. He stops right before he gets to his face.

The second to largest one, and they're all big boys, sticks out his hand and says, "Matthew." Matthew looks tired and a little green. I look at Logan and he nods subtly. This is the one who has cancer and is going through chemo. Paul slaps Matthew's hand away and says, "You're not supposed to be sharing any germs right now."

"Fuck you," Matthew says, and then he walks toward the hallway and goes in his bedroom and closes the door. He doesn't look back at me, but I don't mind.

The last two brothers have to be twins. They're younger than Logan, and they look identical. "Sam and Pete," Paul says.

They huddle around me, and I end up sandwiched between them, which they think is hilarious. They jiggle me around for a minute, until Paul barks at them. "Let her go," he says. He pops them both on the backs of their heads and says, "They don't know how to act when company comes over."

Company? That's what I am? "Nice to meet you," I say. I'm a bit overwhelmed. This is a lot of testosterone in one room. There's shooting and fighting blasting from the television and I look over at it. I know Logan can't hear it, but there are subtitles playing at the bottom of the screen. I don't know why, but that makes me smile.

Logan motions for me to follow him and I do, presumably toward his bedroom.

One of the twins (I can't tell them apart) calls out for us to wait. But Logan can't hear him. I follow him down the hallway, and the other of the twins is standing at the end of the corridor laughing like hell. Something is up, but I don't know what. Logan opens his bedroom door, and steps inside. I follow him. And that's when I see a form move in the bed.

"Who the fuck is that?" a female voice shrieks. Logan turns around and slaps at the light switch, and the room goes bright. A book flies across the room and hits his shoulder just as the light comes on. I step back out of the room, because whoever that is in his room is throwing shit like crazy. She's blonde. And she's naked. Completely and starkly naked. Shoot.

She jumps out of bed and starts grabbing for her clothes. Logan swipes a hand down his face and sticks his head out of the room. He motions toward Paul, who is leaning casually against the wall, a grin on his face. Paul walks down the hallway, his stride full of swagger, and he removes me from the doorway and goes in himself. The door closes with a thud.

"I thought you knew she was coming!" Paul says with a laugh. I imagine him doubled over, because that's how the twins are, they're laughing so hard. They're high fiving each other and listening to what's going on behind the door.

Logan must have signed something to him. Because he says, "She said she was going to surprise you."

Well, she did that, apparently.

Paul heaves a sigh and says, "He wants you to go."

More thuds in the room make me think she's throwing stuff again. Good God.

"He doesn't want you to surprise him again," Paul says quietly, but I can hear it. I want to press my ear against the crack in the door, because things have gotten quiet. I can hear her sniffle.

"You don't have to worry about that," she says with a loud inhale. "I'll never sleep with you again." The door flies open and she steps out it, and then she attempts to crowd me back against the wall. The twins freeze, their mouths falling open. She's almost six feet tall. I'm not.

"Oh, shit," one of them says.

I tolerate her until a piece of spittle flies out of her mouth and hits me in the cheek. "You better back the fuck up, bitch," I say. And I draw my fist back. I don't hit like a girl. I never have. I never will.

Like one of those hooks on the gong show my grandma used to watch, Logan wraps his arm around her waist, picks her up and spins her away from me. He shakes a finger at me. He better be glad he caught her, or she'd have my fist up her ass.

"Don't shake your finger at me," I warn. I'm pushing against him to get to her. "I'll rip every extension from your head." She actually has nice extensions. I'd love to ruin them. "I'll wrap them around your skinny neck and strangle you with them." I'm still reaching for her, and Logan can't sign, because he has her on one side and me on the other. I swipe at my cheek. The bitch spit on me. He hands her to the twins, who try to calm her down.

He holds up one finger at me. I think he wants me to wait. Wait for what? That skinny little no account whore just spit in my face. He shakes that finger at me again. I grab it and bend it back, until he winces and makes me let go. He's stronger than me and I know it. But it felt good. I could get tired of that finger really quickly.

He bites his lips together and sets me back from him. Then he walks to her, takes her by the elbow and escorts her to the door. She slides her shoes on as she goes, and her pants are still unbuttoned. She's going to be doing the walk of shame and she didn't even get laid. I take a good bit of joy in that. I'm more content than a cat in a windowsill. Logan signs something to Paul.

Paul turns to the twins and says, "One of you walk her home. It's late."

They both volunteer by raising their hands and jumping up and down. He calls on the one on the left. "Pete, you take her." He glares at him. "Don't stay long."

"Asswipe," the other one grumbles as he stalks back to the couch. "Pete gets to do everything." He clunks his feet down on the table. Then he changes his mind, stomps down the hallway and slams the door to his bedroom.

"Pete's not a man whore," Paul calls in the wake of his departure, deadpan.

"Since when?" Sam complains, sticking his head back out his door. "I'll have you know-" But he shuts his mouth when Paul glares at him. The door slams closed behind him again.

Logan swipes a hand down his face and then grabs my arm, leading me into his room. He closes the door behind us. "I didn't know she'd be here," he says. His voice is halting and slow.

I pout, crossing my arms beneath my breasts. He looks down at them. He is such a guy. "When was the last time you slept with her?" I don't know why I want to know this.

He holds up three fingers and points behind him. He's not quite meeting my eyes.

"Three days ago?" I clarify.

He nods. "But I didn't invite her tonight."

"Is she your girlfriend?" I ask.

He shakes his head. He holds up that finger again and I roll my eyes.

He leaves the room and comes back with a stack of clean sheets. He jerks the slut sheets off the bed and throws them in the hallway. He motions for me to walk around to the other side of the bed, and then he snaps the sheet open and makes a movement like he wants me to help him. I might as well.

I work quietly with him to make the bed. Then he crosses to me and tilts my chin up. I think he's going to try to kiss me and I'm balling up my fist to deck him again. But he just looks into my eyes. "I'm sorry," he says. His voice is clear. Halting, but clear.

"I'm not sleeping with you," I say.

He jerks his head back, clearly surprised. He steps back and shakes his head, and I think he's biting back a smile. "I brought you here to keep you safe. Not to have sex with you." He smiles again, and then he walks out of the room.

I follow him, because I don't think we're done yet. He goes to the fridge and pulls out a beer, pops the top of it and offers it to me. At the last second, he takes it back. "How old are you?" he asks, his brows drawing together.

"Nineteen," I admit. He puts the beer back and hands me a cold bottle of water. I take it. It's cool. And I'm thirsty. "What now?" I ask. He takes a sip of his beer.

He shrugs, and goes to sit on the couch. I look around. The place is a mess. There are pizza boxes everywhere, and dirty laundry piled up in the hallway. There are dishes in the sink, and the counter is full of clutter. There hasn't been a woman in this place for a really long time.

"Can I use your shower?" I ask. It has been a few days since I had a shower. It's hard to protect my stuff when I'm wet and naked, but I'm not too worried about it now.

Paul looks over his shoulder and then signs something to Logan. Logan looks at me and nods, pointing down the hallway. He makes a two with his finger and points, and I assume he means the second door. So, I grab my bag and head that way.

I open the door without knocking and I find Matthew hunched over the toilet. I move to step back and he looks me in the eye, his watery and red. "Don't tell my brothers," he warns. He starts to wretch again, and I step in the room and close the door. I open the cabinets and find a wash cloth, wetting it with cold water. I pass it to him and he wipes his face. He closes the toilet, flushes it and sits down on it. "Fucking chemo," he says. "It's a bitch."

"Do they know you're sick?" I ask.

He shakes his head and flushes the toilet again when it stops running. "Please don't tell them. They have enough to worry about."

"I won't."

"Did you need to use the bathroom?" he asks. He doesn't look like he has enough strength to stand.

"I was going to take a shower," I say. "But I can wait."

He gets up, groaning. "I think I'm good for now." He smiles a watery smile. "But I might have to barge in on you." He removes a towel from the cabinet and lays it by the sink for me.

"You'll be here to puke and not to look at me naked," I say.

"I don't mess with Logan's women," he says. Then he goes on to say, "Ever. It's a brother thing." He burps and I worry that he's about to toss up his cookies again, but he doesn't. He smiles at me and walks out, closing the door behind him.

"I'm not Logan's," I say more to myself than to him.

He opens the door back up, startling me. "Yes, you are."

Logan

Kit's in my bathroom and she's naked. Or she will be in just a minute. I look down the hallway at the closed bathroom door. If it was any other girl, I'd be in there with her. But with the tattoo this girl wanted, I already know there's a vulnerability there that no one gets to see. I don't want to make her run away. I want to get to know this one. I've never had this kind of curiosity about a girl before. I usually sleep with them. Then I send them home. That's one of the reasons why it surprised me so much to find Terri in my bed tonight. She knew what we did wasn't the start of a relationship. I never bought her flowers or candy or took her on a date. I never bought her dinner. I just said *let's go* with my eyes and led her back to my room. Why she thought I might want a repeat performance is beyond my comprehension.

I go get another beer and Paul glares at me like the time I let the toilet lid fall on his dick when he was seven and I was four.

"How did you end up with her?" he asks.

I shrug. *I found her in the subway tunnel busking for change.*

"And she followed you home like a lost puppy?"

No. I had to carry her. You saw me. Why is he asking so many questions? It's not like I've never brought a girl home before. *I followed her to see where she was going after I bought her dinner. And she stood in line at the homeless shelter until they closed the doors. They were full. She didn't have anywhere to go, so I brought her here.*

He's still glaring at me.

What? I ask.

"I told you not to mess with that one." He sits back, huffing out a big breath. "She's not like the others."

I know that. I'm going to sleep on the couch, dickwad. I'm not going to sleep with her.

His brows shoot up.

Shut up, I sign.

"You're going to sleep on the couch." He might need a two ton jack to pick his jaw up off the floor.

I nod. *How's Matt?*

"Sick." He takes a swig of his beer. "I don't think he wants anyone to know."

I nod.

His brows are still up. "You're really going to sleep on the couch?"

I nod again, raising my hands in the air to say what the fuck.

He shakes his head. "I just don't believe it."

I have a heart.

"Yeah, but it usually gets overruled by your dick." He takes a sip of his beer. "Does she know you put her tattoo on your wrist yet?"

I shake my head. *Not yet.*

"Are you going to tell her?"

Why should I?

"Maybe because it's personal to her. I still don't understand why you wanted it."

He's going to get a permanent crease between his eyebrows if he keeps scowling like that.

I don't understand it either. I look toward the bathroom door again. *Does she look familiar to you? Like you've seen her before?*

He shakes his head. "I don't think so."

I nod and shrug. I would say she just has one of those familiar looking faces, but she's so fucking beautiful that can't be the case. She's gorgeous. She would stand out in a crowd. And that's not just because she's in my bathroom naked.

"How's your nose?" Paul asks.

I shrug. It's fine. Nothing I can do about it either way. And I kind of deserved it.

The bathroom door opens up and she comes out. She's wrapped in a towel and her hair is wet and hanging down over her shoulders. She looks like she just brushed a comb through it. She doesn't have any makeup on. There's no black stuff around her eyes and I see she has a line of freckles across the bridge of her nose. She ducks quickly into my bedroom, and I sit back, forcing myself not to go and see her. She probably wanted to get dressed somewhere that's not all steamy.

I get up and go to the bathroom, closing the door behind me. The mirror is fogged up from the steam of her shower. The countertop is clean for the first time in months, and she even cleaned the toilet and the shower before she got in it, apparently. Everything is all clean and shiny. I assume it's because she's a girl that she felt the need to clean it before she used it. It looks nice and I remind myself to tell her thank you.

She left her shampoo bottle in the shower, and her soap. It smells nice in the bathroom for a change and I realize it's her stuff that left that clean scent in the air. Makes me want to go and sniff her. I want to bury my face in her hair to see if it smells as good as the bathroom does.

She's had enough time to get dressed now, hasn't she? I knock on my bedroom door and I crack it open, peeping in. She's sitting on the edge of my bed wearing the towel. It's open over her thigh, showing a long expanse of naked leg.

I motion to her, asking her silently if I can come in. She grips the towel where it's tucked between her breasts and hitches it higher. But she nods.

She looks toward my closet, which is standing open, and then back at me. I raise my brows at her in question. Does she need something?

"Can I borrow a shirt?" she asks. She looks down at her bag. "All my clothes are dirty, and I hate to put on dirty clothes when I just got out of the shower."

I must have looked at her funny. Because she rushes on to say, "I'll return it to you tomorrow, before I leave. I just want to sleep in it. Do you have a washing machine?"

I nod.

"Which question are you answering? The shirt? Or the washer?"

"Both," I say. She smiles at me. I'd talk to this girl all day long if it means she'll smile at me like that. I take a shirt from a hanger and toss it to her. She catches it and pulls it over her head. After she tugs it down toward her knees, she tugs the towel and jerks it from beneath the shirt. She sits down on the side of my bed and removes a pair of pink panties from her bag.

"Can you turn around?" she asks.

I do, and the fact that I did makes me grin like a kid in a candy store. I hope she can't see me.

I feel her hand on my shoulder and I turn back around. She's wearing my AC/DC shirt, and it hangs down around her knees. Damn she's pretty.

"Can I throw some things in your washing machine?" she asks.

"I can do it for you," I offer.

She shakes her head. "You are not fondling my panties, perv," she says, grinning. "Next thing I know, you'll be sniffing them." She laughs. I wish I could hear it, because it's probably the most beautiful sound in the world. It's not often I wish I could hear, because I can do almost anything I want. But right now, I wish I could hear the sound of her laughter.

I motion to her and she walks out with me to the hallway, where I open the door to the laundry closet. I take what's in the dryer out, and put it on top. Look like Sam and Pete's stuff and they can handle their own clothes. I flip what's in the washer to the dryer, and ask her for her things by holding out my hands. She shakes her head. I step to the side and she starts to take a few things from her bag. She doesn't have much – just a few shirts, some shorts, a pair of jeans, and what she was wearing today.

And the throws in a few pairs of panties. There's more Betty Boop and I grin at her and shake my head.

I dump in some laundry soap and she starts it, and then she walks back toward my bedroom. "Do you have a blanket I can put on the floor?" she asks.

What the hell? "Why?" I ask.

She looks at me like I've grown two heads. "To sleep on?"

"You are not sleeping on the floor," I tell her. "You take the bed. I'll sleep on the couch."

"The couch is about five feet long. You're too tall. I can sleep on the couch." She nods like she's made up her mind.

I grab her arm gently as she goes to walk by me. "No," I say. "You take the bed."

The bed is full size, so it's not the biggest bed in the world. She draws her lower lip between her teeth and nibbles it. That has to be one of the most erotic things I've ever seen. I reach out and touch her lower lip with my thumb, gently pulling it from between her teeth. She licks her lips and looks everywhere but at me.

"Are you sure this is all right with you?" she asks.

I lean close to her and pull her into my chest. I don't know why I feel the need to do that, but I do. She hesitates briefly and then wraps her arms around my waist. I kiss her gently on the forehead. She looks up at me and she looks almost lost. The color is high in her cheeks and she steps back. "Thank you," she says. She stands up on tiptoe and kisses my cheek almost like it's an afterthought.

That kiss touches me like the deepest tongue kiss never has. It's like my breath is trapped in my throat and I can't draw it in or out.

"Are you all right?" she asks.

"Fine," I say. But I'm anything but fine. She raises her arms to lift her wet hair from her neck and her boobs shift beneath her shirt. I'm instantly hard. "Let me know if you need anything?" I say. But I'm not looking at her anymore. I'm walking toward the door as fast as I can, before she notices that I'm getting hard just thinking about the fact that she doesn't have a bra on.

She touches my arm and says, "Logan, please don't tell anyone that I can't read, ok?" She looks worried and I hate it for her. I hate that she even has to worry about things like this.

"That was between me and you," I tell her. I like that it's our secret. Kind of like my talking is.

She closes the door behind me and I hear the thumb lock on the door click. She just locked me out of my own room. I can't say I blame her really. She's in a strange place. And she's surrounded by strange men. But there's a piece of me that's glad she locked the door.

I walk back to the living room, taking a blanket with me from the linen closet.

"I still can't believe you're going to sleep on the couch," Paul says.

I can't believe it either. But I am.

Emily

I've been lying in Logan's bed for what feels like hours, but I can't sleep. I heard Pete when he came home, and I heard Paul tell him to go to bed. Then the apartment got quiet. No one has made a sound for hours, until now. I think it's Matthew, because it sounds like quick, muffled footsteps and then an awful gagging noise.

I open the door and look out, the bathroom door is open about an inch, and I'm pretty sure that's Matthew in there getting sick. He's miserable, and I want to help him, but I also don't want to intrude. I tiptoe into the kitchen because I'm thirsty, and I look over at the sofa, where Logan is sleeping. His feet are hanging off the edge by about a foot, and he's flat on his back, his head bolstered by the arm of the couch. He doesn't even have a pillow.

I open the fridge and bend over see what they have to drink, and when I stand up, Matthew is looking at me over the top of the door. "What are you doing?" he asks. His eyes are rimmed in red and bloodshot, and his face is pale.

"Getting something to drink," I whisper. "Can I get you anything?"

He shakes his head. His gaze darts down to my bare legs, and I tug on the hem of Logan shirt. "Nice shirt," he says. He jerks a thumb toward Logan. "Did you two have a fight?"

I look over at Logan too. He's sleeping soundly, his mouth hanging open. "No," I whisper. "Why would you think that?"

"Wait." He stops like he's thinking about something. "Why are you still here? Are you spending the night?"

I nod, lifting a bottle of water to my lips.

"Logan's girls never spend the night." He looks amused. But I don't understand why.

"He insisted," I whisper.

"Why are you whispering?" he whispers loudly and dramatically.

"Logan's asleep," I reply.

"He's deaf." He grins.

Oh, yeah. I forgot. It's so easy to forget that he can't hear. I laugh and shrug.

Suddenly, he turns on his heel and runs back to the bathroom. He's sick again, but it sounds like his stomach is empty. I open drawers beside the sink until I find a drawer with towels in it. I wet one with some cool water, and I meet him when he's coming out of the bathroom with it. He takes it from me with a heavy sigh and dabs his face with it. "Do you need anything?" I ask.

"Ginger ale," he says. "There's some in the fridge."

I nod and go back in that direction. While I'm there, I grab an empty margarita mix bucket off the counter. I start down the hallway, and assume his door is the one with the open doorway. He's sitting on the edge of the bed, his head in his hands. I put the bucket in front of him. "For later," I say.

"Thanks," he says as he takes a sip of the ginger ale. I take the towel from his hands and go back to the bathroom, getting it cold again. When I go back in the room, he's laying down, so I gently put the towel on his forehead and turn to walk out. "Don't break his heart," he says.

He's puking his guts out and all he's worried about is me breaking Logan's heart.

"I'm just here for the night," I say.

He snorts. It comes out more like a snuffle. But I get it. He doesn't believe me. "I'll see you tomorrow," he says.

I turn out his light as I leave the room, and close the door behind me.

The washer has stopped quite some time before, and I take what's in the dryer out and see that the pile on top of the washer is growing. I can't see letting their things get all wrinkled, so I stand there and fold them, and I fold what's coming out of the dryer, too. I flip my laundry into the dryer, and then I remember the huge pile of laundry in the hallway, so I start a load of their things. Might as well. I'm not doing anything else.

I walk back to the kitchen, and Logan is snoring. His hair hangs all tousled over his forehead, and I wonder if his mother ever used to watch him sleep like this.

The kitchen is a mess, so I grab a trash bag from the pantry and start packing pizza boxes away. Then I put up all the food that's on the counter, and give it a good scrub. The kitchen is all nice and sparkly before I go back to bed.

I yawn and close the bedroom door behind me. But this time, I don't feel the need to lock it.

***

The bed dips in the middle of the night, and I startle awake. My heart starts pounding like a jackhammer and I scoot to the edge of the bed. "What are you doing?" I ask.

It's Logan, and the room is dark, so he can't see my face or hear my voice. He rolls to his side, away from me, snuggling deeply into the pillow. He makes this adorable smacking noise with his mouth as he settles. He reaches back and jerks the blankets off of me, tugging them onto him.

He doesn't really think he's going to sleep in here, does he? I could go and get on the couch, but he's already snoring. He's sound asleep. I lean up and look into his face. He doesn't stir. He's not going to try to put the moves on me. He's just going to sleep.

I roll over, curling into myself, because it's chilly without a blanket. I could go and get the one from the couch, I guess. I know he had one out there. But I'm afraid I'll wake him if I get up. I grab the edge of the blanket he just stole from me and pull it back over to my side, just enough to cover half of me. He doesn't move. So, it must be all right.

Logan

I wake up slowly, immediately aware there's a warm body pressed against mine. I raise my head and look down at the leg thrown across my thighs. There's a delicate arm wrapped across my chest, and a black head of hair with a blue streak tucked under my chin, right beside my heart.

Her thigh is naked and it feels so fucking good that I don't want to move. Her shampoo tickles my nose and I wonder how I ended up in bed with her. I know all we did was sleep. My guess is that I got up to pee in the middle of the night and came back to my bed by accident. How she got wrapped around me is another story.

I lay my head back against the pillow and look up at my cracked ceiling. I didn't mean for this to happen. And I don't want her to think that I just want her in my bed. That I only want to sleep with her. But I do want to sleep with her. Right now, I want to roll her over and slide the pink panties she made me turn around for last night slowly down her legs. I want to kiss her from the soles of her feet to the insides of her thighs. I look down at her thigh again. I can't resist it. I reach out and lay my hand on it. She wiggles and presses harder against me, her breasts cushioned by my chest.

I'm so freaking hard that all the blood in my body is pulsing in my dick. Shit.

The sun is coming up, so my brothers will be moving around soon. They'll never let me hear the end of it if they find me in here. I started off on the couch, and swore I would stay there.

Shit.

I just wanted to keep her safe and now she's in bed with me. Or I'm in bed with her.

Involuntarily, I clench her thigh in my grasp. I turn onto my side to face her, and hitch her thigh up higher over my hip. I need to slide out from under her arm. But then her brown eyes blink open. We're face to face. She doesn't seem startled. "You stole the covers," she says.

She has morning breath, and I've never wanted to kiss someone so bad in my life. "Why are you in my arms?" I ask.

She looks around like she's not quite sure, and she bites her lower lip between her teeth again. I pull it out very gently with my thumb and she licks her lips, just like she did last night. "I was cold. And you were warm."

"I started out on the couch," I say.

She nods, leaning close to me, burying her face in my chest. She inhales deeply, her breath moving through the thin material of my t-shirt when she exhales. Did she just sniff me?

"You smell good," she mouths, looking up at me so I can see her lips.

She did just sniff me. I can't help it. I palm her ass and draw her closer to me. "Do you always wake up so sweet?" I ask. She's like cotton candy in my arms. She smells soft and clean and she's not shoving me away.

"I'm not awake yet," she mouths. She spins over in my arms, facing away from me. My forearm is under her head and her bottom is tucked against my groin. Her head is beneath my chin, and I can't see her face anymore. But I doubt she's talking. She's soft in my arms, and her breath rushes out of her open mouth with every exhale, searing my forearm with her every breath.

The bottoms of her feet are cold against the tops of mine, so I unfurl the blanket over us both, tucking it around her, throwing it over our feet.

I don't want to let her go. But I know I need to get up. I need to go back to the couch. I close my eyes and brush her hair down between us.

She lets me wrap around her, and by her own admissions she's still asleep. Will it hurt to stay there? I keep holding her. I've never had a girl sleep the whole night in my bed before. Ever. I've never woken up with someone. I've never wanted to. Until now.

I settle my arm around her waist. I'll just stay a few more minutes.

***

My bedroom door slams open, and I feel its *thwump* as it hits the wall. Paul is a bear in the morning, and he doesn't wake anyone up easily. He goes around, throwing open doors and turning on lights until the twins are up and ready for school. They're both seniors in high school and have to be there early. I look up at him as he stops in my doorway.

I knew you wouldn't stay on the couch the whole night, he signs to me. He doesn't say it out loud. Probably so he won't wake her up. Kit's asleep on her stomach, her hand tucked beneath the pillow and one leg pushed out to the side. I sit up and look down at her. My AC/DC shirt has risen up around her waist, and one side of her pink panties has migrated to tuck in the crack of her ass. Her left ass cheek is on display, the firm, round globe taught but relaxed. I toss the blanket over her bottom as I get up.

Shut up, I sign to Paul.

I reach over and grab my jeans, shoving my legs into them quickly. I put on my boxers before I went to sleep last night.

Paul is wearing a pair of lounge pants and no shirt. When I get to the kitchen, the twins are eating bowls of cereal, both in their boxers.

Put some clothes on, I sign to them. *Kit's still here.*

"That's her name? Kit?" Sam asks.

I shake my head. *I don't think so.* I'm pretty sure that's not her name. *It's what some guy on the street called her.*

"Where's she from?" Pete asks.

I don't know. She won't tell me.

Paul motions to the couch. "How'd you sleep?" He grins.

My neck still hurts from being on the couch. *Fine*, I say.

"She slept in your bed. With you." Paul's grin has turned into a glare.

I nod. *Not the whole night. Just part of it.* I fumble for a cup of coffee, but the coffee pot's not where we left it. What the fuck happened to the kitchen?

Paul has his hip hitched against the counter top and he's staring at me. "We woke up to it looking like this." He motions toward the expanse that is our clean countertop. I can't remember the last time I saw the Formica.

Where is all the stuff?

He opens the pantry door and points inside. She put it all away? The sink is empty of dishes, until Sam puts his bowl in it. *Put it in the dish washer*, I tell him. If she worked this hard to clean the kitchen, we can try to keep it looking like this, can't we?

"Aww, man," Sam complains. But he opens the dish washer and puts his bowl in there.

"You two get to school," Paul says. He shoos them toward their room so they can get dressed. "Next time, put some clothes on before you come out of your rooms," he warns. He looks at me. "How long will Kit be here?"

Paul looks over my shoulder and smiles at something. I turn around and see that it's Kit. She's all rumpled and she has a dent in her cheek from the crease of the pillow case. "I'll leave today," she says. She walks toward the coffee pot, which is now on a different counter. Granted, it's more convenient where she put it, but it's still not where it goes. She takes out a coffee cup and pours herself a full mug, and then she turns and says, "Thank you for letting me stay last night. I appreciate it."

I want to ask her about cleaning the kitchen and tell her thank you, but I can't use my voice in front of my brothers.

"She cleaned the bathroom, too," Sam says as he comes around the corner. His hair is wet and he leans toward me. "Do I smell too much like a girl?" he asks. He looks slightly abashedly at Kit. "I used your shampoo. And your soap."

Paul shoves him in the shoulder. "He would have used your tampons if you'd left any in there."

Her face colors prettily.

"Stay out of her stuff, dickwad," Paul warns.

Paul adjusts his jeans. "She folded my jeans. It doesn't feel quite right wearing something that wasn't rolled up in a ball in the basket in the corner of the room."

I glare at her. She did all this while we were sleeping? I want to tell her she doesn't have to work to stay here.

"What?" she asks. "I couldn't sleep."

She was sleeping pretty well in my arms. I don't want to think about that, because I can't get over the fact that I liked it as much as I did.

Sam leans over and kisses her on the cheek, just as Pete kisses her other cheek. She scrunches up her face, but she doesn't slap either of them. "I vote that we let her stay another day," Pete says. He looks down at her naked legs. Honestly, I've seen women at night clubs show a lot more skin than she's showing. "She's cute," he says. Then he grabs a banana off the counter and runs for the door. Sam is right behind him. He closes the door behind him and Sam sticks his head back in. "I second that vote," Sam says. Then the door slams and they're gone.

Kit smiles and looks over my shoulder. Matt is up, and he looks like death warmed over. "I third," he says as he sits down in a chair and puts his face in his hands.

Paul shrugs. "It's fine with me," Paul says. "But it's Logan's call. It's his bed."

Paul leaves to get ready for work. I have to do the same, but I don't have to go in until eleven. Paul goes early every day because he has to do paperwork.

Kit gets a ginger ale from the fridge and pours it into a glass. She hands it to Matt and he smiles faintly, and says, "Thank you." She doesn't say anything back, but she squeezes his shoulder. What's going on with the two of them? He won't let us do a damn thing for him, but he's letting Kit get him something to drink?

She smiles and walks back to the bedroom, taking her coffee with her.

"She's going to break your fucking heart, man," Matt warns after she closes the door.

I know. She's going to break my fucking heart. Because I've never wanted anything with anyone the way I want something I can't even define with her.

Emily

Waking up in his arms was one of the best moments of my life. I didn't want to wake up. I wanted to stay like that forever. So when he asked me questions about how we came to be tucked into one another, I pretended like I was asleep and rolled over, hoping he would wrap his arm around me. He did. He wrapped his whole body around me. I purposefully chose to turn away so I wouldn't have to explain. Because I didn't want to tell him about how I felt him when he got in bed with me. Or how I reached out to touch him in the night, and he let me put my head on his chest.

I didn't intend to wrap my body around him, but he didn't seem displeased by it. If the tent in his boxers was any indication, he was very pleased by it.

But even after, he was nothing but respectful about my body.

I come out of his bedroom dressed in my school girl outfit. It's clean now, so I didn't mind putting it back on. Aside from the fact that putting it on means I'm leaving his apartment. My bag is over my shoulder and my guitar case is in my hand. No one is there aside from the two of us. Paul went to work an hour ago. And Matt is staying home today, I'm sure. He's too sick to hold his head up, much less go work with the public. He must be in his room, because Logan is sitting at the table reading the newspaper. He looks up when I walk out of the bedroom, and his face falls.

He makes a gesture with his hands like he's asking me what.

"I have to go," I explain. I hold up my guitar. "I have to go to work. And you have to go to work. And I'm sure you don't want me hanging out while you're not here. What if I steal something?" I try to laugh it off, but he's not amused.

"You don't have to go," he says. "Stay." He gets up and comes to stand in front of me.

I hold up the guitar again. "I can't. I have to work." I only have thirty two dollars to my name. I can't find a decent place to stay on that. Not even for a night.

Like he can read my mind, he pulls out his wallet and flips it open. He takes money out of it and tries to press it in my hand. I can't take his money. "Stay," he says. He wants me to stay instead of going to busk for change.

I shake my head. It's hard to explain it to him. I want so badly to stay. But I can't. I can't get comfortable anywhere. Because tomorrow, I might have to leave again. "Thank you for letting me sleep here," I whisper. I know he can't hear the quality of my voice, but he can still read my lips. He tips my chin up with his forefinger under my jaw so that I look at him. "Thank you," I repeat.

"Come back tonight?" he asks. He's holding my hand, his thumb swiping back and forth across the surface of it. "I'll sleep on the couch. I promise."

I look up at him, swallowing hard. "I liked it when you were in the bed with me," I admit.

His eyes narrow and he looks closer at me than I think anyone ever has. But he doesn't say anything else.

"I think I'm in like," I admit softly. That's probably the wrong thing to say. But I need to tell him. I didn't just use him for a place to sleep. I genuinely could care about him if my situation was different. But it's not. And I can't.

He doesn't understand the terminology, I think, because he looks confused. "What?" he asks.

"I think I'm in like," I repeat. But he still looks just as confused.

He looks like he's going to get Matthew to translate. I stop him by jerking on his arm. "I like you," I say clearly. "That's why I'm leaving. I wouldn't be any good for you or for your brothers. I like you too much to stay."

"That's ridiculous," he says.

Yeah, it's ridiculous. But he doesn't know where I come from. He doesn't know how many people are looking for me and why. And when he does find out – I have no doubts that he will – he'll hate me for not telling him everything up front.

"Have dinner with me?" he says, his brows shooting up. He looks hopeful, and that's not what I want for him. He bends his knees so he can look into my face. "Dinner?" he repeats, like I might not have understood him. "A date," he says. "Go on a date with me."

I shake my head. I shouldn't like him so much after such a short time, but I see possibilities there where before I had none. He makes me believe I could have a real connection with someone. Well, maybe if I was someone else. But I'm not. So I can't.

"Thank you for letting me sleep here," I say. "And do my laundry and take a shower. I really appreciate it. Will you tell your brothers thank you for me?"

His hand falls away from me, and I feel like someone just untethered my anchor and I'm going to float away. He nods. He walks back over to the table and sits down, and begins turning the pages of the newspaper. He's not looking at me anymore and I feel the loss like someone chopped off my arm.

I let myself out and lean heavy against the wall outside his door. I can't bring him into my life. It's not good for him. Not for any of them. This is the way it has to be.

***

My ass is cold again, even though I'm wearing black leggings under my plaid mini skirt. It's freezing in the subway, and I'm sitting on my bag to keep my butt off the cold concrete. But it's still seeping into me. I have made forty-two dollars today, though, and it's a good day. I must have looked utterly miserable, because people have been putting money in my case like I'm homeless. Well, I am, but it's not like I'm holding a sign that says "I'm hungry."

It's a little after seven o'clock, and I've been here since I left Logan's apartment. My hands are tired, and I can't help but think to myself that I had better get moving. The after-work crowd has passed, and the drunks tend to come out after dark. So, I never feel safe in the subway when it starts to get late. I gather up my things and put my guitar away. I pocket the money I made today. It's getting colder outside as fall settles on the city, and I don't have a coat. So, I can either use the money I have to get a motel room, or I can go to the thrift store and try to find a used coat that I can use to keep warm as the weather changes. If I do that, I'll be sleeping in the shelter again, provided that they have room.

So, it's coat, shelter, and back to the subway for me tomorrow.

Someone calls my name as I walk up the steps of the tunnel and I turn to find Bone standing by the lamppost. "How's it going, Kit?" he asks. His eyes rake down my body, and my insides revolt.

"Fine," I say quickly. "Did you need something?"

He shakes his head, biting his lips together. "You have somewhere to stay tonight?" he asks.

He asks me this every time he sees me, like he's going to catch me at a vulnerable moment and I'll take him up on whatever he's offering. I don't even know what he's offering, but I know it won't do me any good. "I do, but thanks for asking."

"Any time, Kit," he says. He turns and walks away, his arm around some girl's shoulders. She looks strung out. And I'd be willing to bet that's how he likes them.

I walk through the city, wandering toward the shelter. I know it's right around the corner from where Logan works. I can't help but walk by there. The lights are on inside and there are still people walking around. I slow down, hoping I can get a look at him. I just want to see him. I know he probably hates me. But I want to see that he's walking around, breathing and maybe even laughing.

The neon sign over the building says Reed's. Makes me wonder if that's their last name. Paul walks to the door and lifts a hand at me without opening it. He tilts his head and looks at me. A bit too closely. He pushes the door open and speaks through the crack. "Are you coming in?"

I shake my head. "I shouldn't."

He nods. "You shouldn't. But you are." He motions me forward. "He's in the back."

It's like my feet have a mind of their own. I walk toward the back of the store, and the girl at the front desk shoots me a heated glance. I ignore her. There's a curtain in the back of the shop, and I'm guessing that's where he is. I push it slowly to the side. He can't hear me and he's facing away. But there's a woman on the table who's naked from the waist up. He's standing in front of her with his arm wrapped around her; his hand is busy around her right breast.

"Shit," I say. I feel like someone has just punched me in the gut. The lady on the table startles and Logan looks up. I have no choice but to leave. I've done nothing but think about this man all day long, and he's with one of his skanks. I knew he had them. But seeing his hands on one of them is worse. I have no right to claim him. I didn't even plan to come and find him. Paul insisted. Did Paul know what I would walk into?

Paul steps into my path as I run toward the door. "Kit," he says, blocking me from leaving with his body in front of me.

I put up my hands to ward him off. I can't take a deep breath, much less stop to talk to him. Before I can get to the front door, Logan runs from the back of the shop to the front, chasing after me. I can hear his feet on the laminate floor.

Logan reaches for me, taking my elbow in a tight but gentle grip.

Tears are stinging the backs of my lashes. I don't know why they are. But they are. And I don't want him to see. He holds up a finger telling me to wait. I can't wait. If I wait, he'll see me break down.

He takes my hand in a firm grip and starts to tow me toward the back of the store. He pushes the curtain to the side, and I see that the woman is still sitting exactly like he left her. Only now she's holding a thin piece of paper over her breasts. "Hi," she says. He points toward a chair and indicates that he wants me to sit.

I shake my head. "No."

He points toward the chair again. I drop into it because I feel like my legs won't hold me up anymore and that's the only reason.

He turns back to the woman and urges the paper down. He's tattooing her nipple. I look away. "It's all right," the woman says. "He did beautiful work. I don't mind if you see it."

He's doing a tattoo. Of course he is. All the breath rushes from my body in a huge exhale. He's doing a tattoo. I look over his shoulder as he's finishing up. He's not just tattooing her nipple. The tattoo is her nipple. What the hell?

"Double mastectomy," she explains. "Logan does free tattoos for mastectomy patients." She arches her back, pressing her breasts out. "What do you think?"

They look like real nipples. The shading around the edges is perfect, and he's drawn a simple nipple with a large areola. But there's nothing simple about it. It's a work of art. The color is the same shade as her lips, and I can't believe how real they look. "Wow," I say. What do you say? Nice nipples? Beautiful boobs? "That's amazing."

Logan holds up a mirror for her, and she looks from one to the other. "They're perfect!" she squeals. She throws her arms around his neck, and he hugs her tightly, smiling over her shoulder at me. He steps back from her, and bends down, softly placing a kiss on the top of her breast. Her eyes fill up with tears, and so do mine. "I'm going to show everybody," she says. She holds the paper over her breasts as she walks out into the shop. The girl that runs the front of the shop comes over to admire them, and Paul pretends to look everywhere but at her boobs. There's no one in the shop, but I get the feeling she wouldn't care if there was.

"She wanted to feel sexy again," he says quietly, yanking the curtain so that we're behind it.

"You did beautiful work." I bat my guitar case against my shins, not sure what else to say. It really was remarkable how lifelike they looked. The shading and the colors and the way they fit the size of her new breasts – it was all perfect.

"She needed them." He shrugs. He's so humble.

She bounces back behind the curtain, looking so pleased. She tugs her shirt over her head and takes money out of her purse. "I don't have much," she starts.

He presses it back into her purse, shaking his head.

"He won't take it," I say.

She narrows her eyes at me. "Who are you?"

"No one."

She nods. She kisses Logan on the cheek, waves at me and leaves.

He starts to clean up his supplies. He looks over at me out of the corner of his eye and says, "Why are you here?"

I open my mouth, but can't think of the right thing to say. I close it again. He stops and leans his hip against the table, crossing his arms over his chest.

"Can I buy you dinner?" I blurt out. I have no idea where that came from. But there it is.

He smiles. "Yes."

Logan

"What do you want to eat?" I ask as we leave the shop. Kit asked Paul to join us, but I think he saw the pleading in my eyes when I looked in his direction. I need some time alone with her. I need to take her on a date. Technically, she asked me out, but I'd never let her buy dinner for me. Ever.

"I don't care," she says with a shrug.

I realize I have no idea what she likes. "Italian?" I point to an Italian restaurant on the corner by my apartment.

She nods, smiling at me.

"I didn't think you were going to come back." I hold the door open for her, and she walks into the dark restaurant ahead of me. The waitress leads us to a corner booth and she slides in across from me.

"I shouldn't have." She puts her guitar under the table, banging me in the shin with it in the process. "I'm sorry," she says, wincing. She's suddenly uncomfortable with me.

Is she sorry for knocking me in the shin or for leaving me this morning? "What did you do today?" I ask.

She makes a face and points toward her outfit. "Playing in the subway."

"How did it go?"

She shrugs. "It was cold. My butt is still freezing," she admits. I get an immediate and strong image of me helping to warm up her ass. I saw that perfect globe that is her ass cheek this very morning. "What?" she asks.

My thoughts must have played out on my face. "Nothing," I say. But a grin tugs at the corners of my lips.

"What's so funny?" she asks, her head tilting to the side.

I shake my head. "My mind was in the gutter if you must know," I admit. "I'm sorry. It won't happen again. Please go ahead." I motion for her to keep talking using my hands.

"You were thinking about my butt," she says. And now she's grinning too.

Heat creeps up my cheeks. She's so damn pretty.

The waitress comes to the table with menus, and lays one in front of each of us. "Welcome," she says. "Do you want to know our specials?" She blinks at me, trying to catch my eyes. I make it a point not to look at her.

Kit nods in answer to her question. She rattles off some menu items and their prices, and I see Kit reach into her pocket and count her money beneath the table. There's no fucking way I'm letting her buy dinner.

"What can I get for you to drink?"

Kit arches a brow at me and I motion from her to me and back so she'll get me what she's having. "Root beer?" she asks.

I nod. The waitress leaves us with the two menus. I open mine and she doesn't. "Do you know what you want?" I ask.

"What are you having?" She smiles at me.

I open the other menu in front of her and point to the word at the top. "What do you see when you look at that?"

She scrunches up her nose. "I see someone who thinks he can teach me to read." She closes the menu. "Believe me, better people than you have tried."

"Who tried?" I ask.

She takes a sip of her root beer through a straw, her lips pursing around it. "A better question would be who didn't try. I have been poked and prodded and put through special ed and been to therapists who thought they could unlock my brain. No one could."

She doesn't look upset by this. She just looks resigned to it. I open the menu back up, just because I'm curious. I point to the word at the top of the page again. "What does that say?" I ask.

She looks down at it and closes it. "I know words," she says. She looks like she really wants to explain it to me, and I really want to hear it. "I can spell words. And I know what they mean. It's just the way they lay on the page that's hard for me." She shrugs. "I don't expect you to understand." She's looking everywhere but at me now, and I wish I hadn't pushed it.

"So, you know the words, and how to spell them in your head?" That baffles me.

"Crazy, isn't it?" She laughs, but there's no smile on her face. "Dyslexia's a bitch."

The waitress reappears with a basket full of bread and places it in the center of the table. Kit reaches for a piece and I wonder if she ate today.

"Did you decide what you want?" the waitress asks. I point to the chicken parmigiana. She nods and looks at me funny. She's catching on that something isn't right. But apparently, she still finds me intriguing.

"What's good?" Kit asks her. She did this same thing at the diner. It must be how she copes.

"The chicken parmigiana is amazing," she says, smiling down at me. Kit's not impressed. "But the alfredo is my favorite."

I raise my brows at her in encouragement. She laughs. "Ok, but if I don't like it, I'm taking your chicken," she warns. I nod. "I'll take the alfredo," she says to the waitress.

Kit lifts a piece of bread to her lips and takes a bite. A crumb sticks to her lip and I want to reach over and catch it, and bring it to my lips. But I don't dare. I have her at dinner with me. If I push her too hard, she's going to run away.

"Did you eat today?" I blurt out.

Her face flushes and she nods. She's lying. I'm sure of it.

I push the bread basket toward her and say, "Eat." She takes another piece.

She chews silently for a minute and then she looks at me. Her face is soft when she says, "What you did for that woman in the shop, with the tattoos…" I nod when she stops. She's referring to the nipple tats. "That was amazing and beautiful. Where did you learn to do that?"

I shrug. I don't remember learning it. I just knew I could draw it. And if I can draw it, I can run a tat of it. "I think she was pleased."

"Are you kidding?" She slaps the table. "She was ecstatic. And they really were beautiful. Like art. Can I see your tattoos?" she asks hesitantly.

I'm wearing my coat, so I have to shrug out of it to show her. I want to show her my art. I drew most of them, and my brothers put them on me. But I take my coat off and lay my hands face down on the table. She leans over, looking closely. I have full sleeves, which means I have tats from my neck all the way to my wrists.

She touches the lips on my forearm with a light finger. The hair on my arms stands up, but I pretend I don't notice. "Why did you get this one?" she asks.

I smile. "That one goes with this one." I point to my other arm. "It's something my mother used to say."

Her forehead crinkles as she looks at the cross on my other arm.

"From your lips to God's ears," I explain. "In my case, I have a lot of distance between my lips and God's ears. That's why they're on different arms."

"Do you see your mother often?" she asks. She's still eating bread, and that's good. I want to keep talking to her so she'll keep eating. I know she hasn't eaten today.

I shake my head. "She died a few years ago."

"Oh." Her mouth stops moving, and she swallows hard. "I'm so sorry."

I shrug. It was a freak accident.

"And your dad?" she asks.

"He left after Mom died," I explain. This part is always difficult. "There were just too many of us, I think." I laugh. But it's not funny.

"So, it's just you and your brothers?" she asks.

I nod. "Paul took responsibility for everyone when our dad left. He had to so we wouldn't all be split up."

"Wow." That's all she says. Just wow. She looks baffled.

"We make do," I explain. I don't want her to feel sorry for me. "How about you? Where's your family?" I wait, like a kid in a candy store.

But she shakes her head. "No," she says.

"That's not fair," I say.

She holds up a finger, just like I do to her all the time. "I know it's not fair," she says. "But it's better if you don't know."

"Better for who?" I ask. I'm a bit irked that she's keeping secrets. She has a right to them. But I don't have to like it.

"My situation is difficult," she begins. "And I can't explain it to you."

She looks back down at my tats. Her eyes play across them. There are too many to count. But I need to show her the one that's hers. "I want to show you something," I say. "But I'm afraid you're going to be angry at me."

She's suddenly on guard. "Why? What is it?"

I turn my wrist over and point to her tattoo on my inner wrist. It's a bare spot I'd been saving for something special. She leans toward it and all of her breath rushes from her body. I can feel it across my hand when she exhales. "That's my tat," she says.

She takes my hand in hers and lifts it toward her face. "Are you angry?" I ask.

She looks up at me briefly and then back down at the tattoo. She's taking in every facet of it. Her hand trembles as she holds tightly to mine. "You changed it."

"I felt like you needed a way out."

I put it on my wrist because I was intrigued by the secrets inside. It's art. And I appreciate art in all its forms.

She swallows. Hard. Then her eyes start to fill with tears. She blinks them back for as long as she can. And then she gets up and runs toward the bathroom.

Shit. Now I fucked up. I made her cry. She runs by the waitress, who startles. The waitress starts in my direction, a sway in her hips. I get up and follow Kit. I stop outside the door to the ladies' room and press my hand against it. I don't know what I'm waiting for. She's in there crying and I can't hear her through the door to be sure she's all right. Fuck it. I'm not leaving her in there upset. I push through the door and I don't see any feet in the stalls when I bend over.

Where the fuck did she go? I push doors open, but the last one is locked. I stand up on my tiptoes and look over the top. She's standing there with her forearms pressed against the wall, her head down between her arms, and her back is shaking. She's crying.

I knock on the stall door and say, "Let me in, Kit." She doesn't say anything. I wouldn't be able to hear her if she did. I step back onto my tiptoes and look over. She's still crying. "Let me in," I repeat. She doesn't move, so I walk into the stall next to hers and stand up on the toilet. I rock the partition between the stalls gently. It might hold my weight. There's only one way to find out. I hoist myself up and over the wall, bringing my legs over the top slowly and carefully, and then I hop down.

Before I can reach for her, she's in my arms, her arms sliding around my neck. She's still sobbing, and her body shakes against mine. I tilt her face up to mine because I can't see her lips to tell if she's saying anything to me or not. I need to apologize. I didn't expect her to get so upset. I'll have it covered up with something else if it bothers her this much.

My heart twists inside my chest. I really fucked up. "I'm sorry," I tell her, looking down into her face. Her face is soaked with tears and she freezes, looking up at me. I can feel her like a heartbeat in my chest. She steps on the toes of my boots, and then rocks onto her tiptoes. She pulls my head down with a hand at the back of my neck.

Her brown eyes are smoldering, and black shit is running down her cheeks, but I don't care. She's never looked more beautiful to me. I hold her face in my hands and wipe beneath her eyes with my thumbs. Her breath tickles my lips and she leans over even closer. She's standing on my fucking boots, and I don't care. She can do whatever it takes to get her closer to me.

"Why did you do it?" she asks, moving back enough that I can see her lips.

I already told her. I thought she needed a way out. All I added to the tattoo was a keyhole right in the center of the guitar. It's a simple design really. "I don't know," I say. I want to explain it to her, but I can't. Not right now. Her breath is blowing across my lips and she smells like yeast from the bread and root beer. And I've never wanted to kiss a girl so much in my life. But she was fucking crying. I can't take advantage of her.

She pulls my head toward hers and she kisses the corner of my mouth. Then she kisses the other corner. I can't take much more. I chase her lips with every move she makes. She's smiling when she finally presses her lips to mine. I can feel it against my mouth. I keep my eyes open, because I need to see her face. I'm holding her in my hands, and I slide my fingers into the hair at her temples.

I want so fucking bad to kiss her softly. I want to treat her like the treasure she is. But I can't. She smells so good and she feels so good and she's in my arms and I don't know if I can stop. Then she draws my lower lip between hers and sucks it gently. Her eyes are closed, and she's making love to my mouth. I'm afraid if I close my eyes, that I'll realize this was all a dream when I open them back up.

I tilt my head and press my lips harder against hers. She's soft and warm in my arms, and she's pressed against me from head to toe. Kit starts to tug my shirt from my jeans and I raise my elbows to help her. Her hands touch my waist, and I freeze. I hoist her in my arms, wrapping her legs around my waist, holding her up with my hands palming her ass. I press her against the wall and she laughs against my lips. I can feel the sound of it through her throat, like a gentle hum.

Her hands skim up my chest between us, but I'm still making love to her mouth. Her tongue slides against mine and I press inside the cavern of her mouth. This is the first time my body will enter hers, and I want to take it slow. I want to enjoy every second of it, but she's not having that. She's hot in my arms, and wiggling to get closer to me. Her hands stop as she skims up my chest, and she withdraws her lips from mine. I take a moment to try to catch my breath, because I feel like I just ran a five mile sprint. I even have the stitch in my side to prove it. She lifts my shirt up, and touches my piercings with her fingertips.

My breath leaves me. She's curious and I love that she's taking the time to look at me. She's intent upon her task and she explores my nipples, looking down, her bottom lip drawn between her teeth. I pull it free with my thumb, just like I have so many times before. Only this time, I lean forward and draw it into my mouth, nipping it gently. She rolls my piercings between her fingertips, and she's going make me disgrace myself if she doesn't stop. I pull back and bury my head in her shoulder, breathing harder than I ever have. This woman has completely undone me.

A hard wrap on the bathroom stall startles me, because I can feel the heavy shake of the metal partition. Kit looks up and says, "Just a moment."

I'm breathing so fucking hard that I can't catch my breath. But I put her down when she unwraps her legs from around me. She opens the stall door and steps out, wiping her still-wet face. The guy who banged on the door startles when he sees how wrecked she is. She was crying really hard there for a minute. I close the door and let her talk to him, because I need a minute to compose myself. I reach into my pants and adjust my junk. I have to cover it up with my shirt, because my dick is reaching up past the button on my jeans. Shit.

She felt so fucking good in my arms. I lean back against the wall and try to take some calming breaths. But there's not much that can calm me at this point. The only thing that would make this better is if she came back in here and we finished what we started.

I open the door and look out. The man is gone, and she's standing at the sink washing her face. She looks up at me, a soft smile on her lips as she sees me in the mirror. I walk up behind her and put my arms around her, resting my chin on her shoulder. "I'm sorry I made you cry," I say.

She shakes her head and talks to me in the mirror. "No one has ever done anything like that for me before," she says. Her eyes fill up with tears again, and I'm sorry that I came out of the stall. I'll go back in there if she'll stop crying. But I'm not leaving her. I can see that now. I'm not leaving her, no matter what.

"The lock?" I ask. She's leaning back against me, and she wraps her arms over mine.

She nods. She wipes her eyes with a paper towel, swiping the black makeup from under her eyes. Her face is splotchy, but she's never looked more beautiful. For that one split second, she isn't hiding anything from me.

"The minute I saw the tattoo, I knew it needed to be changed. I'm sorry if I defiled your art." She could take exception to my change. But I have a feeling she doesn't.

"It's perfect," she says. She lifts my arm from around her waist, and looks down at it. "It's perfect," she repeats, sniffling. "I don't know how to tell you what I'm feeling."

I'm the one with the hearing impairment and she can't tell me something? I laugh and lift her hair from her neck, and press my lips there. "You don't have to say anything," I tell her.

She turns around and cups my face in her palm, her hand stroking across my five o'clock shadow.

I take her hands in mine and lift them to my lips, kissing them one by one. Then I look into her eyes and open my mouth to ask her the one question I need to know the answer to. "What's your name?" I ask.

She freezes. It's like there's suddenly a wall between us and I haven't even let her go. "No," she says.

I feel like she's kicked me in the gut. I let her go and take a step back. "Why not?" I ask.

"I just can't," she says.

I nod and let myself out of the bathroom. My legs are shaking. The waitress shoots me a glance as I walk back to the table. I sit down. Kit's still in the bathroom and I can't help but wonder if she's ever going to come out. Her guitar is still under the table. So, she has to come back, right?

Emily

I lean heavily on my palms, putting all my weight on the bathroom countertop. My pulse is pounding so loudly that I can hear it in my ears, and drawing in a deep breath is burning my lungs like someone has set a fire inside them. Perhaps that's what he did. Or maybe he'd just shaken the pieces of me loose and now my body had to work to put me back together.

Either way, I feel like someone has torn me into two pieces. There's the one piece of me that wants to give Logan everything he wants. It's the piece that so very desperately wants to bare my soul to him, to tell him all of my problems. He would take them inside himself and then breathe them back out, and all my problems would vanish like in *The Green Mile*. I know he would. But my problems are too big for him. They'd eat him alive. And I can't let that happen. Because there's the other piece of me that knows I need to run like hell. I need to leave him before I hurt him.

I touch the tips of my fingers to my lips. They're red and swollen from his kisses. I've never been kissed like that before. I've never had a man make love to my mouth. I've never had a man try to work his way inside my body, kissing deep inside me, while touching nothing but my mouth. But that's what Logan did.

I need to go out there and collect my guitar, and then go. That would be the fair thing to do. But he put the tattoo on his wrist. He marked himself with my brand, and he changed it. Tears flood my eyes again, and I blink them back, using a wet paper towel to wipe the eyeliner smudge from beneath them. I look like a raccoon.

I heave a sigh. It's no wonder the manager looked at me like I deserved all the sympathy in the world. I told him someone important had died. That's why I looked like this. But in reality, I'm the one who died. When I left home, I died. I like the peaceful existence I've been creating here. I know what to expect. And I expect to face life alone. Now Logan is ruining my almost perfect existence.

I haven't felt hope in a really long time. But I am hopeful. And that isn't a good thing.

I push off the countertop and fluff my hair. His hands have been all over it, and it looks like I'd been tumbled in a drier. Laughter falls from my lips, completely unbidden.

I go back to the table, and he's there. He's eating a piece of bread, and looking up at me, quiet like he normally is. I slide into the booth across from him and settle against the seat back.

"Are you all right?" he asks.

I nod. "I'm fine." I close my eyes tightly, trying to find the right words to explain it.

He takes my chin in his grip and I open my eyes to look at him.

"You don't have to tell me anything," he says.

I shake my head. The words are right there on the tip of my tongue, but I can't force them past my teeth. "I want to talk to you," I start. But then I wince and bite the inside of my cheek.

The waitress comes with two warm dishes, and puts them in front of us. She refills our root beers and leaves.

Logan looks down at his food and smiles. He takes a bite of his chicken, and he's happy. He points to mine with his fork. I don't want to eat right now. I want to hash all this out.

"I'm just glad you're here," he says as I fill my mouth up with alfredo. "I was afraid you'd run."

I was afraid of that, too. And I probably still will. I circle my fork in a pile of noodles and hold it out to him. "Do you want to try mine?" I ask.

His blue eyes get all smoldery there for a minute. Then he grins and leans forward. He leans his head back after his mouth is full and chews thoughtfully. "Yours is better than mine," he says.

I take my fork and dip it into his plate, and he grins and shakes his head. It doesn't stop me. I chew thoughtfully on a piece of his chicken. "Mine's better than yours," I agree.

He shrugs and smiles. "Eat," he says.

We eat quietly, and I steal food off his plate so often that he puts up a fork to block me. But I feed him just as much of mine as he will accept. I like this time with him. But I also liked the time in the bathroom.

When the waitress takes the plates away, I have to force myself not to ask for a to-go box. There might not be anything for me to eat tomorrow, and I hate to see food go to waste. But there won't be anywhere for me to keep it at the shelter. That is, provided that I can find a shelter that's not crowded already.

The table is clear between us, and the waitress comes and leaves a leather-bound folder. I reach for it, but he intercepts it. "No," he says, shaking his head.

"But I wanted to pay," I complain.

He shakes his head again. "No." He slides his credit card into the slot and lays it on the edge of the table.

I reach over and take his hand, and he startles for a minute, but then his grip is strong on mine. I turn his hand over gently, looking at the inside of his wrist.

You can tell it's a fresh tattoo, and it's looking a bit like Fruity Pebbles, all rough and crinkly. But the design is still there. "I love this," I say. "Will you put one on me one day?" I ask. I want one just like this one. And I want the keyhole. "How much does this cost?"

"Nothing, for you," he says.

"I wouldn't let you do it for free."

He smiles. "I wouldn't let you pay for it."

"Do you do tattoos like the one today often?"

His brows draw together like he's not sure what I'm referring to.

I point to my boobs. And then heat creeps up my face when he looks down at them. He grins.

"Oh, jeeze," I say, burying my face in my hands.

He pulls my hands away. "What?" he asks. He must have thought I said something when my face was buried.

"Nothing." I shake my head.

"I don't do those often. Just once in a while. They give my name out at the cancer center."

"You never charge them."

He shakes his head. "I can't. They need it."

"So, how many boobs do you touch a day?" I ask playfully.

He grimaces. "Some," he says.

"Really?"

He nods. "It's a popular place for tats. Even when people aren't getting new nipples." His face colors. I think he's embarrassed.

Our discussion about boobs makes me think of what we'd just done in the bathroom. When I ran my hands up his chest, I'd discovered his piercings. He'd even let me look at them. "How many piercings do you have?" I ask.

He starts to count on his fingers. He stops at seven. "Seven?"

"Where?"

He points to each nipple, then his ears, then the shell of his ear. And then his gaze goes down to his crotch. He's not smiling, and his eyes narrow, like he's waiting to see my reaction.

I gasp, and nearly choke on my inhale. "Down there?" I whisper, a grin tugging at my lips.

He nods, taking a sip of his root beer.

"Did they hurt?" I suddenly have the most obnoxious desire to see every last one.

He shrugs.

"Can you do one for me?" I ask. Then I rush on to say, "Not today. Or any time soon. I don't have enough money."

"Where would you want it?" he asks.

I've only had my ears pierced, and never thought of doing any other part of my body. My nipples go hard just thinking about it. "Did your nipples hurt?" I whisper. Then I realize he can't tell I'm whispering, since he's just reading my lips.

"It hurts a little when you do it. But it goes away. Just like any other piercing."

I can't stop thinking about the one down there. Heat creeps up my cheeks again.

"I could pierce you. Anywhere you want," he says. And his face floods with color.

"Anywhere?"

He closes his eyes and takes a deep breath. When he opens them, he only opens one and he looks at me like he's wincing when he says carefully. "Anywhere." He looks at my boobs again and licks his lips. "Take your pick of places."

Suddenly, I'm curious. "You do a lot of those?" I don't know why that bothers me. "The... ones... down there?"

He shrugs.

I don't like the idea of him touching anyone's private places. Not at all. Although the idea of him touching mine... I squirm in my seat, and he arches a brow at me. "Something wrong?" he asks. He's smirking.

I shake my head, biting my lips together. "Can anyone get a piercing like that?" I point toward my lap. I don't know why I'm being so bold about this. But I'm curious.

"Most people can." He plays with the salt shaker. "We'd have to take a look to see what type of piercing would be best for you."

My face flames at the thought of him taking a look down there. He pushes my root beer toward me and says, "Drink. Before you pass out." He's grinning, though, and I've never seen such a look of confidence on a man. The awkwardness of a moment before has passed. And he's enjoying making me squirm.

"Are there, like, different kinds?" My words don't want to come out of my mouth gracefully.

He nods. He takes my hand in his and drags his thumb across the back. "There are as many kinds as there are types of women."

I take a deep breath.

"Is there, like, a purpose for it?"

He grins. "There can be." He takes a sip of his root beer. "Some people just like the idea of it. Then others like to play with it."

"Play with it?" I choke out. His thumb is still stroking across the back of my hand, and he might as well be touching me right where a piercing might go. Because it's thumping like crazy.

He leans closer to me, speaking softly. "Lips. Tongue. Fingers." He licks his lips again. "Teeth." He arches a brow at me. "I can go on, if you like."

I hold up a hand. If he goes on, I might just spontaneously combust. "No thank you."

"Another time," he says.

He threads his fingers through mine.

"You scare me," I blurt out.

He startles, jerking his hand back from mine. "Me? Why? What?" he asks, leaning forward.

He's worried. I can tell, so I feel the need to fix the error I just made. "I have all these feelings for you," I say.

He sits back, laying a hand on his chest, heaving a sigh in relief. "Oh, you scared me," he breathes. "I thought I offended you with the sexy talk."

"You didn't offend me. But you make me want things I can't have." There. I admitted it. I want him. I want all the things that come with him. But I can't have them.

"I feel like I need to tell you something," he says. He's thinking about his next words, and he's talking very slowly, like the weight of them is hard for him to carry.

"Ok," I say hesitantly.

"I want you more than I want air," he says. My heart starts to beat a tattoo rhythm in my chest. I open my mouth to speak, but he holds up that damn finger. "But I can't act on my feelings. Not while I don't even know your name."

He takes a deep breath and waits for me. I can't say anything. I wouldn't know what to say even if I could.

"I want to take you to bed, and make love to you all night long." He cocks a grin at me. "Lips. Tongue. Fingers. Teeth." He makes a circle motion with his hands. "Should I go on? Or do you understand?"

I nod. I get it. He reaches over and lifts my jaw to closes my mouth. His touch is tender.

"I want to do things to you that you probably couldn't imagine." His blue eyes are dark and the centers big and wide.

"I don't know," I start. I am imagining all sorts of things right now. And the pulse between my legs is thumping so hard I have to push my legs together to ease some of it. It doesn't help.

"But even more than I want to lick you all over and make you cry out my name and swear you see God, I want you to trust me. And you don't. Not yet. But you might one day."

I'm breathing so hard I feel like I just ran a mile. "I trust you," I say.

He shakes his head. "No you don't." He smiles at me, and my heart flips over. "But you might one day."

The waitress brings the receipt to the table, and gives him a pen. I see that she's written her name and phone number on the bottom of the receipt. He tears that part off and gives it back to her. He shakes his head, and tilts his at her, and she looks disappointed. Her heavy bottom lip pokes out.

I look up at her and blink. "I absolutely hate it when skanks try to give my boyfriend their contact information," I say.

Logan chokes, coughing into his fist.

The waitress steps toward me, but Logan gets between us. That's good, because I will take that bitch out. "Have you ever slept with her?"

He looks up at her and takes in her features. "I don't think so," he says quietly, by my ear.

He's slept with that many women that he can't tell one from another?

She huffs away. He tugs me to my feet. "You shouldn't have called her a skank," he says with a laugh.

"What do you call a woman who gives her number to a man who's been holding hands with someone else?" I ask crisply.

"And you shouldn't have called me your boyfriend." He looks down at me as he opens the door of the restaurant for me.

"I'm sorry," I start. "I shouldn't have said that. I just wanted her to go away." And I wanted to stake my claim, even though I had no right to one.

He looks down at me beneath the street light. "You shouldn't have said it because you gave me hope," he says.

I can't speak. I can't utter out a sound.

"Come home with me," he says.

I shake my head.

He sighs heavily. "You know how this is going to end."

"I shouldn't." I really, really shouldn't.

"Fine," he says, and then he bends at the waist and tosses me over his shoulder, just like the night before. Only this time, his hand is on my ass, under my skirt, instead of holding the backs of my legs. It's hot, pressed against my panties.

I can't say a word to him, because he wouldn't hear me. So, I just hang there, all the way to his building, and up four flights of stairs.

He opens the door and walks inside. His brothers are there, and they look up. Sam and Pete snicker, and Paul shoots them a look. Matthew is on the sofa, and he shakes his head.

Logan puts me down. Apparently, I'm not a side show attraction tonight. "Hi," I say tentatively to them all.

"Hi," they call back. They don't get up and rush over to me, not even when he sets me on my feet and steadies me. "You're back," Matthew says as he walks to the fridge.

He looks better tonight. Not quite as green.

Sam walks to the kitchen and Paul snarks at him when he reaches for a beer. He takes a soda, instead, grumbling to himself.

Logan signs something to them. Pete tells him the name of the movie, and it's one I haven't heard of. Logan points to the TV and then to me asking me if I've seen it.

I shake my head. He sets my bag and my guitar on floor, and laces his fingers with mine. He tugs me gently toward the couch. Logan bumps Sam and Pete's knees until they scoot down. There's barely enough space for him, much less for me. "I'm going to go take a shower," I complain.

But he sits down and pulls me into his side, his arm around my shoulders.

Matt gives me a look I don't understand. He doesn't seem completely pleased by my being there. Did I do something to offend him?

But Logan looks down at me and smiles, and then places his lips against my forehead. Matt gets up and goes to his room, but not before shooting me a glance that I couldn't help but take as a warning.

Logan

She fell asleep curled into my side. The credits roll on the TV and I don't want to move. I don't want to set her away from me. My arm is sweating where she's pressed up against me, and her hairline is damp. I reach over and brush her hair back, and she blinks her brown eyes at me. "Is it over?" she asks.

She stretches, her arms raising high above her head.

I nod. The movie's over. But my feelings for her are not. They're just beginning. I like having her on my couch. And I like it even more that she's so soft in my arms.

"Good movie," Paul says.

She looks over at him like she's surprised he's there. Sam and Pete went to bed as soon as the credits rolled, and Matt is in bed, too. "Sorry I fell asleep," she says. She wipes the side of her mouth, and I draw her in to give her a hug. She pulls back all too soon, looking askance at Paul. "I'm going to take a shower," she says.

I nod and help her to her feet. She picks up her bag and goes into the bathroom, closing the door behind her. I flop back onto the couch and cover my face with my hands. This girl will shred me. I already know she will. And I'm jumping in with everything I am despite the fact that I know it.

"Want to talk about it?" Paul asks. Matt comes into the living room and drops down on the sofa beside me.

You too? I sign and then throw my hands up in surrender.

Matt grins and shrugs his shoulders.

You guys like her, right? I ask. Their opinions do matter to me.

Paul nods, while Matt shakes his head. What the fuck? It's like they're at opposite ends of the spectrum.

Matt lays a hand on my knee so I'll look at him. "I like her," he says. He's talking while he signs, which makes it easier to listen. "But how much do you know about her?" His eyebrows draw together.

I don't know anything about her. *Nothing,* I admit. *I don't know a damn thing about her.* I lean forward so I can prop my elbows on my knees. I feel like I can't breathe. *She won't tell me anything. Not even her name.*

"What's she hiding?" Matt asks.

I wish I knew. I flop back against the couch again.

"She looks so familiar to me," Paul says, looking toward the closed bathroom door. He shakes his head. "I wish I could place her."

She busks in the subway tunnels every day, I sign with a shrug.

"It's more than that," Paul says. He shakes his head, like he's shaking his crazy thoughts away. There's no way he could know her from anywhere else.

"She staying over again?" Matt asks.

I nod.

"Don't fall in love with her," Matt warns.

Paul nods his head in agreement. "Fuck her and be done with her," he says.

She's not like that.

Paul exhales heavily. "You haven't slept with her yet, have you?"

I slept with her. I hang my head. *But all we did was sleep.*

"You've never *slept* with anyone, dumbass," Paul says.

I haven't. Not since my mom died. I used to crawl in bed with her when I was young. Her bed was always warm and smelled like her. After she died, I used to crawl in her empty bed just so I could smell her, until Paul changed the sheets and took that room as his own.

I know. I've had plenty of women in my bed. But none of them stayed.

"Stay smart," Paul says, tapping his temple.

"He'd have to be smart to stay smart," Matt says, bumping my knee with his. "He's already half in love with her." He looks down at his fee and then glares at me. "If you don't want her, can I ask her out?"

She's mine! I sign.

He holds his hands up to fend me off. "I know! I know! I said *if*, asshole. I just wanted to see where your head is." He heaves a sigh. "Apparently, you really like this one." He shakes his head. "I don't think she has bad intentions. But I'm worried about you. Be careful."

Matt's in love with April. But she dumped him when she found out he was sick. Self-serving bitch.

"She brought me a bucket when I was sick last night," Matt admits. "It was nice of her."

Paul's eyebrows draw together. "That was you, puking your guts out?" Paul asks.

This is Matt's second round of chemo. The first didn't work. This is his last chance. He nods.

Why didn't you tell us? I ask.

He scrubs a hand down his face. "I'm scared," he admits. He looks me in the eye and then his gaze moves to meet Paul's. "I'm going to fucking die," he says. He grins but there's nothing funny about it. "So you don't have to worry about me asking her out."

"Don't joke about that shit," Paul bites out.

"I'm not joking," Matt says. He's serious.

Paul leans forward and squeezes Matt's knee in his hand. "You have to believe it's going to work. If you don't, you don't stand a chance."

Matt pushes forward to perch on the edge of the sofa. "You guys believe for me, ok?" he says. "Because I'm too fucking tired to do it." He gets up and goes to his room, closing the door behind him.

"When did he start admitting he's afraid?" Paul asks.

I shrug. *It's the first time I've heard him say it.* I look up at Paul. Fear clutches my heart in a death grip. *He's going to be all right, isn't he?*

"I don't know," he admits. He swipes a hand down his face.

I pat my shirt pocket, reaching for my cigarettes.

"Matt has fucking cancer, dumbass," he snarls at me, his hands flying wildly. "And you want to smoke?"

I jerk the pack from my pocket and toss it across the room, into the waste basket.

Paul nods. "Thank you," he signs dramatically. He sags back into the lazy chair.

He's going to make it, right? I ask.

He nods. "Of course he is."

I believe him. Because I can't imagine a life without Matt in it. I won't allow myself to think he's going to die. I just won't. If Matt can't believe he's going to live right now, I'll believe enough for the two of us.

Paul stands up and ruffles my hair, and it quickly changes into a noogie. I brush his hand away. "Don't worry," he says.

The starts down the hallway, and I clap my hands to get his attention. He turns back to me, scratching his stomach. "What?" he asks.

"I want to talk to her," I admit.

His eyebrows draw together. "Yeah?" He shrugs. "So talk."

I want to tell him about her dyslexia, so he won't feel like I've been holding out all these years, but that's not my story to tell. It's hers. I shake my head. It's just too hard to explain. She's making me feel things I've never felt before. She makes me want things.

"I wish you'd just fuck her and get it out of your system. Then you can be done with her. And stop wishing for things you can't have."

She gasps behind him. Her mouth falls open and her eyes fly open wide. I can imagine her gasp, even if I can't hear it. But Paul must hear it. His eyes clench shut. "She's right behind me, isn't she?" he asks. He opens one eye and looks at me.

Kit's wrapped in a towel with another turbaned around her head. Paul turns to her, but I can't hear what he's saying. It had better be a profuse apology.

She glares at him for no more than a moment, and then she ducks into my bedroom and closes the door behind her.

"Shit," Paul signs. "I fucked that up."

He knocks on the bedroom door. He knocks again. His hand wraps around the doorknob, and he starts to turn it, but she's wrapped in a towel. I can't let him in there. I leap over the back of the couch, and put myself between him and the door. I push his chest back and point toward his bedroom door.

"I need to apologize," he says. He's grimacing, and his face is flushed. He didn't mean it. Well, he did mean it. But he didn't. "I didn't know she was there."

I sign the word *tomorrow*. I place my hands on his chest and push him back gently. I couldn't manhandle Paul even if I wanted to. He's a great big son of a bitch. Even bigger than me. And twice as mean. *Tomorrow* I say again. *I got this. I'll talk to her. I'll tell her you didn't mean to hurt her feelings.*

He nods and runs a frustrated hand across the stubble he calls hair. "Sorry," he says.

I nod, and let myself into my bedroom. I lean back against the door. I expect to see her angry and throwing things. Or crying. I really don't know what to expect. I don't know her well enough to have a clue. She's doing neither. She's standing there looking at me. She unrolls the towel from her hair and her locks spill down over her shoulders. Her hair is all wet and tangled and she fluffs it with the towel, blotting it dry. She looks at me, but she hasn't said anything yet.

"He didn't mean that," I start.

"I think he's right," she says. Then she raises her arms, pulls the towel free of where it's tucked between her tits, and drops it to the floor. She kicks it across the room with her delicate little naked toe. She's starkly, completely, beautifully, perfectly, delectably naked. "I think you should fuck me and get it out of your system. Then you can be done with me."

Emily

I'm shaking like a leaf, and I desperately want to cross my arms over my chest. But I force myself to stand there. He looks at my pointed toe as I kick the towel to the side. My heart leaps in my chest, kicking like an angry mule. I expect his eyes to drag up my leg, and then to the rest of me, and my body heats in anticipation of his gaze. But he doesn't. Instead, he rushes to the closet, yanks a t-shirt from a hanger and hands it to me.

I finally do cross my arms, but it's so that I can more effectively glare at him. He looks everywhere but at me, and then bunches the shirt up in his hands, rucking it up until he can slide it over my head. He tugs it down until my hips are covered. Then he steps back, falls against the door and takes a breath.

"Damn," he breathes. Then he grins.

I shove my arms through the armholes of the shirt, and glare at him. He's laughing. Seriously? I arch my brows at him. "Beg your pardon?"

He chuckles into his closed fist, and then shakes his head. "He didn't mean to hurt your feelings." He bends over at the waist, trying to catch his breath, he's laughing that hard. I pick up a pillow and throw it at him, then sit down on the end of the bed and cross my legs. I still don't have any panties on. And I'm too angry to care.

I just stood naked in front of this man and he's laughing. Tears prick the backs of my lashes. "This isn't funny," I say.

He sits down beside me on the bed and turns my chin so that I have to face him. "I didn't see what you said," he tells me. His thumb touches the corner of my eye, and his brows come together in confusion. "Did Paul hurt your feelings?"

I shake my head, pinching my lips together.

He reaches over and lifts my wet hair from the collar of his shirt. "Your hair's still wet," he says, as he picks up a towel. I brush his hand away as he tries to dry my hair.

"It's fine," I say. "Stop," I warn.

"He didn't mean to hurt your feelings," he says.

He thinks Paul hurt my feelings. What crap. Paul didn't hurt my feelings. Logan did, when he completely ignored my offer. And he laughed.

I reach into my bag and pick up my panties, then shimmy into them. Logan looks away, and I roll my eyes. I was naked in front of him. Does he really think I care if he sees me put my panties on? I tug the blanket from the bed and glare at him for a moment, and then I open the door and head for the couch. I'll sleep out there. It's better than sleeping in here with a man who doesn't want me.

Matt's at the kitchen table with his head in his hands when I come out of the hallway. I falter and tug on the length of Logan's shirt. He looks down at my legs and smiles. "I've seen more skin at the club," he says. "You might as well be a nun."

I sigh heavily and throw the blanket onto the edge of the couch. Then I walk into the kitchen for a cup of water. "Can I get you anything?" I ask.

He looks better today. But he still doesn't look good. "No thanks."

"Did you eat anything today?" I ask. Now I sound like Logan, but I can't help it.

"I did," he says with a nod.

"Did you keep it down?" I tilt my head and look at him.

"Some of it," he admits.

Logan walks out of the bedroom and skids to a halt in the kitchen. He looks from Matt to me and back again. He signs something to Matt.

"Dude, you can't talk around her unless you want me to interpret," Matt warns.

Logan clenches his hands together and bites his lips just as hard. He looks like he wants to say something. But he can't. Not with Matt there. "Go to bed, Logan," I say.

Logan shakes his head. He starts to sign, and Matt starts to talk. "He doesn't want you to sleep on the couch," Matt says. Matt sighs heavily. He gets to his feet. "How do you two communicate normally?" he asks, exasperated.

I can't tell him that Logan talks to me. So, I just shrug. Everyone else in this family shrugs all the time. I might as well take up the habit. Become a master at evasion. "He can go fuck himself," I say. "I'm sleeping on the couch."

"Shit, man, what did you do?" Matt asks.

Logan signs something quickly.

"Damn. You should make Paul sleep on the couch." He chuckles. "Seems like he deserves it."

Logan stalks back into his room. Matt looks at me, grinning. "You're turning him inside out," he says.

Apparently not. He didn't even look at me when I was naked.

"What are your intentions with Logan?" he asks. His voice is quiet. He's not threatening me. I think he's genuinely curious.

"I don't have any intentions. He tossed me over his shoulder both times I've been here. It's not like I had much choice in the matter."

"You could have said no," Matt clarifies. He holds up a hand to stop me when I open my mouth to talk. "Paul was just trying to protect him. He's never brought a girl home before. Not one he really likes."

"I'm the first one he won't sleep with, I guess," I murmur, more to myself than to him.

Matt nods. "Yes, you are. That means you're special." He tweaks my nose as he walks by and I make a face at him. He has cancer. I can't be mad at him. Particularly not when he's being so sweet. He turns back to face me. "He's never wanted something real with a girl. Give him time to explore it before you start expecting more from him."

"That's just it," I argue. "I don't expect anything."

"Yes, you do." He looks sorry for me, and it pisses me off.

"Apparently, I'm the only girl in the city of New York that he won't sleep with." I harrumph like a two year old who just dropped her ice cream.

"I can't believe I'm discussing my brother's lack of sexual appetite with his girlfriend," Matt mutters.

"I'm not his girlfriend."

"Oh, honey," he says, shaking his head. "You're his first girlfriend."

I turn to look toward Logan's room. I don't know what to do.

"Don't fuck with him," Matt warns. He's suddenly very direct. And the intensity in his face is almost scary. "And don't break his heart."

"He'd have to love me for that to be an issue."

Matt snorts. "You're clueless, aren't you?" he asks.

"Apparently," I say.

Matt wraps my head in his arm and squeezes me against him, rubbing my head playfully with his knuckles. He stops and sniffs me. "You smell good," he says. He laughs. "We don't have much around here that smells good."

"Thank you," I grumble.

He pops me on the tail and points me toward Logan's room. "Go talk to him," he says.

I yelp and look back at him over my shoulder. I can't believe he just did that.

"That was a 'get your ass in the game' smack. Not an 'I want to see you naked' smack," he warns. I didn't doubt what he meant.

"I don't mess with Logan's women," he says. He told me that the first night.

"It's a brother thing," we both say at the same time.

Matt grins. "Exactly," he says.

When I walk in Logan's room, he's laying back on the bed with his arm laid over his eyes. He doesn't look up when I walk in, so I touch his knee. He uncovers his eyes and lifts his head, looking up at me. His blue eyes blink for a moment, and then he sits up. He tangles his fingers with mine and pulls me closer to him. "Don't sleep on the couch," he says.

"Matt says we should wake Paul up and let him sleep on the couch."

Logan's eyes get wider and he smiles. "I like that idea. But I would rather sleep with you any day."

"You could have fooled me," I spit out.

"What?" he asks. Could he not see my lips? Or did he not understand what I said?

"I was standing stark naked in front of you, Logan. And you didn't have any interest in me." I hold up a hand to stop him when he opens his mouth. "I get it. You don't have feelings like that for me. It's all right."

Suddenly, Logan jerks my hand, rolling me gently onto the bed. His body covers mine, and his face is a breath away from me. "You think I don't like you that way?" he asks. He's looking into my face like he'll find something he's missing there.

"You laughed at me."

"I laughed because the one girl I do want to fuck is naked in my room and I can't have her!" he growls. "It's like divine intervention."

He wiggles a knee between my knees and kicks my legs open wider. He settles there between my thighs and rocks forward so that he presses against my panties. He's hard. So hard.

"I was naked and you wouldn't even look at me," I start. I close my eyes.

"I didn't want to disrespect you," he says.

He rocks his hips against me again, and this time the length of him notches against my cleft. My breath catches.

"I want you so bad it hurts." His voice is quiet, and harder to understand than it normally is.

"You didn't even look at me," I protest.

He sits up on his knees and lifts my leg up by his shoulder. He's not looking at my body. "You have pink toenail polish. And you have a bit of stubble on your legs." He grins. "You can use my razor if you want." His hand slides up my calf, toward my knee, leaving a wake of goose bumps behind. "Your thighs are firm, and you have a generous flare to your hips. His hand slips to the front of my panties, where he drags his thumb back and forth for a moment. "You have this tiny dusting of hair, here." His thumb presses against my cleft and I arch my back to press harder against him. He chuckles. His hands drift up my sides, lifting the shirt. He tugs it up, until it rests just beneath my breasts. He presses a kiss to my belly. My nipples are hard and standing tall. He licks his lips. "Your nipples are pink and puffy and perfect. And your breasts will fit in my hands." He throws the shirt back down, groaning as he lies back down on top of me, rocking his length against me again. "I saw everything," he says. "I was just trying to be a gentleman." He laughs. "You thought I didn't look." He kisses the tip of my nose. "Silly woman," he scolds.

"You looked." That's all I can say. And it comes out as a croak. Thank God he can't hear the quiver in my voice.

"I looked," he admits. "You were naked. And so fucking beautiful that I could barely breathe. Of course, I looked."

"You look at a lot of naked women?" I don't want the answer to that question after it's out of my mouth.

"Not anymore," he breathes against my lips. His lips touch mine, tentatively, and then he retreats. He's making me crazy. His hips press insistently, pushing him closer and closer to my heat. "I haven't seen a single naked woman since the day I met you."

"Do you want to see any naked women?" I ask. My voice is still doing that quavery thing. His hand lies on my throat, almost like he's listening with his fingertips for the sound of my voice.

He shakes his head, looking directly into my eyes. "Just one."

I reach down to tug his shirt over my head, but he stops me with a grunt.

"What?" I ask.

He looks into my eyes. "What's your name?" he asks.

This time, it's me who throws her arm over her eyes. I want to scream. I can't tell him anything. "I can't tell you," I say.

He tugs the shirt back down around my hips. "Then your clothes stay on." He kisses me, his lips nibbling at mine until I'm breathless. "And so do mine."

"Your brother said you should fuck me and get it over with."

He heaves a sigh. "That's because he thinks I'll fuck you and not want to see you anymore. But I can assure you, that's not the case." He presses against me again, rocking against my cleft, the ridge of his manhood pressing against my softness. "Once I get to be inside you, I'll never want to give you up." He kisses the side of my neck, suckling gently as he moves across the front of my throat. His five o'clock shadow abrades my tender skin. But I don't want him to stop.

I reach down to cup him through his jeans, and he stills.

"Don't play with me," he warns. His voice is strong but quiet. "If you want to be my friend, you can be my friend. We can sleep in the same bed, we can have meals together, and we can spend time doing things we both like."

I lift his head so that he's looking at me. "I want to be your friend," I say.

"I want you to be my girlfriend."

"What does that mean?" I cry, slapping the bed with my open palms in frustration.

He looks confused. "I'm not sure. But I think it's the same as being my friend, but I get to make you come." He rocks against me once again. Then he lifts away. I want to scream.

"Where are you going?"

"To get the blanket off the couch. Unless you want me to sleep out there?" He looks unsure.

I want him inside me. But that's not going to happen. "Go get the blanket," I grumble. He chuckles and leaves the room.

My panties are wet. Soaked. I reach into my bag and put on a fresh pair. I'm adjusting them over my hips when he walks back in the room.

"Fresh panties," I explain. "All your fault," I taunt.

He groans, and flops back on the bed. "Why did you have to tell me that?" he asks. He lays there for a minute with his hands clenched. Then he motions me forward and pulls my head down to lie on his chest. He takes a deep breath and hugs me to him tightly, then releases me and relaxes. He picks up a book from beside his night stand and holds it in one hand. He reads quietly to himself.

"What are you reading?" I ask.

He looks down at it and tells me the title. "Will you read it to me?" I ask.

He lifts his head long enough to look at my face and finds that I'm serious. I can learn. And I love books. I just can't read them. I have an amazing memory.

"Start at the beginning?" I ask.

He turns to page one and begins to read. I settle against him, wrapping my arms around his chest, snuggling as tightly against him as I can. And he reads. His voice is strong and sure, and he reads long into the night, long after he's yawning, because I don't want him to stop. When he finally lays the book to the side, I roll toward him and he turns to face me. He tucks me beneath his chin and I can hear his heart beating in his chest. "When you're ready for what I want," he says, "let me know."

I'm ready. I'm ready now. But I'm not ready for the same thing he is. I nod against his chest, and he heaves a sigh. His lips touch the top of my head, soft as a whisper.

***

I wake up the next day and lift my head. Sunlight pours into the room, and I know I've slept much later than I normally would. But then again, we were up really late last night reading. My heart clenches inside my chest when I realize that he hasn't used his voice in eight years, but he spent hours last night reading to me. It makes me feel warm all over, and I look around, wondering where he is. The bed is empty, and there's not even an impression of his head on the pillow. That's probably because we shared the same space last night. I draped myself across his chest, and then we adjusted, and I had my head on his belly. All the time he read, his fingers had trailed across one body part of mine or the other. It was a tiny tickle, but it touched the center of me.

I know he wasn't unaffected by it. He was rock hard, and he had to ball the covers up in his lap more than once. But he ignored it. I ignored it. I wanted to reach over and touch him, but he doesn't want that from me. He wants all of me. And I'm not free to give it away. I'll never be free.

I roll over and brush my hair from my eyes. I still can't get used to the black hair. It's so different from my natural color. Every time I look at myself in a mirror, I have to do a double-take and try to figure out who I'm looking at. Maybe I'll never know.

My eyes land on a sketch pad that's propped against the lamp on Logan's end table. I crawl closer to it on my hands and knees, and close my eyes tightly, wincing when I see that he's drawn a naked woman. She's drawn in pencil, and he has shaded all the parts of her naked body. But what immediately grabs my attention is that there's one streak of color on the whole thing. It's down the left side of her hair. It's blue.

Oh, crap. It's me.

I sit up on the edge of the bed and pick it up. It's me. Definitely me. My arms are down by my sides, and my fists are clenched tightly. There's a look of defiance on my face. I've never seen an artist capture a look like that. But he's done it. There's a towel on the floor beside my toe and my foot is pointed like I just kicked it to the side.

He's drawn shadowing around my boobs, and my nipples are standing tall, sticking out like they've been kissed tight. My stomach clenches and I have to force myself to take a breath. There's a small triangle of hair at the vee between my thighs. I close my eyes. It's almost lifelike.

It's me. He drew me. From memory. At the bottom are some scribbled words. They're written in all caps and the letters are spaced far apart.

I L O O K E D

Yes, apparently he did. There's no doubt about it. He saw me naked. And he remembered every dip, every curve and every strand of hair. Or lack of hair. Yikes. I close the sketch pad so no one else will see it. I'm feeling a bit over-exposed, like he somehow peeled back a layer of me and forced me to look at it as closely as he did.

I can't believe I accused him of not wanting to look at me. He obviously did. He looked closer than anyone ever has. I take a deep breath and sit there for a minute with my eyes closed.

I slide on a pair of jeans beneath Logan's t-shirt and put on a bra. I like his brothers, but I'm not one hundred percent sure who's in the house. And I don't want to walk out there to get a cup of coffee to find everyone dressed appropriately and for me to be the one who's not. Padding around in the middle of the night is one thing. This is different.

I let myself out of the room and look around. The apartment is empty. I'm kind of glad that Logan's not there, since my face is flaming just thinking about how closely he perused my body. If he was there in the flesh, I'd be a puddle on the floor.

I don't think I've ever seen the apartment when it wasn't full of testosterone and male bodies. It's a mess, like usual. I pour myself f a cup of coffee and load the dishwasher, and then clean the countertops. I can't help it. They might not even want me to do it. But I do it anyway. My life is such a mess, and what I want most in the world is to tidy it up. Since I can't tidy my own life, I'll tidy their apartment instead. I remove a rubber band from a stack of mail and twist my hair up out of my face. If I'm going to clean, I'm going to do it right.

I start a load of laundry, and fold what's in the dryer. I don't know which shirt goes to which man, since they're all big boys. So, I just make a neat pile of them and stack them on the kitchen table. The pile grows as the day goes on, and by the end of the afternoon, the house is still empty and quiet, and it's clean from top to bottom. I didn't clean any of their bedrooms, because that would be an invasion of their privacy, and my cleaning at all might be, now that I think of it. I bite my fingernails and look around. They won't be mad, will they?

I go into the bathroom and look beneath the sink. There were cleaning supplies there the other day, and it could use refreshing. I lift a bucket of baby toys out of the way and then I stop. I shuffle through them. There are tiny boats, bath crayons, and a rubber ducky. I give it a squeeze and it goes flat, a hiss of air escaping it. Why do they have baby toys?

The curiosity is killing me. Do they have a little sister? They couldn't possibly. Logan said he lived with four brothers the day I met him. He didn't say anything about a sister. I put the bucket back under the sink, and keep cleaning.

The timer on the dryer goes off, and I fold the last load of laundry, blowing a lock of hair out of my eyes. I look toward the window, and see that the day is nearly gone. So much for busking in the subway. And Fridays are usually my best days, since people just got paid and they're feeling generous. I have wasted the whole day cleaning Logan's apartment, but I feel good about it. I put my hands on my hips and look around the room. I did a good job. I've mopped, and vacuumed, dusted, and put things away. Of course, I had to guess where a lot of stuff goes. The stuff I'm not sure about, I've been putting on the kitchen table with the stacked laundry.

I open a kitchen drawer and stumble back when I see that it's full of condoms. Nothing but condoms. They're in every shape, every size and every color. And every flavor, if the banana on the front of one is any indication. My face fills with heat. Why on earth do they have a drawer filled with condoms? I slam it shut, and walk away. It's none of my business.

I carry the mop bucked toward the sink so that I can dump it. I pick it up, and just as I'm walking across the kitchen floor, the door of the apartment opens, and Logan walks through. Only he's not alone. On his shoulders, there's a blonde with two squiggly pony tails. He ducks to get through the door, and she giggles when he wiggles her feet and pretends to dump her off his shoulders.

He stops in front of the closed door and freezes when he sees me standing there. He must not have expected me to still be there. And I certainly didn't expect for him to have a child. He starts toward me, one hand holding on to her feet tightly at the base of his neck. And the other reaches for me. But I'm so startled by the girl that the bucket of sudsy water slips from my hands.

"Stop!" I warn, because I don't want him to slip with his daughter on his shoulders.

Logan

I'm so damn happy to see Kit that I want to run to her and pick her and spin her around. I wonder if she'd giggle like Hayley does when I jostle her. Probably not. I wasn't sure Kit would still be here, and I was really worried she'd vanished when she didn't come to see me at the tattoo parlor.

Water crashes over the toes of my boots, and Kit rushes to right the bucket. She slumps, looking down at the mess. But her dejection only lasts for a second. She gets herself together and rushes to the table, where there are piles of folded laundry and she grabs towels, throwing them down over the spill.

She's saying something but I can't read her lips. I walk toward her and she warns me to stop, holding up her hands. Her eyes dart to Hayley, and then back to my face, and she doesn't look too happy with me. I set Hayley on the counter and put a cookie in her hands, and she settles there to watch us, her mouth full of chocolate chips. Hayley's three, and she's a cool kid.

I move the towels around with my boots, and Kit drops to her knees to mop up all the water. She pushes the towels around frantically, until it's all cleaned up. Then she throws the wet towels in the mop bucket and starts a load of wash with them in it. She comes back to the kitchen and looks at Hayley, who's still perched on the counter, happily munching on her cookie. Paul's going to have my ass when he finds out I gave her chocolate, but I needed to entertain her for a second.

Kit blows her hair out her eyes with a frustrated breath and glares at me. "You're home," she says. Her hands are on her hips, and she's not wearing any make up and her hair's a mess and she has a line of dirt streaked across her forehead. But she's never looked prettier.

I nod. The knees of Kit's jeans are wet, and her shirt's damp now, too. "What have you been doing?" I ask. I look around. The apartment is clean. And I don't just mean "straighten it up because Grandma's coming over" clean. I mean spotlessly clean. Like showroom floor clean. But better. It smells nice. And it looks nice. And she's here. God, I'm so happy she's here.

She shrugs. "How was your day?" she asks. Her gaze zips between me and Hayley. Hayley's making a mess, but I don't care.

"Better, now," I admit. I feel like someone took a weight off my chest when I walked into the room and saw her here. I reach for Kit, and squeeze her to me, kissing her on the forehead. She scrunches up her face, and pushes back from me, her gaze jumping to Hayley again.

"Who's that?" she asks warily.

I wet a kitchen towel and wipe Hayley's mouth and hands clean. She hasn't gotten it on her dress yet, but I know it'll happen any second. Her mother will shit a brick if we send her back with dirty clothes. I tickle Hayley's tummy and she giggles, her belly clenching as she arches into my hands. "This is Hayley."

Hayley looks a little confused, and I pick her up, putting her on my hip. She wraps around me, and one hand covers my mouth. I kiss her palm and make noises at her. She wiggles in my grasp. She's probably confused about the noises coming out of my mouth. I've never talked in front of her before.

"How old is she?"

"How old are you Hayley?" I ask her, jostling her on my hip.

She holds up three fingers.

"Three?" Kit says, like she's amazed. "Such a big girl." Kit looks at me. "Does she talk?"

"I don't know," I admit. Her lips are really hard to read, so I don't know if she talks or if she's just making noises. She knows how to sign simple words like food, milk, bath, water, and other things she needs. She and I do pretty well together. Most of it is just me trying to figure out what she needs, but Hayley doesn't seem to mind. "She might."

Kit bends down to her level and asks, "Do you talk?" Kit smiles and she's so damn pretty making faces at Hayley that I want to kiss her. I grab Kit quickly around the waist and jerk her into my side with a hand on her hip, and she laughs, looking up at me. I kiss her on the forehead and Hayley bats the side of my face with her open palm. "I don't think she likes that," Kit says, backing away from me.

"She'll have to get used to it." Kit's eyes meet mine, and then they skitter away.

"She's adorable," she says, but she's not looking in my eyes. We'll have to talk about that later.

"What happened to the apartment?" I ask, a grin tugging at my lips. She looks unsure of herself as she brushes her hair back from her face. That streak of dirt is still across her forehead and I reach out to wipe it away with my thumb.

She wrings her hands together and doesn't look me in the eye. "I did a little cleaning."

I take her chin in my hand and tip her face up to mine. "I'm glad you're still here."

"You're not mad, are you?" she asks. She bites her bottom lip.

"That you're here?" I ask softly. "I'm fucking ecstatic."

She scowls and looks at Hayley. "Language," she says. "And I meant about the cleaning. I started it this morning and... well... I couldn't stop."

"You shouldn't have."

"I know," she says with a shrug. "I wanted to. And I sort of feel like I owe you guys for letting me stay here."

"You don't owe us anything," I try to explain. I tug her to me again. I like the feel of this girl in my arms so much more than I should. "I like having you here."

She smiles up at me, and then Hayley starts to jump in my arms. She's excited, and reaches over my shoulder. I look back and Paul's coming in the door. She gets so excited to see Paul.

Kit starts smiling beside me, and then she grins, and air escapes her in one big relaxed breath. I'm not sure what that's about.

"You met Hayley, I see," Paul says to Kit. She nods as Paul takes her from me. "See, Hayley," he says to his daughter, "now you won't be the only girl in the house." He dances around in a circle with her. I'm reading his lips, because it's really hard to sign when your hands are full of baby. I can't see what he says when he dances around in a circle, but whatever it is makes Kit smile.

Kit points a finger at Paul and smiles. "She's yours?" she asks.

Paul looks from me to her. "You're not trying to use my daughter to score with chicks again, are you?" Paul asks, punching me in the shoulder. "I can't let him take her to the grocery store. He gets too much attention from the ladies."

Paul looks around the apartment and grins. "What the fuck happened here?" he asks.

Kit scowls at him, too. "Language," she says, looking toward Hayley. She's smiling now, though, and she looks like she's taking deep breaths, which she wasn't doing when I first walked into the house.

"Who cleaned?" Paul asked. He wipes a spot on Hayley's cheek with his thumb and says, "And who gave you chocolate?" He scowls at me. I shrug my shoulders and grin.

Kit cleaned up. I pull her into my side, and she wraps an arm around my waist, lays one hand on my chest, and looks up at me. *Isn't she amazing?*

Paul looks from me to her and back again, sticks his finger down his throat like he's going to hurl and walks away with Hayley toward his bedroom. He looks back at me long enough to say, "You're going to be late for work if you don't hurry." He looks down at Hayley. "Tell Uncle Logan he's going to be late." He shows her the sign for late and she does it. She's adorable when she signs. They disappear into his bedroom and I look down at Kit. I bend my head and touch my lips to hers. I don't want to pull back, but I do have to hurry. "I have to go out," I say.

Her brows raise, and she looks wary. "Out?" she says.

I nod. "I have to work tonight. Do you want to go with me?"

She looks down at her wet shirt, and brushes a lock of hair from her forehead. "I haven't even had a shower today."

"How quickly can you get ready?" I ask, looking at my watch. I have thirty minutes before I have to be there.

Emily

Warm water sluices over my body, and I force myself to hurry up. Logan is probably dancing from foot to foot in the living room waiting for me so he won't be late for work. Apparently, he's a bouncer at some club around the corner on Friday nights. And he wants me to go with him.

I hear the door to the bathroom open and I freeze. "Matt?" I call. He's the only one who might come into the bathroom with me, and that's only if he's sick.

I open the bath curtain an inch and look out. Logan is standing there, looking at me. He changed clothes, and now he's wearing a pair of jeans, his boots, and a blue t shirt that says "Bounce(r)" on the front of it. It strains across his broad shoulders. His eyes are a startling shade of blue against the azure shirt, and he looks at my face as I poke my nose through the curtain. My hair is full of suds, and soap is burning one of my eyes. "Is something wrong?" I ask.

He shakes his head and smiles at me. He doesn't say anything else, but he stands there with one shoulder against the wall with his arms crossed. "I have a question," he finally says.

I lean back and wash the soap from my face and hair, and then poke my head back through, blowing water from my lips. "Ask it," I say.

"It bothered you when you thought Hayley was mine," he says. His face doesn't change. He's still appraising me closely. But he's not leering, or trying to look at my naked body. He's totally respectful, just like always.

It did bother me when I thought Hayley might be his. They have the same deep blue eyes, and their hair color is similar. And he was so familiar with her. But then she's called Paul Daddy, and everything was suddenly all right. I know he can't read my lips unless I stick my head out of the shower. "What makes you say that?" I ask.

He snorts. "I read people every day, all day, and I have to tell how they feel by the way they hold themselves, rather than the inflections in their voices. And something tells me that you didn't like thinking that Hayley was mine."

He looks closely at me, and I know he's still appraising my reactions.

"Either you don't like kids, or you didn't like the idea of me having a kid." He shuffles his feet. "I just wanted to tell you that I might not be able to hear, but I'm fully capable of taking care of a child. If I wasn't, Paul wouldn't leave her with me."

He heaves a sigh, and then he turns to walk out of the door. I call his name, but he doesn't hear me. So, I jump out of the shower and grab for the towel, letting it fall open in front of me, but I don't have time to wrap it around me. I clutch it to my chest, and grab his arm. He turns back toward me, one eyebrow rising as he looks at me.

"It wasn't that I don't think you're capable of taking care of her," I say. "It wasn't that at all."

"Then what was it?" he asks.

It's so hard to explain, but if I don't tell him the reason it bothered me, he'll go on thinking it's because I think he can't do the kid justice with his disability, and that couldn't be farther from the truth.

"I thought she was yours," I say with my eyes closed. He tips my chin up with an insistent finger.

"What?" he asks.

"I thought she was yours," I repeat. This time, I make sure he can see my lips; although that's the last thing I want him to see me say. "I thought she was your daughter."

He grimaces. "Again, I'm fully capable of taking care of a child. I can watch the lights on a monitor just like anyone else. And changing diapers doesn't require my ears." He's irritated. And I can tell it. "She cries, and I can figure out what she needs."

"It's not that." God, I'm so stupid. I bury my wet face in my hands and he urges them down, watching my lips. "I was jealous," I admit. There. I said it.

"Jealous?" he asks. "Of Hayley? She's three, for Christ's sake."

"I know." I don't know how to tell him. "It made me wonder what kind of a stupid woman would ever let you go." And made me realize someone else has had him. Probably a lot of someone's. A lot of someone's I can't compete with.

He chuckles, the air in the room lightening. "That's all it was?" he asks, his voice incredulous. That's not really all it was. I also wondered how in the world I would do sharing him with someone else. But he's not mine to share, is he? Not really. Not at all.

I nod. "That's all. It's not because you're deaf. I was just jealous." I shrug. "I'm sorry. Really, really sorry. I didn't mean to offend you." I want to tell him that I want him all to myself. But I'm not free to do that.

"I don't have any kids," he says. "In case you were wondering."

The thought hadn't even crossed my mind until I saw Hayley. "All right."

"I want kids someday," he says. His voice is soft and he's looking into my eyes. "Do you?"

"I don't know." The idea of trying to help a kid of my own with homework, and spelling, and school is sometimes overwhelming to me. "I don't think I'd make a great mother."

His lips press against my forehead and he lays his hands on my naked hips. I draw in a breath. My hips are bare and his hands cover them completely as he pulls me toward him. The towel that was draped in front of me gets sandwiched between our bodies.

"I'm glad you came to talk to me," I croak out.

He dips his head, and kisses the side of my jaw. I don't even think about it; I tilt my head to give him better access. "I am, too," he says against my skin.

I could say more, but he's not looking at my face. He's not looking at anything. His eyes are closed. His hands slide around to my bottom and he lifts me against him. "I have never wanted to have sex with someone I care about," he says.

He's hard against my belly, and I can barely think or take in a breath.

I lift up his shirt, and lay my hands on his stomach. The muscles ripple under my fingertips. I want to touch him. I want to touch him so badly. "Pretend I'm someone you don't care about," I say impulsively.

He must have seen my lips, because he stills. "You think I can do that?" he asks, his voice incredulous. He lifts a hand and runs it through his hair. "I don't think you realize how very much I like you."

He likes me a lot if the rather impressive size of him pressed against my stomach is any indication.

He must read my mind, because he sighs heavily, and says, "I don't mean like that." A muscle ticks in his jaw for a moment, and then he steps back from me, lifts the towel and wraps it around my naked body. "I've had sex. Lots of sex. But I've never had it with anyone who matters to me."

He's only known me a few days. "Why do I matter so much? What makes me different?" Now I'm dying to know.

He shakes his head.

"Tell me," I prompt.

"I've been locked in my own world for a really long time," he says. "I have an excuse to keep people away, because of my disability. And then I saw your tattoo." I turn his wrist over and trace my finger across it. He shudders at my touch, closing his eyes tightly. "And I felt like maybe, just maybe, we were each locked in our own little worlds and we could let each other out."

He's pouring his heart out here, and I have nothing of encouragement to say. "But there's nothing wrong with you," I start. I look up at him, and he looking at me with a warning in his eyes.

"That's not true." He shakes his head.

"There's nothing wrong with you. So, we're not on equal footing, and we never will be."

He shakes his head again, like there's something on the tip of his tongue that he wants to say but won't.

"I can't read. I can't get a job. I can't go to school. I can't do any of the things my family wanted for me." Actually, they'd wanted me to get married and have babies, because all I was good for was being a trophy wife. But I refused. That's why I left. They'd compartmentalized me, deciding I couldn't play my music because it was "beneath our class" and I couldn't further my education, because it was too hard for them to watch me struggle. It was all about them. Always about them.

"Don't underestimate your own value, dummy," he says.

I stiffen. I hate that word. Absolutely hate it. He stiffens when I do.

"What?" he asks. "What's wrong?"

"Don't ever call me a dummy, Logan," I say, my teeth grinding together so hard they hurt.

"Oh, God, I'm so sorry," he rushes to say. He takes my face in his hands, holding it tightly as he looks into my eyes. "I didn't mean it." He chuckles, but there's no mirth in the sound. "It's a term of endearment in our family. I didn't mean to hurt your feelings. Really I didn't. I don't think you're stupid. You have a fucking learning disability. But you're not stupid. I know that."

I wish I knew it. He sounds so sure about it. "It's all right," I say, but I'm already pushing back from him. Tears are pricking at the backs of my lashes.

"Don't pull away from me," he warns.

That makes me laugh. "I'm not the one who's always pulling away, Logan," I remind him. I push him back again, but he's not having any of it. Suddenly, his hands clutch my bottom and he hoists me up onto the bathroom countertop.

"Forgive me," he says.

I nod, and he kisses the corners of my eyes where tears have formed. That word hurts me. It always has. And it was the final straw that made me leave my parents' house. That word and others like it. I've heard them for too long.

He bends his head and his lips touch mine. He licks into me, his tongue soft but insistent. I lay my palm flat on the side of his face and he keeps kissing me. He's taking my mind off that word. I already know what he's doing. I applaud him for it. Because he's stealing the pain along with my wits.

He jerks the towel from between us, and looks down at my naked body. I'm perched there on the countertop, and he stands between my legs. He licks his lips, and my heart beats double time. God, he's sexy. I pull his mouth back to mine, and he allows it, but not for more than a moment. Then his head dips, and his mouth moves down my body. He's not gentle. He's rough. His five o'clock shadow rubs against my skin as he touches something inside me that I didn't even know existed.

"Do you want me to stop?" he asks, lifting his head to look into my face.

I shake my head. "Don't stop," I say. I thread my fingers into his hair, and hold him tight to me, tugging his hair gently. My head falls back, and I lean against the mirror, watching his face as he sucks on the turgid flesh. His other hand slides down my belly. Logan raises his head, and buries his face in the curve of my neck as explores my body.

If he doesn't stop, I'm going to shatter. "Logan," I say. He can't see my lips, so I tug his head up until he looks at me. I can barely get the words to form on my lips. "Together?" I ask. I start to work at the button on his jeans and he brushes my hands away.

He looks deep into my eyes and asks, "What's your name?"

I can't answer. I don't answer. I close my eyes tightly and pretend I didn't hear, because the things he's doing to my body are mind-altering.

Logan is pleasuring me without taking anything at all for himself. I bite back an oath. "Oh, God!" I cry as pleasure washes over me.

I lie back limply against the mirror, and pull him up to face me. "Your turn," I say, and I reach for the button of his jeans.

He shakes his head. "No."

"What?" I don't understand.

He lifts me to stand in front of him.

"You don't want me?" I ask.

"Fuck, girl, I want you more than I have ever wanted anyone or anything." He presses his forehead against mine and he's breathing hard. His lips touch mine softly, but there's an urgency there, too. He bends over and picks up the towel, wrapping it around me, tucking it tightly between my breasts. Then he opens the door, shoves me out into the hallway, and locks the bathroom door behind me.

Logan

Fuck!

I scrub my hand down my face, and then run my fingers through my hair, squeezing my head in my hands like a big pimple that's ready to burst. That's not the only thing that's ready to burst.

I've never been as fucking turned on as I am right now. Kit was wet, and warm, and she was willing. She would have let me fuck her right here on the countertop if I'd said yes. I know she would have. And she wouldn't have had any regrets. But I would. Although right now, I'm rethinking my decision to put her outside the door. I reach for the handle and get ready to turn it so I can beckon her back into the room, but I jerk my hand back.

I desperately needed to take that look off her face, and the only thing I could think of was to put her mind on something else. But now I can't get my mind off the look on her face when I touched her. Good God, that girl can undo me.

My junk is so hard I could pound nails with it.

The door vibrates as someone pounds on it. Probably Paul telling me to hurry up so I won't be late for work. But my dick's so hard that I can barely stand up straight, much less walk.

I run my hands through my hair again. Deep breaths.

Shit. I'll never get out of here this way.

I take a towel from under the sink and lay it in front of me, and unzip my jeans. This won't take but a second. Because I know I'll think about her while I do it.

She'd cried out once. I'm sure of it. I could feel her throat move through the side of my cheek. It was a soft vibration, and it makes my heart trip just remembering it.

I shouldn't do this, but I can't avoid it. I'm too far gone. It only takes a second and I sink back down onto my heels, spent. I lean heavily against the door, trying to catch my breath. The door shakes with the pounding of a heavy fist. I wash my hands, and throw the towel in the hamper. Shit. I'm glad I did that. But I wish it had happened differently.

I tuck myself back into my jeans, and I'm still semi-hard, but not so hard that I can't walk. I open the door, and Paul greets me with an arched brow. "Better?" he asks, grinning.

Fuck you, dumbass, I sign.

"Fuck you," he repeats, laughing. "Oh, wait. You already got fucked." He tilts his head at me. "How was it?"

I jerk him into the bathroom with me. *I didn't fuck her.*

He rolls his eyes. "Yeah, tell it to someone who couldn't hear her crying out in here." He pushes against my chest playfully. "Next time, warn a guy so he can leave. That shit was loud."

What was loud? I'm confused.

Very dramatically, he signs, "Oh, God! Oh, God! Oh, God! Logan! Logan! Logan!" He punches me again. This time it hurts. I rub at the spot. "That shit would have been hot if it hadn't been my brother on the other side of the door. As it was, it was just awkward."

I couldn't hear her. Sorry. I am. Well, sort of.

"No shit," he says. He's looking very closely at me. "You all right?"

I nod. Then I shake my head. *Fuck, I don't know.*

"What's wrong?"

She's making me crazy, man. Stark-fucking crazy.

"You just got laid, and you're complaining?" He waves his hands in dismissal. "I don't even want to hear it. Do you know how long it's been for me? Shit, asshole. You don't get to be all torn up inside when you just got some."

I didn't get any.

"Shut up. And stop rubbing it in."

I run a frustrated hand through my hair and close my eyes.

He taps my chest with his open palm, forcing me to open my eyes. "Wait. You're serious."

I nod. *I said something stupid to her. She was crushed. And it was all my fault.*

"So..." he prompts

So, I wanted to make her feel better. I'm not giving you details.

"It's like you're being re-virginized. That shit's fucked up." He has this mock look of abjection on his face.

I can't hold back my grin. *Tell me about it.*

"You're going to be late for work," Paul warns.

Shit. I am going to be late for work. I run out of the bathroom just as Hayley runs in. Paul picks her up and dances around with her in his arms. He has her every other Friday until the next Friday. And he loves every second of it.

Pete's standing beside Kit in the living room. "You ready?" he asks.

Kit's shuffling from foot to foot, avoiding my eyes. I walk over to her, tip her face up to mine and kiss her. It's a kiss full of promises of what could be. And what's not possible yet. She's breathless and clutching my shoulders when I pull back. "Thank you," she says. She signs it at the same time and my heart swells.

Ready, I sign to Pete.

He follows us into the hallway and I catch him looking at Kit's ass. *Knock it off*, I sign to him.

He grins and shrugs. *I can't help it.*

I can, I warn. I mock punching my fist into my open palm.

He looks away somewhat sheepishly. I motion for him to look at me. *Help me take care of Kit tonight? In case I get busy with something.*

Pete nods. He understands exactly what I mean.

Emily

The name of the club is Bounce. Logan leads me by my fingertips through the back door, but on the way from the street, I see a huge line out front, and a few men about Logan's size watching the door. This place is nothing like I expected. It's a lot bigger.

A big, burly guy in an apron stops us as we walk inside the rear entrance and puts a hand in the middle of Logan's chest. He looks at me and lifts his brow.

Logan starts to sign something and Pete translates. "She's with me." Pete sheepishly looks over at me and points a thumb toward Logan. "Well, with him," Pete admits. "She's 19," Pete interprets. The guy motions over a man with a stamp pad and he stamps the word "no" on the back of my hand. I roll my eyes. Seriously?

"It's a bar sweetheart. I'll get in all sorts of trouble if someone serves you when they shouldn't." He has him stamp Pete's hand too.

I nod. I understand.

"Is she deaf, too?" he asks.

Logan shakes his head.

I think he says something like "flavor of the night" as he walks away, rolling his eyes. Pete goes with him.

Logan leads me to the end of the bar and shoves a really big guy off his stool. The man teeters, complains, and turns to find Logan standing behind him. The man holds up both hands like he's surrendering to the cops, turns and walks away. "Why did you that?" I ask.

He shrugs. "You needed a seat."

He says it like I needed a soda. "But you just shoved him off the chair."

Logan follows him with his yes. "He didn't care."

"He didn't care because he thought you would kick his butt if he said anything."

He nods. Like he would kick his butt. Seriously?

"What?" he asks. He pats the stool. I slide onto it slowly and look at him.

"You want me to stay here?" I point to the stool. The bar. The general area.

He nods. He tips my face up so that I look at him. "Don't drink anything unless the bartender gets it for you. Do you understand?"

Not really, but I nod.

"I'm serious," he says.

"Where are you going?"

"To work." He presses his lips to my forehead, holding there for a moment. Then he bends his head and says close to my ear. "Just so you know -- I can still taste you on my lips." He looks down toward my lap. Heat floods my face. I'm probably as red as a tomato, but I force myself to look into his eyes.

"Wish I could say the same."

He groans, pushes back from me, winks, and walks away.

I look down at the bar counter, and see the perky blonde who's making drinks. She shoots me the stink eye and says, "What can I get for you?"

"Root beer?" I ask. She raises a brow, nods, and pours one from the tap on the bar.

"How do you know Logan?" she asks as she slides my drink over to me.

The words "he's my boyfriend" come unbidden to my lips. But I bite them back. "I'm staying with the boys for a bit."

Her brows shoot up toward her hairline. "Really?"

I nod, taking a sip of my root beer. "Thanks," I say absently, pointing toward the drink.

She drops two cherries with stems into it and smiles. "I'm Abby." She holds out her hand and I take it. She has a firm grip. I like that.

"Kit," I say. "So, are you one of the thousands of women Logan has slept with?" I ask. I try to make a flippant sound, but if the look on her face is indication, I fail. I don't really want the answer. But then again, I do.

She laughs. "Honey, I have more respect for myself than that." She looks at me for a moment as she pours someone else a beer with a perfect head. "You?"

I feel much better about her knowing she hasn't slept with him. "No. But girl, do I want to." I force a chuckle that I don't really feel past my lips.

"He has that effect on all the girls." She laughs. "Hang in there."

I don't want to be like all the girls.

Someone taps the bar in front of her rudely, and she looks up scowling. "Don't ever bang on my fucking bar again, asshole," she says, but there's a smile under her words, I can tell.

"Oh, come on, Abby," he says. "You know you love it when I bang you."

Snickers erupt around the bar. He leans over the bar and she stands up on her tiptoes, putting all her weight on her arms, so she can touch her lips to his. She points to me. "Ford, this is Kit."

Ford looks over at me and smiles.

"Kit came in with Logan," Abby explains. She shoots him an odd look and he narrows his eyes at her, and then looks over at me.

"Say it ain't so," he says with a laugh.

I press my lips together, not sure what he's insinuating.

"It's about time somebody caught that bastard." He laughs, rubbing his hands together with excitement. "Payback's a bitch," he says. Then he saunters off into the crowd.

"Ford works with Logan in the front," she explains in between pouring drinks. She takes a twenty from a guy and presses it down her top. I can see the tip of it sticking up from her cleavage. And so can her customer. He licks his lips. "Oh, did you want change?" she asks sweetly. He shakes his head, laughs and walks away.

"Have you worked here long?" I shout. The band is just getting started on the stage, tuning their instruments and playing some snippets of music. I turn around to look toward them. The lead singer is already shirtless. But the crowd seems to love it.

"About a year," she says. She's working quickly to fill drinks, and the club is getting busier and busier. I almost wish I could go and help her. I feel pretty useless sitting on the sidelines like this with nothing to do.

"Who's the band?" I ask, jerking a thumb over my shoulder.

She shrugs. "They're new."

I hear the beginnings of *Free Bird* start to play and my fingers itch. I swipe the tip of my finger across the calluses on my thumb and wish it was me on that stage. But it can't be. They're just doing cover songs, anyway. But they're songs that make my fingers twitch and make my heart start to beat faster.

I turn around to watch them.

They're really very good. But there's one problem. Their lead guitarist is stinking drunk. They barely got through their warm up, and he's already stumbling over the cords. Their bassist turns to glare at him, and he grins and keeps on playing. But he can barely stay on his feet. He motions to a waitress and she brings him a shot. He tips it back and keeps on playing.

The bass guitarist is pissed. I can tell. I would be too. You don't mess with the music. Ever. I'm itchy on the stool, and I want to go and take the guitar from him and take over. I force myself to sit still.

Logan stalks close to me from across the room and stops half way. "You ok?" he mouths. I nod at him and shoo him away with my hands. He grins at me, and stays where he can look my way. I hope he's not planning to hover all night.

I twitch for a completely different reason when I see a girl walk up to Logan. She's wearing a short skirt and a skimpy top, and her boobs are sitting up like they're stacked on a shelf for people to look at. Logan's eyes skim across her chest, and she lays her hand on his arm, leaning close to him. I scoot to the edge of the chair, watching to see how he reacts. He watches her lips for a moment, and then puts his hands on her shoulders and pushes her back. She scowls. He takes a step back from her, and my heart thrills.

"Damn," Abby says. "Never thought I'd see that happen."

I look over at her. "What do you mean?"

"I've never seen him push one away."

Logan looks over at me and winks.

The girl glares at me, and turns to say something sharp to him. He looks at her kindly, but there's no heat in his gaze. At least not the kind she was looking for. She huffs off.

Suddenly, the band's amp screeches loudly and their lead guitarist stumbles, falling to his knees. His buddies stop playing and try to stand him up, but he just lays there laughing.

The crowd starts to shout, pushing toward the stage. They are not happy. And I can't say I blame them.

I motion to Logan, and he rolls his eyes as he walks toward the stage. The crew staggers the lead guitarist to his feet and lifts the guitar strap over his head, but he's too wobbly to stand. Logan bends, shoves his shoulder into the man's middle, and hoists him over his back. Logan winks at me as he walks toward the back of the bar and disappears behind a curtain. The band members are huddled in a circle, trying to figure out if they can continue or not without their lead guitarist.

My fingers twitch and I wiggle my feet, trying to keep away. But it's impossible. I slide from the stool, my legs wobbly as I walk over, and very nonchalantly step onto the stage. My heart is pounding in my ears and I couldn't utter a sound if I wanted to, my throat is so tight. But I pick up the abandoned guitar, slide the strap over my head, and look at the band members. I pull my pic out of my pocket and hover over the steel strings. One of them reaches to take the guitar from me. But I start to play before he can.

Sweet Child of Mine rolls off my fingertips, the sound of it filling the space, and the men step back, aghast at the little girl who's playing the big boys' guitar. Truth be told, it's too big for me, but I don't let that stop me. "We going to play or what, boys?" I yell. But I don't stop playing, no matter what. The crowd is hooting, and I do a quick show for them.

The boys of the band all rearrange themselves, and the lead singer comes to me and asks, "What can you play?"

"I can play anything you can sing," I say with a laugh. My blood is surging in my veins, and the rhythm of the music is taking me away with it.

"Can you be more specific?" he asks. But he's smiling and watching my fingers as they fly around on the guitar. He shakes his head. "Never mind."

He goes back to the mic and says, "We have a surprise for you, folks!" He motions toward me. "She's a whole lot prettier than our usual lead guitarist, don't you think?"

The crowd yells and claps. I keep playing, until I wind down *Sweet Child of Mine*. I stop and look up the lead, grinning. "What's next?" I ask.

He raises a brow. "*Hotel California*?" he asks.

I nod. I was playing that when I was eight. But I wait for the drummer to pick up the beat, and then I fall in with it. Their bass guitar duels with me for a minute and then we find a rhythm.

I haven't had this much fun in a long time. Not since I left my band back home. I forgot how much I missed this.

We finish up the song and the lead singer mouths at me, "*Welcome to the Jungle?*"

I nod, laughing. I look out over the crowd and see Logan leaning against a post in the middle of the room. His arms are crossed over his chest, and his mouth is open slightly. I blow him a kiss and he shakes his head, smiling. Goodness, that boy is pretty. He gives me a thumbs up and walks away.

I wish I could share this with him, because this is the best feeling ever. The fans, the sound, the way I feel complete when I do this... there's nothing that compares. I'm not scared. Not in the least bit. I love this. I love music. I love the guitar. And I'm afraid I'm a little bit in love with Logan.

Logan

I turn around to watch Kit as she plays. Her cheeks are all rosy, and she's smiling. Every now and then, they give her a quick solo, and she strums the guitar, dancing around, her knees bending as she works it. By the way the crowd's going crazy, I'd guess she's really good at this.

I can feel the thump of the music in the floor and on the walls, and I stop and rest my hand on one of the speakers.

Kit's hair is all wet, and her face is shining. She's never looked more beautiful to me. This is obviously what she was born to do. And I can't help but wonder why she's busking in a subway for pennies rather than doing this full time. This is where her future lies. This is her passion.

I'm happy just watching her. And I have to keep reminding myself to keep an eye on the crowd, rather than both my eyes on her.

Someone chucks my shoulder and I look over to find Pete standing beside me grinning. "Damn, she's good," he says. He plays some air guitar, and I can't help but laugh at him. He waves at me and says, "Hell, I'll leave it to the pro." He points a finger toward Kit. "Did you know she could do that?"

I shrug. *I knew she could play. But they apparently think she's really good.* I motion to the crowd.

I watch as the lead singer walks toward Kit and says something in her ear. He's shirtless and sweaty, and she brushes him away like he's a pesky fly. He goes, but he's laughing when he does it, and I don't like it. I don't like it at all. I stand up taller.

"He's not worth it," Pete says.

I know. But I still don't like it.

"You got it bad for this one, don't you?" he asks. He's smiling, but his question is serious.

I nod. I don't need to say more than that. I do have it bad for this girl.

The band breaks, and Kit wipes her hairline with her forearm. The lead singer walks toward her, but I go that direction and hop onto the stage before he can get to her. He nearly bumps into my back. But he stops and goes the other way.

"Oh my God!" she says, excitement in her eyes as she jumps in place in front of me. "Did you see that?" she asks.

Then she grabs my shoulders, jumps, and wraps her legs around my waist. She kisses me. She tastes like root beer and excitement as she licks into me. I hold her ass, and jerk her tighter against me. The owner of the club waves and I catch him out of the corner of my eye. He jerks his thumb toward the back of the club. I nod and carry Kit in that direction. But she's all hyped up on nerves and attitude. And she hasn't taken her lips from mine. I carry her with her legs still wrapped around my waist into the storage room, and back her up against the wall. She's tangling her tongue with mine, and I don't ever want her to stop.

She finally pulls back and looks at me, her hands clutching my face. "Did you see that?" she asks.

"See what?" I have lost all my wits in her kiss.

"Me playing. Did you see it?"

I nod, nuzzling my nose into her neck. "You were amazing."

"I know! Wasn't I? Oh my God, I want to go back out there." She unclenches her legs from around my waist and drops her feet to the floor. She starts to pace back and forth across the room, chewing on her fingernail. I can't see her lips moving at all, but I lean against the wall and smile at her. "What's so funny?" she asks, stopping to look at me.

"Nothing," I say. I walk to her and brush her sweaty hair from her neck. "You're just so fucking beautiful." She shivers as I blow across her neck.

Her hand comes up to cover mine where it lays on her shoulder, and I get more comfort from that little touch than I ever have from a girl I've been inside. "Thank you for bringing me here," she says.

"Thank you for coming with me."

"I haven't had this much fun in a really long time," she admits. She's glowing.

I lean down and kiss her, because she's that damn pretty. She hears something from the doorway, and turns to look that way. "I'll be right there," she says, holding up a finger. She looks up at me. "They're ready to get started again."

"I have to get back to work, anyway. The owner just sent us back here because he was afraid I was going to fuck you on the stage."

She covers her mouth with her hand. "So, they think we're having sex back here. Are you serious?" Her eyes are wide.

I can't keep from grinning. "Probably."

"Do you do that back here often?" she asks.

I freeze. I don't want to answer her. Because I have done it. She doesn't push for an answer. But she heaves a sigh and shoves herself away from me. I feel the loss of her immediately. "Don't do that," I say, taking her face in my hands. "I can't change my past."

She looks deep into my eyes and says, "I know. I didn't ask you to. I just have to go back on stage." She kisses me softly. "Can we come back to this later?" she asks, grinning. She's nearly vibrating with excitement.

She's not mad at me. Thank God. "We can come back to this as often as you want." Any time. Any place.

She darts away from me, and I tug on her fingers to hold her back. She pulls back from me slowly and I ache with wanting to jerk her back into my arms. But she turns and runs away.

She hops back up on the stage and I follow her. The lead singer turns to her, scowling. "You and Logan, huh?" he asks. I can read his lips from where I'm standing.

She grins and nods her head.

He says something that looks like, "Figures," before he scowls and turns toward me. I point to her and point to my chest and mouth the word "mine" at him. He gets it. He totally gets it. He might not want it to be true. But he knows she's not in his future. She's my future.

I go see Abby and get Kit a root beer. She's been sweating up there for an hour, and they have another set to do. I point to the root beer lever on the fountain and raise my brows. "For you?" Abby asks, with a pointed finger as she fills a glass. I point to Kit. She nods and drops two cherries into it. I turn to take it to Kit and Abby tugs on my sleeve. "Where did she learn to play like that?" Abby asks.

I shrug. I have no idea where she learned to play. All I know is that she's good. I can tell by the way the crowd is reacting to her. My heart is filled with pride for her. And it's filled with a lot more. A lot more that she's probably not ready to address yet.

I take her root beer to her and stand by the side of the stage to wait until she's done with the song. But she marches down the steps, her fingers flying over the strings, and she leans over, taking the straw into her mouth. She sucks it greedily, and there's not a man in the room who's not envious of me right that moment. She never stops playing, but she drains the glass. Then she smiles at me, kisses me quickly and struts back up the steps and onto the stage. Great. Now I have a hard on and so does every man within a twenty foot radius. Suddenly, she runs back down the steps. She nods toward a cherry in the glass and I lift it to her lips. She takes it against the tip of her tongue and closes her lips around it. She pops it off the string with a gentle tug. She nods to the other, and looks at my lips. She taunts me with her grin, and I lift it to my lips and open my mouth for it. I tongue it from the stem, taking my time with it, playing with her, until she leans over, opens her mouth over mine, and takes it back from me.

I pretend to look offended, but I'm so fucking turned on that all I can do is look like an idiot.

Emily

I crash onto the stool at the end of the bar I'd vacated when I took over the band's guitar, and lean my elbows on the table. A grin I can't suppress tugs at my lips. Abby clinks a root beer down in front of me. "That was amazing!" she says as she tosses in two cherries.

I nod. It was pretty damn amazing. I'm still trying to catch my breath. I lift my wet hair off my neck and roll it into a lump, then let it go.

"You been playing for a long time?" Abby asks. She wipes the bar down with a rag.

"I think I was playing before I could walk," I admit. I can't remember a time when I didn't have a guitar. "My grandfather gave me my first guitar." My dad was all for it, until it became the only thing I was good at.

"Well, you can tell." She raises a hand to give me a high five. "That was fantastic." She clenches my hand for a second and meets my eyes, smiling. I don't quite know what to do with that. Yet.

I look around the bar. The place is finally quiet and Logan is stacking chairs on tables for the cleaning crew. He raises the tail of his t-shirt and mops his brow with it. His abs ripple as he bends and a whistle escapes my lips. "Goodness gracious," I breathe.

"That boy is one fine piece of man candy," she says, stopping to lick her lips.

"Makes me want to lick him from top to bottom," I reply softly, more to myself than to her. My face floods with heat when I see that she heard me.

She laughs and keeps cleaning. "What's stopping you?"

I point to Logan. "He is."

Her brows shoot up toward her hairline. "Logan won't scratch your itch?" She points a finger toward him. I'm afraid I'm going to have to give her mouth to mouth, she looks that shocked.

I shake my head. "He scratched my itch. But he won't let me scratch his," I whisper fiercely. I have no idea why I'm talking to this girl. Probably because she's a bartender. They have a natural way of making people open up and spill their guts. Consider me eviscerated.

Abby steps back, her chin dropping toward her chest. She regards me like I just grew two heads. Then she smiles. "It's about damn time," she says, throwing her head back with a laugh.

"It's not funny," I pout. "And don't say anything to Ford, ok?" I add.

She holds up a hand like she's raising it to God and says, "I promise not to say a word." She laughs again. "Even though it's the news of the century, I'll keep it to myself."

I look up as Pete walks out of the back, but he's deep in conversation with Bone and another man. I watch them closely. Pete reaches over and shakes hands with Bone. What in the world is that about? You never, ever shake hands with Bone. Ever. That would imply that you made a deal with him. And Bone's deals never turn out well for anyone but Bone.

Logan smacks his hands together to get Pete's attention. He signs something really quickly, but Pete brushes him off with a wave. Logan sets down the mop he was wielding, and steps toward the pair of them. Bone squeezes Pete's shoulder and then Bone walks away from him and straight toward me.

Bone leans back against the counter beside me, and Abby tries to make herself look really busy. I watch Logan as he yells at Pete in sign language. I have no idea what he's saying, but it's not pleasant, whatever it is.

Bone looks at me over his shoulder and says, "You got a place to stay tonight, Kit?"

I nod. "Yep. But thanks for checking."

Bone looks closely at me for a minute. So closely that my skin crawls. "Let me know if you ever need anything."

"Sure will." I don't say more than that. I just play with my straw and wait for him to walk away. It's best not to antagonize him.

Bone stands up tall, nods at me, and walks toward the back entrance. He leaves. Logan is still yelling at Pete. And Pete's finally deflating a bit. Logan's bigger than he is. But that's not all. Pete looked like he wanted to argue with Logan when they first started talking. But then Logan wraps his fist up in Pete's shirt and jerks him into his chest. He's not signing a word. He's just glaring at Pete until Pete holds up his hands in surrender. If looks could kill, Pete would be a dead lump on the floor.

Logan releases him and Pete falls back off his tiptoes onto his heels. He signs something that calms Logan down, but he's still pissed, and he starts shoving chairs from place to place. He was stacking them. Now he's stacking them forcefully. Pete walks toward me and grumbles.

"What were you doing with Bone, Pete?" I ask.

"Nothing," he mutters.

"That man's no good. Don't let him get you into trouble," I warn quietly.

"Why does everyone think I'm going to get into trouble?" Pete asks, affronted. He pats his chest. "I can take care of myself."

"Not with the likes of him," I say.

He looks up at me, and asks, "What do you know about Bone?"

"More than I want to know," I admit. I've seen what he's capable of. I've seen what he's done to girls at the shelters. I've seen how he uses them.

"Mmm hmm," Pete hums.

Just then, the band members walk out from the back of the building. The lead singer walks toward me and slaps a small pile of bills in front of me. He sits down on a stool next to me, his shoulder a little too close to mine for comfort. I shift away. He doesn't take the hint.

I look down at the stack of money. "What's that for?" I ask.

"That's your cut of the door."

"What's that mean?" I ask.

He nods toward the front door. "We get a percentage of the cover charge. That's your cut. We split it five ways."

A grin steals across my lips. "Seriously?"

He smiles and nods. "Seriously." He lays a hand over mine. "You did a good job tonight."

I slide my hand from under his and wipe it on my jeans. He doesn't notice. He looks at me like he's hungry and I'm cake.

I pick up the stack of bills and fan them out in my hand. There's more than three hundred dollars here. My mouth falls open. "Thanks," I say. I can live for weeks on this much money.

He shrugs. "You earned it."

Abby jumps in. She's watching Logan across the room. And warning me by shooting her eyes in Logan's direction. "Logan's girlfriend is an amazing guitar player, huh?" she asks.

"Girlfriend, huh?" he asks me quietly.

I smile and nod. "Girlfriend." I look over and see Logan walking toward us. He's not smiling. He's doing the opposite. I get up and step between him and the lead singer. I didn't even get his name. Nor do I really want it. I tuck the money in my pocket and put my hands on Logan's chest. He looks down at me and tries to brush me to the side, but I won't let him. "When can we go home?" I ask, purposefully tugging him toward me by the loops in his jeans. He finally looks down at me. His brow is furrowed as he glares at me. "What's the sign for home?" I ask.

He shows me, looking into my eyes as he signs it. I point to me and then repeat the sign. Logan nods.

The lead singer walks by us, and says softly so that I can hear, but Logan can't see his lips. "When he's done with you, give me a call, sweetheart," he says.

Abby gasps. He looks over at her and winks and she flips him the bird. He laughs louder, and then he leaves, taking his band mates with him.

Logan wants to talk to me, I can tell. But he won't do it with everyone looking. "When can we go home?" I ask.

He looks around. The chairs are all put up and Ford took over with the mop. Logan claps his hands at Pete and Pete turns around. He makes the sign he just showed me for home and Pete nods. He's still pissy but he comes with us.

I wave at Abby and she waves back. She's lifting her purse from beneath the bar, so I think she's about to leave, too. "Don't be a stranger!" she yells at me. I smile back and nod. She's nice. I like her.

We walk through the bar to the back exit, and let ourselves out. It's after four in the morning, and I'm tired, but the cold air wraps around me, and I feel more invigorated than I have in a really long time. I just got to play with a band for hours. And I have over three hundred dollars in my pocket.

Logan takes my hand in his and looks around. The streets are dark and more than a little scary at this hour. I'm suddenly really glad I'm with these two men. They're both built like mountains, and the tats make them look much fiercer than they are. I want to talk to Logan, but I know he can't walk beside me and see my lips. So I stay quiet all the way to his apartment. He motions for Pete to go up the stairs, and we stand in the stairwell for a moment. He brushes back a strand of hair that's stuck to my lip. "You really enjoyed tonight, didn't you?" he asks as soon as Pete's gone.

I nod, and bury my face in his chest for a moment, squealing inside with excitement. I want to bite his chest, but I lift my head and say, "Thanks so much for taking me with you."

"What did Bone want with you?"

I shrug. "Same thing he always wants."

"Have you ever worked for him?" He appraises me closely, his blue eyes searching my face.

"Never." It's true. I have never fallen that far. Although I came close more than once.

He takes my hand in his and starts up the stairs. I kind of like holding hands with him. It's nice. He pushes me up the steps before him and I turn around to say, "Do you know this is the first time I've ever walked up these steps of my own free will?"

He turns me around, slaps me on the ass, and I hear him chuckle. It's more of a murmuring sound, but it's all Logan and it warms my heart.

Logan

I'm so pissed at Pete that I can barely keep from running up the stairs and strangling the living shit out of him. He has something going on with Bone, but he won't tell me what they were talking about. Bone's no good and Pete knows it. So I have no idea what his purpose is for talking to the loser. He should have stayed far away from him.

But Kit's hand is in mine, and it jerks me from my thoughts about strangling Pete. I stop at the top of the stairs and draw her to me. She laughs and falls into me, her hands landing to lie flat on my chest. Her thumb scrubs across one of my piercings and my breath catches. "Kit," I warn.

"What?" she asks playfully, a grin tugging at her lips. "After what you did to me on the bathroom counter, you still won't let me touch you? Seriously?" She's playing. And I know it. But I don't want to explain it. I cup her neck with my hand, and I feel a soft purr in her throat. God, I want her so bad.

"I enjoyed what I did to you on the bathroom counter," I say as I touch my lips to hers. I lick across the seam of her lips, and she opens for me. Her tongue is a velvet rasp against mine, and I can imagine her taking my dick in her mouth and licking across it the same way. I groan into her mouth, and she steps up on tiptoe to get closer to me. Her hands slide around my neck, her tits pressed against my chest.

She lifts her head so I can see her lips. "When do I get to return the favor?" she asks. Her cheeks color prettily, and I can tell asking the question embarrasses her. God, she's so damn cute.

I shake my head. "Not going to happen."

She pulls back farther, her brows drawing together into a crease. "How long are you going to stick to that rule?" she asks.

"As long as it takes for you to trust me."

"I trust you now," she protests.

She doesn't. If she did, she would tell me her secrets. "No, you don't."

"There are just some things I can't tell anyone." She takes my face in her hands. "Even you." Her breath rushes against my lips and it's all I can do not to press her against the wall and sink inside her right here and now. I could have her jeans off in seconds. Her legs around my waist. She breaks me from my haze of lust when she says, "I want to tell you everything."

"You don't have to tell me everything. But you can't hold back from me."

She lets me go and steps back, her breath rushing from her. I can feel the blast of it against my chin. "You mean like you're holding back from me."

I jerk her back to me, and she pushes away. She's irked. I try to explain. "If I ever get to fucking be inside you, I want to know what to call you. I want to at least know your name. Because when that happens, you're going to fucking own me." I tip her face up so she's looking at me. "Do you understand?"

She looks unsure.

"You're going to own me." I jerk her hips to mine, letting her feel how much I want her. "And there's nothing I want more."

I step back, brush her hair from her face, and open the door, tugging her by her fingertips until she follows me. She's dragging. She tugs on my hand until I look at her.

"I want everything you want," she says. She's not looking me in the eye. So, I wait for her eyes to open. They finally do. She meets my gaze. "I do want everything you want. I just can't have it."

I lay her hand on my chest, and spread her fingers over my heart. "You already have me." I laugh. "You had me from that first moment in the shop." I hold up my arm, so she can look closely at her tat. "I'm wearing your fucking brand, damn it." I tip her face up to mine. "What are you afraid of? You're hiding from something. I know it. But I don't know what."

She bites her lower lip between her teeth and worries it. I tug it free with my thumb and lean down, sucking it between my lips. She steps onto her tiptoes and growls against my lips. I set her back and away from me, and I can feel the rumble in her chest as she moves.

"I'll tell you. I can't tell you everything. But I can tell you some of it," she says.

My heart swells. I take her hand and lead her into the apartment. The whole place is quiet. Everyone is already in bed. "Want to take a shower?" I ask her. She sweated the night away.

"I thought you wanted to talk," she says, looking everywhere but at me.

"I do." And I don't. Now I'm really afraid. "Take a shower and then we can talk until the sun comes up, if you want."

She nods and bites her lower lip, which sends a kick straight to my gut. Then she turns from me. Suddenly she spins back. She grins and jerks her thumb toward the bathroom. "You want to join me in the shower so we can talk in there?"

Something tells me that if we end up in the shower, we won't be doing much talking. "We'll talk when you get out."

Her bottom lip pokes out. But then she shrugs and says, "Can't blame a girl for trying."

Emily

I shower quickly, trying to put my thoughts in order. I have to be really careful about what I tell Logan, mainly because there are so many people looking for me. I still see the lost posters at times. And there are news blasts sometimes with pictures of the old me. They're of the me who had dark blond hair, pretty headbands, and shoes that cost more than the Reeds' monthly budget. I ignore them, telling myself that person no longer exists. It's easier that way.

I miss home with the longing of a toothache. But I've been gone so long now that I can't go back. I left out of anger. And I can't go home out of shame or necessity. I will only go home when I'm strong enough to stand up for myself. And I haven't felt like that for quite some time.

I wrap a towel around my head and one around my body, and I step into the bedroom. Logan's reclining on the bed wearing nothing but his boxers. He tosses me a clean shirt, and I pull it over my head. He closes his eyes as I slide his shirt on and step into my panties. I can hear the hiss of his heavy breaths across the room, and it's a heady feeling to know how I affect him.

"You still want to talk?" I ask. "Or are you too tired?" I shake out my hair and run a comb through it.

"There's no way you're taking back your offer," he warns. "You can't tease me like that."

I laugh. "I'm not taking it back. I just thought you might want to wait until tomorrow."

He sits up and crosses his legs in front of him. I crawl onto the bed and mirror his position.

His gaze darts down to my panties, where he can probably see the strip of fabric between my legs. But I still sit criss-cross-applesauce. He groans. "You're killing me here."

I tug his shirt down over my knees. "You're making me spill my guts. You can take some torture, too." I glare at him until his gaze becomes indecipherable. "What is it?" I ask.

He heaves a sigh.

I hold up a hand to stop his melancholy mood. "If you could do anything, what would it be?" I ask.

His brows shoot up. "We're supposed to be talking about you."

"We will," I warn. "I promise. Just tell me, if you could do anything, what would you do?"

He doesn't even blink. But his eyes darken, and he says, "I'd lay you down, move your panties to the side and slide inside you."

I freeze. My gut clenches and my belly quivers and my face heats up. I want what he wants. I want it so badly.

He laughs. "Oh, you meant the thing I want second-best?"

"That'll do," I croak.

"I'd go back to college," he says over his laughter.

"Back to college? When were you in college?"

He scrubs a hand down his face. "Before Matt got sick. I had a scholarship."

"But you had to come back home because of Matt and his cancer?" I lay a hand on my chest. My heart is breaking for this family. For Logan.

He shrugs. "We had to get some loans against the shop to pay for his treatment. And then he couldn't keep doing tats because of the germs. So, we couldn't pay the loans. Pete and Sam weren't old enough to work there. Not doing tats."

"What school did you go to?" I ask.

"NYU." His brows furrow. "Why does any of his matter?"

"You gave up your scholarship for Matt. For your family."

He shakes his head. "I got a deferment. I didn't give up. I can go back once things are good here."

"Did it cost a lot of money for Matt's treatment?"

He nods. But he doesn't elaborate. I can guess what a lot of money is to them.

"I wanted to do that, too," I say quietly. No one knows this. No one else knows I had dreams once. "Well, not to NYU. I wanted to go to Julliard. But my dad said it was a worthless endeavor and he refused to pay for it." I hold up a finger when he opens his mouth to protest. "But he was willing to pay for a wedding that cost four times what Julliard ever would." I shake my head.

Logan looks a bit shell shocked. "A wedding?" he asks.

I nod, looking up at him from beneath lowered lashes.

His breath hitches. "Please tell me you're not married."

I shake my head. "No. That's why I'm here." I scoot forward so my knees are touching his. I don't touch him anywhere else. But I need a connection with him. "My father arranged a marriage for me. That's all I was good for, being on the arm of a senator or a high powered attorney. I had no worth of my own, aside from being someone's arm piece. Since I can't read, that was supposed to be my future."

"But you said no."

I nod. "I said no. And he didn't like it. So, he went on without me. The wedding was planned. The dress was purchased. The church was decorated."

His brows shoot toward the ceiling. "But you ran away."

I nod, biting my lower lip. He pulls it free with the pad of his thumb and strokes across it. I kiss his thumb, and he leans back. "I ran away," I confirm. "On the morning of the wedding, I ran away. I took a bus from home to here."

"With nothing."

I show him my empty hands. "I took some clothes, my guitar, and bus fare."

"Where are you from?" he asks.

I shake my head. "I can't tell you." Yet. I know I'll tell him eventually. But I can't risk him calling my family. I can't risk them finding out where I am. My father is one of the richest men in the country. He would spare no expense in bringing me home."

He nods. He's not happy about it, but he understands. "Julliard, huh?" he asks, smiling. His thumb trails across the back of my hand.

"Julliard," I say with a smile. "I struggle with reading," I admit. "But Julliard didn't care. I even auditioned for them without him knowing. They wanted me. And offered special services for my dyslexia. But my dad found it to be a worthless endeavor. He's of the opinion that I can't learn. Anything."

"Your dad is an idiot." Logan says it deadpan.

I laugh. It's a watery sound. He believes in me. Logan believes I could do it.

"What's stopping you from going now?"

"My social security number," I explain. "My father is looking for me. And I'm afraid he'll force me back there if he knows where I am. He can track my movements if I go to the doctor or get a bank account or register for school."

Logan shakes his head. "You're an adult. You're not under your father's thumb."

"I know." I'm starting to realize that. "I don't think I'll ever go back."

"Do you miss them? Your family?"

I miss them like crazy. "Almost every day."

"Your dad?"

I nod.

"Your mom?"

I nod, and tears prick at my lashes when I think of her. But she didn't help me when I begged and pleaded for her to do so. She sided with my father.

"Siblings?" he asks.

I shake my head. "My parents didn't have more children. I'm their only one. Poor things got robbed, huh?"

"Don't say that," he warns sharply.

"It's the truth. I've never been what they wanted."

"What did they want?"

Someone else. "Someone who can read. Follow in their footsteps. Someone who doesn't struggle to read street signs or financial statements. I can't do any of those things."

"Have they ever seen you play?" he asks.

I shake my head. "Not like I played tonight."

"Then they're even bigger idiots than I thought. You were amazing tonight. You had the crowd eating out of the palm of your hand."

"Thank you for saying that."

His eyes narrow. "It's the truth."

"I appreciate you so much," I say. I know I've only known him for a few days, but it feels like forever. "Did I tell you enough?" I ask.

"Not by a long shot," he says with a laugh. "I want to know everything."

Maybe someday. "Can we take this slow?"

I can't give him enough info that he could contact my parents. Because I'm afraid he would, thinking he was helping me.

"You're worried that I'll betray your confidence?" he asks. He sits back, affronted.

"Some people have good intentions. I know you do. But you don't understand how much I have to keep my anonymity. I can't trust anyone." If I do, my parents will suddenly have the info they need to sweep down and snatch me back into their world.

He nods. He's somber. I should have known how this would affect him.

"Now that you know where I came from, I understand if you want me to leave." I turn to reach for my bag, so that I can gather my things.

"What the fuck?" he says, his arm snaking around my stomach as he picks me up and lifts me into his lap. I turn to face him, my legs over his thigh. "Where do you think you're going?"

I heave a sigh. "I have no idea."

He tips my face up and looks into my eyes. "I want you here. Will you stay?"

"Will you be satisfied with what I told you?"

He nods. "For now, yes."

His eyes narrow and I know what his next question is. "Will you tell me your name?"

I shake my head. I can't. "I'm sorry," I say.

He nods, settling me against his shoulder. He holds me like that for a minute, and then he jostles me out of his arms. He pulls the covers back and picks me up, tucking me. He climbs in behind me and turns me to face him. "I had hoped for more. But I'll take what I can get. Thank you for telling me what you did."

"Thank you for listening."

I lean forward and touch my lips to his. He's hesitant. "What's wrong?" I ask, leaning back.

He pulls me into him, and I feel the length of him against my hip.

"Oh," I say. My belly clenches. My need matches his.

He brushes my hair back from my face with gentle fingers. "Yeah," he says with a laugh. "It's like this crazy torment, having you this close to me."

"You know we could-" I start. But he puts a finger against my lips to stop me.

"I can wait," he says. He reaches over and turns off the light. He rolls me into him, and the light dusting of hair that's on his chest tickles my cheek.

"I think I might love you, Logan," I say to the darkness.

His head lifts. I can see it in the sliver of light that's falling from the open curtain. "Did you say something?" he asks.

I shake my head, letting my nose brush his chest so he can feel my answer.

"You sure?" he asks.

I nod, my nose brushing him up and down. He kisses the top of my head, and hitches my leg up over his hip. I wrap an arm around him and snuggle in deeply. "Go to sleep," he says softly.

So I do.

***

I wake the next morning to a gentle tap, tap, tap on the side of my nose. I blink my eyes open and startle when I see a face looking into mine. Hayley grins at me. "You sweepy?" she says quietly.

I was, until she tapped against my face like a hungry bird. I scrub the sleep from my eyes and look over at Logan. He's lying beside me with one arm flung over his head, his mouth hanging open. I snuggle deeper into my pillow. "Where's your daddy?" I ask.

"Sweeping," she says. She's dragging a bunny by the ears. "I'm hungwy," she says.

I cover a yawn with my open palm. I probably have awful morning breath. "Can you go and wake your daddy?"

She shakes her head. "He said to go back to sweep."

I look toward the window. The sun is just barely over the horizon. "I want a pancake."

A pancake? "How about some cereal?" I ask, as I throw the covers off myself and get up. I take a pair of Logan's boxers from his drawer and put them on.

"Dos are Logan's," she says, scowling at me.

"Do you think he'll mind if I borrow them?" I whisper at her.

She shakes her head and smiles, taking my hand in her free one so she can lead me from the room. "You don't got to whisper. Logan can't hear," she says.

I laugh. She's right. And what's funny is that it took a three year old to remind me. I hold a finger to my lips, though, as we step out into the hallway. "But your daddy can. Shh."

She giggles and repeats my shush.

She runs down the hallway, her naked feet slapping softly against the hardwoods until she's in the kitchen. I search through the cupboards to find a box of cereal.

"Not dat one," she says, shaking her head. "I don't wike dat one." She points to a different box. One with a cartoon character and the word fruit on it. But I know there's no fruit in this cereal. Or anything else healthy.

"Does your daddy let you eat this?" I ask.

She grins and nods. I shrug my shoulders and pour her a bowl of cereal with milk. She gets her own spoon from the drawer. She knows where everything is. She digs into her cereal, her feet swinging back and forth beneath the chair.

I go and lay down on the couch. I am tired. I think Logan and I got to sleep around five in the morning, and it can't be much later than that now. I lay back with a groan and close my eyes. I am just getting comfortable when two sharp elbows land in my midsection. Hayley crawls on top of me on the couch. I think she must be part monkey. She holds a kid-sized board book in her hand. "Wead," she says, shoving it in my face.

I sit up, tucking her into my lap. I take the book from her and open it, but the words jumble. I turn it upside down. "Once upon a time," I begin.

"Dat's not how it goes," she complains.

She's a smart girl. "I know," I explain. "But books are magical and if you turn them upside down, there's a whole new story in the pages."

"Weally?" she asks, her eyes big with wonder.

No, not really. But it's the best I can do, kid. "Really," I affirm.

She wiggles, settling more comfortably in my arms.

I start to make up a story, based on the upside down pictures. She listens intently. "Once upon a time, there was a little frog. And his name was Randolf."

"Randolf," she repeats with a giggle.

"And Randolf had one big problem."

"Uh oh," she breathes. "What kind a problem?"

"Randolf wanted to be a prince. But his mommy told him that he couldn't be a prince, since he was just a frog."

I keep reading until I say, "The end." She lays the book to the side and snuggles into me. I kiss the top of her head, because it feels like the right thing to do. And she smells good. "Your story was better than the book's story," she says.

My heart swells with pride. "Thank you." If only it was this easy to please the adults of the world.

"Want to watch TV?" she asks.

I yawn. "Sure. Why not?"

She goes over and picks up the DVD. "You go start it," she instructs.

The DVD player is under the TV, and it doesn't look that complicated. I put the movie in and turn the TV on. The movie starts, but it's not a typical kids' movie. It's a movie that teaches sign language to children. I drop onto the floor to sit beside her. There's a lady teaching each of the signs, and there are pictures. There are words at the bottom of the screen for people who can read. But it's an instructional DVD made for kids.

Hayley sits beside me and she starts to repeat the signs. "You do it?" she asks. "We wearn signing for Logan."

I am enraptured. "We learn sign language for Logan," I repeat with a nod.

When the first DVD ends, we move on to the second. I have an amazing memory, because I have to have one. So, I think I can remember some of this. I'm giddy with excitement. I practice some of the more basic signs with Hayley.

We're almost done with the second DVD when Paul walks into the room. "Hayley, what are you doing?" He scratches his stomach. His hair is a mess, sticking out all over the place.

She pats my cheek. "I wearning signing with Logan's girl," she says.

I like that. I like it a lot.

"Did she wake you up?" Paul asks, smothering a yawn.

I wave him off with a breezy hand. "It's no big deal. She was showing me the DVD's."

He nods, his brows arching. "Well, I'm sorry she woke you. You should go back to bed."

"Do you think it would be all right if I watch the rest of them later?" I ask, suddenly feeling shy about it.

He chuckles. "Of course. That's how we all learned."

I nod. He picks Hayley up, jiggling her until she giggles. He laughs at her. "Next time I tell you to stay in bed, I mean stay in bed, little girl," he says. She laughs all the way down the hallway, until he takes her in his room and closes the door.

I yawn. The bed is calling to me. I go back in Logan's room, and he's lying exactly like I left him. I draw the shades closed, so the room isn't quite so bright. Then I take off his boxers and slide back into bed with him. He reaches for me immediately, pulling me into him as he rolls and covers me with his leg, his thigh across the backs of mine. "You all right?" he asks.

I nod. I'm all right. I can't help but think that I'm where I'm supposed to be.

He brushes my hair from my face and nuzzles me with his lips. I settle deeper into him and go back to sleep with him wrapped around me.

It seems like only moments later when the bed begins to vibrate.

Logan

The bed vibrates and I reach over and smack the alarm clock. I hate early Saturday mornings. But I promised Sam that I would go and run some plays with him in the park before the shop opens. Sam's a football player, and he's being scouted by a few colleges. He thinks he might get a full ride, and I couldn't be happier for him. He doesn't have the grades to get a scholarship like I did. But he's capable of getting an education through sports, and that works too.

The purr of Kit's throat tells me that she's saying something. I look down at her lips, but she's laying with her face smushed into the pillow. "Did you say something?" I ask, rolling her to her back. I throw my leg across her.

She doesn't speak, but she signs the word no at me. My heart leaps. She smiles, then her brown eyes open and she blinks at me. "Did I do that right?" She signs the word for right, but nothing more.

"Yes, it's right. Where did you learn that?"

"I watched some DVD's with Hayley this morning when she woke me up." She yawns and turns toward me. "Will you sign with me? I want to learn your language so we can talk around your brothers."

My heart swells.

"I can learn to sign," she begins, like she has to justify her ability to learn. I put my finger over her lips.

"Shh…" I say. "I'll sign with you any time you want."

She's lying on her back with my t shirt sliding up to expose a strip of skin over her panties. I reach out, and run my hand along the seam of her panties, dipping the tips of my fingers below the elastic. She squirms and her eyes open. They're soft and warm and pleading with me.

I should move away from her. But I can't. I haven't been able to get away from her since I met her, and I can't start now.

I bend my head and press my lips to that little strip of skin, lingering there as I kiss my way from one hip to the other. She arches her back, pressing her heat closer to me. If she were anyone else, I would be pulling her panties down her legs by now. But she's not anyone else. She's mine. And she's special. I groan out loud, flip her shirt down and move up to kiss her quickly. I'm sure I have morning breath, so I don't linger. But as I move to roll off of her, she grabs my shoulders and pulls me back to her. "I'm not a virgin, you know?" she says.

I still. I didn't know. And I don't care. "Ok." I don't know what else to say.

She closes her eyes so she doesn't have to look at me as she says, "I just wanted to be sure you know in case that's why you're hesitating so much."

"Ok." I pry her hands from my chest and roll away from her. She taps my shoulder and I look at her.

"It's not like I've been with a lot of guys or anything." She hesitates.

"I didn't ask." I smile at her in encouragement. But I'm sort of reeling from her declaration. I look into her eyes. "Did you ever do it with someone you were in love with?" I drag my crooked finger down the line of her jaw.

"Not yet," she says.

I can't bite back my smile. "Good." Neither have I.

My dick is so hard that I have to shove it down into my jeans. I turn away from her long enough to do it and zip.

"Where are you going?" she asks.

"To toss the football with Sam."

She throws the covers off and her face lights up. "Can I go?"

I stop. "You want to go toss a football in the park?"

She nods enthusiastically, her eyes shining. "There are a lot of things I can't do. But football isn't one of them."

"You play football?"

"Played," she clarifies. She takes on a strong man pose. "Four years with the pee wee league."

I laugh. "Get dressed. You can come with me."

She jerks on a pair of jeans and lifts her hair into a messy pony tail. Damn, she's pretty. She picks up her bra, turns her back to me and hides her arms in the shirt, adjusting the bra beneath the fabric. Within seconds, she's ready to go. She slides on her boots and nods. "Ready?" she asks. "You look like you've never seen a woman get dressed quickly."

"I've never woken up with a woman," I say. She stops moving and stares at me. "So, no, I've never watched one get dressed to start the day." It's usually a quick shrug into clothing after I kick someone out of my bed. Correction – after I make her come and then kick her out of my bed. But one day soon, I hope to watch her get dressed without holding the shirt over the best parts. "It seems really intimate, and I've never paid attention to anyone getting dressed after getting out of my bed." I shrug. "I like it."

"I'm your first," she teases, her face going soft.

I nod, unable to speak past the lump in my throat. "You're my first," I say, walking toward her. She thinks I'm going to squeeze her into a hug, and she leans into me. But I jerk her into the crook of my arm and give her a noogie instead. "That's for messing with me," I growl.

She jerks back, running her hand over her hair. She bends and takes her toothbrush from her bag.

"We don't have time for tooth brushing, woman," I say. "It's time for football."

"I am not leaving here without brushing my teeth," she says pertly. Then she signs the word no.

I point her toward the bathroom and smack her ass. She jumps and turns back to me, walking backward. She shakes her finger at me and I chase her into the bathroom. She brushes her teeth standing two feet away from me while I brush mine. I imagine her humming, and I find that I'm right when I place my hand on her throat. "Don't stop," I say.

She mouths something at me, but her mouth is full of toothpaste and I have no idea what she's saying.

"Don't stop humming," I say.

"Why do you care?" she asks after she spits. "You can't hear it."

"You look happy when you do it. So, don't stop."

She freezes, nods at me and rinses her mouth. I do the same. I grab her by the belt loops and tug her to me. "Is it safe to kiss you now?" I ask.

"Unless you want to be late," she warns, but she's smiling and she's already threading her fingers into the hair at the nape of my neck.

I slam the bathroom door shut. "Let's be late," I say.

Emily

Sam is irked because we're running later than he'd planned. I can't say I blame him. But when Logan kisses me, I can't think about anything but him. He always calls for the stop before I do. I can't figure out what to do about that, aside from giving him time to trust me. We just met a few days ago, but I feel like I've known him my whole life. He's kind, considerate, and he doesn't treat me like I'm somehow lacking because of my dyslexia. He doesn't seem to care.

Ahead of us, Hayley walks alongside Paul, her fist clutching his index finger. She's dressed warmly in a pink coat that has fur around the hood. She's adorable. Paul looks at her like she hung the moon and stars in the sky. Sam and Pete walk side by side in front of them, and they stop to shove one another across the sidewalk every few seconds. Logan tosses a ball in the air as we walk together. I bite back a shiver.

He makes the sign for cold, asking me with his brows raised if I am. I show him my fingers about an inch apart. He hands me the ball, unzips his hoodie and puts it around my shoulders. I pass the ball back to him, tug the hoodie more tightly around myself, and slide my arms into it, and zip it up to my chin. I lift it and sniff. It smells like him.

Why he asks in sign, then he mimes my sniff. Why did I smell it? I know the sign for why, and my heart thrills that I do.

I don't know how to sign the words, so I say, "Smells like you. I like it." I shrug my shoulders. I turn around backward and walk facing him because I'm sure it's hard for him to read my lips from the side. He holds a hand in warning. He shakes his head.

No need, he signs. He mouths the words while he does it, so I get it.

"Don't let me run into anything," I warn. I like looking at him. Apparently, a lot of other women do, too. His arms are naked, his t shirt straining across his shoulders. You can see his tattoos, which go all the way to his hairline on the back of his neck. He attracts a lot of attention. "Women really love you, don't they?" I ask. He's drawn more than one pair of eyes, from the teenagers to the cougars. They all stop to stare as he walks past. And having his brothers with him doesn't help any. They're a good looking group of boys.

He shrugs, looking sort of put out by my question.

When we get to the park, Matt goes and sits on a bench and I drop down beside him. Logan goes with Sam and Pete to toss the ball around. Paul chases Hayley over to the swings. "How are you feeling?" I ask of Matt.

"Fine," he says quickly. He doesn't elaborate.

"You don't look fine," I blurt out. I can't help it. He doesn't.

"Thanks," he says, his voice droll. "I love to hear how bad I look from beautiful girls." He nods. "Appreciate it."

"Why didn't you stay home to rest?"

"Honestly?" he asks, looking at me out of the corner of his eye. He's leaning forward so that his elbows rest on his knees. He plucks a blade of grass.

"No, lie to me," I respond. Then I roll my eyes.

He chuckles. "I don't know how many more moments I'll have to do this. I want to suck every bit of life from the moments I have."

Tears prick at the backs of my lashes. "Are you afraid?" I ask quietly.

"Only every fucking day," he says on a heavy sigh.

"Oh." I don't know what else I can say. "What's your prognosis?" I ask. I don't know why I'm being so nosy. I just want to know what Logan will be up against. And Matt. But mainly for Logan. I might be able to do something to cushion his blow.

"Don't know. I go back in two weeks and they'll tell me if the chemo worked."

I nod. What can you say to that? *Hope it's good news. Hope you're going to live. Oh, you're going to be just fine.* None of those seem appropriate.

He turns so that his knee is facing me, his arm lying along the back of the bench. "I've been trying to plan. For when I'm gone."

Shoot. What should I say to that? "That's smart." I'm an idiot.

"I have letters for all my brothers. I already wrote them."

"Is that what you've been doing all day?"

He nods, playing with the piece of grass, rolling it between his fingers.

"They'll appreciate them if anything ever happens to you."

"*When* something happens to me," he says, correcting me. "It's just a matter of how long I have at this point, I think. I can feel it."

I cover my hand with his on the back of the bench, and give it a squeeze. "Is there anything at all I can do for you? Anything to help you plan?"

He looks at me, hard. His green eyes bore into mine. "If you're still around when it's time, can I give you the letters? To share with them when I'm gone?"

"I'll still be around," I say. I'm not going anywhere. Not any time soon. "And yes, I can take your letters. Just tell me how and when you want them delivered."

He nods. "I have one for this girl, too. April is her name. Logan will be able to find her. But he won't give her a letter from me. He sort of hates her."

"She probably deserves it," I mumble.

He chuckles. "You don't get to pick who you fall in love with." He sits silent for a minute. Then he says, "Don't let them put me on the mantel or anything," he says. "I fucking hate the idea of being stuffed in an urn."

"What would you want them to do with your ashes, if they could?" I kick at a rock that's near my toe.

"I don't give a fuck, as long as I'm not stuck on the mantelpiece." He chuckles.

"Don't give up yet, all right?" I ask.

He nods. "I'm fighting 'til the day I die. But there are things I need to plan for."

I nod. I understand.

Logan walks over and stands in front of me. He signs something. The only sign I recognize is the word *girl*.

"No, I'm not putting the moves on your girl," Matt complains. Then he laughs. "She's putting the moves on me."

Logan turns to me, his mouth hanging open wide. But his eyes dance with laughter. He pulls on my hands until I stand up. Then he bends and tosses me over his shoulder and spins in a circle. I scream, covering my eyes. I know he won't drop me, but still.

He runs around, and Sam and Pete chase us. Pete -- or Sam – I still can't tell them apart – slaps my butt. I flail around, trying to reach out and grab him, but Logan is running with me over his shoulder. He spins, holding tightly to my legs. I cover my eyes and squeal, but I know he can't hear me.

I hit Logan on the butt, but he pays me no mind. Suddenly, he stops and starts to lower me down his body. I slide down him slowly, my body contours rubbing against his until my feet hit the ground. "Hi," he says quietly. He signs it, too, but his free arm is around me holding me against him.

"Hi," I say, and I sign it just like he did. Then I smack his chest. "I can't believe you did that." I turn and motion toward Sam. "Throw me the ball," I say. Sam looks at me like I'm nuts, so I say, "What? Are you afraid to play with a girl?"

He smiles and hurls the ball at me. I take off running with it cradled in my arm. Logan runs after me, but I'm faster than any of them expected. Just before I reach the bench Matt's sitting on, Logan snakes an arm around my waist, swinging me around. While he holds me tightly, Sam wrestles the ball from me. "That's cheating!" I scream.

"Cheating is allowed!" Sam yells back.

"In whose rule book?" I ask, stamping my foot.

"What rule book?" Matt says with a chuckle. He hefts himself to his feet. "Me and you against them?" he says. He grins at me.

"We can take them any day," I say, throwing my arms around him. He squeezes me gently and sets me away from him. He rubs my head, messing my hair all up.

Logan runs down the field, and I chase him. He turns to catch the ball Sam throws, and as soon as he has it, I tackle him. I hit him as hard as I can. He stumbles with me holding on to his shirt, until I can wrap around his legs. He goes down like a big oak tree falling. He lies on his stomach, but he's smiling at me. I climb on his back and sit on him, plucking the ball from his grip. I hold it in the air and cheer, flailing my feet wildly. He lets me sit there on top of him for a minute as his breath heaves in and out under me. But then he upends me. He rolls me under him. "You cheated." He says. His hands hold my wrists in a strong grip.

"There's no rule book, remember?" I giggle when he tickles beneath my ribs. "Stop!" I cry.

He looks into my eyes. "I think I might be falling in love with you," he says softly.

My breath catches. "Yeah, me too," I say.

He smiles and gets to his feet, tugging me up beside him. His face is flushed, and he's grinning.

"If you two are done playing lovey dovey," Matt yells, "we have a game to win." He waggles his brows at me. Suck every moment from life. We should all do more of that.

Logan

It has been almost two weeks since her declaration in the park. She hasn't said it again, and neither have I. But I know she loves me. There's no doubt in my mind. She sleeps in my bed every night, and we spend every waking moment together when we're not working. I'm so used to having her at my side, I'm not sure I'll survive it at this point if she leaves me. I'm hopeful that she'll be ready for what I want soon. Because I want all of her. I want her past, her present and her future. I want to ask her to marry me, but I can't. Not yet.

Sometimes, there's a look in her eye that I don't fully understand. She's longing for something she doesn't have. I'm not sure if it's home or something else.

She's learned to sign in the past two weeks, and she can carry on conversations. She's actually really good at it, and she's found that spelling isn't as hard for her when she's fingerspelling as it is on paper. Something about the spacing of the letters, she says.

She's sitting on the couch now with Hayley in her arms. She's holding a book upside down, and telling a story she has made up. The corners of my lips tip up and I can't bite back my grin. She fits so well into my family.

She still busks in the subway every day while I work at the tattoo shop. And last Friday night, the band encouraged her up on the stage when the crowd started chanting for her. They passed a hat through the audience and she got to keep the money they put in it. It was just over one hundred dollars and she only played one or two songs.

She saves every dime of the money she has made. We won't let her pay rent. My brothers and I had a frank discussion about it and we all agreed. She does too much for us to charge her rent. She cooks often. And she can't seem to keep from cleaning, even though we tell her not to.

Pete's on the couch across from Kit with a girl he met a couple of weeks ago. They've been necking for about ten minutes. I'm standing in the kitchen with Paul. I jerk my thumb toward them and Paul scowls. He says something to Pete, who looks up sheepishly. He adjusts his junk and lifts the girl up, taking her down the hallway toward his room. Paul yells at him, and he comes back and takes a few condoms from the drawer, grins and goes to his room.

"Great," Sam grouses. "I'll have to sleep on the couch."

Paul smiles. "There are two beds in there."

"Yuck," Sam says. "I don't want to have to hear them."

At least the boy is getting some, I sign.

Kit scolds me with a glance from across the room. I rue the day I taught her to speak sign language. I can't keep anything a secret anymore. I shrug at her and she grins.

You would be getting some too if you'd quit being such a prude, she signs to me.

Did you really just call me a prude? I ask as I stalk toward her. She sets Hayley to the side and jumps over the back of the couch. By now, she knows I'm coming for her.

She darts around the sofa and dodges back and forth, trying to avoid my hands. But I catch the tail of her shirt and jerk her to me. Linking my arm around her waist, I pick her up and take her to our room, slamming the door behind us. I toss her onto the bed and she bounces, laughing at me. "Did you really just call me a prude?" I ask, using my voice.

"No, definitely not." She laughs as I tickle her and she squirms in my arms.

"I think you did." I keep tickling her, because I know it drives her crazy.

"Prove it," she says. She's signing the whole time she's talking. So, I don't miss anything with her anymore. She grabs my hands to keep me from tickling her.

I growl as I press my lips to her throat. "Don't tempt me," I warn.

She taps my shoulder until I look up at her. "I want to tempt you. I want to tempt you really bad." She throws her head back on the last word and I can feel her throat vibrating as she growls. "You're making me crazy."

I chuckle. "I think that's my line."

"How much longer will you make me wait?"

I wake up with her wrapped around me every fucking morning. I go to sleep with her in my arms every night. I take long, cold showers every day, just so I can take some of the pressure off. She's making me nuts. But she's not ready for me yet. She's not. She knows it. I know it.

I change into a pair of jeans while she watches. I don't even try to hide my erection from her anymore. She knows it's there. She knows how much I want her. I think she knows how much I love her. I feel certain she loves me just as much. I just don't know why she's still hiding. "I have to work tonight at Bounce. Are you coming with me?"

She shakes her head. "I don't think so. I have a date with Hayley to read a book." She doesn't look at me.

No she doesn't. "Paul has a date tonight and he's taking Hayley with him," I remind her.

"Oh." She avoids my gaze.

"You're worried about Matt, aren't you?" I ask her. I frame her face with my hands and look into her eyes.

She nods. "He's been sleeping too much. I don't think it's good."

We all dance around the fact that Matt will be going back to the doctor two days from now to find out his prognosis. Everyone but Kit. She thinks about it a lot, I think. I try not to think about it at all. "You want to stay home so you can keep an eye on him?" I run a hand down the length of her hair and press a kiss to her forehead.

"Would you mind?" she asks. She looks hopeful.

"You know Pete's here," I remind her.

"Pete's knocking boots in the bedroom. How's he going to know if Matt's ok or not?"

She's right. "Thanks for staying," I say. I kiss her forehead again. "I'm taking Sam with me. Send for me if you need me for anything, ok?"

She nods. She flops back on the bed and I want to climb on top of her. But I have to go. Sam beats on the wall. I can feel the vibration of it. "What do you want, Sam?" I ask.

"Her," he says, grinning. He waggles his brows at Kit.

I punch his shoulder. "She's taken."

Kit grins, shaking her head. She has gotten used to all of us. I walk over to her and tip her head up to look into her eyes. "I'll see you later."

"Count on it," she says.

Emily

I step closer to Matt's door, listening intently for signs of life. He's been really tired for the past few days, and I'm worried for him. I'm *really* worried for him. And for Logan and the rest of them. None of them have come to terms with the fact that Matt is dying. They all overlook it, like pretending it's not going to happen is going to help him.

His voice, weak and tired, funnels through the crack in the door. "Don't just stand there breathing hard. Come on in."

I open the door and smile at him. "You could not hear me breathing."

He chuckles, but it's a hollow sound. "I heard your footsteps. You should learn to be more stealthy. Like Paul. He came in last night and stood over me, watching me breathe for about an hour." He adjusts, fluffing a pillow and jamming it behind his head. "He thinks I was asleep."

"Why didn't you tell him you were awake?" I ask. "You two could have talked."

He harrumphs. "He doesn't want to talk. He wants to fix everything. But I'm afraid I can't be fixed."

"You don't know that."

He heaves a sigh. "I know it."

I can't say anything past the lump in my throat.

"How's it going?" he asks.

I still can't find my tongue, so I nod.

"That good, huh?" he rolls toward me, his arm beneath his pillow.

"Matt," I start. But I stop, bite my lower lip and shake my head. "I don't know what to say to you."

"You still running Logan in circles?" he asks.

I bite back a smile. "I don't know what you're talking about."

He laughs. "It's good for him. Keep up the good work." He narrows his eyes. "He's never had to work for anyone before. Women came easily for him."

My face floods with heat when I realize what he said.

He laughs. "Yeah, that, too." He points across the room. "You remember those letters I told you about?" he asks.

I nod. I don't want to talk about letters. Because when I deliver the letters, he'll be gone.

"They're in my top drawer. My dresser." He nods his head in that direction. "When the time is right, be sure they get them?"

I nod. "I will. I promise."

"There's one for you too."

I don't want mine. "Ok."

He takes my hand in his and squeezes it tightly. I can tell the action takes a lot out of him. "What do you want to do tonight?" he asks.

I shrug. "Sit here with you."

He smiles at me. And I see so much of Logan in him that it hurts. He rolls to the edge of the bed and lifts himself up to sit. "Let's go watch a movie."

I nod, taking his hand in mine to help him to his feet. He lets me, but he groans as he gets up. "You sure you can do this?" I ask.

"Remember when I told you I was going to suck every minute out of life that I could?" He stares at me. I am a little worried that he's trying to gather enough energy to walk into the living room.

"Let's go suck at life," I say. "Do you want some popcorn?" I ask over my shoulder. He's following me.

"Why not?" he asks flippantly. "Popcorn and I'm going to snuggle with Logan's girl." His voice is farther behind me. But he's coming, so I start the popcorn. The steady pop, pop, pop has started when I realize he hasn't followed me into the kitchen.

There's a thud in the hallway, and I jump. "Matt?" I ask, walking back in that direction. But Matt's lying on the floor. He's drooling, and his body is convulsing. "Oh, shit," I say. "Matt!" I yell. I roll him onto his side, because I heard that's what you do when someone convulses. Or maybe it's that you're supposed to roll him onto his back. Shit, shit, shit. I don't know. "Pete!" I yell.

Pete opens his door, he's in a pair of boxers and he drags his shirt over his head. "What?" he asks. Then he sees Matt lying on the floor. "What the fuck?" he says, and he drops down beside Matt.

"Go call 911," I say calmly. When he sits there and doesn't move, I shove him and yell in his face. "Go call 911!"

He shakes out of his fear induced stupidity and runs to the phone.

He gives them the address and stays on the phone with them until the ambulance arrives. He gets dressed while he talks to them, stepping into his jeans in front of me, but I don't care. His girlfriend leaves. She's not worth the air she's breathing, apparently.

Matt calms and I lift his head into my lap. I wipe the spittle from his face with my sleeve and brush his hair back from his forehead. He's still. Too still. I hadn't realized how much hair he'd lost with the chemo. It's thinner than I thought it was. I brush across his face. "Not yet. It's too soon," I whisper to him.

I follow the paramedics as they carry him downstairs. "One of you can ride along," the paramedic says.

Pete looks at me and says, "I need to get my brothers." He runs a heavy hand through his buzz cut.

He knows where they are and I don't know how to get there. None of them carry cell phones because it's not in their budget.

"Go get some shoes," I say. He looks down at his naked feet and nods.

He shoves me into the ambulance and they close the door behind us. The rest of the world falls away, and I can no longer hear the sounds of the street or the blaring horns. All I can hear is the unsteady beat of Matt's heart on the monitor. Every time it stutters, mine flips in my chest, my breath leaving me. I lean over and take Matt's hand.

"It would be better if you don't touch him," they say.

I nod and sit back, buckling the seat belt in the jump seat they pointed me toward.

My hands are shaking and I don't know what to do with myself. They start IV's and look into his eyes and do a lot of things I don't understand.

He doesn't wake up. I worry that he never will.

Paul gets to the hospital first, and he's carrying Hayley on his hip. She's frantic, and she wants to know why they can't finish their date. I hold out my hands and she comes to me, settling against my chest. "What happened?" Paul asked.

"He just fell down in the hallway and started to shake," I try to explain. But I'm trying to be strong since I'm holding Hayley.

"Can we see him?" he asks.

I shake my head. "Not yet. They took him back and they're working on him."

Paul goes to the payphone and drops in some change. He turns his back to me and talks for a minute. Then he comes and takes Hayley back from my arms. "Now we wait," he says.

Hayley pats his cheek, and I see tears well up in his eyes. "Where's Matt?" Hayley asks.

"Matt's with the doctors," he explains, blinking hard.

"Dey gonna make him all betta?" she asks. She's following his gaze with hers, not letting him off the hook. She frowns when he doesn't answer.

"They're going to work hard to make him better," I tell her.

"Thank you," Paul chokes out. I nod. I can't say more than that. Hayley holds out her arms to me again, and I take her to sit down. We read upside down books until a woman comes rushing through the doors. She runs to Paul. Her hair is up in a ponytail and she's almost as tall as he is.

But she's stunning. Hayley has Paul's hair color and eyes, but everything else about her is her mother.

She leans into Paul to her and he hugs her tightly. I hear them murmuring to one another but I can't hear what they're saying. She comes to me and takes Hayley in her arms. "Thank you," she says.

I look into her eyes. She's kind. I can tell. And I can also see that she's head over heels in love with Paul. She walks over to him, whispers something in his ear, and he nods. She kisses him on the lips, and he kisses her back. "I'll call you when I find out what's going on," he says.

She leaves with Hayley. Paul takes a deep breath and sits down beside me, his elbows on his knees. "He wasn't in a lot of pain, was he?" he asks.

"Not that I could tell." He was convulsing. But not in pain. I doubt he was feeling much.

"That's my biggest fear. That he'll be in a lot of pain when it happens. It scares me to death."

"So you've thought about it," I blurt out. I want to take it back immediately. But it's too late.

"Thought about it." He snorts. "It's all I ever fucking think about. Ever." His voice cracks on the last word. "I'm his big brother. I'm supposed to be able to save him from anything that could hurt him. But I can't save him from this."

I just listen, because there's nothing I can say to comfort him.

A tear drop rolls down his cheek and he brushes it away with a hurried swipe. "He knows how much you care," I say. It's probably the wrong thing to tell him.

"The fucker better know how I feel about him. I'd die for every last one of them. I wish it was me instead of him. I'd trade places with him in a heartbeat."

"He wouldn't let you." It's the truth.

Paul chuckles. But it's a sound without any merriment.

The doors of the hospital slide open and Logan, Pete and Sam run in. I hop out of my chair fall into Logan's arms, because I know he'll catch me. He squeezes me to him and rubs my hair for a second. Paul walks over and starts to speak to him. They're all signing, but I can follow it. He explains.

Can we see him? Logan asks.

Paul shakes his head. "Not yet. They'll let us know when we can."

If we can. But no one says that out loud.

Logan drops his arm around me and pulls me into him. His face is in my hair and I can feel the warm caress of his breath against my neck. I lift my head and look up at him. "It's bad," I say.

He closes his eyes and lays the tips of his fingers against his temple. He knows.

Now we wait.

They're all draped over the furniture in the waiting room, taking up a ton of space. But no one else is there, so it hasn't mattered. Any one of these boys would give their seat up for someone else. Pete took Sam's socks about an hour ago, and Sam put his shoes back on with none. Pete was barefoot. I somehow knew he wouldn't go back inside. He went for his brothers instead.

It seems like days later when a doctor comes to talk to the family. It could have been minutes. It could have been hours. It feels like days.

The doctor sighs heavily and starts to talk. I hear snippets of it over the pulse that's pounding in my head.

The chemo didn't work.

He's worse than he was.

They can call hospice.

"There's nothing else you can do?" Paul asks.

The doctor sits down with them. "We've exhausted every opportunity. There are some trials that he could get into, but the chances are small. And the one that would most benefit him is very expensive."

He waits. A pregnant silence falls over the room. "How expensive?" Paul asks.

"Hundreds of thousands," the doctor says. "He doesn't even have medical insurance."

So that's it. They don't have hundreds of thousands of dollars so their brother dies.

I wipe a tear from my cheek. "This treatment, it could save him?" I ask. "Or would it just prolong the inevitable?"

He looks at me like I'm the most ridiculous person he's ever met. "They're having good success with it. There are no guarantees, however."

"But it would give him a chance?"

"The best he could have."

I nod. Logan squeezes me to him. *I'll be right back,* I sign to him. I know what I have to do. My heart is breaking in two. But I know what my choices are.

Where are you going? he asks.

Restroom. I'll be right back.

You ok?

I nod. He watches me walk away, his gaze boring into my back. I can feel it all the way down the hall. I don't stop at the bathroom, though. I keep walking until I find a payphone.

I pick up the handle and a weird sort of peace settles over me. I press the button for the operator. "Collect call to California, please," I say. I rattle off the number. It's Saturday afternoon. My dad will be in the office.

Ring.

Ring.

Ring.

"Mr. Madison's office," a chipper voice says.

"You have a collect call from – caller, state your name?" the operator says.

"I'd like to talk with Mr. Madison, please," I reply.

"We'll accept the charges." There's a stillness on the other end of the line. "Emily, is that you?" the voice says. There's hope in her voice. She's been my dad's secretary for as long as I can remember.

"Can I talk with him, please?" I ask.

The line goes dead for a moment, and then my dad picks up. "Emily?" he asks. I can almost hear the beat of his heart through the phone in the stillness.

"Dad," I say.

"Em," he says on a long sigh, like he's deflating. There's a clank and I imagine him taking his glasses off his nose and laying them on the table. "Where are you?"

"I need some help, Dad," I say. I lay my forehead against the cool tiles on the wall and try not to cry. I want to cry for all that I'm giving up. I want to cry for all that I'm giving them. But mostly, I want to cry for me.

"Anything, Emily," he says. His breath catches. "You're not hurt, are you?"

"No, I'm fine. But I'm coming home."

"Tell me where you are. I'll send the jet." His voice is urgent.

"Dad, first, I need for you to do something for me." Please, please, please do this for me.

He doesn't say anything for a minute. "What do you need, Emily?"

"I need for you to take care of something for me, Dad." I tell him some of the story. "I need for you to get him in the trial. And I want to take care of his treatment. We'll use my money, Dad." I have enough to spare. And then some. A lot more than I need.

He chuckles. "We don't need to touch your trust fund, Em," he says. "Why does this young man matter to you?" he asks.

"He just does, Dad."

I hear his pen click. "What's his name?"

"Matthew Reed." My voice clogs in my throat. He's going to do it. *He's going to do it.* I tell him the name of the hospital. "I don't know more information than that. I don't even know who his doctor is."

He chuckles. "I can get the information I need."

"You're going to do it, right, Dad?" I ask.

"Emily," he sighs. "If I do this, you're coming home."

My voice is a whisper. "Yes, Dad. I understand."

"I'm sending the jet for you now."

"I need a day, Dad. I need for you to handle this now. And I need another day. If you'll give me that much time, I'll come home and I'll do whatever you want." I'm pleading with him now.

He waits. And I hear his pen click over and over. "Ok," he breathes. "I'm sending the jet now. It'll be waiting when you're ready at the airport."

"Take care of this for me, Dad." I roll my forehead back and forth across the tiles. "Please. Promise me."

"I'd do anything for you, Em," he reminds me.

"I'll see you in a couple of days," I whisper.

"Two days, Em," he says. "No longer." And before the line goes dead, I hear him yelling details to his secretary. I hear Matt's name. And I hear him tell her to handle it. It'll get done. I'm sure of it.

I walk back to the waiting room. The doctor is gone and all the boys are standing there with their arms around one another. "What happened?" I ask.

They move away from one another. "They're moving him to a room. He's awake. We can go see him in just a minute," Paul explains.

I drop into a chair. My legs will no longer support me.

A few minutes later, a nurse summons the boys to follow her. Logan takes my hand and tugs me along with them. "I'm not family," I say.

"Shut up," he murmurs. He brushes a strand of hair back that's stuck to my lip.

I let him tow me along.

"You can only stay for a few minutes," the nurse warns.

The boys are giddy with excitement. She pushes back a curtain and Matt's there in the bed. There are tubes and wires and he's hooked up to monitors. "What's up, guys?" he asks. He winces and adjusts himself in the bed.

"The next time you want to die, don't do it on Kit's watch, you sorry fucker," Logan says out loud. The room goes quiet. A tear rolls down Logan's cheek and Matt reaches out a hand for him. Logan grabs it, palm to palm, their thumbs wrapped together like men do, and falls into his chest. Sam and Pete put their arms around one another and Paul is just standing there, so I lean into his side. He throws an arm around my shoulders and pulls me into him.

Matt finally lets Logan go and says, "Shit, when did you learn to talk?"

Logan shrugs.

"This girl is teaching him all sorts of new shit," Paul says, squeezing me tightly.

"What happened?" Logan asks. He's signing while he talks out loud.

"I had a date to snuggle with your girl on the couch and we were going to watch a movie," Matt says. "Next thing I know, she has my head in her lap, instead." He looks over at me, an impish twinkle in his eye. "If you wanted to hold me, Kit, you could have just asked." He chuckles.

"You remember?" I ask.

He grins this unrepentant grin. "I'll never, ever forget the day you threw Logan over to hold me in your arms."

Logan chuckles. Out loud. Everyone looks at him and he shrugs.

"You going to keep talking, bro?" Paul asks cautiously.

Logan shrugs again.

Paul squeezes me.

Suddenly, a team of doctors rushes into the room. "What's wrong?" Paul barks.

The doctor comes in a moment later. "We're going to be moving Matt to a different facility," he explains. "So he can begin that treatment we discussed."

"What?" Matt's dumbfounded. As are the rest of them.

The doctor holds up his hands to silence them. "Don't get too hopeful," he says. "But now there's a chance where there wasn't one before."

"There's a chance he might live?" Paul asks.

The doctor smiles and claps Paul on the shoulder. "A small one, yes."

"How?"

"I'm still working all that out." The doctor looks at me, but I break eye contact.

The room is barraged with activity, and the nurses get ready to move Matt. "There's a helicopter waiting," the nurse explains.

"How?" Paul asks again.

Matt reaches for each of them in turn. He hugs his brothers. Then he hugs me to him last. "Take care of them," he says. "No matter what."

I nod. I'm doing that the only way I know how.

Logan

My brothers are solemn on the way back home. It's early afternoon on Saturday, and I look down at my watch. "Shit," I say.

"What?" Paul asks.

"I have an appointment for a tat this afternoon." Kit's walking beside me but she has been lost in her own world since we left the hospital. "I guess I can cancel."

"Are you too tired to do it?" Paul asks.

Honestly, I'm so full of adrenaline right now I could climb mountains. And pick them up and throw them. I shake my head.

"So, why not do it?" he asks.

"Matt," I say. Just that one word.

Paul claps me on the shoulder. "They won't let us see him for forty eight hours, dummy," he reminds me.

That's right. They are going to do a bunch of tests and scans and shit and told us that he can't see anyone until at least Monday. Until he's settled in. I'm hopeful. I'm so hopeful and I haven't been hopeful for weeks. I've watched Matt decline more and more, and I was at the point where I was coming to terms with it. But hope has bloomed within me. It's not fair. It's not fair at all. What if he still doesn't get better? I have to believe he'll make it.

"He said he'd call when he gets settled," Paul reminds me. "Until then, we wait."

Kit looks up at me, her eyes focusing for the first time since we left the hospital. "I think you should open the shop. Do your tat. You're going to need the money." She doesn't look me in the eye when she says the last part of it. "Can I go, too?" she asks. "I want to watch."

I wrap my arm around her and she smiles up at me. "You ok?" I ask.

She nods and leans in. I can feel the warm wind of her inhale against my skin. "Stop sniffing me, you little pervita," I say.

Her eyebrows lift and she repeats the word. "Pervita?" She laughs. I hug her to me, never wanting to let her go. She's a part of us now. All of us. And she's mine.

Sam and Pete are walking behind us with their heads pushed together, talking softly. When they do that, there's usually trouble brewing. "What are you two up to?" Paul barks. Their heads snap apart, and they try not to look guilty. They're terrible at it, though.

"Nothing," they say in unison.

Paul narrows his eyes at them. "I don't believe you."

They look at him sheepishly.

"I don't believe you either," I say.

"I think I liked you better when you didn't speak," Pete says. Then he grins.

I flip him the bird and he flies at me, jumping on my back. He bounces up and down, and leans over my shoulder so I can see his lips. "My feet are cold," he says, batting his golden lashes at me. "You should carry me the rest of the way."

He's latched onto me like a koala. And he's fucking heavy. It's like carrying a load of bricks. But I hitch him up higher and start walking.

Sam turns his back to Kit and bends down. "You look tired, Kit," he says. "Want a ride?" He waggles his brows at her. She laughs, and jumps onto his back.

"I'm not sure I got the good end of this deal," I croak, as we all walk along together.

I can't help but wish Matt were here. I miss the gentle giant already.

***

I've been working on this tat for weeks. It's a huge bald eagle that goes from shoulder blade to shoulder blade. Not to mention that it's on a really big guy. I drew the outline, and then I started shading it last week. I need to finish it today. It's a five hundred dollar tat, and we could use the money. Particularly now.

I settle down to work on it, and Kit watches over my shoulder for a few minutes. But then she goes to the front of the store to sit down with Friday and Paul. Paul is updating Friday on Matt's condition. Friday adores Matt; if there's one of us she hangs with the most, it's him. She wipes a tear from her eye.

I can read her lips from there. "What are the odds that he gets accepted in that trial? It's so strange," she says. I can't see what Paul says in response.

Kit ambles up to the front of the store and says something to Paul. He looks shocked for a minute and then he pulls her forearm down to look at it. She's not hurt, is she? I move to set my gun to the side, but she looks over her shoulder and smiles at me. She's fine. Paul motions for her to follow him and he takes her behind a curtain. I see his lips when he says, "Keep him out of there," to Friday. Keep who out of where? Then he pulls a curtain around the two of them to separate them from us and I have to put the gun down. I start in that direction. Friday gets between me and them. "She's just getting a tat," she says, turning me around.

"What kind of tat?"

"A tiny little butterfly or something equally as cute. Maybe a Disney princess. She hadn't decided yet." She rolls her eyes. Friday has skulls and crossbones, and turtles, and all sorts of weird shit all over her body.

"I want to help her pick something," I say, trying to push past Friday.

"Stop," she says. "She wants to surprise you."

I run a frustrated hand through my hair.

"Tats mean different things to different people," Friday says. "This means a lot to her and she should be the one to decide what she gets."

I already know this, but I want to be involved. Damn it.

"You don't trust Paul to take care of her?" Friday asks, her brows crashing together.

Of course I trust him. "But this is my girl," I say. I know I sound like a baby. But there it is.

She pats me on the arm. "Suck it up, buttercup," she says. Then she narrows her eyes at me. "Wait a minute! When did you start talking?"

My face flushes with heat. "Don't get used to it," I grumble. "I may never talk to you again."

"I could only be so lucky," Friday says, rolling her eyes. But she jumps up onto her tiptoes and hugs me tightly. "I'm so happy for you," she says.

I can't figure out what she's talking about. Kit? Me? Our relationship? My talking? I brush her off when the guy I was working on starts waving his arms from the back of the shop. I have a lot of work to do. So, I had better get busy.

An hour later, Kit comes out from behind the curtain with Paul. She's smiling, and her forearm is covered with a large bandage. She walks over to me. I finished my tat ten minutes ago and have just been waiting for her. "You're going to wear a hole in the carpet," Kit teases.

Paul walks out behind her. He's smiling, but he won't meet my eyes.

"What did you put on her?" I ask.

He scowls at me and says, "Shut up." He points to a sign on the wall that says, "Tattoos are as individual as the people who get them." Then he points to another that says, "One man's ink is another man's purpose in life." Then he points to a third. "We do not tattoo drunk clients." Then he points to a roll of duct tape below a sign that says, "Keep whining and I'll use it."

"You are not amusing," I say.

Kit falls into my side and wraps her arms around me.

"What did you get?" I ask.

She looks into my eyes. "Something that will keep me from ever forgetting you and what you mean to me."

"It's about me?" My heart lurches and my breath catches and I suddenly can't think.

She smiles and she nods. "It's about you."

"Can I see it?" I'm dying here.

She shakes her head. "Not today."

"When?" Still fucking dying here.

She shrugs and she suddenly looks sad.

"What's wrong?" I ask, tipping her face up to mine.

She reaches into her pocket and pulls out a folded piece of paper. She hands it to me. Her face flushes with heat.

"Is this the tattoo?" I ask.

She shakes her head. "No."

I open it slowly.

MY NAME IS EMILY.

Emily

My heart is pounding so loudly that I can hear it. Logan opens the piece of paper and he freezes. He looks down at it for a long time, longer than I expected. I try to take it back from him. He jerks it away. Then he takes my hand and pulls me from the shop. I don't get a chance to say goodbye to Paul or Friday. I don't even get my feet under me before he's tugging me down the street.

"Wait," I call. But he can't hear me. His gaze is fixed on his route to wherever he's taking me. I tap his shoulder. He doesn't stop. He just pulls me through the crowd. I dig my heels in and stop. He turns to me and reaches for my hand again. I'm afraid he's going to toss me over his shoulder one last time. But I want this to be my choice. I want this to be our choice, together. "Wait," I say, framing his face with my hands. He looks down at me. "Why the rush?"

"Because I want you so fucking bad that I hurt, you silly woman." He makes me smile. He'll probably never call me a dummy again, but I do realize that it's a term of endearment with him, and not a set-down.

"I want you too," I admit.

He looks down at the piece of paper that's in his hand. "You trust me," he says.

I nod.

"Can we go to the apartment and talk?" he asks. "I promise not to molest you the minute we walk in the door. We have some things that need to be said."

Yes, we do. I nod.

He takes my hand in his and raises it to his lips to kiss my knuckles. He walks a little slower this time. He points to my arm. "What did you get?"

I smile. I'm not telling him. It's for me. It's for me to take with me when I go. It's a piece of him. Of all of them really. It's mine. And I'm not sharing it. Not right now.

"Come on," he cajoles.

I shake my head. "Not happening."

He looks crestfallen for a moment. But then we reach his apartment complex and we run up the stairs side by side. He's barely winded.

We step into the empty apartment. No one is there.

"Can you believe that they admitted Matt into the trial program?" he asks as he walks toward the bedroom.

"Amazing, isn't it?"

"So fucking amazing," he says. He's giddy about it and I love the way he wears his heart on his sleeve.

I don't want to talk about Matt because I'm afraid I'll break down crying and tell him what I did. Tell him what I committed to in order to give Matt a chance, in order to be sure Logan's world stays complete and full with all his brothers. "I'm so glad he's going to get a chance," I say. My voice clogs in my throat and I'm glad Logan can't hear it.

He picks up on my feelings, though, because he walks across the room and brackets my face with his fingers. "I'm sorry you were the one here when he got sick."

I'm not. Not at all. I'm so glad I was here. I'm glad I could help. In more ways than one. "I am glad I was here. Wouldn't trade the time I spent with his head on my lap for anything." I can't bite back my grin.

"I love you so fucking much," he says. Then he bends his head and kisses me. His lips are soft, but urgent.

Tears well in my eyes, because I know this is our last day together. "I need to take a shower," I say, stalling. I need a moment to compose myself. Not to mention that we spent the night at the hospital. I need to get cleaned up.

He nods and points at my arm. Shoot. I have a new tattoo and a bandage. "You can get it wet if you take the bandage off," he says.

I don't want to take the bandage off. "Can we just wrap it up?"

"Why don't you want me to see it?" He's looking deep into my eyes. I can't explain it to him.

He heaves a sigh and comes back with some plastic wrap and some waterproof tape. He wraps my arm and says, "There. That'll keep it completely dry."

I'm not worried about getting it wet. I'm worried about the bandage falling off. "Thank you," I say. I kiss him quickly. "I'll be out in a few minutes."

I take off my clothes and step into the shower. Warm water sluices over me and I realize that the fear in my heart has been replaced by longing. I was afraid to love Logan. Now I long to love Logan. And I do. And always will. But I have to give him up to protect something precious to him. I know that. I don't have a choice. The warm water steams over my back, and I lean both forearms against the wall, trying to compose myself. Tears track down my face, melding with the water. There's a draft and I feel the curtain move behind me.

I jump when Logan steps into the bath with me. His body envelopes mine, completely naked. "Logan!" I screech.

A warm chuckle makes his chest move against my back. "I don't want to be away from you," he says, pushing my wet hair to the side so he can press his lips to my naked shoulder.

Logan takes my washcloth from my hands and gets it soapy. Then he drags it down my spine, slowly, ever so slowly. My breath catches in my throat when he abandons the washcloth and runs his soapy hands over my bottom, squeezing my butt cheeks in his gentle grip. He doesn't leave a spot unwashed, his hands finding every crevice and dip, all the way down the backs of my legs, across the backs of my knees, which I had no idea were so ticklish, and over the heels of my feet. I stand there with my eyes closed, unable to look at him. He stands back up and lathers the soap in his palms again. This time, he doesn't take the washcloth at all. He uses his fingers to skim my body. His fingers tickle all the way down my left arm, all the way to my fingertips. Strong fingers lace with mine and he gives me a squeeze before he turns me to face him.

I keep my eyes closed. I am overwhelmed by what he's doing to me. If I look into his eyes, I don't know what will happen right now. I might combust. I might shatter. I might break. I can feel his smile against my shoulder as he presses his lips there. I hear him chuckle. My eyes fly open.

His hair is wet and he's dripping with water. I lean forward and lick his chest. He groans, freezing. "Logan." He looks up at me and stills.

"Did you say something?" he asks.

"I don't know," I say. Laughter breaks from my throat. "I can't even think. You want me to repeat myself?"

"I felt you say something," he says. He grins. "I just wanted to be sure you're all right."

I lay my head back against the wall. I'll never be all right again. He rubs his soapy hands over my belly, and then his fingers dip lower. I reach for his shoulders.

He picks up the wash cloth again, and gets it sudsy. He washes my most intimate places, until I'm squirming and flinching.

"I think I'm clean," I say with a laugh. I can't take much more.

Logan stands up and kisses me. "I want to be inside you so bad," he says. He pushes me under the spray to get my hair wet, and then washes my hair, rinsing it gently. "Your hair is growing out," he says. "Is it blond?"

I nod. "Not platinum. But a dark blond color."

"I'd like to see you like that," he says. "Maybe someday." He smiles and kisses me. He moves me to the side and starts to wash his own body, his movements quick and efficient.

"Let me help you," I say, reaching to take the soap from him.

"If you touch me right now, this will be over," he warns with a chuckle.

My belly flips. "Oh."

He chuckles. "Just stand there and watch," he says.

He washes and rinses his hair, and I let my gaze drag down his body. He told me he had a piercing down there. But he didn't tell me he had a bar through the skin at the base of his penis. "That's the piercing you were telling me about?" I ask.

He nods, blowing water from his lips. I opened the door to all this intimacy when I told him my name.

"Emily Madison," I say. "My name. It's Emily Madison."

He stills. "Where are you from?" he asks. He turns the water off, but never looks away from me.

"California."

"The opposite coast," he breathes. He takes my face in his hands. "Emily," he says again. "It suits you."

I grin. "I'm glad."

Logan steps out of the tub, and comes back with two towels. He dries me off and wraps me in one towel. The other he uses on himself, and then wraps it around his hips.

"Do you want to go to bed?" he asks. He fakes a yawn. "I'm really tired."

I laugh. God, this man makes me laugh. "If you think you're getting any sleep tonight, you are sadly mistaken." I shake my finger at him.

"Promises, promises," he growls as he lifts me from the tub with strong hands around my waist.

Logan

She's so fucking beautiful that I can barely breathe. "Emily," I say. I want to say it over and over and over. She told me her last name, too, but for the life of me all I can remember is what was written on the piece of paper.

"That's my name. Don't wear it out," she teases.

I pick her up, and she wraps her legs around my waist. My dick reaches for her, and I slide against her heat. But I'm not ready yet. I want to savor every second. I carry her into the bedroom. She kisses me as I walk, and I can barely take a step, I'm so wrapped up in her.

"Is anyone here?" She sits back from me long enough to ask.

God, I hope not. "Don't think so," I say.

"What if they are?" she asks.

"Then you're going to have to be quiet." I laugh. Because the odds of her being quiet during all the things I plan to do to her is ludicrous.

She buries her head into my shoulder and I can feel her breath against my neck. She kisses me softly, suckling my skin. "Give me a hicky," I urge. I'm kidding, but then I feel the scrape of her teeth against the tender skin and I really, really want her to keep doing what she's doing. She bites down gently, and then sucks the pain away. "Jesus," I moan. I bite back a groan. I slam the bedroom door behind us and fall onto the bed with her, holding myself above her. My fucking arms are shaking and for the first time in my life, I don't know what to do next.

So I can collect myself, I take a moment to stop and I unwrap the plastic and tape from her arm. I start to peel the bandage back, but she catches me and slaps my hands away. I freeze, burying my face in her neck. I can barely breathe.

"What's wrong?" she asks, taking my face in her hands.

"I feel like a fourteen year old fumbling with his first girl," I admit. "I don't know what to do next."

I lift up and open her towel, and unhook mine, shoving it from between us. "You've done this so many times," she reminds me, rolling her eyes.

I still. "I have never done this before."

Her eyes narrow.

"I've never done this with someone who matters. With someone I'm in love with. Jesus, girl, you make me crazy."

"Can we turn the light off?" she asks. Then it dawns on her that I can't see her lips if we don't keep the light on. "Never mind," she says.

"Will the light bother you?" I ask. I work my way down her body, kissing her all over, just because I can.

Her naked thighs wrap around my hips, and the slickness of her makes this so real. "Shit," I say.

"What?" She freezes.

"I forgot to get a condom."

She counts on her fingers and shakes her head. "It's all right. We don't need one." She stops and bites her lip. "Unless, um, you need one."

I got tested just a few weeks ago when we all had bone marrow testing for Matt. I'm clean. "I've never done this without one." I'm afraid. More afraid than I've ever been.

I don't know what to do next, I want her so bad. My breath falters, and my arms quiver under my weight.

We have a lifetime to perfect this. But I don't know how it could get any better.

I take it slow. I want to remember this moment forever and ever. I can't hold in a groan as I bury my face in her neck and slide inside her.

I look up at her face and there are tears in her eyes. "Have I hurt you?" I ask. I bracket her face with my hands and swipe her tears away with the pads of my thumbs. She shakes her head.

Her skin slides against mine, her breath blowing across my ear. "Emily, Emily, Emily," I chant.

She's saying my name over and over and over. I can see it on her lips. I move inside her until she falls apart with me.

Her arms wrap around me when I collapse on top of her and she squeezes me, but then her arms fall away. She says something. I can feel it. I lift myself up. "What?" I ask. "I didn't hurt you, did I?" Fear clutches at my gut with eager talons.

"If that's hurting me, I want you to do it over and over and over, all night long." She chuckles, her body shaking with laughter.

I roll to my side, but I don't want to be far from her, so I turn her to face me. I brush her hair back from her face with both hands. "I love you," I say.

She smiles at me, hiding her face abashedly in the pillow. "I love you too," she says. "No matter what happens, please know that what I feel for you is real. That I don't know how I could live without you."

I lean back, appraising her closely. Why would she say such a thing? But she reaches for me and pushes me onto my back.

Her body moves against mine, taking me to places I have never, ever been.

When we're done, I roll to the side and pull her to lie on my chest. I place my lips against her forehead and hold them there.

She sits up with her elbows on my chest and looks down at me. "I love you so much, Logan," she says. Then she dips her head, settles against my chest, and falls asleep.

Emily

I wake before the sun comes up. The light is still on and Logan's on his back. I'm lying on top of him, and there's sweat between us. I need to get cleaned up and get out of there before he wakes up. My gut clenches at the thought of leaving him and tears fill my eyes. I look at him through my crying until he's a big blur. A big, beautiful blur. I love him so much. I love him so much that I can't stay. I love him too much to make him do without Matt for a lifetime. I just can't do it. I have to give him up to save Matt. I know it can't be avoided. Someone might as well cleave me into two pieces – it wouldn't hurt any less.

I let my tears fall, not bothering to wipe them away as I go and shower. I move as quietly as I can, and get dressed in the bathroom. I brush through my wet hair, but I don't do much more than that. There's no need to put on any makeup. It'll be washed away by my misery.

I sneak back into the bedroom and look down at him lying there. He's so beautiful. He's everything I want and everything I could ever need. But I'm not sure what he needs. Yes, I am. He needs Matt. He needs for me to see that Matt gets everything he has to have to get better. To live. And I'm giving him this the only way I can.

His hair is tousled over his forehead. I remember looking at him as he slept that first night and wondering if his mother ever watched him like I do. She had to. He's just so pretty. Both inside and out. He took care of me for so long. And I trust him so much. But I need to do this.

I brush the tears from my cheeks and steel my spine. I can do this. I have to do this. I pick up my guitar and my black canvas bag. There's still not much in it. There's not much of me that I won't be leaving here, so I don't guess it matters.

I look down at my guitar. I want to leave him a part of myself. Something that will let him know how very much I love him. I lean the guitar against the wall. He'll take care of it for me. My father will never let me use it again anyway. There will be no Julliard for me. There will be a wedding. There will be me as arm-candy. There will be a future, but not the one I want.

I leave with nothing but my black canvas bag and a few articles of clothing. I don't take anything else, except for his AC/DC t-shirt, the one I wore the first night I met him. I know it's silly, but I want it. I call for a cab before I walk downstairs. In the city, you never can be too careful.

I bounce from foot to foot. I still don't have a coat and it's cold. It's still dark out. There are no stars in the sky because of all the street lights. The cab slows to a stop in front of me and I walk out onto the sidewalk. I look up at his building, and I say a little prayer for Matt. Logan will be all right. He'll survive this. I'm not sure I will, but Logan will have Matt and the rest of his brothers.

I take a deep breath and get in the cab. I tell the cabbie to take me to the airport, and I need to go through a private entrance. He looks at me closely in the mirror. Then he shrugs and takes me where I tell him. I bypass security inside the airport, but we still have to go through security checks. They call the plane, and the pilot assures the security guards that I will be traveling privately, and that they have my identification. I hadn't even thought of that. But my father would have thought of everything.

My father's own security guard is waiting at the bottom of the steps of the plane. "Miss Madison," he says.

"'Sup, Watkins?" I ask flippantly.

He smiles. "I like the hair."

"Look at it while you can, because Daddy will make me change it as soon as I get home." I heave a sigh. I'm so tired. I buckle up, because it's what I'm supposed to do until we take off and stabilize. The pilot comes to greet me. I know him, too, but can't remember his name.

"Miss Madison," he says with a nod. "I'm glad you're flying with me today."

"I'm not," I mutter.

He doesn't respond. He just goes and gets things started. It's early and still dark, so I can't even watch the city pass me by as we take off. I see the lights, but they're not what the city is to me. This city is so much more.

After the pilot says it's ok, I unbuckle and go lay down in the bedroom. "Can I get you anything, Emily?" Watkins asks. I bury my face in my pillow so he won't see my tears. I shake my head. "Let me know if you need anything, Em," he says softly. Then more firmly, "Anything."

I nod, my face still buried in my pillow.

I sob until I am too exhausted to do more. Then I sleep the rest of the flight. They wake me up to buckle when it's time to land. I go to the bathroom and wash my face, brushing my hair and cleaning up. My dad is going to have a shit fit no matter what. But I can at least look presentable.

The limo pulls up beside the plane just as soon as it lands. Watkins opens the door and I slide inside. But then I stop. My mother is inside. She's perfectly put together, as always. Her brown eyes are not the ones I want to be looking into. I want Logan's blue gaze. His are the eyes I want to see. She looks at me, and at Watkins, who closes the door behind me and goes to sit with the driver. He never does that. But my mother can accomplish just about anything with nothing more than a look. "Emily," she says crisply.

"Mom," I reply.

"You look like hell," she says. And her face finally cracks into a smile.

"Where's Dad?" I twirl a lock of my black hair around my finger.

"Your father is in the doghouse I'm afraid. He bungled this terribly. And so he's no longer in charge of this little matter."

My mother never does this. I didn't think she had a spine at all. "What?"

"Your father is the reason why you ran away from home. Your father is the reason why you have been gone for more than six months. Your father and his conniving are the reason why I lost my daughter." Her voice cracks on the last word. My mother never falls apart. Ever. But she does now. Tears roll down her cheeks and she reaches for me. I fall into her. My mother is offering me everything I need right now.

"I'm going to mess up your clothes," I warn, sniffling.

"Mess me up. I don't care." She squeezes me to her. "Tell me everything."

I sit back. "You don't want to hear everything."

She sighs. "I can't help you if I don't know what's wrong."

"Mom," I complain.

"I'll start it for you," she says, smiling. She mocks my bored tone and says, "Well, there's this boy…" She motions for me to finish.

I tell my mother the story about why I left, where I've been, what I've been doing.

At the end of my story, she says, "Your father still expects you to marry that boy."

I nod. "I know."

"But that will never, ever happen."

My gaze shoots to her.

"We're going to the salon. And then we're going to take care of this."

"Mom," I breathe. "I promised Dad."

She pats my hand. "You'll see. Trust me." And for some reason, I do.

For the next four hours, we change my hair color back to its natural shade, paint my nails a glossy pink instead of black, "because we don't want to buck the system but just so much," and she sends someone to get me a new outfit. She has a flock of people doing her bidding.

When we're done, I feel like my old self. But I'm not. I never will be.

We pull up to our home and the gates are open. I'm so confused. There are news vans everywhere. "What's this, Mom?" I ask.

"This is me handling this situation for you." She absently runs a hand down the length of my hair. "You're a smart girl, Emily. You can make your own choices."

Tears prick at the backs of my eyelids. I'm a smart girl. Someone other than Logan said it.

Logan

I'm terrified. Emily is gone, but her guitar is still here. She was gone before I got up this morning. Her black bag is gone. And all of her belongings, except her guitar. She wouldn't have left, would she? Not for good. Paul sits beside me on the couch and he knocks my hand from my mouth when I chew my fingernails. "She'll be back," he says. "Stop worrying."

She won't be back. I'm sure of it. I realized that by telling me her name last night and letting me inside her, she wasn't telling me she loves me. She was telling me goodbye. It hurts like nothing ever has when I realize that, but it's true. I'm sure of it.

The phone rings. I jump when the lights flash, signaling the ringer. Paul runs to answer it. "Matt says to turn the news on," Paul says, as he turns the TV on and flips the channels.

The new anchor starts to talk. I read the captions as they play across the bottom of the screen.

IN CELEBRITY NEWS TODAY, THE PRODIGAL DAUGHTER OF ONE OF THE UNITED STATES' MOST INFLUENTIAL BUSINESSMEN HAS BEEN FOUND ALIVE TODAY.

"What does this have to do with us?" I ask Paul.

YOU MAY REMEMBER THE MEDIA CIRCUS MORE THAN SIX MONTHS AGO WHEN EMILY MADISON DISAPPEARED.

The TV switches to a picture of a blonde.

Paul slaps my chest hard to get my attention. It hurts like a mother fucker but my gaze is stuck on the TV.

EMILY MADISON DISAPPEARED MORE THAN SIX MONTHS AGO, BUT SHE RETURNED HOME TODAY.

"That's my Emily," I breathe. Her hair is blond. And she has on a million dollar smile, along with some million dollar earrings.

Paul smacks me harder so I have to look at him. "That's Kit?" he asks.

I wave at him to shut him up. He turns the TV up. I watch the words at the bottom of the screen. I scoot forward so my ass is balanced on the edge of the couch.

EMILY HAS AGREED TO ANSWER A FEW QUESTIONS, the captions say.

I watch as the woman I love steps up to the podium. She blinks and holds her hand up to block the sun. I can see the freckles across the bridge of her nose, and my heart lurches. She's in California. "Good afternoon," she says.

The crowd starts firing off questions. They only print the ones in the captions that get to her. "Where have I been?" she repeats. "I have been in New York for six months. There's a bit of a story to go with that, but I won't bore you with it. Sometimes a girl just needs a break." The captions indicate that she's laughing. But there's no laughter in her eyes.

ARE YOU WELL, EMILY?

She's not well, but she's alive.

"I'm perfectly well," she says, smiling. "Never been better."

ARE YOU MENTALLY ILL, EMILY? DID YOU HAVE A BREAKDOWN? HAVE YOU BEEN IN REHAB?

She looks at the person with surprise. "The last time I checked, I wasn't." She looks down at her body and pats her hips and stomach. "I think I'm all in one piece."

WAS THERE FOUL PLAY, EMILY?

She shakes her head. "No. No foul play. I was perfectly safe the whole time."

Someone steps up to the podium to pull Emily away, and I ache as I watch her take a step back. One more question scrolls across the screen.

WHAT ARE YOUR PLANS FOR THE FUTURE, EMILY?

She smiles. Then she looks directly into the camera. Directly at me. She might as well have kicked me in the gut. "In the spring, I'm going to Julliard to study music."

My stomach drops down toward my toes.

WHY NEW YORK, EMILY?

Thank God someone asks before she can walk away.

She tilts her head to the side and looks right at me. She raises her hand into the sign for I love you and I see the tattoo that takes up her forearm. It's a key, and written down the center of the key shaft are the letters of my name. I look at Paul. "Did you do that?"

He grins and shrugs. "It's nothing."

It's everything. It's every fucking thing.

The reporter repeats the question.

WHY NEW YORK EMILY?

"That's simple," she says. "It's because I love New York. I love New York with all my heart and I can't wait to get back to it. I needed to come see my Dad so he could take care of something for me. But I'm going back to New York." She leans close to the microphone. "I love you New York. Never doubt it. I'll see you soon."

Then she waves and she's gone.

I fall back against the couch, trying to put it all together in my head.

"Shit," Paul says. "She paid for Matt's treatment."

"What?" I'm still dumbfounded.

"She went back home for you," he explains. He still has Matt on the phone and he's talking to both of us at the same time.

She did it all for me. "She did it for me," I say out loud.

"You lucky fucker," Paul says, punching me in the arm.

"She'll be back for the spring session at Julliard." Warm happiness settles around me like a blanket fresh out of the dryer.

Paul nods. "Matt will be home by then."

We all hope Matt would be home by then. Matt has a chance to come home and it's all because of Emily. I jump up and Paul pulls me into a hug.

"She'll be back?" I ask. I can't wrap my head around it all. "She's not gone for good."

"She just told the whole fucking world how much she loves you, you jackass." Paul punches me in the shoulder again.

She's coming back. To Julliard. To me.

THE END

Made in the USA
Charleston, SC
20 June 2013